The Lady of Light Soon Would Know Her Darkest Hour

The King weakly turned his fevered face toward the lady of his heart and swallowed painfully. "Faris—if I am dying, the Council must be called."

Faris trembled and gripped his hand. "But you will live!" she whispered, her voice edged with terror. "They are praying for you at the College of the Wise, and in the Cities.... Oh, Jehan! You cannot leave me!" She buried her face in the pillow, her body shaking with sobs.

"It may be that I have loved you too much," continued the King, "too much for your own good, or for mine. Faris, you must promise me to guard Westria, or I will be not only dead but damned! Others will help you rule, but only you can be Mistress of the Jewels."

"Oh my love—if you say I must—I will do whatever I can...."

Books by Diana L. Paxson

Lady of Darkness
Lady of Light

Published by TIMESCAPE BOOKS

Most Timescape Books are available at special quantity discounts for bulk purchases for sales promotions, premiums or fund raising. Special books or book excerpts can also be created to fit specific needs.

For details write the office of the Vice President of Special Markets, Pocket Books, 1230 Avenue of the Americas, New York, New York 10020.

LADY OF DARKNESS

—— The Second Book of Westria ——

Diana L. Paxson

A TIMESCAPE BOOK
PUBLISHED BY POCKET BOOKS NEW YORK

This novel is a work of fiction. Names, characters, places and incidents are either the product of the author's imagination or are used fictitiously. Any resemblance to actual events or locales or persons, living or dead, is entirely coincidental.

Another *Original* publication of TIMESCAPE BOOKS

A Timescape Book published by
POCKET BOOKS, a division of Simon & Schuster, Inc.
1230 Avenue of the Americas, New York, N.Y. 10020

Copyright © 1983 by Diana L. Paxson

All rights reserved, including the right to reproduce
this book or portions thereof in any form whatsoever.
For information address Timescape Books, 1230
Avenue of the Americas, New York, N.Y. 10020

ISBN: 0-671-45882-5

First Timescape Books printing September, 1983

10 9 8 7 6 5 4 3 2 1

POCKET and colophon are registered trademarks
of Simon & Schuster, Inc.

Use of the trademark TIMESCAPE is by exclusive license
from Gregory Benford, the trademark owner.

Printed in the U.S.A.

*To my husband,
Jon DeCles*

Acknowledgments

I would like to thank David Hodghead for information regarding the habits and hunting of wild boars, Ken DeMaiffe for data on the capabilities of both horses and carrier pigeons, Clint Bigglestone for suggesting the strategy used in the Battle of the Dragon Waste, and Paul Edwin Zimmer for arguing with me about the right way to do a fighting scene.

Contents

	Prologue	11
I	Harvest	14
II	The Samaine Boar	27
III	A Season of Pain	41
IV	The Sun Road	58
V	The White Queen	77
VI	Maneuvers in a Mist	94
VII	The Queen's Battle	116
VIII	The Chessmaster	135
IX	The Morning Star	158
X	Dream—and Nightmare	179
XI	The Trial	202
XII	The Way to Awahna	227
	Epilogue	247
	Index to Characters	250

LADY OF
DARKNESS

Westria
SEA GATE
Elder
Silvershine River
Rivered
Rushing River
Bongarde
Borrada River
Laurelynn
Red Mtn.
Wilkamsted
Lady Mtn.
Sacred Wood
Misthall
THE ROYAL DOMAIN
THE RAMPARTS
Wildwater River
AWAHNA
Gateway
Stanesvale
Mercy River
Sanjas
LAS COSTAS
Darkwater River
Risslin
Montera
Elk Marsh
N
W
E
S
THE DRAGON WASTE
© 1983 Diana L. Paxson

Prologue

The Master of the Junipers tucked his grey robe under him and settled himself beneath a live oak on the sunny hill above Misthall. Carefully he shook out the silk cloth and laid his deck of tarot cards down. Beyond the silvered shake roof of the hall the land fell gently to the Great Bay. The Lady Mountain seemed almost to float above the water, its lower slopes veiled by autumn haze. With the marriage of King Jehan to the Lady Faris, the past year had been eventful, and it was good to rest.

He took an appreciative breath of air scented with the Harvest feast they were preparing for this afternoon and shuffled through the worn cards. He was seeking the *Queen of Wands*—dark, slender and ardent—to represent Faris. She had been so young and fearful when the King had married her that many had wondered if she would ever make a Queen. But the Master had seen her face when she put on the Elemental Jewels of Power to help Jehan master a forest fire a month ago, and he thought that she understood what it meant to be the King's counterpart at last. No urgency drove him to read the cards for her now, only the knowledge that they were sometimes useful, and lack of practice must not dull his skill.

But perhaps he had not lost it, for the first card the Master drew—the one showing the influence that ruled the subject now, was the Empress, surrounded by the fruits of the field. He thought of Faris, growing more luxuriantly beautiful as her pregnancy advanced, and knew that she *was* the Empress now.

As the pattern required, he picked another card from the deck to cross her. The *King of Cups?* This card indicated a fair man in a position of responsibility. Was crossing the same as reversal of the card? *That* could mean treachery.

More important, whom did the card signify? Westria had its share of politics, but the King and the Seneschal, Caolin, had always kept the worst plotters under control. Brian, the Lord Commander of Las Costas, was agitating for greater independence, but he was more an enemy of Caolin's than of the King and Queen. Did the card point to the Elayans, who were now claiming Westria's southernmost city, Santibar? But how could they threaten the Queen?

With a sigh he went on to the card which should show the best that could be achieved. It was the *Seven of Cups*, and usually indicated the insubstantiality of earthly wealth. Here was another puzzler, but perhaps later cards would make its meaning clear.

The card for past achievements was the *Two of Cups*, whose emblem was a youth and maiden pledging their troth. That was better—the pictured couple even had the look of Faris and Jehan, and the appearance of the *Lovers*, following it, seemed to confirm the reading. If this was the influence that was now passing away, perhaps it showed that their love would now mature.

The sixth card was for the future, and as he turned it over the Master found his stomach muscles tightening, for it was the *Queen of Swords*, and she means mourning. The seventh, for the subject's attitude, proved to be the *Two of Wands*, showing a great man sorrowful in the midst of his wealth.

Keep on, the Master told himself. *Only when it is complete will the pattern become clear.* Swiftly he set out the next two cards that should show the environment within which all should come to pass and the subject's desires, and shivered as he saw the *Tower* and *Death* on his dark horse. *Death* could be interpreted as a card of transfiguration, but there were no hopeful meanings for the *Falling Tower*.

And what of the end? The air seemed to have chilled, though the Master saw no cloud across the sun. He forced his clenched fingers to release and put the last card down.

The *High Priestess* gazed up at him from the silk cloth, her eyes mysterious below her crescent crown. She had Faris' face— why had he never seen that in the card before? But what road could lead from the opulence of the Empress to this? As he stared, the enigmatic features of the Priestess were momentarily dimmed by the flickering shadow of a late butterfly.

It has been too long since I tried this—I have lost my touch with the cards, The Master told himself. He heard his name called and looking down the hill saw Faris herself waving from the garden gate. Beyond her a rider was coming up the road, his fair hair glinting in the pallid sun. It was Caolin.

I will read the cards tomorrow. Surely they will tell a different story then. Briskly the Master began to gather them up and fit them into their case, ignoring the bitter wind that ruffled his thinning hair.

I

Harvest

Fire leaped from the taper in Faris' hand to a twig, exploded in the tinder and flared through the kindling with a soft roar. Startled, Faris snatched away the flowing wings of her orange robe, but the fire's beauty fascinated her, its sunset colors veined by dark branches like the wings of the monarch butterfly she had found that morning, killed by the cold.

I could draw those flames into a cloak to warm me, she thought. Her hands throbbed with the memory of power. She took a quick breath and stood up, careful because of her pregnancy, and turned to the others who were seated in a semicircle before Misthall's great hearth.

"On this day the powers of light and darkness are balanced and we celebrate the feast of hearth and harvest. We honor not only the hearthfire but the earth from which both reaper and harvest come. Therefore let us reaffirm the Covenant that binds us and Earth's other children, our kin . . ."

The words flowed freely, as if some other part of Faris' consciousness were conducting the ceremony. With doubled vision she saw the firelit faces of the household she and Jehan had gathered around them, and her own prismed reflection.

To Jehan's steward Patrick and his wife Carlota she was the stately priestess of the hearth. Her friend Rosemary was seeing herself, tall and fair, at the hearth of Eric of Seagate whom she loved. To her brother Farin, Faris blazed with more than mortal beauty, but the trained awareness of the Master of the Junipers perceived her as the Queen of the Harvest with her hair earth-dark and her body ripening with child.

Curiously her awareness moved onward to Caolin the Seneschal and halted, finding no reflection in his cold eyes. *But Jehan loves him,* she thought, *and therefore I must love him too*—she sought to draw him into their unity and glimpsed a confusion of the glory she had worn when she and Jehan mastered the forest fire and a coarse and animal opulence that was its opposite.

Frightened, she sought Jehan's familiar strength and stilled in his contemplation of a flame-robed Goddess, the Lady of Fire. Dazzled, her awareness expanded to encompass the fire on the hearth and the earth below, the golden hills of Westria and the life they bore. She was a redwood tree breathing in the sun, a salmon thrashing up the stream, a boar that coughed challenge as it scented a sow. She was the Lady of Westria . . .

Then the King's presence balanced her and she realized that the ceremony was almost done. The others were setting before the hearth the offerings of salt and water, milk and honey, bread and wine, and squash and corn.

"We have laid these gifts before our hearth," her words came clearly, "yet we cannot hallow that which is already more holy than we. Let us therefore take these separate elements into our own bodies, and as they become one in us, let us join with each other and with the earth from which we come . . ." She raised her arms in invocation, feeling the air throb around her. She knew herself at once servant and sovereign, and glimpsed a way of transcending the fear of self-surrender that had kept her from matching Jehan's desire.

"Let it be completed in the names of earth and water, air and fire, and in the Name of the Maker of All Things!" With a gasp she brought down her hands and bent to touch the floor, grounding the energy she had raised.

"Now is my Lady Mistress of her own hearth!" cried Jehan. Faris sighed and went gratefully into his arms, ignoring the others' indulgent smiles, while Carlota dashed for the kitchen and Caolin rose stiffly and turned away.

"Make way for the garden! Make way for the feast!"

Caolin stepped backward abruptly as Jehan's squire Philip strode past, hands to his lips as if he were blowing a trumpet, while Rosemary and Branwen staggered behind him with an enormous wooden bowl of salad to match the tureen of shellfish stew.

"Poor Caolin!" Jehan laughed, drawing the Seneschal toward the table. "We will have to put off our discussion of Lord Brian's mission to Santibar." It did not matter, Caolin told himself as he sat down. As long as the lord of Las Costas was in the south there was little he could do against him. He smoothed back his fair hair and sighed.

"You really do have a garden here." The Master of the Junipers hitched up his grey robe and took his place next to Faris at the foot of the table.

"Well, most of it—" she smiled, serving him a generous portion. The wreath of gold chrysanthemums was already askew on her dark hair. *She was like a Goddess when she wore the Jewel of Fire,* thought Caolin. *What is she now?*

He picked at a slice of duck that had been baked in clay and stuffed with wild rice and herbs and waved onward the dish of zucchini sauced with cheese and dill. He had already eaten at this meal as much as he usually did in a day. Jehan was at the sideboard, slicing the haunch of venison.

"This is my contribution to the feast."

"It was a wonderful shot!" exclaimed Philip. "We tracked the buck for five miles, and my Lord was just drawing when the wind changed, and—"

"Peace, Philip!" said the King, "It was the deer's fate, not my skill."

The boy's mouth closed abruptly, and Farin looked at him in sympathy. "There will be more hunting—it has been a fat year and we help maintain the balance like any other predator. I hear that sometimes wild pigs from the coast come into these hills."

"Wild boar!" Philip's eyes began to sparkle again. Caolin toyed with his meat and took another swallow of Wilhamsted wine as fruit and cheese were passed.

Jehan loosened his belt with a sigh. "Surely there has never been such a feast in all this land!" He smiled the length of the table at Faris.

"That's because it's your own, my Lord," said Carlota, setting before him a bowl of raspberry cream.

He clasped her hand. "Thank you, Carlota, for waiting all those years when it seemed I would never bring a Lady to this Hall." He looked around him. "I know when I am a happy man!"

There were food stains on the King's tunic. Caolin saw in Jehan's full stomach the beginning of a paunch, saw a softening of the clear lines of cheek and jaw, and something within him contracted in pain. He remembered too clearly the clean beauty that had been Jehan's long ago. But the memory of the young King's clear skin and slim grace were replaced by a vision of thickening body and greying hair, a face reddened by good living, and eyes that sought nothing beyond a plump wife and children around the hearth. Alarmed, Caolin looked down at his own belt, tighter now than it had been this morning, but still buckled firmly in the same notch that had held it for ten years.

"For me, happiness is being safe among the ones I love," said Faris tremulously. "I haven't felt this way since my mother died."

Farin pushed aside his pumpkin pie and reached across the table to clasp her hand. "I'm happy as long as I have my harp and my sword!"

Caolin listened with increasing irritation. Did they all believe that the purpose of existence was a full belly and a place by the fire?

"Happiness comes to me when I am part of the harmony of all things," said the Master of the Junipers in his voice that was at once both rough and sweet. "But my life has been laid in pleasant places—contentment is no virtue in me."

"Then you must seek a challenge that will make you earn your happiness!" the words burst from Caolin's lips. "It is the struggle to achieve more than one has that proves to us we are alive! Don't you understand that—" he stopped abruptly, seeing the surprise on the faces of those who were still listening, and tried to laugh. For a moment he met the grave gaze of the Master of the Junipers, then looked away, realizing uncomfortably that of them all, the man he disliked most was probably the only one who had understood.

Presently people began to leave the table. Philip and the Master started a game of chess. Farin brought out his harp. Caolin stood apart, watching the colors change while the room darkened around him. After some time, he turned back to the fire, meaning to ask Jehan when they could discuss the report from Santibar.

He found the King sleeping with his head on Faris' lap, her hands upon his dark hair. Jehan lay utterly still, vanquished by the feast and the softness of the woman's arms. Caolin fought an impulse to haul him to his feet and out the door, away from the murmur of women's voices and the warmth of the fire.

But it would do no good. As long as Jehan could seek oblivion in Faris' dark eyes he was lost to him as surely as if the traitor's arrow had found his heart last spring. Faris was as earthbound as the pumpkins that flanked the hearth, her arms like clinging vines that in time could crack stone.

With a stifled groan Caolin strode from the room. His brown mare tossed her head skittishly as he led her from the stall, but he cuffed her and cinched the saddle tight before she had time to swell her sides. The road was dim, but the mare knew the way. Caolin pressed her over the pass and spurred her into a canter as they reached the level ground beneath the walnut groves. They were galloping as they passed Wilhamsted, nearly knocking over a small boy herding sheep along the road.

Caolin's body jarred as the mare leaped forward, and the regular motion imposed at last a kind of order on his memories. *Jehan's slack body . . . Faris' complacent gaze . . . the silver in Jehan's hair . . .* As the road curved over the lower slopes of the Red Mountain he let the mare slow to a walk. The peak bulked dark against the early stars. He controlled an impulse to turn the mare toward the temple he had built there at Midsummer, where he had touched the Mountain's power, the one place where he need not pretend.

Pretend what? The horse paused as Caolin's fingers tightened on the reins. "Since Jehan married Faris I have been pretending that all is well, when every day he loses more of his youth, his beauty, his spirit. When they fought the forest fire they were like a god and goddess, but Faris has bound him to the earth again now." He urged the mare forward again. "Will Jehan be so happy ten years from now when Faris has become a fat sow like her sister, and he realizes that he has thrown his manhood away?"

And yet what could he do? Caolin let the mare amble, staring into the night until his thoughts acquired substance again. The King was required to have a Queen and an heir. It was Jehan's *obsession* with Faris that must be cured. His passion must be killed or turned to something that would kill Faris' smothering need for him. Yes, that would be better, since it would free Jehan from guilt.

But Jehan will suffer . . . Something twisted in Caolin's belly as he remembered Jehan's grief when love disappointed him before. Did he want more days like that, searching frantically for something to bring back Jehan's smile and fearing to leave him alone?

But Faris might betray Jehan in any case. Last spring her heartlessness had been the talk of the Corona. Considering it that way, Caolin realized that he must make Jehan invulnerable to such a loss and let his own love compensate as he had before.

In the library at Laurelynn there were books unknown even to the Masters at the College of the Wise. Surely Caolin would find a way there to turn Jehan's love to hate and save him from his folly.

He dug his heels into the mare's sides and whipped her neck with the reins until they were stumbling down the river road. Then Caolin let the reins slacken at last and eased back in the saddle, feeling the wind chill his damp brow and seeing in the distance the lights of Laurelynn.

"You should take care, my lord. I think that Brian is as much your enemy as you are his." Ordrey eased further down in the soft chair, brushing dust from the muted plaid of the Elayan kilt he still wore. He was a little, gingery man and Caolin's most trusted servant.

Caolin tapped the papers Ordrey had just brought him against his palm, wishing it had not taken the man until mid-October to get them here. Brian's writing sprawled across the page—ill-spelt, but legible enough to one who had an interest in deciphering it. It had been addressed to Brian's lady, Alessia of Moonbay, but its tone would have suited any comrade-in-arms.

> We have done what we can here, and you may expect me back before November ends. I think now that my quarrel is not with the King but with his Seneschal. Caolin is no warrior. When Elaya attacks us, what if I tell Jehan that I will not ride to war—not I nor any man who swears to me—while Caolin bears the Kingdom's keys? Will Jehan choose his Seneschal above his throne?

Caolin stared through the window, his thoughts as fragmented as the courtyard seen through the leaded glass. If it came to a choice, what would Jehan do?

"Brian means to make my head the price of his sword . . ." he said softly.

Ordrey nodded. "It's true Elaya is arming. They are beating crude iron from the desert mines into blanks for swords and the impis are practicing maneuvers below Palomon's citadel. We will need Brian's sword, come spring."

"We will need my head as well!" snapped the Seneschal. "If only to make sure they don't lose at the peace table what they win in war!"

Ordrey shrugged. "I will not argue with you, but why not pretend to let Brian have his way? Agree with the King to 'resign' until this war is done. After bearing the load alone for a time he should be only too eager to reinstate you."

Caolin moved closer to the window. Clerks scurried across the courtyard and carts bore the produce of Westria into the Royal City and the products of Laurelynn out again. He touched the glass as if he could feel the pulse of the Kingdom through his fingertips and knew it was more than a metaphor.

The heart of Westria beat here in his building through which records of all the comings and goings in the Kingdom passed; in this mind that compared, evaluated and understood them all. But would Jehan see it that way?

And what would happen if he followed Ordrey's advice? Would Brian be content with that victory or would the taste of power only whet his thirst for more? King and Seneschal might share the responsibility for a Kingdom, but in an army there could be no divided command.

Caolin shook his head. "I do not think that Brian will let go once he has Westria in his grasp." He looked back at the letter.

> Therefore, my lady, be vigilant, and set our friends to examine Caolin's doings as formerly they watched the King. I do not think he will be cast off easily . . .

Caolin suppressed the desire to crumple the thin sheets and laid them carefully on the desk once more. *You are right in one thing, Brian,* he thought, *I will never willingly give up Westria!*

He turned to Ordrey. "Brian and I have only been playing until now! But Jehan will never be able to rule him without me, and I do not want him free to breed trouble here while Jehan is at war! Brian's own weight will drag him down, but I cannot wait that long—" he went on more slowly, "if Brian will not incriminate himself then we must help him!"

Ordrey grinned. "Oh, indeed! And what happens when Jehan finds out?"

Caolin did not answer. He moved back to the window, staring unseeing at the glass as the day faded to dusk. He remembered Jehan as he had last seen him, supine in the arms of his Queen.

Jehan must never know . . .

> In times past, each god made sacred certain birds and beasts to signify his powers . . . In the north, the god who ruled men's generative powers had as symbol the boar, by reason of his fierceness and fecundity.

Caolin replaced the marker and carefully closed the book, brushing age-powdered leather from his fingertips. Each book on his table had passages similarly tagged, the result of a month's work in the library at Laurelynn. He rubbed at eyes reddened by lack of sleep—he could only do this research after the day's work was done, in the moments when he was not searching for a way to trap Brian.

In his mind the two problems had become the same—to destroy Jehan's trust in Brian, that threatened Caolin's position; to destroy Jehan's obsession with Faris that had diverted his love. The tools for his second purpose lay here.

Beside the books lay the notes on rite and symbol upon which he would base his ritual. He would have liked more time, but Samain was only a week away, and Jehan would be returning to Laurelynn. He must act soon.

It was long since he had applied the principles of ceremonial magic he had learned at the College of the Wise. Still it was simply a matter of patterning the symbols to focus the power of the mind until the alternate reality envisioned achieved an existence of its own. The most effective rituals used many minds bent toward the same end, but a single sorcerer could achieve as much with sufficient strength of will.

Caolin rested his head in his hands, remembering the warnings against solitary sorcery. A man working alone was apt to forget that he was only human and that the power he exercised was a gift to be used for the good of all.

"And so it shall be!" he exclaimed, "though I doubt those fools at the College would say so! Are a flock of sheep wiser than the shepherd just because there are more of them?"

He pushed back his chair and began to pace about the room. He must wait until sundown to begin his work, and though anxiety was foolish, he could not sit still. He opened another box and leaned the stuffed boar's head he had found in the palace at Laurelynn against the wall.

"You shall help me, old tusker!" he turned the head so that its glass eyes glowed red in the sunset light. "This is not so different from the skills I use to rule Ordrey and others . . ." He stopped, remembering that he had not used his ability to control men's minds since he questioned Ronald Sandreson and the man died.

"I misjudged Ronald's weakness—" he addressed the boar's head as if it could absolve him. "That does not mean my technique is wrong! I cannot touch another's mind, but there are things I *can* do. Why should I stop my studies—it is all for the good of Westria!"

The door creaked and he whirled. Then he realized it was only the deaf and dumb woman, Margit, with his dinner. She turned the ruined side of her face away and smiled shyly.

"Well, Margit," he said genially. "You must feed me well tonight, for I've a great work to do—transforming a King's passion for his Queen from love to lust!" He gestured toward the boxes, laughed as she peered at him uncertainly and showed her a tunic of Jehan's, a gown of the Queen's. And seeing Margit next to the gown, he realized how much she looked like Faris, despite her handicaps.

"Oh no—don't go yet, my pretty one . . ." he pulled her toward him, ignoring her trembling. "You live to serve me, don't you—well you shall serve me well! My plan was sound enough, but I think I see a better way!"

"Would you like to be beautiful, Margit?" he went on. "You shall be—as beautiful as a Queen. Put on this gown!" Holding her eyes, he projected commands until she obeyed, modestly pulling the gown over her head as she dropped the last of her garments, as if her body had been as maimed as her face. Then she stood before him, nervously smoothing the green silk that clung to her breasts and sides.

He twitched the kerchief from her head, loosened her coiled hair. "Dark hair, like *hers* . . ." he murmured. "Now you shall *be* Faris."

He closed his eyes, summoning from all his memories the image of the Queen. She was small, her head just reaching his chin . . . her neck was long and her shoulders slim, the bones fragile as a bird's. Dispassionately he reviewed Faris' body, shaped her face with its smooth curves of cheek and brow, and the fold of her eye-lid that gave the almond shape to her brown eyes. She had a little mole just where one straight eyebrow ended, he remembered, and paused, a little surprised he could visualize her so well.

So—that was Faris—an ordinary woman in whom Jehan for some reason saw the Goddess revealed. That was what he wished to change.

Deliberately, Caolin lifted his ring to catch the last sunset light, and held Margit until her eyes focused on the spot of light. Then he began to project into her mind an image of Faris, subtly distorted from that of the woman he knew to the one he wished Jehan to see. And finally he pictured this green gowned Faris looking in the mirror, and drawing Margit to the small glass that hung beside his door, he took away his hand and let her see her own reflection there.

For a moment he wondered if it would work, then schooled his thoughts, knowing that his own disbelief could make it fail. His breath stilled for the long moment that Margit stared into the mirror, until, very slowly, she smiled.

Caolin's breath eased out in a long sigh. The woman's stance was altering now, her spine straightening with shoulders drawn back to display her breasts. The Queen's birdlike turn of the head became a provocative tilt, her smile more shallow and sensuous. Both more and less than Faris, Margit stretched luxuriously and began to preen before the mirror. Caolin found himself smiling as well, and thought that the role he had set himself might not be so distasteful after all.

But the light was fading. Quickly Caolin pulled on Jehan's tunic, picked up the boar's head and pulled Margit after him into the inner room. Soon candles were flickering on the Altar of Fire, lending a malevolent life to the boar's mask which he had set there.

"Lady of Fire—" his voice echoed dully in the little room. "Light in us a self-consuming flame! Lady of Fire—help me take this woman in violence, in pain, until she hates and fears the thing that she has loved."

His voice rolled on as he fired coals and laid upon them an incense that eddied chokingly around the room, rehearsing all the evils men could commit in the name of passion, evoking every image of lust he knew.

He lit candles until the room was blazing and he was sweating. Margit was perspiring too. Did he dare hope that another kind of fire was kindling now? The reek of the incense dizzied him. Margit's eyes were half-closed and a pulse beat heavily at the base of her throat. He had made her believe herself Faris. Now he must make her believe that he was Jehan.

The image of the King's face came to him immediately, every feature memorized. For a moment the memory of Jehan's beauty stilled his spirit, then Margit sighed, and Caolin remembered what he had to do.

Swiftly he searched his memory for every expression he had ever seen Jehan wear, from laughter to the sick anger that shook the King when he encountered treachery. He passed quickly over the memory of the tender amusement that focused the King's face when he was making love—that look would never be for Caolin again, but it did not matter, not if he could separate him from Faris.

In frustration he realized that it was Jehan's inability to look at a woman with greed that made this work necessary now. Margit must simply see the King's face then—its expression would be Caolin's. He sent the image of Jehan to Margit's mind.

I am Jehan . . . he shivered as he dared imagine what it would be like to inhabit that beautiful body, to lead men who loved him, to rule Westria and bear the Jewels.

He ripped Margit's gown sharply from shoulder to knee. Laughing at her attempts to cover herself, he passed his hands over her body, his fingers closing brutally on her shrinking flesh. Then he thrust her to her knees, and hitching up his tunic, pictured to her what he wanted her to do.

He had thought to prolong her humiliation, to enjoy the sight of that dark head pressed against his loins, but the passion he was evoking grew too quickly. With a gasp he threw himself upon her, battering her with his body until the spearhead of his attack found her vulnerable core. Her lips writhed in a soundless scream, but her struggles served only to impale her more securely now.

Caolin felt power build within him, possessing him as he possessed the body beneath him. Lights danced crazily and the boar's head leered with its red eyes. Then the woman's arms tightened, and he saw not Margit but Faris—no, not Faris, but the completion of her transformation.

He had sought to evoke Love's darker shadow, and its Goddess was here—Her eyes were black fire; Her red lips fastened hungrily on his and Her legs vised around him. Something in the depths of his soul that had only been touched by

Jehan screamed, but his flesh belonged to the Dark Lady now. A brazen clangor clamored in his ears, and he was sucked into the heart of a volcano. His body exploded in a convulsion that engulfed his world.

There was a sharp "pop" as the walnut shell cracked. Faris picked out the nutmeats and dropped them into the bowl, and the broken shell into the fire. Carlota was making walnut pastry for the Samaine feast, and they needed a week to prepare. Rosemary missed the fireplace and bent, her golden braid swinging, to cast the shells again. When she straightened her face was flushed.

"Faris . . ." she swallowed, "now that you are so well settled it is time for me to go home." The nutshells crackled, then the fire returned to its steady purring again.

Faris stared at her. "But Rosemary, I need you here!"

"You have Branwen and Carlota to help you and Jehan to love you, and soon there will be the child."

"If Jehan had to be my constant companion even his love might fray! Besides, he spends so much time on business of the Kingdom which I cannot share."

"Cannot, or will not, Faris? Have you tried?" asked Rosemary.

Faris sighed and clasped her hands over her belly. "No, not yet. I suppose you find that hard to understand—you have been managing a great house since you took your name. But I panic at the thought of even ruling the palace at Laurelynn."

Rosemary touched her hand. "Poor Faris—I did not mean to be unkind. Perhaps I too am afraid."

"Afraid of meeting Eric?" Faris saw Rosemary's stricken look replaced by laughter.

"Haven't we had this conversation before?" Suddenly they both were laughing.

"Well?" said Faris at last, "If my dream came true, why can't yours?"

"Oh very well, I promise to stay with you until the baby has its milkname!"

Faris smiled and picked up another walnut, her eyes returning to the glowing tapestry of the fire. Here with Rosemary it was warm, and tonight she and Jehan would kindle another kind of fire. But as she watched she seemed to see painted in lines of flame a boar's wicked muzzle and glowing eyes. The shadows swept around her like dark wings, and she knew a moment's desire to sink into them.

Jehan, her heart cried, *come soon—I am afraid of the fire . . .*

II

The Samaine Boar

Gouts of fire danced across the darkness. Images flickered in and out of focus—the weathered wood of a wagon . . . Jehan's face white above bloodied bandages . . . blood everywhere . . .

Faris shrieked denial, fought the restraints that would not let her go to him.

"Faris! Wake up—it's all right now . . ."

Faris saw shadow and firelight. She relaxed as she realized that Jehan was holding her and turned to him with a shuddering sigh.

"Faris, my darling, don't cry—it was only a dream."

"A dream!" For the past week she had slept badly, haunted by images for which she had no words. "You were hurt and there was so much blood," she said. "Must you hunt the boar on Samaine eve?"

He laughed softly and pulled her against him so that her head nestled in the hollow where his neck and shoulder joined.

"Is that what troubles your sleep? We will be a dozen men against one poor animal, however fierce he may be. You should pity the boar!"

"But he killed a little boy—" she began.

"Yes, the child of one of my people. That is why I must go," he replied as she whimpered and clung to him. "Darling, I am solid—touch me all you will."

She took his head between her hands, feeling the hard bones beneath his skin and the strong neck where the long tendons merged with the heavy muscling of chest and shoulder. Jehan's skin was fine-textured, satiny to her touch, with the faint taste of salt that had become so familiar to her.

She moved down his body, her hands confirming the contours that covert glances had taught her to reverence. She wondered anew at the corded strength of his forearms, and the roughened texture of those long fingers that could control a plunging stallion or stray like a butterfly's wing across her cheek.

Her hands tried to compass his waist, slipped along his thighs. He held himself still, only his breathing growing a little ragged as her hand closed on the velvet skin of his phallus. She felt it swell beneath her fingers and her terror for him turned to tenderness. She bent to kiss him and recognized in her own body the beginnings of a desire that reflected his.

Farin was sharpening the two-foot blade of the boar spear. His hand stopped as he heard a cry from the room shared by Faris and Jehan, and he tensed with the backlash of his sister's fear. Then the murmur of voices blended with the normal night noises of Misthall.

Farin returned to his task, punctuating the other sounds with the steady rasp of stone on steel. A breath of air touched his cheek. He looked up and saw Faris' maid, Branwen, at the door, clutching her robe around her against the chill.

"I heard something—I thought the Queen called . . ." Hesitantly she came into the room.

"Faris must have had a nightmare. It is too bad she woke the King."

"*You* are awake." Branwen knelt, holding out her hands to the fire.

Farin lifted the spear so that ruddy light ran along the polished surface of the blade, forged from a piece of steel that had been dug from beneath the ruins near the shore. "I'm too excited to sleep," he admitted. "I've never hunted boar." Firelight gleamed on the use-smoothed eight-foot oak shaft as he lifted it and tested the blade.

"Be careful!" Branwen twisted her long braid of brown hair. She looked curiously vulnerable, with the firelight lending her its own soft beauty.

"The boar has a thick hide . . ." Farin tentatively touched the tip of the spear.

Branwen shivered and glanced at the window as if she expected the beast to come ravening through. "I wish you did not have to go."

"The boar has broken his own Covenant, killing a man. The

King must destroy him. Well, we will have roast pork for our Samaine Feast!" He blew dust from the surface of the blade.

Low laughter drifted from the King's room and he heard the creaking of the bed. Branwen took wood from the basket and as she leaned forward to place it on the fire her robe fell open and Farin saw the curve of her breast.

Farin felt his face flaming, not wholly because of the refuelling of the fire. He bent again to his work, but he could not keep from hearing the rhythmical creaking of the King's bed, and looking at Branwen's breast beneath her gown.

Jehan's hand slipped across Faris' breasts and over the curve of her belly, leaving a record of its passing in the tingling of her flesh.

"You still want me, even though my waistline has almost disappeared?"

"Is a ripe pear beautiful?"

"But I am becoming too round for us to be comfortable," she protested.

Jehan turned his head and his breath tickled her ear. "There is a way . . ."

Faris raised herself and moved above him, gasping as her flesh encompassed his. For several moments she held her breath, gazing down at the mystery of his face.

"It is all right for you to move now . . ." Jehan breathed at last.

Faris felt him trembling with something more than laughter. She could see him more clearly now, as if his body were becoming luminous. Her flesh radiated heat and she stilled, remembering other times she had felt such a glow—when she danced at Beltane, and when she put on the Jewels of Power. But this time she could choose whether to feed or to snuff the flame, and surrender herself completely at last.

Deliberately Faris set her hands upon Jehan's shoulders and began to move her body against his, riding waves of sweet fire that swept her toward some unimaginable shore until she no longer knew whether it was she who moved or he. She bent over him, seeking his spirit as her awareness of his separate body disappeared. Glimpses of her own face refracted from his consciousness to hers, blazing with a splendor in which her beauty was not so much transformed as revealed.

A cry swelled in her throat and she felt, rather than heard,

Jehan call out her name. Then she was falling, and her shout of triumph vibrated through every level of her being like the reverberations of a great golden bell.

Hearing that cry, Farin dropped the weapon he held. Branwen clutched at his arm, he turned and found himself kissing her. She gave a little sigh and her arms crept around his neck, and Farin, panting from a heat grown suddenly unendurable, tore at his clothing and sank down upon her before the fire.

The Master of the Junipers, meditating in his room on the floor below them, found his thoughts turning to festivals at the College of the Wise and smiled.

Rosemary stirred restlessly in her sleep, and turning her head into her pillow, murmured Eric's name.

Caolin moaned and ground his body against his crumpled blanket. The sound of ripping fabric woke him and he lay still, waiting for his pounding heart to slow and wondering angrily to whom he had been making love in his dream.

After a few moments he stumbled to the window, shrugging into his robe. There was a fresh, dawn smell to the air. He shivered, for the October air was chill, and rested his head in his hands. His body was still bruised from the ritual he had performed the week before, and since then he had known no peaceful sleep. Strangely Margit had been affected less than he . . . what had happened to Faris and Jehan?

When he opened his door, he saw a square of white upon the floor. The graceful writing was Jehan's—someone must have brought it during the night and feared to wake him. But the King was supposed to return to Laurelynn today—could he have learned somehow of the trap the Seneschal was forging for Brian? Caolin tore off the wrapper, cursed as the lines of writing dimmed and swam in the half-light, and fumbled with flint and steel.

"My dear friend . . . a rogue boar at Wilhamsted . . . enough men gathered to hunt the beast on Samaine eve." Caolin's eyes moved quickly over the candlelit paper. "Please make my apologies to the Lord Mayor and the others."

Samaine eve . . . thought Caolin. That was today. Jehan's delay would give him more time to seal Brian's fate. And yet . . . He stopped, wondering why his heart was pounding so heavily, and looked at the letter again.

"I will be going after a rogue boar . . ." An image of the

boar's mask that Caolin had used in his ritual swam before Jehan's words. And Wilhamsted lay at the foot of the Red Mountain . . .

"No!" Caolin swung his head back and forth in denial. "It is only a natural beast, and Jehan is a skilled hunter!" But he whimpered at the vision of the boar's head he had left on the Altar of Fire charging down the mountain to rend and slay.

"It is not my fault!" he cried again. "There is nothing I can do!" But already he was searching his wardrobe for a hunting tunic and hauling out his riding boots. Outside, the mists of morning dispersed before the growing light of day.

Jehan took another bite of bread and cheese, marvelling at the quantities of food with which the folk of Wilhamsted had weighted the table. This time, there was a grimmer meaning to the festival of the dead which they celebrated every year. Two of the men who had promised to help them avenge their son had yet to arrive, and Jehan knew they would need time to get organized. He forced himself to eat, stifling his impatience to get back to Faris. The memory of their lovemaking still shimmered through every nerve—what need had he of food?

"If this were war I would be going into battle with the King."

Jehan glanced across the room and saw his squire Philip standing with a girl of sixteen whose fingers played ceaselessly with the dagger at her belt.

"This *is* a war," she said grimly. "Neither of us has the weight to face the boar, but my father has assigned me to lead the beaters who will drive him into the trap. We will have plenty to do." Sir Walter of Wilhamsted's daughter spoke with a gloomy pride, fully aware of her status as sister of the boy who had been slain.

"My father says I make enough noise to wake the dead— I guess I can scare the boar . . . I hope we can see the men finish him." Philip said eagerly.

Jehan suppressed a smile, remembering how excited he had been to serve as a beater when his father hunted peccary in the south.

"Would you like some ale, my Lord?" A woman with thick iron-grey braids bound about her head stood holding out a tankard and smiling like an old friend. Jehan thanked her, frowning as he tried to remember her name.

"Oh, it was a long time ago, in the old King's time. Your

horse went lame near my holding and you stayed the night." She laughed.

"Mistress Martina!" He took her hand, grinning as he remembered that he had slept that night with her. "Forgive me—you have changed less than I."

"Well, you're a married man now, and with a child coming, I hear."

Jehan smiled. "But for that, I would have brought my Lady with me today." He was aware once more of muffled weeping from the other room. "I wish Faris were here—when I spoke to the boy's mother I did not know what to say."

"You are our own lord here, not only the King. It is enough that you came."

There was a clatter of hooves and sounds of greeting from outside. Jehan turned as the door opened and was surprised to see his Seneschal there.

"Caolin!" The King's steps slowed and he frowned as Caolin put back his hood. "Is something wrong?" The Seneschal's pale hair bristled about his ears and his tunic was half unlaced. But it was his face that stirred the quick throb of alarm.

Faris! he thought, then realized that Caolin had come not from Misthall but from Laurelynn. "Are we invaded?" he laughed with relief. He held out his hand and Caolin pressed his fingers as if to reassure himself of the King's solidity.

"No—why should anything be wrong? You wrote you would have some sport today and I thought I might join you. I know the countryside hereabouts fairly well." The Seneschal straightened and passed a restraining hand over the disorder of his hair. The King peered at him, wondering at the marks like old bruises beneath Caolin's eyes. Even the flesh of his face was subtly altered, as if it were losing its hold on his bones.

"Have you been ill?" Jehan handed him a tankard.

The Seneschal shook his head quickly. "I've been having trouble sleeping. Perhaps I need exercise."

"Are you sure that is all? You must have *some* other reason for coming here." Jehan looked at his friend narrowly but could not interpret the color that came and went in Caolin's face. "I can't believe you don't intend to seize this opportunity to talk politics!"

Caolin took a long drink and shrugged. "I have no papers with me, but there is always news." Jehan raised an inquiring eyebrow. "The Lord Commander of Seagate is ill again, and this time he is not expected to live."

The King sighed. "I shall be sorry to lose Hakon, and the lordship will be a heavy burden to come to Eric so young—I should know."

"And the Commissioners from Santibar will be returning soon," Caolin went on.

"Yes, I expected that," said Jehan absently, his thoughts still on Eric. Perhaps he could send the Master of the Junipers to him for a while.

"I thank you all for coming to me in my need—" Sir Walter's voice boomed around the room and Jehan and Caolin turned. "The afternoon is passing, and I have sworn not to lay my boy in the earth until I can bury the boar's head at his feet!"

Jehan stared, somewhat appalled at this passion for vengeance. *But what if one of mine were killed?* he wondered. *How would I feel?*

"You have marked the boar's run?" he asked quickly.

Sir Walter nodded. "He lairs on the slopes of the Red Mountain, but there is a gully through which he comes to wallow in the stream. We have the nets to span it and entangle him—"

"And *we* have the spears to pin him once he is caught!" said Farin.

"And the hounds?" said the King.

"Fifteen of them—the pack that I keep for the valley," said Jaime of Palodoro, a neighbor. "They will track anything on legs."

"And we have something to give them the scent," said Sir Walter with grim pride. He was holding out a boy's knife to which a few reddish bristles clung. "My boy marked him, and I swear that I will kill his slayer without delay, without pity—"

"Without breaking the Covenant." Jehan's quiet voice stilled the others as they remembered who and what he was.

"Then make the petition, and let us go!" whispered Sir Walter hoarsely.

Jehan lifted his weapon from the rack of spears, clasping his hands around its shaft, and the others followed his example with their own. The King took a deep breath and closed his eyes, reaching out to the men who stood with him.

"In the name of the four elements whose balance signifies the proper balance of all things; in the name of the Lord of All; may that Being who rules the Pig-tribe hear us now," cried the King.

"Hear us now!" the others echoed him.

"Upon these blades we swear that we begin this hunting not in malice nor for idle sport, but to enforce the Covenant that sets for each creature his own bounds. With our weapons we will come to grips with this boar, body to body, tusk to steel. And if he should prevail, we forgive him our deaths, as we ask thy forgiveness for his." In the silence that followed, the speartips touched with a succession of metallic clicks. Outside the dogs yapped eagerly, but the Red Mountain waited, unmoved.

"How long must we sit here?" Caolin peered through the screen of laurel branches at the slope of the Red Mountain above them.

"Have patience, old friend—" said the King in a low voice. "This hunting is not unlike war—a great deal of marching and waiting and a few flurries of action that finish before you quite know they've begun." He had not moved.

"Sir Walter says that every evening for the past week the boar has come this way to feed." Farin was sitting on a pitted curve of concrete that had been part of some ancient wall. "They are holding the dogs upwind until he enters the gully."

Caolin looked at Jehan's bright eyes and calm face and wondered if this was how he appeared to the men he led to battle. Both duty and inclination had always assigned the Seneschal what he considered the thornier problems of supplying the King's forces or negotiating a conclusion to his wars. Here was an aspect of Jehan's nature he had never had a chance to know.

Jehan smiled. "The waiting galls me too. My Lady and I have achieved our full joy at last, and I would be home again."

Caolin winced at the triumphant wonder in Jehan's eyes.

"Why not come home with me, Caolin?" the King went on. "We can give you a good meal and a soft bed."

The scraps from your table and a pallet by your door . . . how long can I live on the leftovers of your happiness, my Lord? The words trembled against the barrier of Caolin's lips.

Before he could voice a reply, the stillness was broken by the hysterical yammering of the hounds.

The three men sprang to their feet, reaching for their spears, all senses subordinated to hearing as they tried to interpret the confusion of barking and shouting and the boar's occasional deep grunt of rage.

LADY OF DARKNESS

"What's happening? We've got to see!" cried Farin. He swung himself into the bay tree and Jehan's protest was lost in the thrashing of branches. "Lord of Battles! He's a monster! They're all around him now, trying to drive him this way—" They heard a yelp of agony. "He's got one of the dogs . . . another . . . oh! Philip barely got out of the way!"

"Farin, get down! We must be ready—"

Jehan's order was interrupted by Farin's moan, "He's broken away!"

"What?"

"The boar—he charged straight up the bank!" The tree shuddered as Farin danced on his branch.

"Which side?" snapped the King.

"Ours!" Farin's voice squeaked unexpectedly.

"Down!" cried Jehan, "He must not catch us here!"

Caolin followed the King to the comparatively open ground of the canyon floor while Farin flung himself from his tree and crashed after them. They listened again, tracing the boar's progress by the yapping of the hounds.

"Sir Walter—" cried the King, "the boar is past the net! We must cut him off further down the canyon!" He drew his short hunting sword and began to hack at the ropes that held the net. In moments Sir Walter and his three men had joined them. When it was free they dragged it after them, hoping they could still use it to entangle their foe.

There was a patter of footfalls and Jaime of Palodoro stumbled around the bend behind them with Philip and the other beaters.

"Walter, I'm sorry—he's too crafty—" Jaime broke off as a dog burst from the bank beyond them, bleeding from a gash along his side.

"My Lord, we'll run down the canyon. You follow if the dogs flush the beast and we'll surround him—" Sir Walter led his men at a trot around the bend.

Caolin leaned on his spear, glancing nervously at the tumbled rocks of the gully's sloping sides. They were glowing now with the fiery light of the dying day.

"Jaime says that sometimes a boar will turn and hunt his hunters. They can move silently, he says, and—"

"Farin, be still." Jehan's quiet voice cut off the harper's babbling and steadied Caolin so suddenly that he wondered if the King could control the boar too. Then he jumped at a sound like a covey of quail taking flight—the noise of a heavy body penetrating brush at high speed.

The red boar erupted over the edge of the slope in a flurry of dogs. But before the hunters could seize the advantage he was on his feet again. Crimson-tusked he faced them, swiveling as they circled him, ears flicking and head swinging to track his enemies. His shoulder bore the festering wounds of some mating fight. Had that pain maddened him to invade the lands of men?

Caolin met the animal's furious gaze and took a step backward. Sir Walter shouldered past him and only the King's restraining hand kept him from charging the boar alone. The dogs danced about their foe, deafening the men with shrill yapping, but those that remained were more cautious now. The boar moved only enough to keep them from hamstringing him, rumbling his defiance at the men.

Sir Walter's daughter and Farin ran forward with the net, but the boar's rush drove them back again, tripping on the loose stones. Caolin felt the spear haft grow slippery in his grasp; every taunt with which Brian and others had ever questioned his courage echoed in his memory. Surreptitiously he wiped his palms—no one should doubt him now—but the reality of the boar was worse than its image in his ritual. His desperate glance sought the King.

Jehan balanced on the treacherous ground, spear poised, lips curving in an interested smile, his eyes never leaving the boar. "Drop the net," he said softly. "We will have to attack *him*."

"Then he'll charge for certain!" gasped one of the men.

"Jaime! Can you call the dogs to one more attack?" asked the King.

"Well, my Lord, I'll try." Jaime whistled sharply. His pack leader, a brindled bitch whose flanks were already splashed red, whined unhappily, then leaped forward, snapping at the boar's tender ears.

"Now!" shouted the King as the boar's head jerked and the dog was flung over their heads. Sir Walter screamed his battle cry.

Caolin found himself running forward with the others, aware of a blur of rocks and the vivid bulk of the boar. His spear hit as if he had struck a stone wall, the boar heaved and he felt his foot slip. Frantically Caolin tried to hold on while the boar twisted himself further onto the spears.

Battered by the struggles of the beast as he had battered at

Margit in his ritual, Caolin clung to his spear. The remaining dogs leaped in to hamstring their hampered enemy. The boar jerked convulsively and Caolin's mouth shut with a snap. There was a sharp crack and Jehan flew backward with a broken spearshaft in his hand.

The King rolled to his feet and drew his hunting sword. The boar swung to face him, eyes glowing furiously. The hunters swore, knowing they had not the strength to hold him if anyone withdrew his spear to try a new stab and give the King a safer opening.

"Don't attack from the front, my Lord—" called Jaime. "They cannot stop him if he goes for you!"

"Use the net!" screeched Farin.

"Jaime cannot throw it without tangling you. If I wait he may break loose and savage you all." The King crouched, still smiling. "Hold fast!"

The blood drummed in Caolin's ears. "Jehan, don't!" he found his voice as the King lunged. His swinging steel flared in the light of the setting sun.

Time expanded with a terrible clarity as the bright blade fell. It struck the vulnerable crease where the boar's neck and shoulder met. Then the fury in the boar's eyes dazzled Caolin with flame and darkness and his fingers lost their hold on the spear.

The boar surged forward, his bright blood spattering the men who were no longer enough to hold him, and struck the King. The huge head lowered to gore his foe. Sir Walter tugged the axe from his belt and brought it down with all his strength upon the animal's spine. The boar seemed to rock upward, then dropped, jerking until the mortal message of his wounds finally reached his limbs.

Blood covered the boar, the ground, Caolin's eyes. He groped for a twitching foreleg and found other hands beside his, hauling the body of the boar from the King. *I did this . . . it came of my ritual . . .* Accusations reverberated in his brain. Then the red bulk was gone. Caolin collapsed to his knees.

"Caolin—" Jehan was breathless. "Now you can use what you learned of healing at the College of the Wise. Quickly, before I begin to feel the pain."

The tumult in Caolin's mind stilled. "Yes, Jehan," he heard his own clear reply. Dark blood was welling from beneath the King's leather tunic. Caolin lifted it and saw the red tear cutting raggedly from his groin up his side.

"First we must stop the bleeding. Give me your shirts—" He pressed the wadded cloth they gave him against Jehan's side.

"Is he dead?" Farin's voice wavered. Caolin's heart thumped as he saw that Jehan's eyes were closed.

"It is the Feast of the Dead!" said one man with a superstitious shiver. "He is the Sacrifice!"

"He's just fainted!" said Sir Walter bracingly, pulling his shirt over his head.

Mechanically Caolin cast away the soaked rag and applied another, putting all his weight upon it, willing the bleeding to ease. If the boar's tusk had torn the femoral artery there would be nothing he could do. His lips moved soundlessly in the first petition he had made since he left the College of the Wise.

"Do you need another bandage?"

Caolin looked up and felt an obscure pang of sympathy for the terror in Philip's face. Then he realized that the stain on the pad pressed against the King's side had ceased to grow. He took Philip's shirt and swiftly used it to replace the one that had stanched the wound.

"The bleeding is under control," he breathed. "Give me strips to bind the bandage on." Caolin felt down the King's body for other injuries.

As their shock eased the others began to talk. Caolin heard the dull, regular blows with which Sir Walter was hacking off the head of the boar.

"By all the Guardians, Jaime, why didn't you stop the King?" asked Farin.

"I couldn't reach him in time! Why didn't you all stand fast? The beast shook you like dogs and the Seneschal let go of his spear."

Caolin tensed, but Farin was already protesting, describing the boar's strength with a bard's flow of imagery that silenced dispute.

"I believe the King's leg is broken—" Caolin finished his examination. "Let me have the broken spearshaft to splint it before we move him. And we will need a litter to carry him home."

"Bind that damned net to some spears to make a hammock," suggested Sir Walter. "We might as well get some use out of it."

Caolin bent over Jehan, gently stroking his hair. The King's head turned restlessly and his lips moved.

". . . forgive him our deaths as we . . ." the blue eyes opened and focused upon the headless body of the boar, ". . . ask thee to forgive us his," he finished. "How badly am I hurt?"

"I have done what I could, Jehan," said Caolin. "Your leg is broken and there is a hole in your side, but I think there is nothing that cannot heal."

The King breathed in carefully. "You must get me home, to Faris. Take me to Misthall!" He was growing paler, and sweat beaded his brow.

"Yes, my Lord," said Sir Walter. "We are making a litter, but it will be a rough ride and I am afraid we will cause you pain."

"Never mind—" said Jehan with a ghost of his old grin. "If I am lucky I will faint again."

They stumbled homeward through the gathering dusk, Caolin walking beside the litter with his eyes on the pale face of the King while his feet found their own road. An east wind chilled the back of his neck as if the Mountain were sending its cold breath after them. Caolin looked back and shivered, for the slope above him reproduced the silhouette of the boar against the dimming sky.

A cold wind was blowing through the open door of the Hall. Faris drew her shawl more closely around her, wishing she could close it, but on this night every household in Westria left open one door, as they set candles flickering on their window-sills, to guide the returning spirits of the Dead and to welcome them home.

The scent of Carlota's walnut pastry wafted enticingly from the kitchen. She should be in there, gossiping with the others, not waiting here alone in the darkened hall. They would have a fine feast tomorrow, with a ham from their own cellars if Jehan did not bring home a haunch of the boar.

But where was he? Whether or not they had killed, he should have been home before dark. Was he so excited by the hunt that he had forgotten her? He had never had a wife to consider before. But how could Jehan forget her after last night—when even the warm flush of memory felt as if it would melt her bones?

"Faris—what are you doing here?" The Master of the Junipers was like a shadow himself in his grey robe. She turned to him, wordless, and he put his arm around her. "It will be all right, Faris—Jehan is too courteous to rush away from his hosts, no matter how eager he is to be home."

He brought her a cloak and built up the fire since she would not go to a warmer room. But it was long past sunset, and the rest of the household had joined them there, before they finally heard the sound of hooves on the road.

Faris went to the doorway. Torches were bobbing through the mists that blanketed the hillside without visible support, as if they were being borne by the spirits of the dead. The damp air caught in her throat and she coughed.

"They don't seem very jubilant—" said Rosemary brightly. "Do you suppose the boar got away?"

"Be quiet, Rosemary." Peering through the shrouding fog, Faris stepped slowly across the porch, down the first stair . . . the second . . . Then she waited, unable to move.

The Master of the Junipers hurried past her as the procession neared. Like images in some evil dream Faris saw Caolin's haunted eyes, saw the wagon beside him and the blood, blood everywhere. They halted. Carefully they lifted a litter from the wagon. She saw Jehan's white unconscious face and the moisture glittering on his hair and beard.

Faris tottered forward, screaming his name. But they would not let her go to him.

III

A Season of Pain

> My greatest pleasure has become the simple release from pain . . .

Jehan's pen slipped and carefully he moved his good leg to brace the Journal in which he was writing. The wound in his groin still throbbed dully, though the boar hunt had been a month ago.

For convenience they had put him in the old King's bedroom on the first floor of Misthall, with its great carved bedstead and heavy curtains of faded blue brocade. Jehan turned a page, marvelling that he had filled two-thirds of the Journal since June.

> I dream that I am in my own bed with Faris beside me—
> just holding her, breathing the mountain-flower scent of
> her hair. And then I wake in darkness and remember that
> my parents both died in this bed . . . Farin's music would
> help me, but I don't want to wake him in the night.

Farin was playing for him now, his fingers wandering across the harpstrings in a seeming random pattern through which a melody threaded like the gold in the curtains' brocade. Through the window beyond him Jehan glimpsed morning sunlight glittering on the blue of the Bay, very welcome after a week of rain.

The King put down his pen. "What is the tune?"

Farin looked up, color rising in his cheeks. "Just a harpsong, my Lord."

"It sounded like a love song to me."

"I suppose, in a way, it is . . ." Farin's fingers caressed

the gold inlay of the harp's frame a moment before they settled once more on the strings and he sang—

> *"My little harp, for thy great gift of music,*
> *I offer now this faltering song to thee.*
> *More faithful hast thou been than any lover,*
> *And sweeter thy companionship to me.*
> *I seek thy touch when worn by fear or sorrow,*
> *And ever comes thy answer cheerfully—*
> *For thee I must forgo all tears and anger—*
> *Thy nature knows no bitter harmony."*

Farin played the harp as though it had become a part of him, modulating the end of his first verse, then continuing—

> *"To me thou art the very shape of beauty,*
> *Thy weight against my breast delights my heart.*
> *And when my roving fingers wake thy music,*
> *My ears rejoice. Obedient to my art,*
> *Thy sweet response is yet more sweet unbidden,*
> *And when, unwilled, I hear thy singing start,*
> *I know not which of us has made the music,*
> *Or if the god of love plays now a part."*

Jehan remembered times when he and Faris had made such harmony . . . He roused as the last notes died away and looked at Farin.

"Don't you ever want a human being who can return your love?"

Farin rested his forehead against the smooth wood of the harp. "I have been with women, and it was good, but when I am playing Swangold sometimes music comes that I never heard before. I don't know what we are reaching for, but I think that together Swangold and I may find it, someday . . ."

Faris and I found it, the night before I hunted the boar . . . thought Jehan, *But now she seems so far from me, and it is all to do again.* He sighed, remembering how he had feared he would never succeed in giving her joy, and now he feared she might tire of waiting for him to be able to make love to her again. Human beings were so vulnerable—perhaps Farin had made the better choice.

"I am selfish to keep you here, Farin," Jehan said abruptly. "You should be studying at the College of Bards."

"Oh my King, let me stay!" Farin exclaimed. "Perhaps one day I will follow the Bard's road, but not yet, not now!"

"Where is he going?" Faris gently closed the door behind her. She was wearing a loose gown of a blue as pale as the rain-washed sky and her arms were full of chrysanthemums whose spicy scent filled the air.

"I only suggested . . ." began the King, but Farin's "Nowhere!" interrupted him.

Faris shook her head in exasperation and began to remove the old flowers from the vase beside the bed.

"I've no need to ask what you've been doing this morning," Jehan smiled.

"Oh, it's a beautiful day! The poplars are all pale gold, and the firs look black against this sky. After a rain everything glows and you forget how dreary it was before." She kissed him and he breathed in scents of damp leaves and rain-fresh wind. There was a splash of mud on her sleeve.

"Yes, and I suppose you have forgotten to change your shoes, too."

"Oh Jehan! They will dry soon enough. You are the one who has been ill—why do you worry about me?" Her voice came muffled through the fall of her hair as she bent over the vase. "I could nurse you as well as Rosemary . . ."

"You were always sick when we were children—" said Farin.

Faris dashed her hair from her eyes and turned on him, "And *you* were always breaking bones—but now you go to war."

Jehan stared at her uncomfortably. He had told the Master of the Junipers to keep her away because he feared to let her see him weeping with pain.

"Faris," he faltered, "we wanted to spare you, because of the child."

"Spare me!" She slipped to her knees beside the bed and hid her face against his arm. "Perhaps you are right! I might have begged to be allowed to go away! But you never gave me the chance to try . . ."

Jehan turned on his side to stroke her hair, murmuring her name, and she twisted suddenly to meet his lips. He felt a familiar stirring in his loins, and though it was a faint reflection of remembered fires, his arms went around Faris exultantly. For a long moment they remained so, until the strained position tired his weakened muscles and he lay back on his pillows.

"Is everything ready for Eric's ceremony?" he asked a little breathlessly.

"As ready as we can make them," said Farin. "I wish he could wait."

"Eric could wait, but he should not," replied Jehan. "Every day we put off his investiture as Lord Commander will make it harder for him to step into his father's shoes."

"I think Eric will be happier with a small ceremony." Faris smiled.

"It won't be that small—" her brother replied. "Eric's family is coming, and people from Seagate, and the other Commanders. At least Robert of the Ramparts will come, and Lord Brian if the Commissioners get back from Santibar in time."

"Yes, and Caolin will be here too. I will be glad to see him again." said Jehan.

Caolin picked up the letter and compared it with the one on his desk. The sprawling writing was the same, and the signature that covered half the page. Even the seal showed a realistic variation in depth and angle. The man whom Ordrey had found to write the letter was indeed a master of his craft. Brian himself would have cause to wonder if he had penned these words. Caolin flattered himself that he had fairly caught Brian's blustering style. It was a pretty style for treason.

But would Jehan believe it?

The Seneschal rested his head in his hands, kneading the taut muscles in his forehead. After the first shock, Caolin had realized that Jehan's accident gave him time to prepare a weapon against Brian. And it must be used. With Jehan too ill to control him, Brian was even more dangerous.

But his plot was horribly uncertain. What if Brian's agents learned of the forgery? What if Brian evaded arrest and led the south into rebellion, or even joined forces with Elaya?

Tomorrow he must go to Misthall to see Eric of Seagate invested as Lord Commander of his Province. Caolin fingered the forged letter, wondering whether he would have the courage to give it to Jehan. Brian had left Santibar with the other Commissioners over a week ago.

He was running out of time.

It was time to begin.

Jehan nodded to the herald of Seagate, and the old man stepped out before the company whose bright robes glowed in the afternoon sunlight, the petition trembling in his hand.

"We, the people of Seagate, having lately lost our beloved lord . . . do now desire Jehan, King of Westria to give to us another, to be our gracious governor in time of peace and our leader in time of war . . ."

"Whom do the people of Seagate ask for their Lord?" The Seneschal's calm reply carried the ritual forward.

"They ask for Eric of the Horn, accepted by the landholders of Seagate as Lord Hakon's heir." The herald bowed to the King.

Jehan shifted uncomfortably in his cushioned chair, avoiding the eyes of the Master of the Junipers. Caolin turned to him.

"My Lord, is it your will to grant this request?"

"It is my will."

Caolin shifted smoothly to face the company. "Then let Eric of the Horn come into the presence of the King."

Jehan pulled himself upright—Eric must not see him slumped in his chair. The far doors of the Hall were flung open and the steward of Bongarde entered, followed by two men and three women who represented the landholders of the Province. After them came Eric's mother, the Lady of Seagate, and his sister Astrid.

There was a silence as Eric came through the door, robed in white. Jehan flinched before the exaltation in his eyes as the young man knelt before him and bowed his head. *Lord of All!* he thought, *Did I ever look like that?*

The Master came to stand beside the King's chair, his almost ugly features made beautiful by some inner light above the splendor of the green cope he wore.

"My Lords and Ladies—" he said gently. "To make a man responsible for the welfare of part of Westria is a heavy thing. It has been long since you needed a new lord, so it is meet that we consider the reasons for this ceremony."

Jehan relaxed a little, listening to the harsh sweetness of the Master's voice repeating the words they had prepared together.

"In the time of the Cataclysm, most of those men who had survived the onslaught of the elements wandered naked and desperate, for without their machines they did not know how to live. But even in the time of the Ancients' power, some had sought other ways. And in the land we now call Seagate they gathered, and in the Sacred Wood they signed the Covenant. Thus the oldest names, and laws, and faith became new, and this was the foundation of Westria."

Jehan remembered the beauty of the Lady Mountain, and of the Sacred Wood at its feet. If only he could go there now, surely peace would come to him.

"Westria is like a body," the Master went on, "all of whose parts must be healthy if the whole is to survive. But each part of the body has to have its own health too. If the Kingdom, the Provinces and the holdings are well-nurtured, then all will thrive. The animal kindreds are governed by the wills of their Guardians, but men have need of more formal bonds than they."

The King tensed, knowing what was coming now.

"Yet paper laws are easily forgotten," said the Master, "and so we live by words sworn, hands clasped, eyes meeting without fear. Holders swear by their land and bear responsibility for it to the Lord or Lady commanding them. The Commanders, having responsibility for the Provinces, are protected by the King or Queen, who stands for Westria before the Maker of All Things! By each to each the bond of faith is sworn, a chain of loyalty that is the strength of Westria . . ."

And the whole weight of it rests upon the King, Jehan thought bitterly.

"Knowing to what you commit yourself, are you, Eric of the Horn, ready to pledge your faith to the King of Westria this day?" asked the Master.

Jehan leaned forward to meet the young man's clear gaze.

"I am ready, my Lord . . ."

The King gripped the clasped hands that Eric offered him. "Eric, swear now to me these things—" his voice strengthened as Eric echoed his words. ". . . to provide such support in goods or men as I may need to preserve Westria . . . to obey my lawful commands in peace or in war . . . and to speak only truth to me, whatever may befall!" The King swallowed and took a firmer grip on Eric's hands. "By what will you swear these things?"

Eric looked up at him and smiled. "I will swear by the land of Seagate that bore me, and by the sword which I have never drawn in an evil cause, and by my love for you. May my own sword turn against me if ever I fail!"

Jehan's breath caught. "Listen to me well then, for the things I promise you must swear in turn to those who will call you lord . . ." His voice trembled.

"I, Jehan of Westria, do pledge to you, Eric, these things: to come at your call and support you with goods and men, saving only the greater need of all Westria; to rule you according to the Covenant and traditions of Westria, to judge you mercifully; and to answer your truth with my own."

His eyes were dazzled by golden light. He felt the strength of Eric's hands between his, and as he went on, it seemed only natural that he should for a moment feel the firm pressure of another pair of hands clasped over his own.

"This I swear to you, Eric, by the Four Jewels of Westria, and by the help of the Guardian of Men. And may all who have sworn to me deny me if I fail!"

Eric's hands slipped from his grasp and Jehan fell back in his chair, the words of his own binding ringing terribly in his ears. The sun had gone down and he could see nothing in the sudden dimness of the room.

"By what tokens shall the people of Seagate know that Eric of the Horn is truly their lord?" asked the steward of Bongarde.

"By the token of the sword—" Robert of the Ramparts stepped forward, solid as one of his own mountains, and held out the blade that Eric's father had worn. "Your forebears never used this weapon but with all their strength and never bore it in flight from a battlefield. Now it is your turn—use it well!" He bowed and gave the sword into Eric's large hands.

"By the token of the mantle—" Faris shook out the folds of a cloak dyed so dark a green it was almost black and draped it across Eric's broad shoulders. "As this mantle covers him," she said softly, "so shall he spread his protection over all beings committed to his care."

"By the token of the coronet—" said the Master of the Junipers, bringing out a roundel of twisted gold. "As it crowns the Lord Commander, so shall he be the head of his people, as the King is above him, and beyond the King the Lord of All." Gently the Master set the golden band upon Eric's brown curls.

"And by the token of the ring, which I give to him as symbol of the contract made this day between him and me," said Jehan, drawing from off his thumb a heavy golden ring. The last person for whom he had performed this ceremony had been Brian of Las Costas. How could he keep his oaths when those to whom he had sworn them were at odds? Even the Jewels had no magic to deal with this. Carefully he slid the ring onto the little finger of the younger man's left hand.

"Eric, Lord Commander of Seagate, rise!" he said then, and

Eric got to his feet, looking around him as if he wondered how all those people had come there. Gold shone on his head and on his hand, and the dark folds of his cloak set off the golden hilt of his sword, but none of the gold shone as brightly as his eyes.

"People of Seagate, behold your lord!" cried the herald. "Recognize the tokens of his leadership, and as you return to the west tell all what you have seen." There was a blast of trumpets from somewhere outside the Hall.

"Hail Eric of Seagate!" cried the steward, and others echoed him. Robert gave his new peer a hearty hug, then stepped back to let Eric's mother take him in her arms. Jehan saw Rosemary watching them wistfully and wondered if Eric could be persuaded to marry her. A babble of congratulation filled the air.

"My Lord, we should get you back to your bed," said Patrick in his ear.

"Very well, but give me those crutches. I'll not have them see me being carried out of here."

Jehan managed to leave the Hall with fair grace, but by the time he had hobbled down the corridor to his room he was sweating. He rolled himself onto the great bed and lay waiting for the pounding of his heart to slow.

"Jehan . . ." It was Caolin's voice. The King opened his eyes and made out the gleam of the Seneschal's fair hair in the shadows by the door.

"Please my Lord—can't you see he is exhausted?" protested Patrick.

"Yes. I know . . . but this cannot wait," blurted Caolin, coming toward the bed. Jehan had a fancy that the shadows were following him, and knew that he must be very tired. If he pretended to be asleep, Caolin might go away.

"Jehan, I need to talk to you."

The King sighed and opened his eyes. "Let him stay." When he heard the door close he rolled over. Caolin still stood in the middle of the room. "Well—pull up a chair so I can see you—quickly, or I *will* go to sleep!"

Slowly Caolin came to the bedside. "While our Commissioners were collecting evidence in Santibar, the Elayans seem to have been searching too. They hold to their accusations, and this paper was sent to me."

Shadows swam before Jehan's eyes. "Light a candle—do you expect me to read it in the dark?"

The flickering light made a mockery of the planes and hollows of Caolin's face, but the words on the paper were only too clear.

> . . . the time has come now for the move we agreed on when I visited you in Balleor. The King is grown weak and thinks only of this woman he has found in the north. Therefore raid into Elaya now. Help me, and you shall have the holding I promised you, and I . . .

Jehan's gaze jumped down to the signature, but he had already guessed what it must be. The note was addressed to Sir Miguel de Santera, Commander of the fortress at Balleor.

"I suppose that Brian did visit Balleor last spring?" he whispered hopelessly, and then, "I cannot believe it. I did not know he hated me so."

"Jehan, Brian must be punished." Caolin said gently.

"Why? No one can stop Elaya from attacking now . . ."

"Jehan—Brian is dangerous to *you!* He gave Ronald Sandreson that gold!"

"What?" Jehan seized on the distraction of Ronald. "You mean you found him?"

Caolin's face was in shadow. "It was just after your wedding, my Lord. Ronald was weak already, and . . . he died. I was the only one who heard what he said, and I had no proof. I did not think you would wish to be bothered then."

Jehan stared at him. The news that Ronald had died while a prisoner connected with something that had happened in Laurelynn last summer. He struggled to remember, but the significance slipped from his grasp.

"Caolin, are you sure that Ronald got that gold from Brian?"

"My Lord—" the Seneschal sounded faintly offended. "I will swear if you like."

Jehan sighed. "No. I have had too many oaths—only look at me . . ." He gripped Caolin's arm as his eyes fixed the other man's and saw what might be relief there, but no wavering. "Have I been so poor a judge of men?"

"You must execute or imprison Brian now."

"His peers will judge him, not I."

Caolin turned his ring of office around and around. "What of Las Costas? Shall a traitor's spawn hold the power?"

"A boy of six? He has done no wrong, and his mother is a strong woman who can rule until he is grown. I will not interfere with another man's inheritance."

Caolin drew another paper from his pouch and Jehan turned his head away.

"No, Caolin, no more. Have you not shown me treason enough for one day?"

"This is the order to summon Brian for questioning," the Seneschal spoke softly. "Jehan . . . I swear I did not *want* to do this to you . . ."

The King could not answer him. The candlelight seemed powerless against the darkness in the room. He grasped the pen Caolin thrust between his fingers and without really focusing on the words on the paper managed to scrawl his name.

The Seneschal picked up the mug that Patrick had left and slipped an arm beneath the King's head. "Drink this now, my Lord. Now you can rest."

"Sleep perhaps . . . but I will get no rest unless I wake to find that Brian's treachery was only a dream. Oh, Caolin—I trusted him!"

The Master of Junipers shut his book of medicine with a snap. "I trust my own skill less and less the longer this illness of Jehan's goes on!" he exclaimed, moving restlessly to the window of his chamber and staring out through the narrow panes of old glass. Low clouds rolled across the Bay and over the hills. He had gone over his notes and the books sent from the College of the Wise, and found no certainty. One passage echoed in his memory—

A hidden pocket of infection can sap a patient's strength.
If found and lanced it may be cured, if not, it may burst
and poison him, causing fever and death . . .

But how did one know if that were the cause of the trouble, and how could one find such a spot once the wound closed? Something had weighed on the King's mind ever since Eric's investiture. He was a more cooperative patient now, but he would not tell them what troubled him, and he did not heal.

The Master tried to think of someone who might know more. His own teacher was dead and the College presently had no one who specialized in healing. Though every landholder knew enough to deal with ordinary maladies, few studied the curing of more subtle ills.

"In Westria we are like the beasts with whom we share the land. Either we recover quickly or we die and let others take our places here," he told himself wryly. "But no one can take Jehan's place . . ."

He rested his forehead against the cool glass. Once he had been linked with the Mistress of the College, but remembering how they had parted in Laurelynn, he did not know if she would respond to his call.

"And I do not even know if pride makes me hesitate to call her, or fatigue makes me wish that I could . . ." Jehan had awakened him with a nightmare the night before, and he had found it hard to sleep afterward. He had even sought comfort in laying out the tarot, but the cards were all at odds with one another, and they ended with the *Moon*, whose reflected light showed only error and uncertainty.

But now it was time for him to return to the King. The day was still gloomy, but his heart lightened as he heard the cheerful murmur of women's voices from the Hall, and he was smiling as he opened the door to the King's room.

"I feel as if it has been cloudy forever, and as if I have been pregnant forever!" exclaimed Faris, hunting through her workbox for a skein of green silk.

Carlota laughed. "I know, but spring will come, and when it does the baby will come too!" Her foot continued its steady pressure on the spinning wheel and the cloud of wool in her capable fingers twirled into an even thread.

"And the cold season is half gone—next week will be the Midwinter holiday." said Branwen. "The King sat in his chair most of yesterday, do you think he will be well enough to preside over the feast?" she looked at Rosemary.

Rosemary finished threading her needle and smiled reassuringly, but Faris did not think the smile reached her eyes. *I will not ask her why, if everything goes well, the shadow stays in her face*, Faris told herself. *Jehan has made it perfectly clear he does not want me in his sickroom, so I will be good, and hold my tongue.*

"Yes of course Jehan will be well," she said aloud. "If Eric's ceremony had not exhausted him he might be up now! Why couldn't he wait?" She jerked her needle through the fine cotton of the baby gown she was embroidering.

"It wasn't Eric's fault!" exclaimed Rosemary. "The King insisted . . ." she stopped, realizing that Faris had not accused Eric.

"Oh, my lord was always willful—even as a lad," said Carlota comfortably. "But so well-mannered you'd done what he wanted before you thought. I daresay he doesn't realize himself how much he's had his way."

Oh my beloved, I wait upon your will . . . the needle trembled in Faris' fingers, scattering light from the little fire. *I wait for your child to be born and I wait for you to return to me.*

"Is that thunder?" asked Branwen. Carlota took her foot from the spinning wheel. "No, someone's coming up the road from the Bay, and fast, by the sound."

Rosemary dropped her mending and went to the window. "There is a horse-ferry down at our pier. The banner . . . is blue," she finished in disappointment.

"From Las Costas, then," said Carlota.

"Has Lord Brian come a week late for the investiture?" Branwen giggled.

Without conscious decision, Faris folded the baby gown and replaced it in her sewing bag. She stuck her needle in its case and latched her workbox shut. Did she hear hoofbeats, or only the thudding of her heart? What did the horseman want? Was it someone who would drain the strength Jehan had so hardly regained? Faris straightened her skirts and moved slowly to the entrance hall.

The great door crashed against the wall and Brian strode through, head down like a bull looking for something to charge. Faris braced herself.

After a moment he focused on her and sketched a bow. "My Lady—I must see the King."

"My Lord is ill—if your affair is urgent you should go to Laurelynn." Faris lifted her chin as she saw a yellow glow begin to smoulder in Brian's hazel eyes.

"To Caolin? Nay, Caolin's master must answer me now!"

"*Must* answer you?" Faris heard a rustle and knew Rosemary was behind her.

"He must answer me or be forsworn—it is a matter of my honor, and if you cannot understand what that means you are no fit mate for a King!"

"Your honor will have to wait! I am fit mate enough to protect my Lord, and that is all that matters to me!"

"Could you write your message, Lord Brian?" asked Rosemary.

Brian seemed to see her for the first time. "Nay—I cannot put such a thing into scribe's talk! It must be my voice to his ears—my eyes meeting his. Paper can carry too many lies!"

Farris barred the passageway, her hands clenched in the

skirts of her gown. "Go back, my Lord—you shall not enter here!"

"If you wished to spare the King you should have kept your voices down—" said a tired voice behind her. Faris whirled and saw the Master of the Junipers.

"King Jehan says that he will see the Lord Commander of Las Costas now . . ."

Brian hesitated as if suspecting some new obstacle, but Faris stepped aside, still trembling with rage. Lowering his head, the Lord Commander stalked past the Master toward the open door of the King's room.

Faris covered her face with her hands. "I tried to help him! Why is there nothing I can do?"

The Master put his arms around her and she leaned gratefully against him, feeling his concern as she felt the rough texture of his robe.

"I know . . . my dear, I know. He has shut me out too . . ."

"You *are* ill!" exclaimed Brian. "I thought it was a tale to keep me away!"

"I am well enough to deal with you!" said Jehan icily. "If the Queen has taken any harm I *will* have your head!" He struggled to push himself upright, Faris' furious voice still reverberating in his ears.

Brian shut the door of the chamber and took a few steps into the room. "You did ask me to come in . . ." he said a little more quietly. "But you have little cause to chide me, since you ordered me imprisoned without cause."

"I ordered you held for trial—" said Jehan bitterly. "If you are innocent that should be no heavy thing. And how did you know what the order was?"

"Not all in the Seneschal's Office are his creatures. I have friends who would not see injustice done." Brian dragged a chair to the King's bedside, but remained standing, gripping its back.

"Friends like Ronald Sandreson?" Jehan saw Brian's look of scorn tempered by surprise. "That touches you, does it?"

"If Ronald implicates me, bring him to trial—if he *does* accuse me . . ."

"You would rather be tried for what you and Ronald did than for what you wrote?"

"Wrote? Where?" Brian sat down.

Jehan stared at him. He would not have thought that Brian

could feign such honest indignation. "The letter you wrote to Sir Miguel de Santera at Balleor, ordering him to raid Elaya and provoke a war," he said very distinctly.

Brian's cheeks went pale and red again above his beard. "I see that you think me a traitor, Lord, but do you think me a fool? I dealt with Ronald Sandreson, but do you think I would have set my seal to treason?"

"You might think treason to the Kingdom worse than treason to the King . . ." said Jehan tiredly. "But do you think the lords of Westria will acquit you of paying Ronald to assassinate *me?*"

Brian surged to his feet. "That's a lie! That . . . I gave the man gold to gather support for my petition—if he tried murder it was on his own, and if Ronald said I ordered it he is trying to save his own skin." He paused for breath. "Or Caolin has made him implicate me! Let me face Ronald and we'll have the truth."

"That's a safe request . . . Did not your spy in Laurelynn tell you that Ronald died?" said Jehan softly. "And I have seen the letter myself."

"He died! How fortunate for you!" said Brian sarcastically. "And I wrote no letter . . ."

"Brian! I have *seen* it!" cried Jehan, no longer able to suppress his pain. "It was in your writing, with your signature and your seal!"

For a long moment Brian stared at him and the King saw the fire fade gradually from those yellow eyes. He sat down and remained still for several minutes, slowly shaking his head.

"All the way here I was storing up accusations . . . thinking you had broken your oath to me . . ." Brian whispered at last. Jehan felt suddenly dizzy, as if he stood on the edge of a precipice.

"Oh my dear Lord—I see that we are equally betrayed."

Jehan shivered. What had Brian said?

"My Lord, I swear to you by my knight's honor and by the head of my son, I paid Ronald only to persuade men to my cause." Brian leaned forward, forearms braced on his knees, eyes fixed on Jehan's. "Oh Jehan—my writing is an ill-formed scrawl that anyone could imitate, and impressions can be taken from seals!" Brian's rough head bowed and the rest of his words came muffled through his beard. "But if you cannot believe me, I will go into exile from Westria . . ."

Jehan felt his spirit swing like an unmoored boat. Caolin

had not said that Brian wrote the letter, he had only given it to the King. He had not said that Ronald accused Brian—only that Brian had given Ronald the gold. He had told only the truth, but that truth added up to such an overwhelming lie . . .

"I meant to spend the winter repairing the southern fortresses . . . somebody should . . ." his look was suddenly piteous. *"Do* you believe me?"

Jehan stared at him. It would contradict all he knew of Brian, all he knew of men, to think that this man could dissimulate. To serve the Kingdom's good, was Caolin capable of denying all that Westria was good for?

"Yes, I believe you . . ." Jehan whispered at last. "I did not wish to condemn you, Brian—you always opposed me honestly, and I trusted you. But you see, I trusted *him* too . . ." With a kind of dim wonder he saw the other man's fierce eyes brighten with unshed tears.

"My Lord!" said Brian, "We have had our differences, but I have always been your true man!" He dropped to his knees beside the bed. "Jehan, King of Westria—I, Brian of Las Costas do swear to you . . . to spend my goods, my men, my very life for Westria . . . and to speak only truth to you, my Lord, whatever may befall!"

"And may all who have sworn to me . . ." Jehan's voice broke on the words from the ritual of investiture and he reached out blindly to the other man, bruising his fingers on the ring he had given Brian so long ago.

"It will only be justice if I fall in this war . . ." said Brian at last. "I should have kept Ronald under control."

If it be a crime to trust one's servants, then I am guilty too, thought Jehan. A memory of a morning in Laurelynn when Caolin's face had looked like a badly erased manuscript surfaced suddenly. Caolin had said that a man had died under his questioning, and Jehan's heart cried, *How did Ronald die?*

The King shook his head. "No, Brian—is such a price required of lords whose men do ill? Live, Brian! I think you will be needed soon."

Brian met Jehan's gaze and his face twitched as if its strong lines were about to disintegrate. "Jehan, you are tired . . . I have stayed too long. But we will sort this thing out somehow." He stumbled toward the door.

"Brian—say nothing of this . . ." called Jehan.

The Lord Commander turned. "I understand, and I trust you, my Lord."

But do I trust myself? I trusted Caolin—there must be some explanation, something he can say . . . Jehan's mind flinched from the thought. Rain pattered against the windows. The King's hands and feet twitched with reaction. He swung his feet over the side of the bed and pulled himself upright as the Master of the Junipers came into the room.

"Jehan, what is going on? What did Brian say to you?"

The King shook his head and made his way to the window. Hoofbeats thudded dully on the muddy ground outside and he heard Farin half-heartedly wishing Brian a good journey. How could he tell the Master what had happened today? He was no longer sure what was true.

Lanterns glimmered down the road—Brian's men must have come to light him back to the pier. Jehan peered through the rain. Someone shouted, the King fumbled for the catch and threw open the window.

". . . name of the King!" he heard, and then, more clearly, Brian's deep reply, "I have just come from the King! Stuff your damned order of arrest . . ."

There was more yelling, then the clash of steel.

"Treachery!" cried Brian, "Las Costas, to me!"

"No!" muttered Jehan, "Not treachery, not mine . . ." he stopped, remembering the order he had signed for Caolin without reading it. He flung open the door to the porch, anger burning all awareness of weakness away, then hobbled across it and swung himself down the half-flight of wooden steps to the rock garden.

His picked his way through the darkness, cursing the clumsy cast. When he fell he clambered back to his feet, ignoring the shouting behind him. The Master would not know this path, they could not stop him now. Lanterns bobbed before him. Jehan heard the dull smack of a sword biting a wooden shield. Brian was the Kingdom's champion, but he was alone. How many were attacking him? Gravel pricked his bare feet and he forced his legs to carry him forward.

"He resisted—cut him down quickly in the King's name!" A small man reined a piebald horse around the edge of the fight.

"In my own name I command you—put down your swords!" Jehan cried in the voice he had trained for the battlefield.

"It is the King!" shouted Brian.

"The King . . . the King is here . . . but they said . . ."

voices faltered as the riders fell back to either side and they saw Jehan standing in the road.

The man on the piebald horse was Ordrey, still clutching a bit of paper in his hand. "But the order . . ." he began.

"The order is void! Lord Brian is under my protection." The lights dimmed and whirled around him. "Go back and bid your master come to me!"

Ordrey's horse squealed as the man reined it sharply around and slashed at its haunches with his riding whip. In a moment he was clattering down the road. One of his men swore, then followed, and the others went after him.

Footsteps splashed on the road as Farin ran toward him, then the bulk of a horse blocked the light. Brian threw himself from the saddle and caught the King in his arms.

"Oh my Lord, my Lord, what have you done?" murmured Brian, lifting the King as easily as if he had been a child.

That is a silly question, thought Jehan. "I have honored my oath to you . . ." The pain slashed through him, freeing him from consciousness at last.

When Jehan became aware again he was in his own bed, washed, rebandaged, clad in a clean robe. He knew that it must be very late, for the Master of the Junipers lay asleep in the chair and the candle was nearly burnt away. Pain nibbled at the edges of Jehan's awareness and there was a bitter taste in his mouth. If he moved the Master would wake and give him another dose of willowbark tea. But the candlelight illuminated all the weariness etched in his old friend's face.

No . . . thought Jehan. *Let the pain come. Relieving my body will only open my mind to a less endurable agony. Caolin has lied to me. Time will heal my body's wounds, but what is the cure when the soul is in pain?*

IV

The Sun Road

The north wind lashed the windows with whips of freezing rain, but inside Misthall everything was still. The Master of the Junipers closed the door to his chamber quietly and turned to Rosemary. "I think the King will sleep now."

"I wish you would not try to contact the College of the Wise now, when we are both tired," she replied.

The Master knelt by the hearth, building up the fire. "Rosemary, you are enough of a healer to understand what I tried to do just now . . ." His nerves were still twitching from the blacklash of energy he had tried to project into Jehan. "The King's mental shields are like the walls of Laurelynn! And when I tell him so he only apologizes and asks me to wait. What for? What does he fear I will see?" He drew the curtains more closely across the window, shivering again.

Rosemary sat down beside the bed. "I will remember to keep up the fire and keep you covered . . . and call you back if Faris needs you, or if you do not return by dawn," she repeated his instructions to her.

The Master removed his belt and sandals, drew off the golden chain with his circled cross, kissed it and laid it on the mantelpiece. He wore no other metals nor anything that would constrict his body. Then he pulled the blanket over himself and closed his eyes. *In the Name of the Source of All I set out . . . by the power of the Source of All I travel . . . may the mercy of the Source of All bring me safely home again . . .*

He mastered his breathing, systematically released each muscle, strove to drive from his awareness the messages of his senses and the crowding visions of the day. But it was hard to banish the image of Jehan's haunted eyes. What if he could not get free? Hastily, the Master thrust his awareness outward.

LADY OF DARKNESS

He flinched as he touched a current of energy, then reached again and jerked as successive rings of energy passed along his body and waves of fiery sparks exploded in the darkness of his mind. Then all was suddenly, blessedly still.

The Master opened his eyes. Below him he saw his own inert body and Rosemary, looking around her with an uncertain frown. He stretched, relearning the senses of this second body, then he dove outward, focusing his sight beyond the physical surfaces below him to the patterns of energy that defined them.

Between the Red Mountain and the Lady Mountain to the west of it ran a vein of light. Other lines rayed out from them, crossing and connecting to form a network within the body of Westria. Flowing beneath him the Master saw the energies which were the life of the land, as he had traced the energies within the King's body a little while ago. The lines of light gave him a map to follow, over the curve of the horizon to the white radiance of the Father of Mountains, and the pulse of power on its breast which was the College of the Wise. The Master focused his will on the College and sped toward it.

The Mistress of the College was asleep when he came to her. He drifted downward, hoping to arouse her energy body with his. A tremor shook his spirit as he remembered the times when their bodies had joined physically and he paused, knowing that such feelings could draw him back to his own body.

"*Madrona . . .*" he called her by the old name only they two knew now, sensing her weariness though he could not afford to pity her. "*I need your help! Answer me!*"

She stirred. He drew away and saw her other body emerge from her sleeping form. "*Calm yourself! Why have you disturbed my rest?*"

He was still for a moment, ashamed of his fears. "*The King has ceased to try to heal himself and he will not let me try. There is evil there whose source I cannot identify, and I am afraid.*" he said at last.

The Mistress turned a little away. "*What would you have me do? I cannot force the King to love his life, and neither can you.*"

"*If his body has time to heal he will be able to rule his own soul.*"

She nodded, but she would not meet his eyes. "*Men should take responsibility for themselves . . . We can form a healing circle here and send you our power, but we have now no regular link with the priestly communities in the towns.*"

The Master moved uncomfortably. When he had first come to the College of the Wise a network had linked all the adepts of Westria. But he had done nothing to keep it up—why was he surprised?

"*At least you can call to Awahna!*"

"*I can call, but Those who dwell in the Secret Valley answer in Their own times and ways. Why do you always look for help to others? Pray to the Source of All!*"

He wanted to protest, but his uneasiness distracted him, as if someone were tugging at his sleeve. He found himself drifting toward the wall and realized that Rosemary must be calling him back to Misthall.

"*Madrona—I will do all I can. But come to me—I will need you so very badly if I fail!*"

"You called me, my Lord . . . and I am here," said Caolin, entering the King's room. Although the curtains had been opened to let in the early morning light, the great bed was still shadowed. Jehan did not move. Had he heard?

Caolin struggled with a desire to turn and run, his mind replaying alternate visions of confrontation or flight as he had been doing ever since Ordrey had returned to him the previous morning, without Brian. He could not forget the vivid picture Ordrey had given him of Jehan, dominating them all as he stood mud-smeared and half-naked in the rain.

A board creaked in the corridor behind him. *That upstart Farin*—thought Caolin, *or the Master of the Junipers—spying on me!* He struck at the door, then turned again as the click of its latching was echoed from the bed.

"Caolin . . ." the King's voice was almost bodiless, but very clear. Caolin remembered countless other mornings when he had come into the King's chamber. For the first time in all these years he did not know what to say.

Before he reached him, the King spoke again.

"Caolin—did Ronald tell you *why* Brian gave him that gold?" Jehan moved his head on the pillow, and the Seneschal stopped short as he saw the King's face. "Did *you* believe that Brian had written that letter you showed to me?"

Caolin knew that little frown of bewildered pain. He had seen it before, when the King found men less noble than he believed them to be. Long ago Caolin had vowed to keep Jehan from ever having to look like that again. *And this time it is me* . . . His fingers closed blindly on the bedcurtains.

"Caolin, I *will* have truth from you!"

The ancient fabric parted in Caolin's hand. He brushed dust from his palm, staring unseeing at the King. What was the truth? *I loved you, my Lord* . . .

"Jehan, I was afraid!" he said aloud. "Brian meant to make my dismissal the price of his support in the war!"

"But you lied to me—"

"I did what you forced me to do!" Caolin flinched from the flash of Jehan's eyes, but he could not hold in all the resentments he had never realized he bore. "There has always been some reason for me to carry your load—"

"You tricked me into breaking my oath—" Jehan's words crossed Caolin's.

"Who would keep the Kingdom in order if I were not here?"

"—I would have had Brian's blood on my hands!" Both men paused. The King's face was flushed and he breathed rapidly as he glared back at Caolin.

"Did you hear me?" shouted Caolin suddenly. "Have you *ever* listened to me?" The high color began to fade from Jehan's cheeks. Caolin pressed the heels of his palms over his eyes. "No, that's not true. Once you heard what I did not even know how to say . . ." He dropped his hands, moved awkwardly to the chair by the bed.

"Are you saying this is all my doing?" whispered the King. "Whatever I laid upon you, you only smiled and asked for more . . ."

Caolin looked down at his tightly clasped fingers. The garnet in his ring of office caught the light as they trembled and he turned it to hide the stone. "Yes . . . power is a heady draft for one who had none. You set the cup to my lips, my Lord, and I cannot cease from drinking now . . ."

"Have I indeed done this to you?" Jehan asked again. "I thought our strength was that we both had our desire . . . And Faris—how have I failed with *her?*" His last words came almost too faint for Caolin to hear. "It would be better for me to die now and leave you all in peace!" the King cried then.

Caolin looked up quickly and saw Jehan's face contorted, his cheeks frosted with tears. His own turmoil resolved into a single fear. "Jehan, no! Don't you understand that you also gave me the only real joy I have ever known?

"When I came to you after the College of the Wise had rejected me, my life was no good to me," he continued with some difficulty. "But you cared about me, you courted me even, and when you took my body—an easy thing for you—you also touched my soul. No one had ever been able to do that for me before . . ." This was not the time to tell Jehan of his rituals on the Red Mountain and the other power that had touched him there, scarring his soul. He went on, "You gave me something to do with my life, and a reason for wanting to do it!"

Jehan's face twitched painfully. With a pang Caolin saw how the new silver in his hair glistened in the merciless morning light. He brought the King's hand to his lips, stroking the thin fingers that lay inert within his own.

"Jehan—if I have erred it is because you seemed so far from me. I need your trust . . ." Jehan's gaze met his at last and Caolin's tongue faltered. The King's eyes seemed more black than blue—pools of darkness where he could drown.

"How can I give my trust to anyone? I have no faith in my own judgment now."

"I need you, can't you understand?"

"Then you must give me truth . . . Oh, Caolin, your face is like a locked room—" Jehan's voice shook. "I must know what you have done."

Caolin stared at him. In nine years in office he had done so many things. How would they look through Jehan's unpracticed eyes? Truth, like beauty, lay so often in the beholder's view.

"My Lord, where shall I begin?" he said wryly. "Shall I raise all the little veils with which men cover the nakedness of reality? This sin of mine—if it is a sin—is what has allowed you to live with your conscience unstained!"

"Until now—" replied the King bitterly, "when I find that I must bear the guilt for what you have done without ever having chosen what you would do! Caolin—" he shook his head despairingly, "can't *you* understand?"

Caolin rubbed at his eyes. "To understand what I have done you must know why. You read my soul once, Jehan—do it again now!"

Jehan's strained look eased. "Will you open to me?" he asked wonderingly.

Caolin tensed, knowing that this time there would be no ritual or sexual arousal to help them. "My Lord," he whispered, "I will try." He closed his eyes, seeking to darken his mental vision. He counted until his breath was regular again. In all the world there must be no reality but the warm pressure of Jehan's hands.

He checked a surge of joy as something brushed his awareness like wind ruffling the surface of a pool. He marshalled his memories—all his strategies and decisions, all the skirmishes in his war with Brian, all his paths to knowledge . . . And the memory led inevitably to the Red Mountain and the boar's head that still gathered dust on the altar of the Lady of Fire.

He shuddered with vertigo, as if the floor had slipped, and clung to the King's hands. His ears buzzed. In a moment—if only he could open himself, it would be as it had been when Jehan came to him before . . .

The sense of self-awareness being overwhelmed shook him in sickening reiteration of the climax of his ritual—the infernal Lady's embrace that had poisoned all sexual or spiritual contact for him now. Past and present terror resonated through his mind and body and the fear that he had learned on the Mountain wrenched his hands and Jehan's apart.

Caolin's next thought was a dull awareness that someone was pounding on the door. He jerked upright, focusing on the King's still face, grasped his wrist and felt the pulse flicker like the heart of a wounded bird.

"Jehan!" he cried aloud. The door slammed open and the Master of the Junipers hurried past him and bent over the King.

"Who screamed? What have you done to him?"

Caolin shook his head. "The scream was mine. We tried—he wanted to touch my mind . . ."

The Master's hands were passing swiftly above the King's body. After a moment Jehan stirred a little and mumbled, as if in sleep. "Fools, both of you! He had not the strength for this now . . ." The Master laid a hand on the King's brow.

Caolin's head bowed. "Save him—" he whispered. "I need . . ." his voice failed.

The Master's expression softened. "We all need him, Caolin." His hand brushed the Seneschal's shoulder, then he turned to Jehan once more.

Faris bent to take the folded cloth from Jehan's forehead, wet and replaced it, then picked up the half-knitted sock she had dropped beside her chair. But for the sound of Jehan's harsh breathing the house was very still.

As she began to knit, Jehan muttered Caolin's name. She tensed, but in a moment he was still once more. Four days ago, when the infection of the King's reopened wound turned to fever, he had struck at anyone who tried to restrain him. Now he could no longer even stop her from nursing him. She focused her mind on the repetitive movements of her fingers and the irregular spatter of sleet against the windowpanes. On the mountaintops there would be snow. She could bear this waiting as long as she concentrated on the surface of things, knowing that beyond it howled a darkness deeper than the night outside. As long as Jehan was alive she could hold madness at bay.

"Faris . . ."

For a moment she thought that Jehan was speaking in his delirium. Then she heard her name again, faint as if the air had shaped itself to words.

"Why are you here? What is the hour?"

"It is nearly dawn. I am here because I could not sleep and the others needed rest! Oh Jehan—is that all you have to say to me?" Her shawl slipped from her shoulders as she rose awkwardly and bent over him. "Are you better?" She took the cloth from his head and smoothed back his lank hair.

His gaze seemed to turn inward. "No . . ." he whispered at last. "My left side doesn't seem to belong to me, and everything else—Faris, if I am dying, the Council must be called!" He swallowed painfully.

"The Master sent for them three days ago—" she started, then the sense of his words got through to her and a spasm of terror stopped her breath. She gripped his hand. "But you will live—they are praying for you all over Westria!"

"He sent for them . . ." For a long moment Jehan lay very still. Then he gave a faint sigh and what could have been a nod. "Who is here?"

"Lord Robert and Lord Brian, and Frederic Sachs of the Free Cities, and Eric . . ." she answered slowly. "But the Master did not say—"

Jehan shook his head. "If the Master has summoned them, he knows already that this body is too poisoned to heal," he said heavily. "How he must hate to admit that, after he has tried so hard. Everyone has tried, except me."

His eyes closed tiredly. Faris stared down at him, willing herself to see the browned skin she remembered instead of this face that had no color but the fever spots on his cheeks. She took his head between her hands and pressed her lips to his as if she could breathe life into him with a kiss. He lay unresisting, but as she let him go she saw he was weeping, soundless tears that channeled through the fever-sweat on his face until they were lost in his silvered beard.

"I have faced death in battle—" he groaned, "why is it so hard now . . . is it because I have left so much undone?" He paused, fighting for breath.

"You cannot leave me alone!" Faris exclaimed. "I would have been your mistress gladly, but I cannot be Mistress of Westria!" She slid to her knees beside the bed, hiding her face in his pillow. She felt the clumsy touch of his fingers on her hair.

"Faris . . . I accused Caolin of sheltering me too much, but I have done the same to you. My beloved—we cannot change it now! You *are* the Lady of Westria!" She felt him trembling. "Have I failed my trust also in choosing you?"

She wept into the pillowcase, still shaking her head. He could not mean to leave her to carry the burden that had brought him down! His breathing hoarsened and he coughed convulsively. Faris sat up and held the cup to his lips.

He swallowed painfully. "Faris, you must promise to guard Westria or I will be not only dead but damned! Others will help you rule, but only you can be Mistress of the Jewels!"

Faris shuddered as she saw his face twitch spasmodically. Surely nothing could be worse than to remain a powerless audience to his pain.

"Oh my love—if you say I must . . . I will do whatever I can . . ." She kissed his brow, thinking, *now I am doomed too* . . . Jehan's body grew limp, and Faris felt a moment's terror, but she could still feel the life in him, trickling unevenly like water in a polluted stream, but there, still there.

"I must do what I can to order the Kingdom . . ." he murmured after a little while. "Take my Journal from under the table and write out what I say . . ."

Mechanically Faris noted his words, but they made no sense. How could a body exist without its head? How could Westria exist without her King? How could she exist alone? When he seemed to have finished, she laid the book on the table.

"Jehan, do you want something to drink now?" She bent over him anxiously.

He smiled a little and laid his hand upon her breast. "The source of life . . ." he murmured, but his touch was as sexless as that of a child. His smile grew vague, but when she straightened his fingers closed on the front of her gown. Gently she eased down beside him, cradling his thin body against her own. After a little his fingers relaxed and she turned to him in alarm.

But he was only asleep.

Faris hesitated in the doorway to the Hall. Her brother lay fast asleep on a bench by the wall; Eric sprawled in a chair nearby. Before the fire at the near end of the room Lewis the herald was playing a listless game of chess with Speaker Sachs, while Lord Brian and Robert of the Ramparts maneuvered troop counters across a map of Westria. In the far corner Caolin gazed out at the falling rain. Then Eric saw her and sat up suddenly. The others, hearing the scrape of his chair, stared anxiously. Faris swallowed, for to speak would give her words reality.

She was doing Jehan's bidding, though every act thickened the film of ice around her heart. Did she still hope that if she did everything correctly Jehan would relent and get well?

"The King is awake now and his mind is clear."

"Is he better?" asked Brian hoarsely.

Faris barriered herself against the tide of grief she felt from him, from all of them, and spoke coldly, knowing it was the only way to survive the next hours. "He . . . summons the Council of Westria to hear his will." Abruptly she turned back across the hallway and down the corridor to the King's chamber, hearing by their heavy footfalls that they followed her.

The Master of the Junipers sat at the head of the bed, his grey robe falling in carven folds. Faris took her place on the stool next to it. Jehan breathed shallowly, gathering his strength; the curtains had been looped back, making it only too clear how small and still he lay. Benches scraped as the others sat down.

Caolin entered last, marched up to the bed and halted, his face going ashy as the winter sky. "Jehan . . ." he whispered, "how is it with you?"

The King's clear gaze held him. "I do not blame you, Caolin," he said softly, as if continuing a conversation interrupted a moment before, "only you must forgive me, too . . ."

Caolin began to tremble so violently he could not reply. He shook his head and made his way to the back of the room. The others looked at him in wonder, but to Faris it seemed natural that when so much else was disintegrating, the Seneschal's iron composure should shatter too. For a few minutes the only sound was the drumming of rain on the roof of the porch outside.

"Councilors of Westria—" said the King at last, "I will not sit in the high seat at Laurelynn again, and it is my duty to order this Kingdom as best I may." He waited for their silence. "My heir is the child that stirs in my Lady's womb. The Queen will be his regent and rule this kingdom until he is grown. If he does not become Master of the Jewels you must choose another Sovereign. But I think that the child will be a greater King than I! By this token I declare my will . . ."

The royal signet slipped easily from Jehan's finger and he held it out to Faris. After a moment's hesitation she clenched it tightly in her fist, still warm from his hand. "Under Faris, Caolin shall exercise the supreme civil power," added the King. Brian stirred angrily and Caolin jerked upright.

"My Lord—" the words seemed wrenched from his lips. "You must not—you must not give me such power . . ."

"Who else can teach Faris what she will need to know?" Jehan answered gently. "You will be each other's safety. It is for Westria, Caolin . . . If you have loved me, swear that you will serve the Queen and her child!"

There was a long pause. "I swear to serve . . . the Queen . . . and her child . . . as I have served you." Caolin's words seemed chipped from the stone mask of his face.

Jehan sank back and the Master gave him a spoonful of something from a vial of blue glass. Faris held up the book where she had written his notes.

"To lead the Kingdom's armies I give you Robert, Lord Commander of the Ramparts, for I believe there will soon be war . . ." Lord Robert sighed and nodded. "Elaya will think Westria weak now, and they will attack us in the spring . . . attack *you*," he corrected, adding, "may the Lord of Battles protect you, since I have failed." Rain thundered suddenly outside like galloping hooves.

"Brian of Las Costas will be second-in-command," the King continued. Eric stifled an exclamation, but Brian's head came up proudly. "If any of you have heard rumors against Lord Brian you must forget them, for I say to you, while I am still your King, that I have examined him and find his loyalty unstained."

Brian's amber eyes fixed on Caolin. Faris could feel the Lord Commander's defiance even through the shield of her abstraction, but the Seneschal did not move until Jehan murmured his name. He roused then, and bowed to Brian, but there was no recognition in his eyes.

"Brian, you must remember your promise to me." said Jehan. The Lord Commander stiffened, then returned Caolin's bow. Jehan frowned a little, seeming about to speak again, then closed his eyes in exhaustion. After a few moments Lord Robert rose to go.

"No—" said Faris. "He only rests. There is more . . ."

"My Lady Queen—" Robert nodded acceptance. Faris slumped beneath the authority with which his deference had invested her. The room grew brighter as the rain thinned.

Jehan's eyes opened. "Eric—will you be my Lady's champion?"

"My Lord, you asked this of *me?*" Eric stammered. Rosemary winced and looked away.

"I would ask it of no one else," Jehan answered gently. Mechanically Faris held out her hand. Eric knelt before her awkwardly and kissed her fingers, but as he rose the King spoke once more. "Eric . . . there is no more time for rivalry. Offer Lord Brian the embrace of peace. You are both true men and I think that you will know it before the end."

Eric flushed again and stiffened, but as Brian stood he cast a swift look at the King and quailed before the pleading in his eyes. They gripped each others' arms like two mastiffs whose masters have ordered them to be friends.

Jehan coughed spasmodically and the Master gave him more medicine. For a moment he breathed harshly, then appeared to ease, trying to smile.

"Lord Robert—I thank you for the loan of your son. And Rosemary, give my farewell to your father. You already have my gratitude for nursing me—such an effort should have had a better reward. But I will leave Faris with less pain, knowing that you are near her . . ."

Rosemary stared at him, her face working, then turned blindly to Eric, who after a moment's surprise held her against him, patting her awkwardly.

"And you, Lewis, and Master Sachs . . . and all those others who have served me and Westria so well. Receive my thanks for it now." Jehan sighed. "My Lords and Ladies, I have done what I can to leave you in good order—to cover my retreat!" he added with a glimmer of humor. "I see now how often I failed you. Sometimes I shrank from the resolution to steer a safe course. Where I have been blind or unjust . . . I ask you all to forgive me now!" he looked around the room.

"Forgive you!" cried Brian, "Oh my dear Lord do not go without forgiving us!"

"What is there to forgive? I was your King . . ." Jehan's tone held faint curiosity. His voice faded and his eyes closed and for a moment Faris thought he slept again. Then he spoke once more. "Now you will have to be responsible for yourselves . . . Preserve Westria until my child bears the Jewels. Serve the Queen!"

"I swear now to be faithful to your Lady and your heir—I and my heirs after me!" cried Brian.

"And I!" said Lord Robert. The others echoed him.

Jehan sighed a little then and looked at Faris like a child wishing to be told that his work is all done and he may go out to play. Somehow she was able to smile at him, but her voice broke as she turned to the others.

"The Council is ended. You may go."

Crystal drops still flashed from the eaves of the porch and the window frames, but the clouds had gone. Golden light streamed through the western windows to light Jehan's sleeping face. The fine bones of his hands and skull seemed veiled rather than covered by flesh, as if he were illuminated by some light within.

Faris' own pregnant body seemed grossly physical in comparison. *Oh my beloved,* she thought, *how can I dare to try and touch your spirit now?*

"They say we have an immortal body hidden within this one . . ." whispered Rosemary. "I think that his is very close to the surface now."

The King's household had remained in his room to keep vigil while the other members of the Council waited in the Hall, speaking to the steady stream of people who had come to wait for the news that no one could, even now, quite believe. As they watched the peace of the King's face was broken by another ripple of pain, as a fish swimming in the depths disturbs the still surface of a lake.

"He suffers!" Eric accused the Master. "I thought you gave him something to stop the pain!"

"He said he would shut it away no more. It is the body laboring so that the spirit may be born," the Master said wearily.

Faris felt his gaze turn to her, but she would not meet it. *You could not save him and you are helping him to leave me now . . .*

As the sun descended they waited silently, hating each passing minute even as they hoped it would bring Jehan to consciousness again. The storm had washed all impurity from the sky and left it a glowing gold.

There was a sudden indrawn breath from Caolin, and Faris saw that Jehan's eyes were open and the lines of pain smoothed from his face at last.

"My Lord, how is it with you?" Farin asked shyly.

Slowly the King focused on him. "Very well . . ." he answered, as one answers the silly question of a child. They flinched beneath the clarity of his gaze.

"Faris . . ."

She reached out, but did not quite touch him. "I am here."

"You have done more than I deserved. Now I think that I can at least end my life well. Remember your promise to me, my darling. And if I can . . . I will be with you . . ." His hand moved, just a little, so that it touched hers. Faris bit her lip to keep from crying out a denial that would break his peace.

"Have you no word for me?" said Caolin with an odd desperation.

The King smiled a little. "Only remember that I have loved you, Caolin . . ."

The Seneschal turned away abruptly and seemed to collapse until Faris could see only a huddle of robes at the foot of the bed. She felt the Master of the Junipers trembling behind her.

Jehan shifted his head on the pillow to look at the older man. "Be still—you know better than anyone that this parting is not forever. Will you link with me to set me on the road?" The Master nodded silently, but his face showed his struggle for control.

"What day is this?" asked the King.

"It is the eve of the feast of Sunreturn," said Rosemary, surprised.

"The longest night . . ." Jehan sounded faintly alarmed. "Open the windows!"

Eric looked to the Master, and as he nodded, moved reluctantly to force outward one of the windows that faced the Bay. Cold rushed in and they shivered, but Jehan breathed deeply. The setting sun laid a path of gold across the Bay.

"The darkness shall not have me!" Jehan exclaimed. "See—

the sun road is prepared and I must follow the light . . ." His eyes fixed on the descending sun.

Faris shut her eyes against that brilliance. Shimmers of light and darkness pulsed across her vision in time to the heavy pounding of her heart. Though her ears buzzed with pressure, she heard the change in the Master's breathing as he slipped into trance. Desperately she cast her consciousness outward, seeking Jehan's spirit as once she had sought it from the Father of Mountains.

Jehan's fingers quivered in her own, and through her eyelids she felt a sudden brightness in the room. Faris opened her eyes.

Figures moved before her like ships on a sun-dazzled sea. The Master . . . and Others, whose radiance burned away her fear. She stood up. The air around her vibrated with her name. She turned. As if she had tasted the sound of his voice, or felt the blue of his eyes, she knew Jehan . . .

She took a step forward, but the other figures were swirling around him, drawing him away.

Faris cried out, and her vision was lost in a blaze of light.

"Now indeed is our long darkness come." Caolin repeated the words softly, finding an odd satisfaction. He had said them to himself many times in the two days since he had looked on the empty shell that had been Jehan. He rested his crossed arms on the sill of the window next to the hearth, watching three riders pick their way down the Misthall road to the King's road that edged the Bay. The King's funeral procession had passed that way, only a few hours before.

He heard the door to the Hall open and turned angrily, blinking as his eyes tried to adjust to the shadows. He glimpsed dark hair and a shapeless blue robe.

Jehan's robe . . .

He stood up too suddenly, groping for the solid stone of the hearth as the blood left his head. When he could see again he recognized Faris.

He struggled to school his face, but the Queen looked blindly past him as she stepped into the room. Except for her pregnancy she was as he had first seen her in the north, her face colorless, the skin stretched across her cheekbones. There was nothing here of the voluptuous quality that had offended him at Harvest—the thing he had simulated in his ceremony.

He must have made some sound, for her head came up like a startled doe's and her shadowed eyes slowly focused on his face. "I . . . I thought that everyone had gone . . ." She pulled the robe more closely around her and turned.

"No, stay—" Caolin found himself moving to stop her.

The Queen looked as if she expected that the carved timbers of the Hall, the pewter and brass dishes shelved along the walls, even the needlepoint cushions on the benches at the sides would be different now.

"I thought you had gone to the Sacred Wood with the others," she said.

Caolin shook his head. "Someone had to speak to those who come for news." In reality, someone else could have stayed, but Caolin could not have watched earth cover Jehan's body, knowing what must happen to it now.

Faris held out her hands to the fire. There was gooseflesh on her thin arms. "I did not want to see his body . . ." she said slowly. "I told the Master I was too tired to go to the burial, but I cannot sleep, and I cannot lie awake in that room, remembering . . ." She shivered violently.

Caolin nodded. "They will lay him in the earth of the Sacred Wood, and sing songs, and come away comforted. But Jehan will still be gone!" For the first time he met her gaze fully. There was nothing she could take from him, now.

"He went away and left me alone." Faris said in a still voice. Caolin felt suddenly dizzied, as if his own soul had spoken to him through her lips. She moved restlessly away from the fireplace, realigned the game table, then began to replace the tumbled chess pieces. One had fallen, and she bent awkwardly to pick it up.

But Caolin was there before her. He knelt to reach the piece and held it out to her. It was the queen. Still kneeling, Caolin set the bishop beside it on the board.

"Our King is taken," he said softly, "and Queen and Minister must fight on alone . . ." His fingers clenched on the chessman.

"You loved him too." Faris' words pierced Caolin's darkness.

He stared up at her, reading in her eyes a kind of grief he had thought no one else shared. Surely it was true that they had both loved Jehan, and perhaps received from him something which that much-loved man had not given all the others as well. He had built his life on that belief, but now Jehan was gone, his honors fallen to this thin woman who huddled in the King's old robe.

"My Lady, I am *your* servant now—what is your will?" he exclaimed. Eyes burning with unshed tears, he kissed her hand. *This is what I promised Jehan . . .*

The Queen tried to smile. "I have no will. I do not know what to do." She began to straighten the cushions on the benches against the wall. Caolin got to his feet. She must speak—she must tell him what to do!

Faris pulled something from behind one of the pillows and stilled, staring down at it. It was a doeskin glove, the fingers molded by use to the shape of a man's right hand.

"Everywhere . . . everywhere I turn I find his things, as if he had only gone away for a day's hunting!" she exclaimed. "I cannot bear it—I must get away!" She looked at him, pleading, her fingers digging into his arm.

Caolin braced himself and put a tentative arm around her shoulders. "Yes . . . In the morning we will go to Laurelynn."

"It seems very far from the high seat in Laurelynn to a scrape in the earth beneath a tree," said Lord Theodor harshly.

The Master of the Junipers, struck by the pain in the old man's voice, turned from watching for the wagon that bore the body of the King. The meadow was full of people who waited to see Jehan enter the Sacred Wood for the last time as once they had waited to see him put on the Jewels.

"The journey from Hall to Hallows will be the same for you or for me . . ." said Brian grimly.

"I know that, but Jehan could have been my son! If these old bones could keep me from reaching here in time to see him, I have lived too long!"

"You are not old! I saw you swing a sword in the north!" exclaimed Eric, but the Master noted the lines graven so deeply into Theodor's face and the new hint of fragility in his bearing, and knew that he *was* old, now.

If a simple hunting accident could destroy Jehan, what can be counted on to endure? The Master wondered. He shivered in the chill wind and moved toward the Mistress of the College, but she was deep in conversation with the Priest of the Wood. He had not spoken with her alone since she had arrived with Lord Theodor the day before. His stomach knotted, and he wondered what she could say to him that would be worse than his own self-blame.

There was a murmur like distant surf from the crowd as the wagon appeared, and the Master struggled to barrier himself against the intensity of their sorrow. Robert of the Ramparts climbed down from the driver's bench, his face set. Brian touched his arm in brief sympathy, then bent to remove his boots. When all were barefoot, the lords of the four provinces went to the wagon and lifted out the bier on which the King's body lay, scattering the flowers that covered it.

"How can he be so light . . ." whispered Eric as they settled the poles on their shoulders, but no one answered him.

The green-robed priest had taken his place between two redwood trees that stood like pillars at the entrance to the Wood. "Human kind, why have you come?"

"We bring Jehan, King of Westria, for burial," replied Robert gruffly.

"What is the King of men to the People of the Wood?"

The Mistress of the College stepped before them. "We come to return the body of the Master of the Jewels to the elements from which it came."

"Enter then. A place has been prepared for him." The priest stepped aside and the little procession moved into the darkness of the wood.

The Master of the Junipers took his place behind the bier, his bare feet feeling the way. The forest sighed around him as if it too were lamenting for the King. The Priest of the Wood chose the easiest way through the trees where since the Cataclysm no path had been made. As they moved more deeply into the forest the cries of the people faded and even the wind diminished to a distant rustling. The air stirred with the sharp perfume of new redwood needles and the richer scent of decaying leaves. Sunlight was slanting through the branches and kindling the trees with rich tints of carnelian and green when the procession entered a circle of young redwoods and halted at last.

This clearing was much like the one in which they had buried Jehan's father, but landmarks shifted strangely in a Wood where some of the trees could take the forms of men. Once they had gone, only the Lord of the Trees would know for certain where Jehan's body had been laid. In the midst of the circle was a trench just wide enough for the naked body in its linen shroud.

The pallbearers knelt to set their burden down. The Master reminded himself that there was nothing on the bier that he would wish to retain—not when he had seen the living soul depart—but still it took an effort of will for him to help the Mistress ease the body into the grave. She stood looking down at it for a moment, then began the prayer.

"Mother Earth! We bring to you this form of flesh whose substance is your own. As each bodied creature consumes the bodies of others, so each has the same debt to pay. Receive then what remains of him we loved, that from it new life may spring."

The others linked hands and chorused—"Give the flesh to the earth, the blood to the waters, breath to the winds and the fire of life to the Maker of All Things—we go as we have come!"

The Master scattered a handful of damp earth across the shroud. The others followed him, their fingers furrowing the soil as their faces were furrowed by tears. The shallow grave was soon filled. But as they knelt, redwood twigs began to shower down upon the scar in the earth, though there was no wind. The Master felt his skin prickle and saw looming over them a redwood tree that had not been there before, and with another kind of vision, a green-crowned, red-robed figure whose eyes comprehended all the sorrow the world had ever known.

"My Lord of the Trees . . ." he whispered, bowing his head until the last needle had settled to the ground and there was nothing to show where the grave had been.

When they emerged from the Wood it was dusk and most of the mourners had gone. Robert and Eric began to hitch the horses to the wagon again. The Mistress of the College waited, her dark face unreadable. The wind whipped back the cowl of her hood so that the Master saw her profile outlined against the dim sky.

"You must go back with them to Misthall," she said.

The Master shook his head. "I failed Jehan. He had some sickness of the soul that I did not understand. Since I saw him depart I have not been able to meditate. Perhaps if I go to Juniper Cottage alone I can restore my soul. As I am, I have nothing to give to anyone!"

Her fingers closed on his arm. "Do you think so? I have lived in that darkness for five years! But you can still walk even if you walk blind. If you failed the King, that is between you and the Maker of All—but you must not fail Faris as well! I no longer see clearly," she murmured, "but I think a great wind is coming that will sweep away much that we have known. That may be just as well, but if there is anything you want to preserve, you must not run away!"

Abruptly the Master remembered how he had read the cards

for Faris the morning of the Harvest Festival, and the cold premonitory wind that had chilled him then. Thus far the reading was proving itself—Faris was the Queen of Swords now. He stared at the Mistress of the College. "Is my task then to stand against the wind?"

"To stand against it or to ride it . . ." the Mistress replied.

V

The White Queen

Firelight flared on the bronze harpstrings as Farin shifted Swangold in his lap. He dipped his rag in the oil jar and smoothed it along the sound box's polished sides. The interlace of golden wire edging the soundholes shone softly like the embroidery on a King's gown. His hand stilled. He remembered how Jehan had shone in his Council robes the summer before. But now January was half-gone—they had come back to Laurelynn without the King and everything was changed.

A footstep echoed on the stair—Faris, coming from the entry hall below, followed by Caolin.

"—and so when Lord Robert returns from speaking with the holders in the south, we must hold a council of war," said the Seneschal.

Farin returned to his work, his polishing cloth caressing the pillar's curve.

"Yes, I suppose so—" Faris said in a low voice. She slipped off her white cloak. Her gown was of undyed wool as well, the mourning color. "I did not know what it all meant when the Elayan envoys spoke at the Council last July, and afterward . . . I suppose Jehan did not want to tell me . . ." She leaned toward the fire, holding her arms and shivering.

Caolin looked down at her. "We *can* win," he said softly. "We *will* win, if hotheads like Brian listen to reason."

"Jehan trusted Brian . . ." said Faris, her eyes fixed by the leaping flames.

"He said he did." Caolin stared into the shadows of the entry hall below.

"But Brian broke into Jehan's sickroom," she continued, "and when Jehan went out to him, afterward—"

Two strings spoke softly as Farin's cloth brushed them. Caolin whipped around, his eyes flicking to the golden gleam of the harp on the table by the windows.

"You have chosen a strange place to practice in!" the Seneschal said sharply.

Farin's hand paused in its downward stroke. "These tall windows give the best light."

"Not at this hour," replied Caolin, looking out at the bare branches of the plum orchard that sloped toward the central lake of Laurelynn. The pink light of sunset was already fading into the dim winter dusk.

Farin's hands tightened on the harp. "Then if I play, it will be in darkness, now."

For a moment Caolin stared at him in silence, his hands hidden in the folds of his robe. "I must go back to my offices," he said suddenly to Faris. She nodded and held out her hand. Caolin bent over it, then pulled his cloak around him and went softly down the stairs.

Farin picked up a clean cloth and began to wipe down the harp. The wood glowed as if it had absorbed the light of the fire. He looked at his sister, wanting to speak to her, and noted with shock how the firelight glistened on a new veining of silver in her earth-dark hair. Her silence walled her from him now as it had since the death of the King. Once he would have been able to touch her without words.

The stairs creaked deeply beneath a rapid tread. Eric sprang up the last step and stopped short as he saw Faris by the fire. "My Lady!" She looked up, her eyes wells of shadow, as Eric knelt to kiss her hand. Farin plucked the bottom note of the harp, then the other three that made the octaves, but he did not turn. After a moment Faris smiled vaguely, rose and fumbled for her cloak. She allowed Eric to help her to put it on, then, still without speaking, went to the stairs that led to the plum orchard.

Eric stood looking after her, his big hands hanging open at his sides. "Should we let her go out there? It is getting cold."

Farin shrugged, plucked a string and made a minute adjustment with the tuning key. "She will not freeze. Are *you* going to order her to come in?"

Eric slumped. "She smiles past me as if I were not there . . ."

Farin considered him and thought wryly that it took uncommon abstraction to ignore something Eric's size. "I think she listens to Caolin . . ."

Eric snorted. "I suppose she has to! His conversation certainly wouldn't amuse me!" He paced back and forth along the gallery, then paused by a chest beneath the windows. "Jehan used to keep a chess set in here—I wonder . . . yes, here it is! Farin, will you play a game with me?"

Farin shook his head, remembering the many games of chess he had played with the King. "No—" he saw Rosemary and the Master of the Junipers coming up the stairs. "No, but you might ask Rosemary."

Eric looked surprised, but after a moment Rosemary agreed, and he began to arrange the chess board on a bench before the fire.

The Master of the Junipers came over to Farin and ran a gentle finger along the curved top of the harp. "Was Faris here?"

"She has gone to walk in the orchard again," Farin replied. He plucked a minor chord, adjusted two of the strings. The Master sighed, and Farin thought that for the first time since he had known him the chaplain seemed old. He went to the windows and stood staring down at the orchard, his robe blending with the shadows of the coming night.

Farin's left hand lifted to the strings, touched a note, then two more. No—not that tune. He had played that one the afternoon before Jehan died. He tried another combination, but the notes throbbed to silence as his fingers stilled. The fire glowed like the King's eyes, and there was no tune he knew that did not carry its own bitter harmony of memories.

The lord I loved is gone . . . and he has taken all my music away. He rested his head against the curve of the harp and his closed eye-lids stung with hot tears.

Faris eased back in her chair, feeling her aching feet throb against the softness of the sheepskin rug, letting the lassitude of exhaustion still her body. To achieve this numbness she had walked in the orchard until the damp cold bit to her bones—perhaps tonight she would sleep without dreams. Branwen hovered by the door as if looking for some further excuse not to leave the Queen alone.

"I need nothing else, Branwen—you may go—"

"My Lady—" the girl drew from the pocket of her apron a book covered in green leather. "I found this with the things we brought from Misthall." She set the book on the table and turned away.

If it was a book, it should go to the library or to Caolin, thought Faris. Then she opened it, and Jehan's graceful writing flashed up at her.

"My Beloved, I dare not wake you, and yet there is so much I need to say . . ." The date was Midsummer, when he had brought her home to Misthall as his Queen. Faris whimpered and let the Journal close, but Jehan's words resonated in her mind, shattering her illusory acceptance of his loss. She covered her face with her hands.

"You had so much to say to me, and yet you could not stay till everything was said . . ." She opened the book again.

Today we set out for the Ramparts. Has Westria always been so beautiful, or is it Faris who lends beauty to all I see in her company? Was it cowardice that made me leave Caolin to deliver my instructions regarding Santibar to Brian? The land dreams under the summer sun and I want only to lie beneath the oak trees with my wife in my arms. We must avert war with Elaya! The land needs peace, and so do I . . .

Faris remembered those days, when the sickness of her early pregnancy had passed and she flowered beneath the sun of Jehan's love. Now wind rattled the windows. Soon the clouds she had seen overwhelming the sunset would bring sleet or rain. She shivered and reached for her shawl. Golden summer was only a fantasy. Reality was cold, and a lonely bed, and the threat of war.

I try to find words to describe you, my beloved, but all my words have been tarnished by too much use. Your brother Farin has the words and the music, but no love . . . and so in the end I can only climb back into bed and praise you with my body like any other man!

No! She could not bear to remember the acts with which he had praised her, not now . . . Swiftly she turned the page and stopped, seeing not words but a picture—a few simple strokes which resolved themselves into the curve of a woman's bent head. Her own ivory comb was in the figure's hair. She wondered, *How could Jehan find in me such serenity?*

The mural on the wall above her swam in and out of focus as her eyes filled with tears—a woman and a harper, facing a wolf-shape with three fierce heads . . . She recognized the old tale, more ancient than the Ancients, of Orpheus, who had won his lady back from the Lord of the Underworld. If only she could do the same!

The woman in the painting stood with bent head and lifted hand. The style of the drawing was the same as that on the wall of Jehan's chamber at Misthall and in the book on her lap. This room had been the old Queen's, and Faris found herself smiling as she imagined Jehan painting the walls of his mother's room.

Still smiling, she set the Journal aside and snuffed her candle.

One by one, the Master of the Junipers put out the candles in his room. He had learned to fear the shadows this past month, and yet darkness was his only road back to the Light. It was still early in the evening, but the palace was already quiet. He remembered how it had been filled with light and laughter when Jehan was there and sighed as he sat down on the matting, crossed his legs and laid his hands open upon his knees.

"In the Name of the Source of All!"

That was the key, the phrase with which he had been taught to begin. Did it show him his error as well? Has he been seeking his own desire instead of that of the Maker of All Things? He breathed in and out, out and in, easing his body muscle by muscle until there was no distracting strain.

"Ruler of earth and heaven, of the world without and the world within—hear now my prayer!"

So the litany began, the first thing he had learned at the College of the Wise when he sought to chart a path to the Glory that had overwhelmed him spontaneously at times since childhood. And he had succeeded—the ecstacy that had flooded him, unexpected and unwilled, had become a fountain to nourish him whenever he had need. Until now . . .

"Thou art the Foundation of Being, in Whom all times and places are One—therefore hear now my prayer!"

The Master closed his eyes, reaching for stillness, letting

the senses go. He knew that the darkness which had come upon him was no uncommon thing. Indeed, it was an expected obstacle if one pursued the Way. If even the Mistress of the College suffered it, why should he complain? But why must it come to him now, when Faris wandered in her own darkness and needed him?

"From Thee have I come and to Thee will I return—therefore hear now my prayer!"

Surely that was true—he had been blinded by the brightness of Those who had taken Jehan away, and he remembered it as a man in a dungeon remembers his last glimpse of the day. But then the sun had gone down.

"I will seek the Darkness that is the gateway to Thy Light—so hear now my prayer!"

The Master voiced the words and let them go, let his thoughts dwindle and drift until only the fact of his existence remained, sinking through the darkness . . .

Into Nothing . . . There was no foundation, no boundary, no gateway. He fell through the gulfs he had once traversed so easily, and That which was Not began to dissolve his soul.

No! Awareness exploded in terrified rejection. *I exist . . . I am*—his Name reverberated through his returning consciousness. His body convulsed as all senses resumed functioning simultaneously, and he collapsed.

After a time, the Master painfully opened his eyes. It was still dark.

Faris stirred in the great bed, half opened her eyes on the darkness, then slipped back into sleep. The shadows in her chamber changed to shapes—columns soaring to a hidden sky. A forest deeper than the Sacred Wood surrounded her, and hushed all hint of sound.

Why am I here? she wondered suddenly and answered, *I am looking for Jehan.* And at the thought she turned her head and found him walking at her side . . . *He is not dead! I knew it was not true!* Her spirit sang.

"I only fainted when they thought I died—" he said, "and never lay within that shroud—"

She looked at him and said, "I've made no change . . ."

"How does the kingdom?"

"Well enough," she said. "But southern skies still rumble threats of war."

He held her arm. "I would not have them know that I am here—you must still hold my place. But I will tell you all that you must do!"

"But I cannot command your men, my Lord—"

She was being shaken, and brightness stung her eyes.

"My Lady! My Lady Queen!"

Faris stilled, reaching inward to Jehan. But he was gone, and daylight dissipated the shadows of the trees. She sighed and smiled. At least Jehan was not dead. It had all been a mistake after all.

Then she opened her eyes upon sunlight, streaming into the Queen's room in Laurelynn, and knew that not her dream but reality was the nightmare.

The clouded sky filtered a dull, even light into the small council chamber overlooking the river, revealing without illuminating the faces of the four people in the room. Caolin found it comforting.

Faris sat huddled in the King's chair at the head of the table. With her wan face and pale gown she looked like a ghost herself, but at least not like Jehan's ghost. Indeed they were all sombre today—Robert of the Ramparts in grey and Brian in scuffed leather. Caolin had instinctively chosen a robe whose red was so dark it was almost brown. Only the memory of Jehan held brilliance now.

Robert set down the report he had been reading aloud. ". . . and so I was at Elk Crossing when I learned that Prince Palomon is mustering his men," he said. "I had thought that they would want to negotiate when they learned of our loss . . . I wish I knew where and when their attack will come!" He looked to Faris.

Say something! thought Caolin. *This man is waiting for you to command him . . .*

"The road to Santibar has been open all winter," said Brian. "It is obvious they will strike there!"

"The winter has been cold, it's true, and though it is the beginning of February, the Dragon's Tail pass is still blocked with snow." Robert rubbed nervously at his greying beard.

Caolin cleared his throat, thinking of the coded message that lay locked in his desk. "Nonetheless, they will come that way as soon as they can."

Brian's yellow eyes began to glow. "Have you read Palomon's mind? Or perhaps you are such great friends that he tells you his plans?"

Caolin stiffened and looked to Faris for support, ignoring Robert's shocked exclamation. The Queen's clasped hands whitened, but she remained still.

"Lord Brian, I remember *my* promise to the King . . ." he said softly at last. "I suggest that you do the same." Brian's whole body quivered, but the fire in his eyes dimmed and he eased back into his chair.

Robert looked at them both conciliatingly. "It is true that knowing the source of the information would help us to evaluate it."

Caolin frowned, thinking of the patient effort that had developed those sources. Could Robert and Brian be trusted?

"There is someone in Palomon's court," he said carefully, "who talks very freely in a certain tavern where he is never asked to pay for his wine. The inn-keeper passes what he hears to someone who sends it to me." He shrugged. "I cannot swear to its truth—but the information has always been good before. I knew that Elaya had decided on war a week ago," he finished baldly, watching Brian.

The Lord Commander of Las Costas leaped to his feet, leaning across the table. "You should have told us!"

Caolin smiled slightly. "Why Brian, can I do nothing to please you? First you doubt my sources, then you criticize me for wishing to check them!" He turned deliberately to Robert. "I have made what preparations were in my power, my Lord, awaiting your return." His glance flicked back to Brian. "I informed the Queen Regent—I did not know I was accountable to *you*."

"*Someone* will hold you to account one day . . ." growled Brian, his hands clasping and unclasping as if they hungered for Caolin's throat.

"My Lords, be still!" cried Robert. He ran his fingers distractedly through his hair. "Save your hostility for Elaya, in the name of the Lord of All!"

"Robert . . . Brian . . . Caolin . . ." Startled, they turned to Faris, who went on, "This is no pleasure to any of us, and I . . . am becoming tired . . ."

Or ill—thought Caolin, considering her. The Queen had drawn her cloak about her as if she were cold, but perspiration beaded her brow.

"What decisions can we make now? We must make plans for either attack—where does the greatest danger lie?" Faris went on.

Caolin swallowed—for a moment she had sounded like Jehan. Robert nodded gratefully and straightened in his chair.

"If they come up the coast they can attack Santibar immediately and it will take us longer to move an army to meet them. But they will find it hard to pass beyond Santibar to the rest of the kingdom."

"Do they want Santibar?" asked the Queen.

"What else have we been fighting over for the past twenty years? Palomon and I are old enemies." muttered Brian.

You are good at making enemies, my Lord . . . thought Caolin.

"And if they come through the Pass?" Faris went on.

"A heavy storm could delay them, and our fortress below the pass can hold for a little while. But once through, in two weeks they could reach Laurelynn."

"Santibar has been regarrisoned and the fortifications at Balleor improved," said Caolin quickly. "They should be able to defend themselves. We cannot leave Laurelynn unprotected."

Robert nodded slowly. "That makes good sense . . ."

"But I promised the people of Santibar—" Brian began.

"You promised? In whose name?" snapped Caolin. "Will you break your oath to the King to defend your own lands?"

"Brian—we cannot divide our strength!" protested Robert.

The Lord of Las Costas seemed to wilt. "I know . . . I know . . . but it is hard when they are depending on me . . ."

Robert touched his hand in comfort, but his eyes went to Faris. "My Lady—you must decide . . ."

"How can I know what to do? I have never held a sword!" She was shivering.

Brian shrugged. "I obey my lord's will, and he gave you the power. But you will have to lead if we are to follow you!"

Caolin realized wryly that he and Brian agreed on that. But if Faris would not, or could not, exercise her power, someone else must guide her. He took a deep breath.

"We must gather our own armies . . ." whispered the Queen before he could speak. "We must be ready to relieve Santibar or to defend Laurelynn." She stared through Robert, who shifted uneasily in his seat and looked away.

"It will take at least a month for everyone to arrive . . ." he said.

"War . . ." Faris spoke again. "Slaughtered people and burned homes . . . Cannot we send to Prince Palomon and ask for peace?"

Brian gave a bark of laughter. "Peace, with Palomon?"

Robert shook his head sadly. "This is an old quarrel, and now they think themselves stronger than we. What price would we pay for safety? Would you give Prince Palomon the Four Jewels to adorn his wives?"

For a long moment the Queen was still, her eyes dilated and unseeing. "But there will be a price . . ." she said in a dead voice. Caolin watched her intently, feeling a stir of excitement as he recognized the fixed stare of trance.

Faris seemed to focus on Brian. "You desire battle, but I see only blood and death and the arrows of treachery . . . Blood—" She shuddered violently and recognition came back into her eyes. She clutched at the table's edge and looked fearfully around her. "What—what have I been saying? Brian . . . I'm sorry—"

"Why?" replied Brian with surprising gentleness. "I would not grudge the price if I paid it with sword in hand and it brought victory."

"I will send out the battle summons . . ." said Robert at last, shuffling his papers uncertainly. Faris nodded bleakly. Her eyes were bright with tears.

Caolin considered her with a wonder beyond envy. All the gifts of the spirit and all temporal power had been given her, and she seemed neither to value nor to have the will to use them.

Faris looked up, her gaze going from Robert to Brian and resting at last on Caolin. "Help me . . ."

The Seneschal rose, pity and triumph warring in his heart. "Yes, my Queen. Now you must rest. But be easy—I will make sure that everything is done."

For a moment she rested her face against his shoulder, then straightened and held out her hand to the other two men. "Thank you for your counsel, my Lords."

Robert and Brian stood up and bowed. Caolin took the Queen's arm, but he could not keep a gleam of triumph from his glance as, just before the door closed behind them, he looked back and read the smouldering anger in Brian's eyes.

* * *

"What is it?" asked the Queen. The Master of the Junipers followed her into the chamber, cradling a wooden box in the crook of his arm.

Faris sat down, relief from the chronic ache in her lower back momentarily distracting her. The child within her roused at the change of position, his movement ridging the round of her belly. It was almost mid-February, and her delivery was little more than a month away. The Mistress of the College had said it was a son. His birth would lift her physical burden, but what weight would he place on her heart?

She sighed and looked up at the Master. "Is something wrong?"

Only his eyes seemed to be alive in a face which was not so much aged as used-up, his hair and skin as nondescript as his grey robe. Carefully he set the box on the table between them. "I should have given you this before."

Something about the box nagged at Faris' memory. The front fell open and stepped trays slid back as she touched it. Gently she lifted a corner of the silk cloth. There was a glimmer from within. Faris flinched from the blaze of leaf green and mud brown and gold.

"The Earthstone! You have brought me the Jewels!"

The Master nodded. "You will need them for the Feast of the First Flowers."

She fell back, her memory invaded by the fragrance of plum blossoms and the vision of the King coming to her through the sunlight, a crown of flowers in his hands. "I won't wear them. I won't go to the Festival."

"The people have lost their King—will you deprive them of their Queen?"

Faris remembered her promise to Jehan. "Very well, but I will not need the Jewels for the ceremony." Her gaze moved unwillingly to the redwood box. She could *feel* the presence of the Jewels tickling the edge of her awareness like the roar of a waterfall so distant it was sensed rather than heard.

The Master was silent, his hands twisting in the folds of his robe.

"Well?" she asked bitterly. "Is that all you had to say?"

"What do you want me to say? You are now the only guardian of the Jewels, and you have barely begun to learn their powers. When you left the College of the Wise we agreed that you should continue to study. You know what you should do!" His voice held harshness, not honey, now.

She gripped the arms of her chair. "If I do not it is not for want of being told. Caolin wants my approval for supplies, and Robert my orders for those who will consume them. Petitioners come from all over to present requests they did not dare show the King, or just to gape at the kingdom's prize broodmare!

"I am not the King! Whenever I must act in his place I know that people are thinking what a poor substitute this pale misshapen creature is!" She bit off the rest of her complaint. She must not tell him that every night she dreamed that Jehan had come to her seeking an accounting, and every morning she faced the pain of losing him again.

"And if a time came when you must put on the Jewels?" the Master forced the words from his silence into hers. "Could you rule them?"

"Alone?" She shook her head. "Once more Jehan has left me alone with you, as he did when I went to the College of the Wise, and again you are trying to make me grasp power. But this time you cannot threaten me with his need; you cannot force me to do anything! As you reminded me, I am the Queen." Her laughter became a sob and she covered her face with her hands.

"Then let me go!" the Master cried. She thrust out her hands futilely as his barriers slipped and she felt the full force of his despair. Darkness . . . darkness . . . different but in its own way no less dreadful than her own.

From some yet unknown well within her came a swift rush of compassion, diverting the tide of his pain. Rising awkwardly, Faris put one arm across his thin shoulders.

He shuddered, and the pressure of his emotions abruptly eased. "I'm sorry—" he whispered. "I never meant that to happen . . ."

Faris pushed him back down into his chair, but remained leaning against the table, holding onto his hand. "Where would you go?"

Awahna . . . She scarcely noticed that he had not said it aloud. Then she caught her breath as images rushed from his mind into hers—massed trees greater than those in the Sacred Wood, through which clear streams ran sparkling to green meadows where the frisking deer grazed unafraid. Above the meadows sheer cliffs of stone dwarfed the trees, and everywhere one heard the distant whisper of waterfalls . . .

Faris trembled, recognizing those trees, and the meadows

in which she walked nightly with Jehan. "Awahna . . ." she said aloud.

The Master sighed. "As I am I think I would never reach it. The Guardians only welcome the worthy, and the way to the Valley is never twice the same."

"Stay with me—" Faris murmured. The baby kicked sharply and she set her hand to her side. "Stay at least until the child is born." That would be soon enough, now, and perhaps she would die of it and be free.

The Master looked up at her, a memory of his old smile warming his face like sunlight reflected off a stream. "When you need me, I will be here . . ."

When the Master of the Junipers had gone, Faris stood for a long time gazing down at the Jewels. Her shielding had been breached by her contact with him, and she felt their proximity as an almost painful attraction. Without willing it, she found herself putting them on. It was very still in the palace. In this moment, when no need, no other presence distracted her, Faris felt for the first time the undiluted power of the Jewels.

Earth . . . Water . . . Air . . . Fire . . . Her body throbbed with their untapped potency, poised in a moment uncompelled by either fear or desire.

Slowly she turned to face the mirror. The Jewels were awakening, colors shifting, radiating a deepening glow until her body was bathed in rainbow fires. She stared at the terrible beauty of her image in the glass.

This is not me . . . She felt something waken within her soul as the child in her body stirred, some Other that smiled mockingly with her lips and sparkled with a reckless excitement in her eyes.

I am Power . . . it said. *I have always waited within.*

Images pulsed through her awareness: darkness that heaved with emergent life, nameless forms that flowed outward on irresistible tides, tossed in the winds, flared in incandescent fire, and sank into darkness only to be born anew.

I am the Lady of Darkness . . . the voice within her said then.

Faris gasped as the child in her belly kicked sharply. For the first time she felt the touch of his mind, like a flare of clear light. Suddenly terrified, Faris fumbled to free the Jewels from her body and flung them into their box.

Then she sank shuddering into a chair. The right side of her head had begun to throb sickly, but she welcomed the pain. Now she understood why Jehan had feared the Jewels, but more than their power she feared that of the Shadow-self who had desired it.

Caolin grimaced at the paper in his hand and crumpled it, wishing he had the power to do the same to Brian. This was the third time in a week that one of his requisitions to Las Costas had come back with a note that the Queen must sign it before it could be obeyed. The Seneschal sighed and ran his fingers through his fair hair. Damn Brian! Whether this interference was meant to keep him from performing his duty to provision the army by the beginning of March or merely to remind him of his dependence on the Queen Regent, it was irritating him.

"It is your men who will go hungry, my Lord, if I fail!" Caolin muttered, getting to his feet. Faris was presiding over the Feast of the First Flowers this afternoon. He slipped the requisition into the folder of things to discuss with her and began to pace restlessly to the shelves of files and back to the desk. The wolf Gerol's ears pricked and he lifted his grizzled head, watching the man. There was more sound outside the Chancery today than within—even with a war approaching the Seneschal could not deny his staff their holiday, though he had managed to hold a few to their tasks. But none of them could help with the decisions he had to make now.

"Our army can best Palomon's . . ." Caolin said aloud, considering the forces that were already swelling the encampment outside the city. "And Brian will return a hero. Will that satisfy him? Or will he use his popularity to try to divide me from the Queen?" Gerol's head sank back upon his paws, but his amber eyes continued to follow his master back and forth across the room.

Caolin moved to the window and looked down at the revellers crowding the streets, crowned with early apple blossoms or wreaths of silk flowers. Three soldiers went by arm-in-arm, singing raucously.

"Palomon has rivals at home. If he does not conquer outright he will not dare to press a campaign. But Robert and Brian do not know that—Palomon will seem strong to them. Brian accused me of being Palomon's friend when it was not true, but I think that he and I might have some interests in common.

LADY OF DARKNESS

There might be subtle advantages I could grant him without endangering Westria, in return for concessions that would support my claim to power . . ."

His gaze unfocused, as if he were trying to see all the way to Elaya from Laurelynn. "Such a contact would be too delicate to entrust to Ordrey or to Ercul Ashe, yet I dare not compromise myself . . ." He saw his own face reflected dimly in the windowpane. *I must be myself and not myself, as I was to Margit in the ritual* . . . Time was dimming the memory of that ceremony, and he found himself longing for the Red Mountain again.

Across the roofs of Laurelynn he could see its peak and part of the southern slope, still dusted with snow from the last storm, though fruit trees were beginning to bloom in the sheltered orchards of the Valley. The westering sun stained the peak with rose. He had not been there since Samaine.

A shift in the wind brought him the sound of women's voices massed in song and he moved back to his desk and sat down. Could he change his semblance while retaining his will? He closed his eyes, thinking. First he must make his barriers an opaque surface upon which to paint the persona he wanted others to see. Then he would withdraw so that only the simulation could be seen. If he visualized the other identity sufficiently vividly, the strength of his will might be enough to impose that impression on others.

He pictured the face of a little clerk who logged in documents at the Chancery, a foxy-haired man with a missing front tooth. Caolin must slump in his chair—so—and wet his lips with his tongue as he hunched over his work . . .

Gerol whined perplexedly in the silence. The man at the desk reached for a pen and began to trim it with clumsy twitches of his knife.

The door swung open. "Waren, what are you doing here? I thought you were off today!" A stocky young woman with an armful of papers and a pen stuck behind one ear stepped into the room. "Don't let Lord Icicle catch you in that chair."

A flare of triumph breached Caolin's concentration. He lifted his head.

"Oh, my Lord!" Papers spilled from the clerk's arms in a crackling waterfall. "Forgive me—I didn't realize—this dim light!" stammering, the girl scrabbled for the papers, thrust them onto the Seneschal's desk and fled.

Gerol snorted disgustedly and began to scratch while Caolin threw back his head and for the first time in months, laughed aloud.

"I can do it! I *will* do it! Ah, Brian, how will you plot against me now? I may be anyone . . . beware, Brian, lest I creep into your bed and you tell me the secrets you intend for your own wife's ear!"

For a little while he sat smiling as the winter day dimmed around him. Then he rose, and lighting his lantern, prepared to go. His reflected image winked at him from the slubs and swellings of the window glass. He peered at it, moving the lantern slightly, projecting a score of images on the pane—

—Until he glimpsed for a moment a face with dark hair and eyes like blue stars. Caolin's hand moved of itself to shutter the lantern, and he turned and went quickly from the room.

Farin stared into the candle flame, but he saw only the image of the King. It had been two months since Jehan died—two months since Farin had been able to make Swangold sing. He had come to his own chamber tonight just after dinner and now it was past midnight, and silent, still silent, with no music at all.

The strings shimmered gold as his grip tightened on the harp. If he could not break this paralysis he might as well smash the instrument and destroy himself afterward. He would be going to war soon, death would be easy to find. But once a fisherman from Seagate had told him, *You must go through the breakers to reach the open sea* . . . If only he could fight this sorrow with song!

The lord I loved is gone . . . The phrase echoed in his mind. Farin turned abruptly from the candle as once more he realized Jehan was dead, but the brilliance of the flame still dazzled him. His fingers moved blindly on the strings.

"But he is *not* gone!" Farin exclaimed. "If he were gone, we would be able to forget him. My own heart harbors the ghost that haunts me!"

His vision was clearing now, but he was not focusing on the chamber around him. His silver-streaked hair fell across his face as he bent over the harp, testing phrase after phrase of music, shaping and setting the words that lay waiting within. They had always been there, but he had not had the courage to look for them before.

Words and music linked with the sweet simplicity that one felt sometimes when the arrow sang true from the bow, and Farin knew that it was not he, but that Other within whom he and the harp were joined, that made the song.

> "The lord we loved is gone
> His brilliance dimmed by death,
> But in our hearts his image does not die;
> Just as a candle flame
> Is snuffed out by a breath,
> But still its after-image fills the
>   eye . . ."

VI

Maneuvers in a Mist

"Soon we will know who is to have the mastery of Westria!"

Caolin half-turned to glance at the doorway to the grain shed, thinking he recognized that deep voice. Hoofbeats clattered and faded on the packed ground outside—another company off to the muster on the plain outside Laurelynn.

"My Lord, this wagon's full," said the black-bearded man from Las Costas.

"Yes, yes, go on then." Caolin ticked off another space on his tally sheet as the next wagon rolled into place. The loaders were already heaving twenty-pound bags of corn onto their backs and staggering forward. He glanced down the line— only two wagons to go—they could be finished by the time the army moved out this afternoon. He wiped his brow on his sleeve. It was only the tenth of March, but the air inside the shed was very warm.

"Well! I hardly expected to find you here!"

Caolin whirled and saw Brian's dark bulk silhouetted in the doorway. The Lord Commander passed through a shaft of light that barred the dusty air and paused, surveying the Seneschal with a broadening smile.

Caolin returned his stare impassively and flicked chaff from the scarlet wool of his sleeve, uncomfortably aware of the dust in his hair and the perspiration running between his shoulderblades.

Brian was already dressed for the formal departure of the army of Westria. The rivets that held the steel plates beneath the russet suede of his hauberk had been gilded, and gold thread outlined the crimson arrows that flashed across the black shield embroidered on his breast. Light glanced from his golden spurs.

"I promised that your supplies would be loaded. One of my clerks fell ill so I came in her place . . ." The Seneschal checked off the last of the wagons and waved it on. The loaders picked up the weapons they had stacked in the corner and trooped after it. "Are your men as ready to fight as they are to eat?"

Brian grinned. "Prince Palomon will be sorry he challenged us . . ."

"Indeed?" Caolin closed his notebook and slipped it into his pouch. "They have two thousand foot soldiers, three hundred crossbowmen from the eastern desert and a brigade of axemen from the mines, besides their light cavalry."

"But we have more—" Brian stopped, his yellow eyes narrowing. "My last report gave them only fifteen hundred foot!"

"Well, perhaps they lost some when they took the fortress at the bottom of the pass . . . Good hunting, my Lord," said Caolin agreeably.

Brian thrust his head forward and grinned, his teeth surprisingly white in his brown beard. "Good hunting indeed! But you need not play-act now, Master Red-robe—we are alone. I know well that you hope I will not return!"

Caolin stilled, straining his ears for any sound beside their own breathing. Warpipes wailed in the distance, summoning some contingent from the Ramparts or the north, but inside the shed there was only the buzzing of a fly that faded as it flew out into the sunshine. The Seneschal's gaze paused uneasily on the heavy sword that hung at Brian's side.

"I should be sorry to see Westria deprived of such a strong arm . . ." he said unevenly, and truthfully.

"Would you?" Brian laughed shortly. His advance brought him from sunlight to shadow again. "Then no doubt you will rejoice when I present the Queen with Palomon's coronet. You seek to become her only councilor; I will not allow it . . ."

Caolin's eyes narrowed, suspecting this restraint, but he must not let Brian think him afraid. "I can defend myself—is your own place so secure?"

"Are you threatening me?" Brian's eyes began to glow and he straightened. "I have never yet drawn back from a fight!"

"I know that." Caolin smiled slightly, seeing his enemy revert to type. This automatic response to provocation could be Brian's greatest weakness. "Fortunately I am not so constrained. Fight or flight are equally valid if they serve my purpose."

"Or treachery and subterfuge?" Brian spat.

A pulse began to pound in Caolin's temple, but he held his features still, forcing himself to ignore all the provocations of the past three months. "Did you come here to quarrel with me? There has never been love between us, but we promised Jehan to cease our enmity. He left us both in positions of trust. Help me do my job, as I have helped you to do yours . . ." He gestured toward the empty storage bins, trying to read the smouldering in Brian's eyes.

The Lord Commander shook his head. "How very reasonable. I think you even believe it yourself, for now! I begin to see why Jehan believed in you for so long." He set one foot on a grain sack and leaned forward, resting his gauntleted forearm on his knee.

"But do you think I would trust anything you say?" he went on. "Did you think Jehan trusted you? I know that you forged evidence against me, and he knew it too!"

A warhorse trumpeted and the ground trembled as a troop of cavalry went by. Caolin felt the tremor pass through his body. A muscle twitched in his cheek and he could not make it cease . . . Jehan *had* trusted him—Jehan had loved him! He could not afford to doubt that, now.

"I might even forgive your attempt on my honor," Brian's deep voice battered at his ears, "but I saw Jehan's face when he understood what you had done . . . *you* killed him, Caolin, with your treachery!"

"No!" Caolin's shout sent dust motes swirling to kindle in the light. This was the one accusation that could break his control. He saw again the boar's mask on his altar, felt the spear give way between his hands, heard Jehan's voice pleading . . . pleading . . . His hands shot out and Brian recoiled.

"No one shall say such things of me!" hissed Caolin. Brian retreated before him, step by step, his hand hovering above his sword. "Your own words have released me from my oath to spare you!" The Seneschal's voice lowered, focused, till it vibrated the tines of the pitchforks in their racks.

"You have warned me—now I warn you! If you trip, do not laugh, for I will have dislodged the stone . . . If thunder rattles in the sky, beware my lightning bolt! And when you feel your death upon you, then curse me, for I will be its cause!" He stood trembling, glaring at his enemy.

Brian straightened, his eyes glinting with something halfway between astonishment and satisfaction. "Hah—" he barked, "so the worm can turn? Do you bear the Four Jewels of Westria, that you think to bend all Nature to your will?" He shook his head. "Perhaps I should kill you now, but I will let you live to see my victory!" He threw back his head like a bear scenting the breeze, turned abruptly, and strode away.

Caolin collapsed to his knees in the dust, feeling the sweat chill upon his skin. What was happening to him? He had never given way to such fury . . . never, since the day he found the gates of Awahna closed to him. He was changing—nothing was certain, now. He heard Brian speak to his horse as he mounted, then a shout of greeting.

"You should have killed me, Brian . . ." Caolin whispered through teeth that chattered with cold. Pipes keened in the distance, bittersweet as the promise of revenge.

In the shock of the silence after the warpipes had ceased to play, the banners of the Army of Westria snapped like whips against the turquoise sky. All morning the forces of Westria had been maneuvering across the plain near Laurelynn. The reviewing stand trembled as the wind caught at its canvas sides. Faris shaded her eyes and tried to hear what Robert of the Ramparts was saying to the soldiers ranked before him.

". . . and whatever the price, we will accept only Victory! Those who sought to take advantage of our loss must fear our sorrow!" Robert paused for breath as a murmur swept the massed troops he faced. The sun caught their mail in myriad twinkling points of light.

Faris' shielding tingled with the force of their emotion. *Do they think to punish Elaya for the death of Jehan?* she wondered. *But perhaps they are fortunate to have a physical enemy upon whom to expend their grief . . .*

Robert's horse tossed its head with a clashing of bits as the Commander went on—"Our King swore to defend the people of Santibar, but we cannot help them, for the enemy has taken the fortress at the foot of the Dragon's Tail Pass, and they march northward even now. We must redeem King Jehan's oath! We must defend our land!" He stretched a gauntleted hand to Faris as the cheering deafened them. "My Lady," he cried. "I present to you this Army of Westria!"

Faris felt the attention of the Army transfer from Robert to her, as if she had become the focus of a burning glass. The clamor stilled. The three wings of the Army rayed out to form a half circle with the pavilion as its hub. How could she reach them all?

Her thoughts raced in panic, but Caolin had already explained to her that the canvas sides of the platform would reflect her voice outward. Her white gown would stand out against the colors of the other ladies—Rosemary, Jessica of the Ramparts and Alessia of Las Costas. Eric's mother and sister were there too, and her own sister Berisa who had come down from the north with Sandremun. Caolin had even written out a speech for her to memorize.

As she hesitated, she felt Caolin's hand beneath her elbow, helping her to rise. There was a smudge of dirt on his brow. Faris coughed, and Rosemary handed her a cup of wine. It went down like red fire, easing her throat, but burning in her belly. She moved to the railing.

"Warriors of Westria—the Prince of the South has come against us, and now indeed we feel the loss of our King . . ." her voice wavered, then steadied. "But the strength of a King is in his people—" light flickered across the field as the crowd moved forward, and she felt their attention intensify.

"My lord foresaw this war, and it grieved him more than his wound . . ." Faris forced herself to continue. "But he made what provision he could against this day. Come forward Lord Robert, and Lord Brian, whom my lord appointed second in command."

The two leaders turned their mounts until the horses' noses touched the stand. Lady Jessica and Brian's wife Alessia came forward to stand by the Queen, purple gown and blue, one on each side. Faris took from Jessica a baton of polished wood whose ends were adorned with knobs of gold. She held it out to Robert.

"My Lord, receive from me now the insignia of your command. Come back to us victorious and unharmed." She glanced sidelong at Lady Jessica as she spoke, and drew strength from her sister-in-law's steady gaze.

Faris turned to Lady Alessia a little shyly—she had met her only the day before and found her competence unnerving— took from her the silver-ended baton, and held it out to Lord Brian.

"My Lord, take this baton as the King desired, and serve Robert and Westria well," she said quickly.

"My Queen, we will drive the enemy from this land even if we must spend our lives. We swear this by our homes and families, and by the memory of Jehan our lord, and by the Guardian of Men!" The voices of the two generals sounded as one, and as one they wheeled their horses to face the Army again.

Faris took a deep breath. Rosemary offered her the wine, but she waved it away. "Let Eric of the Horn come before me . . ."

Thunderfoot danced and sidled toward the stand, half-rearing as the streamer of white Faris had drawn from her sleeve blew out in the wind. Eric reined him down severely and brought him to a halt before the platform.

"I accepted you as my Champion at the King's word. Here is my token . . ." Faris said faintly, holding it out to him. Eric took it as if she had put a white butterfly into his hand, and held it against his heart.

"Wear it into battle as a true knight, as my lord would have done . . ." she whispered brokenly.

But Eric had heard her. Faris felt Rosemary stiffen beside her, and through her faltering barriers came a momentary picture that was Rosemary's sight of Eric's face. Faris blinked away tears and saw him herself, less beautiful than in Rosemary's vision, but wearing the same look of ecstacy. She shook her head, rejecting that adoration, but Eric had already reined Thunderfoot away.

Faris clung to the railing. Her back ached, and there was a pain behind her eyes. "You must go out to battle," she said, "and I must stand in the place my lord left me to hold until his child can take his throne. But as your time of testing comes, remember that my time is close as well. As you labor on the battlefield, remember that I will soon be fighting to deliver your new King . . ." She set her hands on her belly and added, "Pray for me then, as I will pray for you." Her hands dropped to her sides and she swayed a little where she stood.

A hush stilled the host, as if they had been the mirage of an army. Then Eric bowed low in his saddle, and the movement swept through the lines with a flicker of multi-colored surcoats and a flash of steel like sunlight on the wind-ruffled surface of the Great Bay.

Robert turned in his saddle and held up his baton. "My Lady, is it your will that we depart?"

Faris leaned forward. The tension was building, building, and only she could give it release.

"Go forth to victory!" she cried with breaking voice, "In the name of the Lord of All!"

Robert swung down his baton.

"Faris! Faris!" Trumpets blasted on her left. Robert reached his men and they began to move—forward, then a wheel to the right that resolved itself into a steady southward flow. The beat of their marching feet pulsed in her blood.

Robert, the commander, cantered in the van. Above him flared his banner, with its golden bear, ramping over horsemen who laughed and shook their spears. Behind them the holders from each mountain vale marched in loose formation, axes in their belts. Spears were in their hands and bows across their backs; they wore scale or leather, and bright steel caps. Cavalry came with them from the sloping plains that spread between the mountains and the river's edge. Hoofs dancing in the dust their mounts curvetted by and the pennons on their lances fluttered cheerfully.

Faris raised her hands to salute them, received back a flood of exultation that dizzied her. Lady Jessica abruptly returned to her place.

But Lady Alessia, still standing by the Queen, stirred suddenly and Faris saw Lord Brian's forces—the folk of Las Costas, come forward, wheeling to join the march. Caolin took the place Jessica had left, his robes crimson as blood in the March sunshine. Faris felt him and Alessia trade glances above her head, but the cheering of the warriors before her claimed all her attention.

Brian sat his mount at ease and laughed, motioned with broad arm sweep to his men, reined in to rear in homage to the Queen. The southern coasts bred bowmen, lightly armed, and mounted on scrub ponies good for miles. Each bore a shield and sword—both men and girls, with steel caps covering tightly braided hair, and they were no less fierce, for being fair.

They cheered as they passed, and Faris felt the hairs lifting on the back of her neck. Her heart pounded to the beat of Brian's drums, and she suppressed a desire to leap from the stand and follow them. She thought, *What have I begun? Is this what Jehan felt when he led his men?*

As the last of Brian's forces passed, Caolin gave a little sigh and moved away, his robes clashing violently with Berisa's berry-colored gown as she brushed by to take his place at the rail. Faris looked around and motioned to Rosemary and to Eric's family to join them as Eric signalled the third wing into motion, Sandremun of the Corona by his side.

Out of three smaller forces the last wing had been formed. Their van was bright with banners, led by Seagate's green, black and white for Theodor's men and blue for the Domain. Eric led the horsemen, well-armored for a charge, mounts glittering with plates of steel and strong enough to bear their own weight and the weight of men with sword and lance and mace. He led also Jehan's own men as champion of the Queen—picked men, grim-faced with grief, for they had known and loved their King and lost him to an enemy they could not meet with sword. Behind them came the northerners—above the hoofbeats' drum, they heard the swift chords of a harp, and suddenly a song—

> *"With hearts aglow to strike the foe*
> *The warriors sally forth,*
> *And their delight shall be to smite*
> *For the Lily of the North—*
> *Oh, 'For the Lily of the North'*
> *Our battle cry shall be,*
> *And our refrain, when home again,*
> *We come with victory!"*

They paused as they came by the stand, and Eric wheeled and turned. They saw on his lance fluttering the favor of the Queen. White it burned against the sky and Eric cried again—"For the Lily of the North we fight, and for our lord, Jehan!"

The northerners echoed him, and the cry spread forward to the contingents from Las Costas and the Ramparts. Waves of sound rolled across the plain until it seemed to Faris that the earth itself was shouting her name. Her name, and Jehan's . . .

Berisa sniffed. "I thought they were fighting for Westria! I hope Farin comes home in better frame than he did last time, and my dear lord too . . ."

Faris' exaltation vanished. She shuddered and groped for the rail, the brightness before her warring with the darkness surging within. She felt Rosemary's firm hands assisting her to lie down.

"I told you it would be too much for her—" said Berisa

with gloomy satisfaction. "But at least she did not have to watch her lord ride off to face those savages . . ."

"Berisa!" came Rosemary's shocked whisper. "That was thoughtless, even for you!"

But Faris only shook her head and turned her face against the cushions. *Oh Thou who made life and death as well,* she prayed, *help them all through the next weeks. Oh Lady, help me!*

But though she covered her ears against the sound of their going, still Faris felt the vibration of marching feet through the wood of the platform and the bench, through the very earth of Westria.

"I think that tonight the Army will camp here—" Ercul Ashe's finger brushed the map of Westria to hover above a bend in the Darkwater. "Lord Robert's message was dated noon today, and it would have taken the pigeon something over an hour to bring it here. They are going so slowly!"

Caolin peered at the map. "For a newly formed army, fifty miles in three and a half days is not bad time. They could go a few miles further today—why do you think they will stop there?" Ashe seemed oddly concerned for so dispassionate a man.

"There is a ford and a meadow that would make it easy to water and graze the horses."

"You seem to know the country well," observed the Seneschal.

"I was brought up in Risslin, my Lord, and my parents live there still. Naturally I want to know whether our forces will arrive in time to defend it from the enemy." Ashe said stiffly.

Caolin nodded. "They are nine days' march from Risslin. If Palomon persists in stopping to capture everything in his path, they will meet somewhere in the Dragon Waste south of the city. Your family should be safe." He smiled. Was there some way he could use Ashe's interest in the campaign?

"Thank you, my Lord." Ercul Ashe did not quite hide his surprise at being answered so kindly—Caolin had never encouraged his staff to confide in him.

The Seneschal was rolling up the map with swift, precise twirls. He slipped it back into its niche. "When is your next meeting with Hakim MacMorann?"

"Tonight, at the Three Laurels Inn. He returned to Laurelynn two days ago. I suppose he has an answer to the letter I gave him when he left in January . . ."

Caolin looked at the other man sharply. He had enclosed the letter in a blank outer wrapper, to be opened only when the trader reached Elaya. Could Ercul Ashe have opened it and seen that it was addressed to Prince Palomon?

"Things have changed since then . . ." he said abruptly. "Do not meet with the Elayan tonight or again."

Ashe nodded. "Good. There seems little point in secret diplomacy now that we are at war!"

Caolin looked quickly away lest the other man should read suspicion in his eyes. Inwardly he blessed the instinct that had inspired him to remove Ashe from any part in the communications that, far from ending, had hardly begun.

In his letter, he had offered Palomon a kind of alliance—a chance to trade Elaya's recognition of the Seneschal as spokesman for Westria, for Caolin's help in arranging a generous settlement after the war. There were concessions that would impress the Elayans without weakening Westria, and his own position would be strengthened if he were the only Westrian leader who could handle Elaya. How would Palomon reply?

Afternoon was fading into evening before Ercul Ashe gathered up his papers and left Caolin alone. The Seneschal went to the cupboard and exchanged his crimson robes for a plain gown of brownish wool . . .

The clerk at the side door looked up as he came down the stairs. "Master Ercul, how can you be leaving again so soon? Have you found a way to do two days' work in one?" She laughed. "Surely even our master does not require such efficiency!"

Caolin stilled, concentrating on the image of Ercul Ashe, willing the young woman to hear the other man's dry voice as she obviously saw his thin shoulders and greying hair.

"I came back in by the other door." he said stiffly. "There was a paper I had not put away."

Her laughter followed him as he started down the street toward Ashe's rendezvous at the Three Laurels Inn.

"I am the broodmare of Westria, bound to her service more surely than any slave in the Barren Lands . . ." murmured Faris bitterly. Her distorted reflection stared back at her from the dark waters of the lake of Laurelynn.

The sliding surface of the water revealed nothing. If Faris should cast herself in she would vanish without a trace . . . She sighed, knowing that they would only pull her out again and add reproaches to the weight she bore. She knew that she was watched. Even now, if she should turn to look across the expanse of lawn to the Palace, a face would flicker at a window or a door would click shut. They watched her as avidly as a farmer watches his best cow.

But with the Army gone a week, what else was there for them to do? Faris knew that today there were only two questions being asked in all Westria—Has the Army met its foe? Has the Queen delivered her child?

A mallard swam quacking from among the reeds. Faris turned away abruptly and began to walk along the shore. The messages Robert sent to Caolin told them that the Army was two days north of Risslin and had seen no enemy. Sometime in the next week then their course would intersect with Palomon's.

Sometime in the next week . . . A cramp rippled across her belly and Faris froze, holding her breath. Was it to be now? The child within her kicked painfully and turned, but though she waited, her own body remained still.

Faris glared up at the eyes of the Palace and cried suddenly, "You will have to wait, damn you! Nothing is happening—stop looking at me!"

Caolin put down Palomon's letter, finding the same meaning there on the twentieth reading as he had seen when he received it from Hakim MacMorann three days before.

"If I should need to trust anyone, why should it be you?" wrote Palomon. *"How will you prove your good faith to me?"*

How indeed? Both commanders wanted a great victory, but the Westrians still outnumbered the forces of Elaya. What if something happened—some mischance to Brian's little army, for example—that would even those odds until the margin of victory would be narrow no matter who won. Both sides might be glad of a mediator then. Could he win over Palomon and destroy Brian with one blow?

If only he could go south—he would know his chance when it came . . . The Seneschal smiled ruefully, recognizing an impossibility, for though he might pass unknown in the Westrian camp, he must be known to be here in Laurelynn, and no one could impersonate *him!* He must take the riskier way of making another his instrument.

The opening of the door cut short yet another iteration of his figuring.

"My Lord—I have been in the library, and—"

"Ah, Ercul!" interrupted Caolin. "I am glad you are here. The dispatches for you to carry to Lord Robert are ready." He slipped Palomon's letter unobtrusively into his desk and pulled out the green dispatch case.

"I found some books on strategy, just as you thought—but no one has opened them for centuries!" Ercul Ashe came forward, a surprising amount of color in his worn face, and set two mouldering volumes on Caolin's desk. Dust rose in a visible cloud. Ordrey, entering after the deputy, coughed loudly and sat down on the other side of the room.

"In the dispatch case is the analysis of the Elayan—oh very well, Ercul—" Caolin gave in to his Deputy's eagerness to speak feeling that he had frustrated Ashe sufficiently for the man to be certain that the idea he wanted to discuss was his very own.

"Thank you, my Lord." The deputy opened the book and began to carefully turn the pages until the volume fell open as if its back had been broken at that spot.

"Here is an analysis of battle plans for different weather conditions," said Ashe. "I know the lower valley, my Lord, and I have found accounts of battles of the ancients which duplicate anything our forces are likely to face!"

"That's all very well . . ." said Caolin patiently, "but I doubt that Lord Robert will have time to come here and consult them."

Ashe shook his head. "You don't understand. I could take the books with me . . ."

The Seneschal began to laugh. "Very well, Ercul—take them. Perhaps they will add enough weight for the horse to know you are on its back. If Lord Robert finds he doesn't have time to read up on strategy, you can tell him all about it!"

"Yes, my Lord!" Ashe collected himself with an effort, resumed his customary imperturbability. "I will be ready to leave in the morning. It should take us a week to get there, and allowing a few days for me to visit in Risslin, another week to return. You may expect me back within three weeks, my Lord Seneschal." He picked up the two books and the dispatch case and turned to Ordrey. "I will meet you at the Chancery stable tomorrow then, at six o'clock in the morning promptly." He bowed and went out.

Ordrey bent in his chair, his shoulders shaking with silent laughter.

"Did you have to pour quite so much dust on those books?" asked Caolin, brushing off his robes.

For a moment Ordrey simply shook his head, unable to speak. "At six o'clock promptly!" he gasped finally. "Does he think I keep a clock in my chamber? Oh my Lord, what have you saddled me with!"

Caolin smiled a little, knowing that Ordrey was quite capable of waking up in the middle of the night if necessary, but that he would complain no matter what time he rose. "It's the horses that you will be saddling. I hope you have good ones— it will be hard to make the trip in that time."

"We should be able to make thirty miles a day on those roads," Ordrey replied. "Your plan seems rather complicated—" he went on, "why not just send a description of the strategy to Lord Robert?"

"Because Robert will discuss it with his other commanders, and as soon as Brian knows where it comes from he will reject it out of hand."

"But he will know that Ercul Ashe comes from you," objected Ordrey.

Caolin sighed. "Yes, but Ercul's honesty is so transparent that even Brian should believe him when he swears I had nothing to do with it . . . You *will* remember the strategies?" he added anxiously.

"I wore out my eyes on them last night," said Ordrey cheerfully. "I memorized everything that could possibly apply. A word from Ashe will let me know which one they choose."

"They may not choose any of them. You will have to wait and see how the troops are stationed before you slip away to Palomon. And remember, be careful what you say to Ercul Ashe!"

Ordrey looked hurt. "I understand." He smiled a little wistfully. "Ercul Ashe only serves Westria . . . I serve *you*, my Lord."

The ground was wet. Farin could feel its dampness even through the thick wool rugs covering the floor of Lord Robert's

LADY OF DARKNESS

tent. He drew his knees up and clasped his arms around them, trying to stay awake. He wondered whether Faris had started to have her baby yet. The commanders were making their reports, a soporific account of men and supplies, and their lieutenants and couriers had been ordered to listen to them.

A draft of cold air struck his face and he looked up as someone pushed the tent flap aside. He glimpsed a cloaked figure outside, ghostly in the mist.

"My Lord Commander—" Robert's squire poked his head through the door. "Here's a messenger from Laurelynn." The cloaked man bent to come through and straightened as the flap fell behind him, pushing back his hood and blinking at the light. His hair was as grey as his cloak, his face like an old shoe.

"Is it the Queen?" asked Robert anxiously. Farin dropped his arms and leaned forward.

"She is well, but there was no news when I left six days ago."

"They will light the beacons when the child is born," Brian reminded them.

The messenger fumbled at his belt for a green leather case. "I come from the Lord Seneschal."

"Of course—" said Robert as Brian stiffened. "I believe I remember you. You are one of the deputies, and your name—"

"Ercul Ashe, my Lord." The deputy bowed and handed the case to the Lord Commander, who unlocked it, drew out the papers within, and began to read. Farin's heart sank as he saw Robert's normally dour expression become graver. At last the Commander looked up, sighed and passed the paper to Brian.

"I could wish that your master had given me this information sooner . . . but I suppose it makes no difference. We have already done all we can."

Farin shivered, remembering the cruel pace of yesterday's march, the confused maneuvering to take advantage of this ground, and the shock when the dark line of the enemy army appeared suddenly on the southern horizon in the afternoon. For a while they had thought they would have to fight them, but the Elayan advance had stopped a mile or two away, and they appeared to be settling in for the night. Now their campfires glowed like a line of fire in the shadowed fields.

"I am sorry, my Lord," said Ercul Ashe. "We had to wait until all reports were in before we could make this analysis."

"You know what it says? Then you may as well stay," said Robert as the Deputy Seneschal nodded. He sighed again and looked bleakly around.

"I hope that you have not all been feeling overconfident because we outnumbered the enemy two to one. The Seneschal informs me that a better estimate of Palomon's numbers would be 3,500 men, and as you already know, he has had all winter to train them."

"But surely invaders will not fight as well as men on their own ground, defending their homes!" exclaimed Eric.

"Our own men are courageous and willing, but they are more used to skirmishing with bandits than fighting pitched battles. We still outnumber them, but I beg you to give up any notion that this makes us the superior force!" Robert snapped.

Brian shook his head with a pitying smile. "Spirit is valuable, but if you think it a substitute for skill you are even more naive than I thought. Courage can turn to panic only too quickly when they are untried and the enemy is strong. Even a veteran would be foolish not to tremble when the *Impis* advance."

"I have fought these people before—" said Eric sullenly, "three years ago below Santibar!"

"That was no war! That was a formal exercise. Besides . . ." Brian added more soberly, "then we had the King."

Farin dropped his face against his knees, overwhelmed by memories of the King fighting in the snow, hawking in the hills above Misthall, falling beneath the tusks of the boar. *Oh my Lord . . . my dear Lord . . .* his spirit cried.

In the silence he heard Ercul Ashe cough dryly. "My Lords, forgive me—I have no right to speak here, but I have been searching the military library at Laurelynn . . ."

"Speak, man! This is no time to worry about etiquette!" said Robert.

"I brought a book with me, my Lord—" Ashe gestured toward the door.

"I'll look at it later if the idea is a good one!" Robert growled. "What does it say?"

Ashe took a deep breath, his dull eyes beginning to glow.

"In a distant land, there were two armies that waited to do battle on a night when there was a great fog—and you see, my Lords, the mists are already rising here." He twitched the door flap aside and they saw the moisture in the air glitter in the lantern light.

"They were encamped facing one another, as you face Palomon, ready to charge in the morning. But one of the commanders had an idea. He left his campfires burning, and that night he sent part of his force, perhaps a third, to one side, on a little rise where their numbers could not be clearly seen. He marched the rest very silently in a large circle, so that they emerged, still hidden by the fog, behind their foes." He paused.

"Well, what happened then?" asked Sandremun, pushing his fair hair from his eyes as he leaned forward.

Ashe smiled a little. "In the morning the enemy saw the lesser force before them and attacked, thinking them easy prey. They never knew about the rest of the army until it fell upon their rear. They were caught between hammer and anvil, my Lords—they were destroyed."

"We would have to find a guide who knew the country here very well . . . or we might get lost ourselves." said Robert after a few moments' thought.

"Elnora of Oakhill's holding is a mile back up the road . . ." said Esteban Swift, Brian's lieutenant. "And she is with us here."

"Well Brian, what do you think?"

"I think . . ." said the lord of Las Costas slowly, "that we should look very carefully at any plan that comes from the Seneschal . . ."

"Brian!" Robert's shocked reproof crossed Ercul Ashe's protest—"But it came from the book!"

"I dare say!" Brian turned on the Deputy. "But where did the book come from? Who sent you to tell us about it when we would have no time to think it through?"

"Brian—I know that you and Caolin are not friends, but do you really believe that he would betray the Army of Westria?" said Robert in frank wonder.

"Not friends!" Brian shook his head and laughed, and Farin felt hairs lift on the back of his neck at the sound. As it faded, everyone in the tent turned to stare at the Seneschal's Deputy, who still stood in their midst, twisting his hands.

"My . . . my Lords!" he stammered, then continued with a curious dignity. "I am no warrior, but my integrity is dear to me. I will swear by my honor, by anything you like, that I found the book in the library with the dust of centuries thick upon it. I tried to tell my Lord Seneschal what I had found, but he would not listen. It was my idea to tell you—*you* do not have to listen either . . ."

He straightened and looked at Brian. "I have served in the

office of the Seneschal since I took my name, and with the Lord Caolin for seven years. You who rule the Provinces know something of what government requires, but can you imagine what it is to keep watch over the entire Kingdom? I have seen Lord Caolin laboring while other men slept—if you think that such a man would betray what he has served so long I think that you are fools!"

"But he might try to betray *me* . . ." muttered Brian.

"It *is* a good plan . . ." Robert sounded as if he were pleading.

Eric's eyes were shining with excitement. "Lord Robert! Let me be the anvil, let me take my men and hold the hill!"

Robert frowned down Brian's bark of laughter. "You would do it well, Eric, but we must not waste our heavy cavalry so. We will need you to spearhead the charge. No—for the anvil we must have infantry, a wall of spears!"

"As Commander you should stay with the main force," said Brian abruptly. "But I have forty companies of spearmen from the lands along the river—it is their lands that these vermin have been wasting—give the honor to them!"

Farin's heart lurched as he realized that the decision had been made. The waiting would be over only too soon.

"I think you are right," nodded Robert. "And you have archers to make the welcome hotter. Give me your light cavalry and I will hold my foot soldiers in reserve. In exchange you may have my mountain men. They have spears too, and heavy axes, and they like close work best."

Through the murmur of comment that followed Farin could hear Robert giving orders to specific commanders—they must let the men sleep until midnight, move the main force out first, leave the campfires alight. He tried to listen.

"I thought you disapproved of the plan—" said Sandremun to Brian. "Why did you volunteer for the most dangerous post?"

Brian laughed, and Farin felt the force of his lust for the coming fight. "Do you think I will let that man go back and tell his master that I was afraid?" He pointed at Ercul Ashe, who still stood in the midst of the commanders, a reed among oak trees. He saw Brian's gesture and turned to go.

"Oh no!" growled Brian. "I have not lost all sense—you will go guarded to my tent," his great hand crushed Ashe's shoulder. "The one thing that would certainly bring disaster would be for this plan to be betrayed!"

Ashe began to protest feebly as the Lord Commander marched him out into the night.

It was night in the Queen's garden. The air was rich with the smell of wet earth and growing things. Faris breathed deeply as she walked. They had tried to make her stay inside, but her arms and legs twitched with an energy that had no outlet. She walked quickly, as the Army had marched on its way south, but the latest pigeon had brought the message that the Westrians were resting now, about to face the enemy. Only she could not rest, tonight.

Faris reached the wall and paused. Where was she going after all? No haste of hers could bring her more quickly to her own battle. She reached out to touch the velvet surface of a leaf, but her legs wanted to move. She turned, breaking off the leaf and rubbing it. It was mint, and the sharp scent was heady in the darkness.

Jehan's child would be born soon . . . She felt it move within her and tried once more to imagine it as a real being made from her flesh and his, a new person whom she could learn to love. But she had only wanted the baby because Jehan wanted it . . . He had written—

> The child has begun to move. I can lay my hand against Faris' belly and feel a flicker of movement like the birth of a candle flame. I think it will be a greater thing to hold this child in my arms than to bear the crown of Westria . . .

But now she must bear the child and the crown of Westria too. Muscles cramped deep within her, but she did not pause. This was weaker than the warm-up contractions she had been having for weeks. She only stopped when a second, slightly stronger pang made her gasp.

Was it to be now? Was this rainy March night the culmination of that golden afternoon at Midsummer in the Sacred Wood? She shivered and began to move forward again, but more slowly now. Another contraction stopped her, then she went on.

She ought to go in and tell them that it had begun, but she could not. Perhaps it was only a false alarm—was she to upset the entire kingdom for no cause? And if it was not . . . She knew how they would close in on her, fussing, questioning. If she went in, the belief of the others would make this thing that was happening to her real, and there would be no escape.

Somewhere in the darkened city, midnight tolled.

Faris walked determinedly, shutting thought away, while the ache that periodically rolled through her belly became harder and harder to ignore. It came again and she gasped and fell heavily to her hands and knees in the mud of the path.

She let her head sink upon her crossed hands, bowing before the plum trees as she had bowed to them at the Hold the day she met Jehan. Wind sighed in the branches, or was it only the blood roaring in her ears? Wind touched her damp forehead like a caress.

Her body ached in protest at a new contraction and the seal that had held the waters within her womb broke. As they flowed to the earth on which she knelt there came a roaring in her ears like waves upon a distant shore.

"Oh Lady, help me! Help me . . ." Panting, she tried to get up. Faint as a whisper of wind in the trees she heard a chiming of sweet bells. Warm hands helped her to rise, and for a moment she thought it was the Lady. Then she heard Berisa's voice, as gentle, surprisingly, as her hands.

"You are a walker like me, love, and now your labor is well begun—come, sister, it is time to go in . . ."

The Army was moving out of its encampment, through fog that rose from the river like steam. It drifted from hoof prints sunk in the mud where the spring rains had fallen and the waterlogged earth had let it stand. From the foothills of the Ramparts to the first swellings of the coastal mountains, from the sodden earth fifty feet upward into the sky, fog covered the Great Valley, and from its misty depths the campfires of the two armies glowed like angry eyes.

Shivering, Farin pulled his cloak around him, watching the fog writhe about the hurrying forms of men. The air rustled with confused whispers, for only the commanders knew why they were moving at such an hour.

"Farin—find Lord Brian and tell him he can have two hundred of my archers, but I need to know where he wants them to go!" called Sandremun.

Farin nodded and set off to the knoll where Brian stood in the torchlight, compensating with dramatic gestures for the force he dared not put into his voice. Droplets of fog glittered in his bristling beard.

Farin waited while Brian thought, then answered, "Have them join Dorothea of Montera's troop, toward the end of the line." Farin sketched a bow, but the Lord Commander was already turning away.

"To be under guard is an insult, but to be bound and left here is an infamy!"

Farin saw Ercul Ashe spluttering at the man-at-arms who was looping rope about his ankles. As the soldier began on his wrists, another man paused beside the tent, shaking his head sympathetically.

"What's the trouble, Ercul? Didn't the lords like your plan?"

"Oh they liked the plan well enough—but Lord Brian doesn't trust me or the Lord Seneschal!" Ashe began to struggle in new indignation.

"Brian doesn't like the Seneschal? You astonish me!" said the other man. The soldier laughed, made fast a final knot, rose and walked away.

"Ordrey! Untie me—you cannot leave me here!"

"My dear man, if I let you go, Brian would never forgive *me!*" Ordrey also laughed, and still grinning, stepped back and disappeared into the mists.

Farin repressed a smile and remembering his duty hurried off toward Sandremun's tent. It did seem cruel to leave the poor man helpless while a battle was raging, but the chances were that the fighting would not come that way. Ercul Ashe was more likely to be safe than any of them, he thought, but he made a mental note to check up on him after the battle. *If I survive* . . . and suddenly his belly was cold.

With a murmur of creaking leather and jingling mail Brian's forces moved out toward the hill where they would huddle through the rest of the night, regretting their abandoned fires and longing for dawn. Soon they were gone.

Farin checked his saddle girth and his weapons and swung up onto the chestnut horse, swearing under his breath as the excited animal snorted and plunged. He urged him quickly into the line of Robert and Eric's men who were already moving, like an army of ghosts, southward through the mists.

They had been cautioned to keep silence, so when the dank air caught in their throats they stifled their coughs. Jingling mail was muffled by heavy cloaks, and even the bits of the horses had been wound in strips of wool. What sound they did make was swallowed by the fog as their own forms were engulfed by the darkness. Presently even their own campfires disappeared.

Fire leaped fitfully on the broad hearth of the Royal bedchamber. Caolin paused in the doorway, blinking away the darkness of the corridor. The room was full of women, moving purposefully about like soldiers preparing for battle. Caolin smiled a little at the simile—he was preoccupied with warfare tonight—then realized that it was true.

Rosemary saw him, bent over the bed for a moment, then stepped away. Faris was lying there, the sheet drawn over the distorted mound of her belly and up to her chin. As the Seneschal hesitated, she moaned and bit her lip, turning her head against the pillow, and her belly changed shape beneath the cloth. Her face was puffy and her hair lank with sweat.

Shocked, he turned to lady Jessica. "Is she dying?"

Jessica raised an eyebrow, then her lips quirked. "I suppose you never have seen a woman in childbed before. Doesn't a man at hard labor look the same?"

Caolin's eyes moved back to Faris. Her spasm seemed to ease, she sighed and relaxed while Rosemary sponged her brow. Then she opened eyes that were like smudges of shadow in her white face, and looked at Caolin.

He made himself go forward and sit down in the chair beside her bed. He took her hand. "How are you?"

Faris grimaced. "They tell me I am doing well . . . I am glad that you came." Her eyes fastened on his as if she could draw strength from his soul. He fought an impulse to pull away his hand.

The Queen caught her breath and her gaze turned inward. Her hand tightened painfully on Caolin's and he looked quickly away from the heaving of her body to the pure flickering of the fire.

Berisa bent from her seat by the hearth to pick a new ball of wool from her basket, and turned to lady Jessica. "I had trouble with my legs when I was carrying my first child and my third. But the second one was the hardest to deliver. I was in labor for two days . . ." she said proudly, then glanced at the writhing figure on the bed. "Something always seems to go wrong."

Caolin swallowed and shut his eyes, but he could not keep from smelling the sharp odor of sweat, the too-sweet scent of the women's perfumes, the musky female smell that permeated the room.

Faris' hand relaxed and he snatched his own away, rose and stood looking down at her. Jessica had said that all was well, but what if something *should* go wrong? Jehan on his deathbed had been more beautiful than Faris was now.

"You should go—" said Rosemary softly at his elbow. Caolin fancied he saw pity in her eyes, but at that moment did not resent it.

"Will the child come soon?"

Rosemary shrugged. "I am a maid among mothers, and so no expert, though I have midwifed animals often enough. From all accounts a first child takes a long time. It will be tomorrow before the baby comes, I think—we will call you."

"Be grateful—" said lady Jessica, grinning. "If you were the child's father we would make you stay!"

Caolin shuddered and turned away, nearly running into the Master of the Junipers at the door. The Seneschal stepped back and bowed. "This is one task I will gladly leave to you," he murmured as the Master went by him into the room.

The darkness of his own chamber was a refuge from the sights and sounds of the labor room, but not from his own thoughts. He could not forget the Queen's racked body. Women did die in childbed—What would become of him then? Desperately he lit a lamp and rummaged through the papers on his desk—records of stores sent with the Army which had not been tallied yet.

He forced himself to the work, figuring where he would find grain to replace what had been used . . . how many bushels from which holdings . . . how many harvests . . . But he could not keep from glancing at the window, from listening for footsteps in the hall. In the Palace the Queen was laboring to bring forth an heir to Westria. In the mists south of Risslin, the Army was preparing to meet the challenge of Elaya. By this time tomorrow, the answers to so many questions would be clear—whether Brian would live to torment him, whether the Queen would live to uphold him as Seneschal and whether or not a living child would make her own position secure.

Surely tomorrow would decide who was to have the mastery of Westria. He had only to wait.

VII
The Queen's Battle

The rising sun blazed like a beacon on the high edge of the eastern mountains. Farin wondered how long it would take to burn away the fog that suffocated the Valley below. A sea of mist still lapped the hill where Brian's command waited for the day. People were beginning to stir, stretching legs grown stiff with damp, wiping the dew from swords and bows. An archer combed out her brown hair and braided it again; dawnlight glistened on the silky strands.

Farin flexed his cold fingers and longed for his harp. But by the time he got Swangold tuned, he thought wryly, the battle could be lost or won!

He heard Brian's deep voice and turned. What he had seen of the Lord Commander of Las Costas at Misthall had left him with a hearty dislike for the man, but his army obviously adored him.

Brian paused to speak to an axeman from the Ramparts, and there was a gust of appreciative laughter from his mates. At the noise Farin jumped, then remembered that there was no need for silence any more. Even if the enemy heard them, it was too late to change position now.

"So, Sir Farin—I see you are still with us." Brian came toward Farin and glanced approvingly at the chestnut horse, who was pulling eagerly at dewy hummocks of grass. "Well, I daresay Robert and Eric slept no softer than we . . ."

"Slept?" said Farin in wonder. Even if his body had been at ease, visions of the coming battle would have kept him awake.

Brian shook his head. "I hope you got some rest—you will need your strength today!" He peered down the hill.

The archers were unwrapping their bowstrings from around

their waists and fitting them to their bows again. One offered Farin some of his bread and cheese, but he shook his head and wondered if his belly were cramping from fear or if Faris had gone into labor and he was picking up some echo of her pangs.

The silver veil of mist drew steadily away, revealing hummocks and standing pools carved by the feet of cattle now eaten by the Elayans or driven away from the path of the war. The new grass glistened in the growing light.

"*They* are sleeping soundly enough, the bastards—" said an axeman near Farin, gesturing toward the enemy camp. "You would think they'd be stirring by now."

They listened. Farin's horse shook his head and began on another clump with a juicy sound of tearing grass. A bird flashed out of the mist, twittering cheerfully, and sailed over their heads into the sunny upper air.

Brian frowned. "What's that down there—the black spots on the grass?"

"Cow pats?" suggested somebody, sniggering.

"They're too big . . ." Brian ignored the laughter as he squinted into the thinning fog. Farin was reminded oddly of a herd bull alerted by a shift in the wind. Silence spread around Brian like ripples in a pool.

"Those are Palomon's watchfires . . ." came the whisper at last.

"Cold . . ."

"Palomon may have slept soft last night, but he did not do it here!" Brian's voice grated on Farin's ears as if someone had scraped a fingernail across his soul.

"My Lord! My Lord!" There was a clamor from the troops on the other side of the hill. Farin dashed in Brian's wake as the Commander plunged toward it through the buzzing ranks of men. Then he halted. Farin swerved to keep from caroming into him and slipped to his knees in the wet grass.

For a moment his eyes were dazzled by a glimmer of light that grew momentarily more brilliant as the mists drew away. Then he realized that the dim shapes on the grass below him were figures, warriors, whose spear points sparkled cruelly in the sun. The Elayans! Rank upon rank of them were formed up on the Westrians' left flank about a quarter of a mile away. The outlines of a great crescent were emerging from the fog— surely Palomon's entire force must be here!

"So . . ." said Brian very softly. "The worm *has* turned!" Sorrow flickered across Brian's face so swiftly Farin could scarcely believe it had been there. Then the Commander seemed to root himself into the earth and turned to Farin.

"I see that Palomon can also play at strategy. Lord Robert was going to march behind them—behind where they used to be—and he should be somewhere beyond the abandoned camp by now. Find him! In a moment they will charge us—we are outnumbered, and not properly formed up to meet them. Robert must bring the rest of the army quickly or there will be none left here to aid!" He gripped Farin's shoulder for a moment.

Farin swallowed, shivering as the murmur around him swelled to a roar. As he made his way back to the chestnut horse he heard Brian's voice lashing through the tumult—

"Everyone, face me! Everyone on the end of a line begin moving to your left—you others, follow—march, you fools!"

With surprising coordination, Brian's force shifted to face its enemy. As Farin mounted, a shiver of movement rippled through the ranks of the Elayans beyond them as they readied themselves. For a moment both forces were still.

Farin wrenched his gaze away and slashed at the horse's neck with the reins. The indignant animal squealed and plunged down the hill, bounding erratically among the hummocks toward the abandoned campfires. Farin did not dare to look back, but he heard the ominous *clack, clack* of spears beating on shields as the *Impis* advanced.

"How long will this go on?" asked Faris shakily. She gasped for breath as she felt another contraction begin, then fought to keep from breathing, to avoid any movement that would conflict with the wrenching that was reshaping her body.

Jessica sponged her brow as the pain eased and smiled. "The gate is only half-open, my dear. For nine months your body has been learning to carry this child—it takes time to reverse the process!"

"What is the hour?"

"Near dawn—" replied her sister-in-law.

"Morning!" corrected Rosemary, pulling open the curtains. Lady Alessia of Las Costas had taken Berisa's place by the fire. The midwife from the Community at Laurelynn was adding water to the pot that had been heating over the fire.

Pale light filtered into the room, silvergilt on Rosemary's head, lighting a stray strand of silver in Jessica's darker hair. In the cradle by the window Jessica's three-month-old son stirred, made faint sucking sounds, then slept again.

LADY OF DARKNESS

Faris shuddered. "I thought it would be over by now . . ."

"If your brother were here he could play us a tune to pass the time," said Jessica.

"I expect that Farin must wish he were here too, by now!" Rosemary came back from the window. "Unless he can find music in the clashing of swords."

Branwen looked up from her needlework. Jessica's face stilled and her glance crossed Lady Alessia's, then she smiled resolutely.

"Here we are concerned with the *giving* of life! Branwen, you have a sweet voice. Why don't you sing for us?"

"What shall I sing?" stammered the girl.

"Why not a lullaby?" suggested Alessia.

Their voices blurred as Faris' body reasserted its dominance. When the contraction eased, Branwen was finishing the first verse—

> *"Here there is peace, though the weather be wild—*
> *Sleep in my arms, oh my darling, my child."*

Jessica rose, lifted her own child from his cradle and sat down in the rocking chair to nurse him. The creaking of the chair kept time to Branwen's song.

> *"If your father were with me, then close to my breast*
> *I would hold him, and singing, watch over his rest.*
> *But now he has left me for war's bitter field,*
> *Where my love is no guard and my arms are no*
>   *shield . . ."*

The last note was choked off as Branwen realized what she had sung. Embroidery silks cascaded to her feet as she stood and ran from the room. Jessica's baby whimpered as her arms tightened around him, and Lady Alessia's hand closed on her marriage-ring.

"The song was ill-chosen for this company—" said Lady Alessia at last. "But why did she run away?"

Rosemary had gone rather pale, but she replied steadily, "She loves Farin, and he went to war without saying goodbye."

Faris turned her face against her pillow. *Why should they be spared?* She thought, *My own lord will never return to me . . .*

"May the Lord of Battles hold them all within His hands . . ." said Alessia.

Brian's hand closed on the hilt of his great sword and he drew it in a single shining motion. His gaze focused on the bright array of the Elayan army below. Still watching them he turned a little so that his own men could hear his voice.

"Warriors of Las Costas and the Ramparts!" he cried. "We, who have suffered most from this enemy, were chosen to bait a trap for them. But it seems that they can be clever too. Soon we shall learn if they can fight as well. If we can hold them until Lord Robert comes they will be surprised indeed. Stand fast, therefore, for the honor of Westria!"

He was shouting at the end, his voice ringing across the rhythmic thunder from below as the Elayan infantry banged their spears against their shields.

"Archers, release your arrows when I drop my hand!" His great sword flickered in the morning sunlight like a living flame.

The *Impis* were moving now, the men almost hidden behind oval cowhide shields. Their leather corselets gleamed with oil and the bright plumes of their helmets tossed above the rims of the shields. There were cavalry on either side of the main body of foot soldiers, their brimmed helmets glinting in the growing light. There would be mounted archers among them as well as the lancers with their great round shields. Brian motioned to the man at his side.

"Douglas, find Sir Edgar Whitebeard and tell him to turn four companies of archers—whoever is in back—to guard our rear!"

The enemy were beginning to climb the hill now, their deep chanting seeming to vibrate from the earth. He glimpsed a glitter in the midst of them. "Palomon . . ." muttered Brian, "Palomon and his household in their silvered mail . . ."

From the corner of his eye he was aware of Palomon's horse archers drawing ahead of the rest, swinging wide to circle the Westrian rear as the infantry advanced. He had one moment in which to hope that Sir Edgar's archers were ready for them, then he saw that the infantry was within range and swung down his sword.

The archers, positioned behind the Westrian spearmen on the highest point of the hill, drew and released. Arrows buzzed toward the foe like a flight of angry bees. In the moment the cowhide shields bristled with their stings. Some of the plumed helmets disappeared, but there was no faltering in either chanting or advance.

Arrows swarmed again and again while the enemy came on. Brian could make out individual features clearly now. The blood raced in his veins, his feet seemed to sense the pulse of the earth below him. Now he remembered—only this immediacy of destruction could make one feel so alive! Grinning savagely, he swung round the shield from his back and slipped his left arm through the straps.

They were very close now.

"First rank, ready—" Brian cried, "and—*charge!*"

He leaped forward, his sword swinging up as if lifted by the shout that burst from his chest. He was carried forward on a wave of sound as his men echoed him, their feet beating a thunderous undertone as they used the slope of the hill to gain momentum.

The enemy swirled around them. Black eyes glared into his, but already Brian's sword was lashing forward. He barely felt the shock as the Elayan's shield rim crumpled; the honed edge sliced through leather armor and flesh to be stopped finally by hard bone. White circled the dark eyes as they widened. A scream tore at Brian's ears as he ripped his blade free and ran on.

Faris cried out as the giant's fist squeezed her again.

"Relax your muscles! Take a deep breath! Ride with it, my Lady—don't fight! Now pant—the contraction is coming, now breathe deeply, and again . . ."

Faris tried to relax, for a moment moved with the contraction as if she were poised on an enormous wave, then lost the precarious balance and plunged into a sea of pain.

"No!" She threw out her arms as if she were indeed drowning. Hands pressed her back with gentle force and her body tensed, muscles of back and abdomen tightening in a vain attempt to block the mighty constrictions of the womb that was working to bring its burden into the world.

The contractions strengthened, peaked, and a scream rasped Faris' throat, faded to a moan, rose again and again. She gripped Rosemary's and Branwen's hands and never felt them wince.

"Faris—the first part of your labor is almost over, but you

must get back in control. What do you think those exercises were for, girl? You know what to do! Relax, count, breathe!" Berisa's face swam before her.

"Jehan . . . I cannot do it." Faris murmured as the agony receded a little. "I cannot rule the pain . . . Jehan! I eased your dying, can't you help me now?" She whimpered, feeling her womb begin to tighten once more. Something cold touched her lips, but she had not strength even to sip the lemon-water Rosemary was offering her.

She jerked as the midwife applied hot cloths to the birth opening, hoping to relax the muscles. They had removed her nightgown to ease her and when Faris realized that she did not even care if the other women saw the scar on her arm, she knew how completely this agony now governed her. Then pain slashed through her again and she forgot even to be afraid.

"She is bleeding again . . ." the midwife's voice sounded very far away. Faris closed her eyes.

"Master! Can't you give her something to ease the pain?" cried Rosemary. "She has not the strength to endure so long!"

"It is too soon—" his voice was strained, "it would harm the child . . ."

"But there must be something you can do!"

"If she will let me . . ." Faris felt the cool touch of the Master of the Junipers' hands, and for a moment a memory of stillness eased her torment. *Awahna* . . . Her spirit groped for the Valley's silence, the cooling mist that veiled its waterfalls. Mist engulfed her. She heard the Master calling her name, but she was already beyond him, as if his touch had given her the excuse she needed to break free. The sound of frantic voices faded, and then, awareness of pain.

Farin reined in the chestnut horse, batting futilely at the mist that swirled around him. He peered over the horse's sweating shoulder at the trampled ground. Clearly a large force had been this way, but whose? The hoofprints of Westrian and Elayan horses looked the same. He tried to remember the details of Elnora's map. The chestnut shook his head and took a few steps forward, tugging at the reins as he reached for grass.

"You hog—" muttered Farin. "If I am killed will you push my body aside to get at the grass I'm lying on?"

A glint of silver in the mud caught his eye and he swung down from the saddle to see. It was a medallion of the Mother, bare-breasted with Her child upon Her knee. On the reverse was the circled cross of Westria.

Something cold and sharp pricked the back of his neck. Farin stilled, drew breath again as the pressure eased, then turned. For one moment he thought he saw an Elayan's plumes beyond the short shaft of the lance. Then he realized they were quail feathers and recognized Sir Randal of Registhorpe.

"Randal—where's Eric?" his voice cracked and he steadied it. He scrambled to his feet and hauled himself into the saddle, still talking. "The Elayans marched around us and everything fell apart—"

"This way!" Sir Randal was already jerking his mount's head around. Farin felt for his swordhilt and realized he still held the medallion in his hand. He thrust it into the breast of his tunic, thinking suddenly of Faris. "Mother of All! Protect us both today!"

Free at last, Faris floated forward through the dim swirls of mist that became the spray of waterfalls flowing over towering cliffs of grey stone. For a time it was enough to be there. Then Faris remembered why she had come and called out Jehan's name.

"My beloved . . . I am here."

This was not like her other dreams of him. Just as this Valley was vaster than the Awahna she had seen before, its very stones pulsing with light, so Jehan seemed taller and more beautiful than he had been.

"Has it been so many years?" he said wonderingly. "I waited here, though they wished me to go on. Are you dead too?"

"I . . . do not know," she answered slowly. "I had been laboring so long."

Jehan's features twitched, but the memory of her own pain was too vivid for Faris to pity him. "My darling, I never wanted you to have to bear that alone!" he paused. "And what of the child?"

"Let them tear it from my womb!"

"Can they?" he said doubtfully, not seeming to hear her bitterness. "Would they be in time?"

She stared at him, anger replacing her awe. "You would send me back to that torture? Not alone, my Lord! Not alone!" Her hand closed on his.

She felt herself moving then as if the mist had become a

current. But still she clung to Jehan's hand, making it the focus of her consciousness even when she heard the Master of the Junipers calling her name.

"For the Lily of the North!" cried Eric. Even through the heavy saddle he could feel Thunderfoot's muscles surge as the stallion leaped forward, glorying in freedom after the long hours of waiting in the cold. At his heels thundered all the heavy cavalry Westria possessed.

Words echoed in Eric's memory as hooves beat out the rhythm of the charge—Farin's gasped message. He remembered the stricken look on Lord Robert's face and the orders that Eric was turning to obey before they were past Robert's lips. It hardly registered that this was Brian he was riding so furiously to save. He only knew that he was free to fight at last.

Thunderfoot charged over the last rise and Eric saw the hill on which Brian had made his stand. The sun, almost overhead by now, glinted wetly on blood-slick swords. The pitiful remnant of Brian's command were still struggling in the midst of a sea of waving plumes around which horse archers circled like wolves.

"Westria! Westria and Jehan!" The battle cry swelled from five hundred throats. The enemy horsemen saw them now and came swiftly toward them, their arrows glancing off the heavy armor of the Westrian knights.

The two forces shocked together. One of the lighter southern horses squealed and went down as the black horse crashed into it. Another was before him now, throwing up his shield in a hopeless attempt to ward off Eric's spear. As they sped past the spear struck, stuck, and was jerked from Eric's fingers. A horseman came in from the side. Thunderfoot swerved and his iron-shod heels lashed out, the rest of the Elayans whirled helplessly aside and they were through.

Eric felt Thunderfoot's stride lengthen as they shot toward the beleaguered Westrians. Beyond them Palomon watched with his reserves. Eric wrenched his sword from its sheath and reined to the right, burning with desire to reach that silver figure and run it down. The air hummed around him and something flickered by his head. Startled, Eric took his eyes from Palomon and saw beside him a group of men on foot—sturdy bearded men with leather jerkins, steel caps, and faces burnt red by the sun. They carried crossbows.

The air sang again and the black horse shuddered. Eric cursed as Thunderfoot faltered. There were cries behind him as bolts pierced plate and mail. The horse rocked at the impact as another arrow struck him in the flank, just missing Eric's thigh. Thunderfoot threw up his head with a scream and Eric saw a fourth bolt transfix his neck.

Eric kicked his feet from the stirrups and cast himself from the saddle as the stallion fell.

For a moment there was no one near him. With stinging eyes Eric knelt by Thunderfoot's head. He remembered kneeling in the straw beside the newborn black foal and giving him his name.

"Brother, forgive me for bringing you here," he said swiftly. "May I fight as well as you have done . . ." He laid his sword on the grass, ran his hand one last time along the sweated neck, and drew his dagger for the mercy stroke.

A shadow dulled the blade. Eric's hand shot out to close on an arm and jerk the attacker down across the body of the fallen horse. In another moment his knife had sliced through the man's throat.

"Here's an escort for you, old friend!" he said harshly, but the stallion's eyes were already dull.

Eric picked up his blade and got heavily to his feet, swearing with grief for the horse and for himself, because he knew he would not get his chance at Palomon now. But above the clang of swords and the screams of dying men he could hear Brian's battle cry, and up the hill, he saw the blurred swing of a great sword.

Eric settled his shield more securely on his arm, and shouting, he began to run toward the fight.

"For the Lily of the North, Jehan, and Westria!"

"Jehan!" Still calling his name, Faris felt herself sucked downward. Colors whirled madly around her, but he was still there. She felt his presence even when she opened her eyes and found that she was clutching the Master of the Junipers' hand.

"Thanks be to the Lady!" murmured the Master. His brow was beaded with perspiration, but his face was very pale.

"I brought Jehan . . ." said Faris clearly, ignoring the shock on the faces of the women who hovered at the foot of the bed.

"I know . . ."

Faris felt her body begin to tense and tried to withdraw into the mist again.

"No—The waiting is over and you must work *with* your body now!" cried the Master. "Are you willing to link with me and let me help block the pain?"

Faris nodded, biting her lip as the contraction lifted her. *Jehan!* Her spirit still held his.

"My Lord!" the Master echoed her.

"I am here . . ."

Faris moaned, feeling the pain begin, but another presence slipped between it and her awareness of it. Was it Jehan, or the Master, or both of them? It did not matter now.

"The contractions are changing!" exclaimed the midwife, laying her hands on Faris' belly. "The door is opening at last. Breathe in now, my Lady, and hold . . ."

Let the ocean bear you to shore . . . the Master filled her mind with the image of a vast surging sea on which she rose and fell. Faris reached out for Jehan, and thought she felt his lips touch hers.

She was vaguely aware that someone was thrusting cushions behind her back until she was half sitting, and placing clean cloths beneath her on the bed. Jehan guided her while the Master helped her bear her pain and the waves grew higher and faster, seeking the shore.

Suddenly she understood their urgency. She was not riding the waves, she *was* the wave. Her moan became a grunt and she bore down.

For a moment she was free. She opened her eyes and looked around her, seeing with unusual clarity the strained faces of the women around her, sunlight pouring through the windows, the Master of the Junipers' bowed head.

"Well, it's about time!" exclaimed Berisa.

"Now we can begin to fight!" said the presence within her.

Faris hesitated, her whole being poised as the contraction began.

"Now!" The command rang from without and within. Faris cried out as fiercely as any man upon the battlefield and bore down. Light flared and shattered from the windows, on the sea, in Faris' eyes.

The air seemed to glitter as swords rose and fell. Eric squinted against the noon glare and hewed downward with his sword.

A spear thrust at him, he lifted his shield to knock it aside, staggered and set his feet again as Brian was thrown against him. Eric could feel the other man's muscles bunch against his back as Brian recovered and swung. Eric slashed at a contorted face, missed and realized that the man was retreating. They were all retreating.

Dazed, he stared around him. A breastwork of heaped bodies bore mute testimony to a stand that had lasted, how long? One hour? Ten? He glanced up and saw the sun directly overhead, and against the sky's pure blue tiny specks that circled waiting for their time to come.

Eric's arm ached from striking and he lowered the tip of his sword to the ground. He was covered with blood, and though he knew that some of it must be his own, he felt only a vast weariness. He heard a long sigh from behind him.

"Hmmn—would you agree this is a better place to compare our skill than the dueling field?" Brian asked with a tired grin.

Eric blinked, forcing his muddled brain to remember his challenge to Brian the summer before. After a moment he shook his head and smiled hesitantly. "I think you are the winner, my Lord."

"The pile is as high on your side as on mine."

"Yes, but I feel nearly done, and you were fighting for hours before I came." He looked at Brian's profile, the hazel eyes sunken, the brown beard matted with blood, and felt a sudden jolt as if he had seen his own reflection.

"I'm glad you came. *Bare is brotherless back.*" Brian repeated the old slogan of fighting men.

"Brian . . . I'm sorry we quarreled. I . . ." Eric stammered and fell silent.

Brian grinned. "You will make a man, cockerel—if you get the chance. Jehan predicted this, but I do not think we will enjoy our friendship long."

They looked around them. Beyond the piled bodies there was an area that was almost clear, and beyond that the men who had drawn off from the attack with Palomon and his reserves behind them. Eric nodded, trying to accept the fact that he would be dead soon, but the idea did not seem real. He could imagine himself fighting on and on, but his mind shied away from the darkness at its end.

"If by some chance I should fall and you survive," Brian said quietly, "take the ring, the King gave me, and give it to my son to wear until Westria has another lord." Eric realized that it had been hours since he had even thought of the Queen. Her child could be born by now . . .

"Yes . . ." he said hoarsely. "And you take mine."

They were silent for a little, gazing at the waiting enemy. They could not see southward beyond them to tell if Robert and the army were on the way.

Suddenly Brian laughed. "Well—at least we can make our last fight a thing for the poets to sing about. That lad—the Queen's brother—perhaps he will do it." He began to murmur an old battle chant.

> *"The foe gathers round us, red run their spears*
> *With blood of our brothers slain in this battle.*
> *Strike, men of Westria! Swords cease not swinging*
> *While valiant warriors' will does not falter . . ."*

They could see Palomon clearly now, his silver mail unstained, his black eyes gleaming. Brian fell silent, staring at him.

Eric nodded. "I tried to reach him too . . ."

"I don't suppose he will accept a challenge, but I must try . . ." Brian stepped forward, lifting his sword.

"Palomon of Elaya, I call you to combat," he shouted. "This quarrel is chiefly between you and me—why should these others suffer too?"

Palomon continued to look at them, no change in his face to show if he had heard. Then he raised his hand and called out a command. There was a movement in the waiting ranks and a file of men appeared and took up position facing the two Westrians. Eric growled deep in his throat.

"The crossbows . . . the crossbows! Faris saw it, poor lady—my doom!" Brian said softly. He turned to Eric. "I have no proof, but if you live, remember this—Caolin did this somehow! He swore he would kill me. I never thought he could succeed . . ." he shook his head like a wounded bear. "The cowards! I owed Jehan my life, but not like this—" He gripped Eric's arm.

"They shall not do it! Brother, come with me and let us charge *them!*"

Eric nodded and the sick feeling in his stomach was replaced by a fierce joy that ran along his veins like wine. The two men clasped hands briefly and then, as the crossbowmen raised their weapons, turned to face their foes.

Brian shook his head and started forward, and he chanted as he ran—

> *"Strike now, my comrade, closer than kindred—*
> *Foemen who fell us will weep ere night falls!"*

Close behind him, Eric cried, "For the Lily of the North," once more, and the arrows came.

Brian stumbled as a bolt struck him, but went on. Eric heard a bee snick past his ear and pounded after him, remembering the courage of his black horse. Then he felt the shock himself as an arrow nicked the top of his shield and grazed his shoulder. The missiles were coming fast now, but still Brian staggered forward and Eric followed him.

Some of the arrows bit into Eric's shield. He was hit in the arm once more, and the legs. He did not count the arrows now, but only thought of that line of men he must reach somehow.

His legs did not want to carry him. He swayed and slipped to his knees. Ahead of him he saw Brian stopped at last, saw the sword drop from his hand. More arrows pierced him, then he spread his arms as if to crush his foe and toppled face forward into the mud.

Eric crawled toward the fallen man. He shook his head, trying to get rid of the black patches that crawled before his eyes. It was only a few feet, but his head was swimming when he got there.

He crouched over the body and carefully touched the face. There was no response, no change in the other man's grim smile. Ignoring the roaring in his ears, Eric tugged the ring from Brian's finger and thrust it onto one of his own.

He tried to get up, but the darkness rose about him like a sea. His limbs gave way and he sank down on Brian's body instead. The black wave burst over him, but just before it drowned all awareness he heard, as from a great distance, the sweet music of Robert's horns.

"You are the sea . . ." Faris heard the Master as the bright wave lifted and receded again. They had tied a rope to the bedposts for her to pull on, and Jessica and Rosemary were bracing her feet. She felt the child being forced through her

body—outward and then back again as the surge faded away.

"You are the earth, and the child a sapling striving for the sun . . ." said Jehan. Faris braced herself with the strength of earth, visualizing a shaft of light that streamed upward from her body until it took the shape of a broad-shouldered man with Jehan's features and her own dark eyes.

"I see the baby's head! It has dark hair!" cried Rosemary.

"Just a few more heaves now—" Berisa bent to check her progress. The midwife was already crouched by Faris' knee with hands outstretched. The contraction eased and Faris let out all the air she had left in a shuddering sigh.

"Take a deep breath now, my Lady—" said the midwife calmly.

"You are the wind!" cried the Master.

Faris filled her lungs, felt air rush through her, tingling in every vein. She braced herself, hauled on the rope and pushed, and her breath exploded in a shout that rattled the window panes.

"Now, my darling, now! We are fire!" Pain and ecstacy were one.

Faris' body convulsed and her spirit flared. And in that brilliance she saw a woman whose body glowed, whose hair rippled like flame. She felt Jehan and the Master cower before that Presence, but she opened her arms to embrace the fire. Then the Light grew, until Faris saw only a pair of eyes that were neither male nor female, but something more than either, incandescent with love.

She felt a tug and something slippery against her thighs. The flame that enfolded her eased to a steady glow and her body stilled at last. A warm weight was laid upon her belly. The midwife moved quickly around her.

Then she heard a smack and a thin outraged cry. Faris' eyes focused and she saw the midwife lift high an infant whose face was contorted in protest and whose genitals, seeming from that angle unnaturally large, were unmistakably male.

"A boy! An heir for Westria!" cried Jessica. "Faris, see!"

"Jehan, we have done it . . ." murmured Faris. "There is your son . . ."

"Yes . . . he is beautiful."

From Jehan's thought came a hint of sadness and Faris wanted to ask him why, but every nerve was relaxing in the golden glow. *Our son . . .* she thought drowsily. The women around her were laughing and crying out, a hubbub that spread to those waiting in the corridors and ran along the streets of Laurelynn like flame.

"The child is born! The waiting is over! At last! At last!"

"At last!" shouted Sir Randal. "Look at them—they are running at last!"

Farin squinted at the dark figures moving across the glare of the plain. Someone tossed a sword glittering into the air and caught it with a shout.

"Victory!" the cry was repeated up and down the ranks of bloodstained men who paused, panting, realizing that they held the field.

"You men from Las Costas and the plains—anyone whose horse is fit to run—get after them. I want Palomon!" Lord Robert gestured toward the fleeing foe.

Farin dug his heels into his horse's sides. The chestnut shook his head and took a step forward, stumbled and stopped, whickering unhappily.

"You'll never catch Palomon on that one, Farin—he's gone lame in the off foreleg," said Randal.

Farin swung down from the saddle and inspected the strained leg, then patted the horse's bronze neck. "I'm sorry, old hog . . ." he looked up at Sir Randal. "I didn't notice it before, and I don't think he did either."

A raven sailed overhead, cawing disconsolately, and settled on a dead horse. It looked at them watchfully with its yellow eyes as if wondering whether they would dispute its meal.

It is over . . . Farin rested his head against the shoulder of his horse, who was nosing distastefully at the bloody grass.

"Well, there's plenty of work for us here . . ." Sir Randal looked at the wreckage of the field. "They can't all be dead."

"Where's Eric?" asked Farin suddenly. He and Randal had been sent on to guide Lord Robert's men since neither was armoured heavily enough to join Eric's charge. "Could he have gone with the riders after Palomon?"

But Randal's gaze had fixed on the raven, which was beginning to tear at the black flank of its intended meal. Randal urged his tired horse toward it and Farin ran after him, flapping his arms to drive the bird away.

"Sweet Lady! It's Thunderfoot!"

With an identical motion they turned to look at the little hill upon which Brian had made his stand, then started toward it through bodies strewn haphazardly as if some insane reaper had been harvesting corn. For every Westrian whose face Farin bent to see there were two from Elaya, their bright trappings trampled into the mud. Crows flapped away resentfully as he passed, then hopped back to resume their meal. He saw a condor as well, and heard coyotes howling in the hills, waiting for the protection of night to claim their share of the feast.

He shook his head. How could there be so many dead here and yet have been so many left when Robert and the rest of the army had arrived? His arm ached from striking, but except for a few gashes he had come through without wounds. Had the bards who wrote so cheerfully of battles ever seen one?

Swallowing, Farin plodded determinedly on. In the west the sky was beginning to glow with rosy streamers, and the coastal hills were shadowed. Soon it would be dark, and how could he recognize anyone then? Across the field he saw men with wagons, gathering the dead for the pyre.

Farin paused as he came to a ring of piled bodies, Elayan infantry, and wondered what brave man had raised such a monument. Shuddering, he climbed over them to see who lay in the center and stopped, puzzled, because there was no one there, only the marks of two pairs of feet sunk deeply into the mire.

He stood still a moment, wondering. To the east he could see the place where Prince Palomon and his reserves had awaited Robert's charge. His gaze moved downward and across the curiously empty space between Palomon's knoll and where he was standing now. A flicker of movement caught his eye. Farin's breath stopped, he stared, then clambered over the corpses and began to run.

What he had seen was two bodies, lying quite alone. They both looked dead—with so many arrows in them they must be, and the movement he had seen only a garment fluttering in the wind. Then the one on top moved again.

Farin threw himself down beside it and with trembling hands heaved it over to see the face. Even in the rosy evening light it was pale, but not cold—not yet.

"Eric . . ." he breathed. "Eric!"

". . . the bastards! Go on!" Eric muttered without opening his eyes.

"The Lord of Battles be praised! Randal!" Farin lifted his head to shout. "He's over here!" He bent to the wounded man. "Eric—it's me, Farin! It's all over, Eric—we've won!" Eric's arm fell limply as Farin moved him so that it rested almost protectively across the body on which he had lain.

"No . . . no!" he murmured, "Don't touch him."

Farin lifted the head of the dead man and saw Brian's face. After a moment he laid it down, confusion and wonder struggling in his heart.

"Is he dead?" panted Randal, stopping next to them.

"No! Not yet . . ." Farin added, "but Brian is. Get the wagon over here—get a healer—get someone!"

Somewhere across the field men were cheering Robert, cheering their victory. Farin shook his head and stroked back the matted hair from Eric's brow, wondering whether they would still cheer when they learned its cost.

Even in the palace they could hear the cheering that swept the city, mixed with smatterings of song. The Prince was born and there were rumors of victory in the south.

"Well, they have waited for their festival," said Rosemary, turning away from the sunset glory of the window. "If I were not so tired I would be out there too!"

"Tired!" exclaimed Branwen, "But Lady Faris did all the work!"

Faris, lying warm and euphoric with her child nestled in the crook of her arm, closed her eyes again. They had washed her and dressed her in a clean gown. After the Master of the Junipers had blessed the baby they had swaddled him and laid him beside her. Now she wanted only to sleep. There was a rustle in the doorway and the Master of the Junipers came in, robed in a cope of green damask.

"Don't disturb her—" cautioned Jessica as the Master bent to take the baby in his arms. Faris stirred and half-opened her eyes.

"I will return him safely my dear, sleep now . . ." He smiled with almost his old serenity. The baby nuzzled hopefully against his breast and he laughed. "No, my cub, there is nothing here for you. Let me show you to your people and then you may go to your mother again." He turned to Jessica. "Has someone told Caolin? He will want to light the beacon fire."

Faris heard the door shut behind them. Sunset blazed beneath her closed eyelids like a memory of the Lady's fire. "Jehan, do you hear them rejoicing for our child?" she murmured drowsily, but she was asleep before she could wonder why he did not reply.

* * *

The last light of sunset was fading above the western hills when Farin came out of Lord Robert's tent where the physicians were still fighting for Eric's life. Across the way lights shone in Brian's blue and gold pavilion, whose lord now lay in state with torches at his head and feet. But Brian's horsemen were still away after Palomon, and of the archers who had stood beside their lord, pitifully few survived to mourn him. There would be weeping up and down the Great Valley when this was known.

At least Farin had been able to rescue Ercul Ashe. The man had been gibbering after that long day without food or drink, or news, and was pitifully grateful to his liberator. But Farin had hastened him out of the camp, afraid that Brian's men would blame the man who had brought them this disastrous strategy.

He gazed northward, wondering vaguely whether the rest of Westria had heard the news. On the brow of the hill beneath the pale glitter of the early stars he saw a point of orange light. Another star? But surely it had not been there before.

As he watched, light flared and he saw a second orange glow. It was larger—nearer, perhaps? A third blazed from the hill before him, and Farin realized stupidly that he was looking at bonfires—beacons signalling each other from hill to hill all the way from Laurelynn.

"Faris—" he muttered in confusion. "She's had the baby and I didn't even know!"

All around him men were pointing at the mountain tops, swearing delightedly and pounding each other's backs. "The child is born!"

Farin looked beyond them to the growing mound which would shortly become a pyre to rival the fires on the hills, and wondered whether the lives of so many men and women were a fair exchange for the one that had come into the world. It was the kind of question he would have asked the Master of the Junipers if he had been there. Or, he thought unhappily, the King.

He stood alone, staring at the cheerful twinkling of the beaconfires. "Fire burn bright and light us all to hope again . . ." he murmured at last.

VIII

The Chessmaster

The shadows of the scattered chesspieces wavered across the board in the candlelight. Caolin wondered why he had thought that working through the deliberate strategies of a chess game would calm him. The wolf Gerol lifted his great head as his master turned restlessly to the window, then laid it on his forepaws again.

Outside the night sky glowed with light from the beacon fire. Caolin had come to the top of the Red Mountain to light it as soon as he knew that Faris' child was born. He fancied he could hear the rejoicing all the way from Laurelynn, but it was only the crackling of the great fire. Here there was only stillness. But there was no peace.

He turned back to the little bare room in which the chess set was the only thing of beauty. Why had he stayed here instead of returning to the revels in the city? He had not used his temple since Jehan died—since that terrifying ritual to the Lady of Fire. Had he come to the Mountain because he knew he needed the power that waited here? Perhaps, but he was not yet ready to re-enter that room.

Idly, the Seneschal picked up one of the white chess pieces—a rook, and turned it between his long fingers. Light warmed the polished ivory of the little tower as he set it down in its proper place at one end of the board.

"One rook—Lord Robert of the Ramparts, that worthy man . . ." he murmured. "He moves in a straight line to his goal, once he knows what it is. He is the hero of the day—will he know what to do with his popularity?"

Gerol's eyes followed Caolin's movements, but he could

tell when the man was speaking to him and when he was only making noises and he remained where he was.

Caolin searched out the other rook and set it on the opposite end of the board. "Two—Theodor, the bastion of the north. Here he is set and here he stays, mourning because he has outlived his powers."

Caolin's hand hovered above an intricately carved knight. "And here is our champion, Eric." He lifted the piece in the knight's move, three squares ahead and one to the side, "who never knows where he is headed until he gets there." His eyes sought the other knight, which had fallen on its side, and he thought of the message which Ordrey's pigeon had brought him that afternoon.

"And the other knight?" he picked up the piece. "Sir Brian . . . is off the board!" There was a faint snap as his fingers tightened on the chess piece and the helmed head rolled across the floor. Caolin smiled, just a little, and set the torso aside.

"Now we must have our bishops—the Mistress of the College . . ." he set one hooded figure next to the knight, "and the Master of the Junipers . . . who finds no comfort in his own counsel anymore." He set down the second bishop, remembering the lost look he had seen lately in the Master's eyes. He understood the other man's pain but could not pity it.

Nonetheless his face grew very still as he looked down at the two places left empty in the center of the line.

"The king . . . no King—" he shook his head, gently placing the white king on the table beside the board. "But we do have a queen—" he added swiftly, his fingers moving caressingly on the intricate detail of the gown.

Now there were only pawns scattered upon the board. Frowning, Caolin picked one of them. "And the child—" he said then, remembering the red-faced thing he had seen squirming in the Master of the Junipers' arms. "Will the child be a pawn, or a king?" Shrugging, he put the piece on the king's empty square and swiftly began to set the other pawns in place before the line of principals.

Then he repeated the process with the black figures, pausing only when he came to the ebony king. "Palomon . . . " he muttered, setting the figure down. Caolin smoothed back a strand of pale hair and considered the chessboard.

"And what about me? Well, Gerol—what is my place on this board?" Caolin leaned back in his chair as the wolf got up and padded across the stone floor to nose at his hand. Smiling, Caolin began to stroke the rough-furred head, his knowing fingers moving over the smooth dome of the skull, scratching behind the flattened ears, sinking into the thick fur that hid Gerol's throat.

The wolf made a deep sound of pleasure, then, as the caresses grew more abstracted, sighed gustily and lay down again with his head across Caolin's foot. The Seneschal was staring at the board. In the wavering light the black and white ranks seemed waiting for the signal to charge.

"They are waiting for someone to move them, Gerol, though they may never recognize the touch of his hand," said Caolin at last. He remembered another chessboard, at Misthall. Then as now, Faris had been the Queen, but Caolin had identified himself as a bishop, her chief counselor. And he had tried— surely he had tried to play the role of one piece among many on the board.

He picked up the white queen, fancying he saw a resemblance to Faris in the tilt of her carven head. "The queen is the most powerful piece on the board, but even she is vulnerable . . ." his glance went to the headless knight.

With Brian gone Caolin had no great enemy—strange, how now he almost missed that blustering bully of a man! At least Brian's hostility had been open. Now there remained only a host of pawns who could be turned against him. And he had no ally but this vulnerable Queen! If Faris had died in childbirth what would have become of him? Lady Jessica was next heir, and she would surely have leaned on her stupid husband rather than on her brother's Seneschal. Even now, Faris could choose some other counselor.

"No!" Something in Caolin's voice brought Gerol's head up, ears twitching for sound of an enemy.

"*I* must be the chessmaster!" Caolin picked up the black king and weighed the two pieces in his hands. "Faris and Palomon must both move at my will . . ."

Westria's victory in the battle of the Dragon Waste would force Palomon to negotiate. And once he had met the man Caolin would know how to manipulate him. But before Caolin could make the peace he must make absolute his power over the Queen. He set the black piece back on the chessboard, but kept the white queen, turning it over and over between his strong fingers, considering how it might be done . . .

How can I be father and mother to this child and rule Westria too? Sighing, Faris looked down at the baby's dark-fuzzed head. Oblivious to her doubts the child butted his head against her breast and seized her nipple again. This was all he wanted from her now—from being the broodmare of Westria she had become its most exalted cow. And the worst of it was, they all expected her to *like* it.

Her arm began to cramp. She shifted position against the cushions with which they had padded the big wooden chair so that she could lie on the terrace in the early April sun. The lawn that ran down from the terrace behind the Palace to the lake was starred with dandelions across which the Master of the Junipers was walking with Rosemary.

Over the roofs of the city Faris saw the slopes of the Red Mountain flaring with the varied golds of mustard and poppy fields. Everywhere she looked new life was bursting from the earth even as it had sprung from her. Why then could she not rejoice? *I would rejoice if Jehan were here* . . . She stopped herself from forming a mental call to him. He would not answer now. He had waited only to see his son safely into the world and then he had left her once more.

"Praise the Lady for this fine weather!" said Jessica from her chair. "Soon we can put the babies on a blanket and let them tumble like puppies in the sun . . . Now that my lord has defeated Elaya we will soon be going home. Faris, why don't you visit us in Rivered? You spent so little time there, and in the spring one can see at a glance the snowfields and the flowers . . ."

"Your lord had help with the Elayans," said Rosemary with some bitterness. Her eyes sought the room in the Palace where Eric lay. After a week of her careful nursing he was out of danger, but it would be long before he could ride again.

Faris shook her head. Weakness from her own battle weighted her limbs and she winced where her torn body was still healing from having given birth.

Jessica interpreted her gesture and smiled. "Of course you're still weak—you had a hard time—but you'll mend."

Faris closed her eyes. "What is there to recover for?" She felt the easy tears run down her cheeks. She waited for a scornful answer but felt instead Jessica's swift kiss on her brow.

"I know, you're depressed—well, that's natural just now." The chair creaked as Jessica sat back down. The other woman continued, "It will pass."

Rosemary laughed. "My mother told me there was one day when she was so discouraged she nearly dropped me out the window!"

Faris let their chatter wash over her without bothering to reply. Jessica's husband had returned to her, and Eric, however oblivious to Rosemary's love, was still *there*. But Faris had lost her own love when he died and again when his presence was withdrawn from her, and now she was condemned to live at the mercy of this mewling creature who champed in frustration on her breast.

"I think he's still hungry—try shifting him to the other side," said Jessica.

Wearily Faris complied, rearranging her gown to expose the smooth curve of her right breast, bursting with milk like the bosom of the Mother in a statue. Faris bit her lip as the baby's mouth clamped her nipple and braced herself against the pang in her breast as the milk began to flow.

"Master—can't you persuade her to treasure this time? He will grow up so soon!" said Jessica.

He laughed. "I am only an honorary member of your company, and though few men have shared the privilege of giving birth, among womenfolk I am no expert!"

Faris looked at him in wonder, gingerly recalling the confusion and agony which were all she remembered of her lying-in. Did he consider *that* a privilege? The baby had fallen asleep, his head tipped back in satiation, pink mouth pursed and lashes lying like smudges across his cheeks.

"Let me take him," said the Master. "Having helped you bear him should give me some instinct for the task!" He eased his strong hands around the child's head and bottom and laid him against his shoulder, patting industriously.

"He is probably wet . . ." warned Faris, lacing up the front of her gown.

The Master explored the wrappings. "A bit damp perhaps—let's wait until he has digested a little before disturbing him." He began to walk up and down.

"Have you decided on a milk-name yet?" asked Jessica. "His Naming ceremony is only a month away. *Star* is traditional in the family . . ." her sister-in-law went on, "after Julian Starbairn. Goodness knows who Julian's father really was, but it's a pretty title, and this child is certainly our morning star!"

Rosemary laughed. Faris leaned back against her cushions, watching a stray gull sweep down to the lake to rest before returning to the sea.

"Good morning, my Queen . . ."

Startled, Faris looked up and saw Caolin, his crimson robes glowing like a pillar of fire, his hair a golden cap in the morning sun. Seeing his elegance, she was suddenly glad she had done up her gown and wondered how badly the wind had tangled her hair.

"Here is your daily tribute, my Lady." He bowed and held out to her a bouquet of miniature irises, ivory mixed with an almost slate blue, as delicate and precise as his gesture presenting them. The day before it had been multi-colored poppies, and before that, violets.

"They are beautiful," she said smiling.

"No more so than the hand which receives them."

Her eyes went to his face. Did he really think so? Perhaps now that she was regaining her figure men might find her fair . . . The women had kept him from her when she was in labor, so he had no memory of her in her agony . . . he had not seen her scar . . . On his face she saw only the look a man wears when considering a finely crafted jewel.

Faris laughed suddenly, looking down at the irises. How beautiful their colors were, and how bright the air! She was vaguely aware of Jessica rising and moving away, but when she thought of saying farewell the other woman had gone.

"Have you nothing better to do than turn compliments, my Lord Seneschal?"

"I have been preparing to talk to Elaya, my Lady." He handed her a paper at which she glanced as he went on. "This letter invites Palomon to come here for negotiations two weeks from today."

"It seems well enough . . . what does Lord Robert say?" asked Faris.

"Robert?" He raised one eyebrow mockingly. "Robert is warleader—the council table is *my* battlefield. The decision is yours, my Queen, not Robert's. If they come here your beauty will finish the conquest that Robert's sword began."

She shook her head. "I doubt I will be well enough to appear."

He offered her the paper again with a pen and inkwell and she rather shakily signed in the space he showed her.

"But you must come, even if only for a little while. I will have the cleverest seamstresses in Laurelynn make you a new gown."

"I had no idea that the duties of a Seneschal extended so far!" she mocked him. "Perhaps I will attend, if only to see what kind of a dress you would design for me!"

"A dress that will make the Elayans know that indeed we have a Queen in Laurelynn!" Caolin replied, kissing her hand.

"The Elayans are very fine . . . you would think they had never been near a fight!" said Farin, looking down on the first rank of Prince Palomon's guard.

"They looked pretty on the field too . . ." muttered Eric.

Farin turned from the window to glance at his friend, bound and bandaged so that little of him was visible. But Eric's eyes were very bright, and there was a flush on his cheeks. Rosemary frowned and put her hand to his forehead.

The tramp of feet gave way to a clatter of hooves on cobblestones. Farin looked back to the street as the plumes of the guard disappeared around a corner and the Elayan envoys appeared. Mail glittered from beneath their silken robes and Farin blinked as their silvered helms cast back the sun.

"They do well to come armed," he said, listening. "Hear the crowd . . ."

From the people who lined the street came a murmur like the sound when the wind changes and one hears the thunder of a distant waterfall. The Westrian soldiers who had been stationed along the way looked around them uneasily.

"Can you see Palomon?" asked Eric.

Farin waited while the first four horsemen went by. Another came after them, sitting like a statue on his dappled mare. "I see someone . . . a dark man with a face like an eagle and silver brocading on his blue robe."

"Palomon . . ." Eric sighed. "I wish I could see him up close—I tried to get to him on the battlefield, but they shot Thunderfoot and then afterward . . ."

"Eric! It's over now—please don't try to move!" Rosemary gripped Eric's shoulders, holding him down. He quivered for a moment then stilled, tears of weakness glistening on his cheeks. Rosemary's hand moved gently over his brow and slipped behind his head to smooth the pillow.

"They ride in honor . . ." she said bitterly. "They should enter this city yoked and in chains!"

"Well, they did come in under truce—we never captured them." Farin pointed out, though he found his own hand twitching as if it wanted his sword.

"Whose truce?" Eric's whisper strengthened. "Did the Council meet while I was ill?"

The last of the Elayans had passed from view. Farin frowned and closed the window. "I don't think so." He picked up his harp again.

"Well who decided it then? Robert? Damn this weakness!" Eric added, "I should know what is going on—I should be there!"

"You're here—you're alive! Be grateful for that," exclaimed Rosemary. "The Master says that if you lie still now in a few months you will be riding again. Even fighting, if that's all you want to do!" She bit her lip and turned her face away, but Farin saw how she struggled to regain her usual placid smile.

Eric's eyes rested on her golden braids. "I know I have been lucky . . . But you see, I have never had to lie still before," he said simply.

Rosemary reached blindly for the half-full bowl of broth on the table and began resolutely to spoon it into Eric's obediently opened mouth. Farin, lowering his head to hide a smile, struck up a cheerful melody.

"I know you hate being fed—" said Rosemary, "but soon you will be strong again!" She leaned over him, clutching the empty bowl. "I saw the King slip away from us, but I shall not give up until you are well again!"

"Nay love—I'll not doubt you! If you had been with us in the south the enemy would have run for fear!" Eric grinned as the hot color rose in Rosemary's cheeks and watched appreciatively as she stalked to the other end of the room. She stepped backward suddenly as the door opened and Branwen came in.

"Why are you here?" she snapped, "Have Faris and the child no need of you?"

"Rosemary! Let the poor girl at least get through the door!" said Farin, rising to shut it behind Branwen and reddening in turn at the warmth of her grateful smile. Jehan's sickness had driven memory of the night he had lain with Branwen away, but lately it seemed as if she would like to recall it again . . .

"The Master of the Junipers is playing with the baby—" explained Branwen. "Sometimes I think he is more a mother to him than the Queen! As for my Lady, she is with Caolin." She sat down on the stool that Rosemary had vacated and gave Eric a cheerful smile.

He stared past her. "Caolin . . ." his eyes focused on Farin. "Did I ever tell you exactly how Brian died?"

"Eric . . ." began Rosemary, but he shook his head.

"No, I'm not raving—it will ease me to talk about it. Anyway I must tell *you*, Farin, because Brian hoped you might make it into a song . . ."

Farin tried to laugh. "I thought he didn't like me—" but Eric was already speaking. Farin leaned forward as passion colored Eric's fumbling phrases with the hues of an epic from the ancient days.

"And so I took his ring and promised to avenge him if I lived." Eric lifted his hand and they saw Brian's ring glittering on his middle finger, next to his own.

Farin rested his forehead on the smoothly curved top of the harp. Indeed the tale was worth telling, but could it be told by him? He had never ventured more than a ballad before.

"And you say that Brian accused Caolin of causing his death?" asked Rosemary in the silence that followed. "I don't understand—Caolin wasn't even there . . ."

"I don't know how he did it—neither did Brian—but he did say that Caolin had sworn to kill him. Remember, Farin, how he suspected treachery even when that Deputy of Caolin's first suggested the battle plan?"

Farin nodded, hearing again Ercul Ashe's precise voice warm to enthusiasm as he explained the fatal strategy.

"But I still cannot believe it!" repeated Rosemary. "I have never *liked* Caolin, but . . ."

"Faris likes him," said Branwen suddenly, twisting the end of her brown braid.

"What do you mean by that?" Farin set down the harp.

"Sir Farin! Don't be angry with *me*. It's just that he visits her every day and brings her flowers . . . and she laughs at his jokes . . ." her voice trailed off.

"But Branwen, what's wrong with that?" asked Rosemary. "If he cheers her, why not be grateful? It is more than we have been able to do!"

Branwen shrugged resentfully and fell silent. Farin sighed, wondering why he had been so angry.

"If there was no Council meeting . . ." said Eric after a

little while, "then it must have been Caolin. With Faris' consent, of course, but the idea would have been his."

"Well, she *has* had other things to think about . . ." said Rosemary.

Farin shut his eyes, remembering how Jehan had galloped up the road toward the Hold, and the bright splash of the Seneschal's robe as he followed the King. Caolin had always been there a step behind his master, always serenely in charge.

"But . . . the King was always going off and leaving Caolin to run things . . ."

"The King is gone," said Eric bleakly. "Do you think Faris can rule such a man? I am her champion—I should protect her!"

"But—this is ridiculous—do you realize what we're saying?" Rosemary blinked and rubbed at her eyes. "If Caolin is such a villain, do you think you can protect Faris with the edge of your sword? Brian's sword didn't protect *him!*"

Farin watched Eric's eyes brighten as the idea took hold. He tried to picture his friend skulking in corners spying on Caolin, and began to laugh.

"You are laughing at me and you are right," said Eric. "I don't have the right kind of mind to be a good conspirator. I could never out-think Caolin by myself—but together we might . . ." he looked at them with eyes as bright as those of a dog hoping to be taken for a run.

"I'll help you," said Branwen. "I don't like the way Caolin makes the Lady Faris laugh."

Rosemary was still shaking her head. "Even supposing Caolin is guilty of—something—how do you propose to find him out?"

"Well, what about that Deputy we were talking about before. Did he betray the plan to Palomon?" asked Eric.

Farin frowned, pushing back the silver lock of hair from his eyes. "I think he offered that plan sincerely, Eric—he really believed it was brilliant. And he had no chance to betray it afterward. I should know—I untied him myself after the battle was all over. Poor man, he had spent all day trussed in Brian's tent, wondering whether he would be spitted or rewarded, and by which side."

"Then you know him, and he would be willing to talk to you again . . ." said Rosemary thoughtfully.

"Well yes, but . . . He is loyal to his master."

"At least you can talk to him, Farin. It's hard to believe

that the Elayans just *happened* to move that way!" said Eric.

"Talk to him, and we might find out," added Rosemary.

Farin gave her a sidelong glance. "It sounds as if you have joined the conspiracy."

Rosemary looked at him, her fair brows lifting in surprise. "Are we a conspiracy? Caolin would die laughing." She shook her head.

"I only want to learn the truth . . . for Faris . . ."

But her eyes went to Eric's eager face, and Farin thought that her decision had been made more for his sake than for the Queen's.

"I appreciate the trouble you have gone to, Caolin. The gown is beautiful," Faris lifted a fold of brocade, watching the afternoon light pick a new pattern from its gold threads, "but I am not going to wear it." She let the fabric fall and the gold rippled back into the swirl of opening butterflies whose wings fluttered across the brocade in shades of scarlet and deep purple and rose.

Faris looked up at Caolin. His grey eyes were a little hooded so that she could not tell what he was thinking. But then Caolin's thoughts were rarely apparent even when one met his gaze.

"But you will receive the Elayan envoys . . ." It was not quite a question. Was he disappointed because she had refused the gown?

"I suppose so . . . yes . . . they are all expecting me to go," she replied wearily.

He turned to the window, sunset flaring in his ring of office as he latched it against the cooling air. "What will you wear then? What do you want the Elayans to see?" he asked quietly.

Faris shrugged, looking down at the gown that hung loosely about her. "They will see me as I am." She was abruptly conscious of the scar hidden beneath her sleeve, her pallor, and the silver that was beginning to weave through her hair as gold threaded the brocade. "Why should I put on a show for them?"

Why indeed should she put on a show for the Elayans or for the Master of the Junipers and Rosemary and the rest? They could force her to do this job but not to enjoy it!

Caolin took her hand and turned her toward the window, kissing her curled fingers respectfully. The garnet in his ring glowed like the Jewel of Fire.

"Faris . . ." Caolin's voice was very even and low. "Let

them see a Queen . . . Listen to me Faris, and do as I say." She waited, eyes held by the ring, while he lifted the brocade overdress with the midnight purple of its undergown folded inside and held them up to her.

"See a Queen, Faris!" he repeated. His eyes, grown suddenly luminous, held hers. For a moment she saw herself reflected in their surface.

"You are beautiful and proud—" he went on. "Make them bow to your power!"

Faris straightened from the slump with which she had walked since her delivery and raised her chin. *Yes . . . let them all remember that I am the Queen!* The door to the chamber clicked open and Faris started. Caolin swung away from her, still holding up the gown.

"Branwen, you are come in good time! I have brought the new robes for your mistress to wear tonight and you must help her into them." He smiled brilliantly.

Faris twitched at the faded dress she was wearing with sudden distaste, wondering how she could have considered wearing it.

"Yes, Branwen, and quickly!" she said as the girl hesitated, watching Caolin. She began to fumble at the lacings that closed her gown.

Caolin bowed. "I will return within the hour to escort you to the Hall."

In the Great Hall of the Palace at Laurelynn, candles had been lit in the sconces along the walls. But not all of them, so that the light was not quite sufficient to drive the shadows away. On the musician's balcony a consort of stringed instruments were playing something soft and low without marked rhythm or melody to catch the ear.

Farin listened to them with part of his attention, giving the rest to Rosemary's commentary.

"I wonder how Caolin got people here—" she looked around, nodding to Mistress Gwenna, the Mayor's wife, as she passed. "Everyone was saying that to feast the enemy would betray the dead . . ."

"Is this a feast? It does not seem very festive somehow." The muted music and the shadows lent a sombre air to the proceedings and no food had been set out, though servants were circulating with goblets of a pale chill wine.

They stopped for a moment while Rosemary greeted Lady Elinor of Fairhaven. But when Farin would have gone Rosemary tugged at his sleeve.

"Look at them!" She pointed to the glitter of Elayan brocade below the great banner of Westria that hung on the wall. Farin stiffened as he recognized Prince Palomon and his men.

They were easy to see, for the other guests had left a space around them like the plowed strip that brakes a fire. Palomon chatted easily as he sipped his wine, his manner as unconcerned as if he had been in his own hall.

There was a pause in the music, then the consort began a pavane.

"Oh! Why must they play so mournfully!" Rosemary shook her head as if the music pained her.

Farin focused on it and recognized the tune of an old love song. "Surely the musicians know better than to play a pavane as if it were a funeral march, unless . . ." Rosemary looked at Farin curiously as he slowly smiled. "Unless they are doing it on purpose. I think that Caolin has planned it this way."

"Well he has succeeded, then. I feel almost too hopeless to be angry. If Eric were here he would not be so patient. Maybe it is as well he was too weak to come!"

Farin nodded. Eric's sister was representing him at this reception, as the steward of Sanjos represented Las Costas. It should have been Lady Alessia, but she had refused to come.

Rosemary sighed as if the thought of Eric were finishing what the music had begun.

"Eric is getting better every day . . ." said Farin consolingly. "He will reward your nursing soon."

"What do you mean?" she asked sharply.

It was Farin's turn to be embarrassed. "Well . . . I don't think he loves Faris anymore . . ."

"Am I so transparent then?"

"No!" protested Farin. "But I know you very well." He looked at her, thinking how strange it was that he should feel more at ease with her than with his sisters. "Besides, it's nothing to be ashamed of. You've seen how Faris has lost her beauty since Jehan died. I doubt that Eric's memories will be able to withstand the living presence of a woman who loves him."

He tried to see Rosemary not as his familiar friend, but as Eric might do. Rosemary was too tall for him, but she would be just the right size to fit into Eric's embrace. She was wearing a jade-colored gown tonight with a pattern of eucalyptus leaves woven into the hem. The vivid shade set off her golden hair. But she looked tired. Maybe as Eric recovered she would get some color into her face again and he would see that she had a beauty of her own.

The music was growing fainter, receding like a departing tide and leaving only the low murmur of conversation to fill the space where it had been. He wondered why they had stopped. Then massed clarions called and sound cascaded into the gap like a returning wave. An astonished babble started as the echoes faded, but stillness spread again from the doorway like ripples from a stone thrown into a pond.

"You were telling me how Faris has lost her beauty?" whispered Rosemary.

Farin shook his head mutely, watching his sister and Caolin enter the hall. He had forgotten how Faris looked dressed in bright colors, and he had never seen her wear anything like this. The brilliant reds and purples of her gown flamed against the underdress, which was of a shade somewhere between black and violet, like the skin of a grape, that echoed the darkness of her hair. Tiny gold buttons marched downward from the throat of the high collar to disappear where the brocade bodice was clasped across her breast, and from wrist to elbow where the undersleeves emerged from the square hanging sleeves. Oversleeves and skirts rippled like the enameled wings of some exotic artificial butterfly.

A soprano recorder began to play all alone. After a few measures, the alto joined it, then the tenor and base, following their leader in a fugue as the members of the court fell into step behind their Queen.

The procession circled the Hall. As it passed, servants lit the rest of the candles. By the time the Queen reached the chair that had been set for her on the dais at the end of the Hall, light blazed from every corner, displaying the sheen of velvets, the glitter of gold or silver thread, the luster of a cabochon jewel glowing on hand or breast.

From his place near the Queen Farin looked around him at the color that flushed men's cheeks, the new light in their eyes. He leaned over to whisper to Rosemary, "Whatever you may think of Caolin this is surely brilliant choreography!"

"Yes, but for what end? Look more carefully at that gown."

The Queen's smile remained etched on her pale face as she

spoke to those around her. She leaned in front of Caolin to greet Lady Jessica and the scarlet of her brocade seemed to bleed into his crimson robe; its metallic traceries could have been drawn from the polished gold of Caolin's hair. Suddenly Farin felt cold.

Plumes waved above the heads of the crowd, as Prince Palomon and his escort approached. The Herald stepped forward.

"My Lady Faris, Mistress of the Jewels and Regent of Westria—I present to you now Palomon, Lord of the Tambara and Elected Prince of the Confederation of Elaya."

Faris rose in a rustle of silks, held out her hand for Palomon to touch in greeting, then sat down again.

"Had you commanded Westria in the south, your beauty alone would have vanquished us." Palomon's teeth flickered white among the black curls of his beard. He nodded to Lord Robert with the faintest hint of mockery. "My Lord Commander, my congratulations on your victory."

"It was a narrow one," said Robert, bowing slightly. "You maneuvered very cleverly."

"Not cleverly enough it seems," Palomon said silkily. His gaze moved from Robert to the Seneschal, then back to the Queen, and he stepped aside to introduce his entourage. Then the Herald brought forward those members of the Council who were to participate in the treaty negotiations. When the introductions were complete some invisible signal set the musicians playing again. There was a general movement toward the food.

One of the Guildmistresses brushed by Farin, talking to her husband. "And did you notice those sleeves?" she said, "Elayan cut! And no weavers of Laurelynn ever patterned that brocade!"

"But dear, perhaps the cloth was booty taken in the war . . ." said the man, as the couple passed out of hearing.

Rosemary frowned. "I hope there's not much talk of that kind."

Without answering Farin steered his companion toward the table and managed to abstract two goblets and a pitcher of wine. Rosemary scooped up some cakes and they withdrew to a window seat.

This time the musicians were playing the pavane at the proper speed. Faris and Caolin led the line of dancers dipping and swaying the length of the Hall. Faris' eyes glittered feverishly. Caolin's strong hand guided her through the variations as the music, precise and brilliant, elaborated on its basic theme.

They danced well together, given the differences in their heights, but Farin remembered how Faris had danced with Jehan, like two halves joining again.

"Farin—who is that man—the one standing by the door?" Rosemary's question brought him to the present again. He looked around and saw Ercul Ashe munching a cake with a complacent smile.

"Yes, that's Ercul Ashe. *He* seems to have recovered from the battle well enough!" said Farin. Certainly, with his greying hair sleeked back and his fur trimmed tunic buttoned demurely to the chin, the Deputy Seneschal bore little resemblance to the tattered creature Farin had rescued from Brian's pavilion.

"He looks too secure," said Rosemary. "Why should he be so easy when everyone else in Westria is either angry or anguished. Go talk to him, Farin—"

Farin's own smile faded as he remembered ravens conversing with the dead in the grey dusk of the battlefield. "Ercul Ashe left the camp as soon as I released him . . . he never saw what his words had done . . ." he said slowly. He gave Rosemary's hand a squeeze and moved toward the door.

The guests were drawing aside to leave the center space clear. Farin edged around them as a troop of performers bounded onto the floor brandishing short wooden swords and handbucklers painted red or blue. The bells fastened to their wrists and ankles chimed merrily as they paired off for the stylised sword dance. Ercul Ashe looked up as Farin approached him, his smile becoming a trifle more open as he saw who it was.

"Sir Farin!" the Deputy bowed deeply. "I have not thanked you for my deliverance—indeed I was so distraught it was some hours before I realized who you were! I have not wanted to intrude upon you, and of course I have been much occupied." A discreet nod indicated the dancers and the crowd. The dancers were whirling and weaving, opposed swords tapping a counter-rhythm to the drums.

"Yes, it is a brilliant affair," agreed Farin carefully, wondering how to lead up to his subject. When he had seen Ashe before the man had been reeling with fatigue and fear. What motivated him now that he was secure on his home ground?

A boy came by with a pitcher of wine. Farin held out his goblet and motioned to the lad to refill that of his companion. It was red wine this time, a heady vintage from near Sanjos. Well, perhaps that was fitting, thought Farin, feeling the strong stuff ease the tension in his throat.

"Thank you—" Ashe acknowledged his compliment. "It was not easily accomplished in so short a time." He sipped at his wine.

"I can imagine," replied Farin, "the Seneschal must have driven you hard."

"Driven? My lord has no need to *drive* his staff. They know what he expects of them," Ashe said proudly. Farin was reminded of the tone in which women boasted of their labor pains.

"But there was so much to do . . ." he offered encouragingly.

"My lord anticipates all contingencies," said Ercul Ashe.

Rat-a-tat-tat went the wooden swords. The bells of the dancers jingled like mail.

"I wish he had anticipated Palomon's maneuvering on the battlefield!" Farin fought to keep his tone merely regretful; this was as hard as pitching his voice to deliver a difficult song!

Some unknown emotion curtained Ashe's gaze. Farin felt his heart begin to pound, sensing that his words had slipped past the other man's guard as the dancers' swords slipped by their opponents' parrying. Could he make it easier for the Deputy to blame Caolin?

"I am glad that I got you out of the camp when I did—" Farin said meditatively. "When men are grieving they do not always stop to weigh the evidence. Some spoke against you when they heard who had suggested the battle plan . . ."

Ashe's face did not change, but he became very still. "And what of you, Sir Farin? Do you think I intended treachery?" he said quietly.

Flushing a little at the baldness of the statement, Farin shook his head. "I was there when you spoke to Lord Robert. I believe that you believed the plan would work." he said, a little more strongly than he had intended. The dancers wheeled, and the red-clad warriors began to drive the others the length of the room.

"Someone else could have betrayed the plan. Were you the only one who knew what you intended to say?" Farin went on.

Another man would have laughed or grown angry. Ercul Ashe only pursed his lips and lifted his thin brows.

"If you heard me at the camp you also heard me say that I have worked with my Lord Caolin more than seven years. After serving such a master, do you think a child like you will trick me into betraying him?"

Farin blushed in earnest now, realizing how transparent his attempts to manage the conversation must have been. The red dancers beat their foes around the room with regular smacks of sword against sword or shield. Farin had heard just such a terrible music in battle. But it had been silent, afterward.

"Did you see the battlefield?" he asked sharply, meeting Ashe's eyes for the first time. "The pasture was churned to red mud, and the horses stumbled on severed limbs. I saw a coyote dragging off an arm whose hand still gripped a bow. It was a woman's arm . . ."

"Such things happen in war—" Ashe began weakly, but Farin cut in.

"Do you wonder that I want to know if our movements were betrayed?"

"No . . ." Ashe sighed and took another swallow of wine. "But the book where I found the plan was in the oldest part of the library with the volumes that tell of the devices of the ancients—The book was thick with dust, and I told no one about it on my way south. Even Caolin was too busy to listen to me."

Farin felt his heart sink. They had been so sure Caolin was at fault somehow. But, Farin did not think that Ercul Ashe could feign such sincerity.

"I have wondered too . . . I would not have men think me a traitor . . . but it *must* have been chance . . ." The words came almost too low for Farin to hear.

With shouts of triumph the dancers in the red tunics drove the blue-clad warriors from the room.

"Think about it still, Master Deputy. There may be something you have forgotten. For if someone has hidden behind the shield of your integrity, then traitor is the name you will surely bear!" Farin's words were lost in the burst of clapping with which the audience saluted the end of the dance, but Ercul Ashe turned away abruptly. Farin knew that he had heard, and did not have the heart to call him back.

The dancers had come forward to take their bows, red robes interspersed with blue. Idly, Farin wondered why those colors had been chosen. Blue might indicate Elaya, but then the winners should have worn Westrian green. When everything else about this evening had been calculated so carefully it was hard to imagine the colors were pure chance. The crowd swirled, making a path for Caolin to lead the Queen to the door. His crimson robes glowed in the blaze of the candlelight, almost overwhelming the splendor of her brocade.

Red is the Seneschal's color . . . and the banner of Las Costas is blue! Anger shriveled the pity Farin had begun to feel for Ercul Ashe and he looked quickly around him. But the room was emptying. The Elayans had left in the wake of the Queen, and the Deputy Seneschal was also gone.

"Your servants have gone . . . that is good. I hardly hoped to find you alone . . ." Caolin spoke from the shadows by the door.

In a single fluid movement Prince Palomon came to his feet, already drawing the sword that had been leaning against the wall. The door latched gently as Caolin stepped into the light. Palomon stared at him for a moment, then let his sword slip back into its sheath like a cat withdrawing its claws.

"I did not hear my guards announce you—" the Prince said dryly.

"Your guards do not know that I am here." Caolin drew a second chair up to the low table and sat down. The table bore an inlaid chessboard whose filigreed pieces stirred Caolin's envy even now, when all his will was focused on his purpose here.

Palomon's expression became subtly more ironic. "Shall I display a common curiosity," he asked, "or question my guards? You have succeeded in interesting me, Master Seneschal, or else I would call them now. Men name you sorcerer . . . is this a demonstration of your skill?" The candelabra on either side of the table flickered uneasily and shadows danced and scuttled around the room.

Caolin smiled, refusing to be disturbed by the other man's veiled mockery. When the Prince did question his guards he would find that they thought they had admitted Rodrigo Maclain. He might well begin to wonder, then.

"Do you believe that I am a sorcerer?" he asked blandly.

Palomon's shoulders twitched in a movement too delicate to call a shrug. "Such a title has no meaning for reasonable men—Will you have some wine?" Without waiting for an answer he filled a second goblet and pushed it across the table to Caolin. With one tapered finger he caressed a chess piece of colored ivory. "Will you play with me?"

Caolin sighed and shook his head. "If only we had the

time . . . But though my errand is less pleasant it may be more profitable—It seemed to me that a meeting of minds might be desirable before we meet on the Council floor."

Palomon's finely arched brows lifted again. "You expect me to make promises unadvised?"

"Do you mean without listening to your advisors mouth opinions and then turning the words until they believe that your ideas are their own?"

Palomon's eyes sparkled suddenly, but he did not reply.

"Besides," Caolin went on, *"I* am alone."

"You are not the Lord of Westria."

It was Caolin's turn to shrug. "Not in name . . ." He wondered if Palomon, who had inherited the rank that gave him the right to wrest power from among the other princelings of the Royal House, resented the Seneschal's assumption of authority.

The Prince gave him another oblique glance. "You imply that you control the Queen—are you her lover?"

Caolin stared at him, unable to keep the blood from leaving his face and returning so swiftly that the shadows swirled around him like a dark tide. He remembered . . . Faris in Jehan's arms . . . the simulated Faris struggling beneath him on the Red Mountain . . . the many other women who had come from Jehan's bed to his own . . .

Why was he so shocked by Palomon's suggestion? Why had he never consciously considered the possibility on his own? A hidden doorway in his own mind gaped suddenly, like the mouth of a well, and he dared not look in. And yet there could be no better way to keep power than by seducing—by marrying the Queen!

"Do not be offended—" the Prince said delicately. "Since the lady has lost her husband it would be a natural thing— though I understand that your Westrian women often take a man's role and rule alone . . . For instance," he went on, "Who will hold Las Costas now that their belligerent lord is gone?"

"His widow, according to custom." Caolin took a long swallow of wine, realizing that Palomon's comment about the Queen had only been made to lead up to this.

"And do you think that the Lady of Las Costas would suffer your governance if she knew whose messenger had betrayed Lord Brian's position to me?"

"I had thought you understood . . ." Caolin said patiently. "Elaya and Westria hold each other in check. We can only gain from this Council if we are both prepared to make a sacrifice . . ."

Palomon waited silently. His face seemed carved from some dark wood.

"And I have no need to beg your discretion in any case." Caolin continued. "You cannot prove that the messenger was mine. You rule alone, but you were elected. Those who raised you to the throne can cast you down." Caolin sat back, searching the Elayan's face for any response. A gust of wind rattled the window, then passed on.

"You have called us both reasonable men . . ." the Seneschal added. "Surely we are too reasonable to deal in threats or mysteries." He leaned across the table, striving to hold the other man's gaze. "Listen to me, Palomon. We can gain no more from this conflict. Though it will be some time before you can threaten us again, we cannot afford to follow up our victory . . ."

Palomon laughed shortly, turning his goblet back and forth by the stem. "You are being very frank—do you want to be *my* minister?"

Caolin shook his head, weighing his words. "Men like the late Lord Brian must be driven, but I had hoped to speak with you on equal terms."

The Prince raised his head and he stared at Caolin beneath half-closed eye-lids, giving somehow the impression that he was looking down at the Seneschal.

A vein throbbed painfully in Caolin's forehead. Just so had Brian looked at him. *Softly now*—he told himself, though his fingers had closed around his ring of office until its facets bit painfully, *this man traces his ancestry back farther than Jehan could do. He would be a King if Elayan pride would suffer so public a lordship. But he has the reactions of a chessmaster. He will not be obvious . . .*

He met the Elayan's scornful gaze, held it, passionless, until Palomon shrugged and looked away. Caolin picked up an ivory knight from the chessboard.

"Palomon . . ." he said softly, "is there anyone in Elaya who is your equal on this board?"

The Prince's eyes sparkled suddenly and he laughed. Caolin set down the chesspiece and eased back in his chair.

"Very well—" said the Prince as if continuing the previous interchange, "but if Westria and Elaya are equally impotent, why have you come to me?"

"Our nations may be immobilized, but you and I are not. I will not quarrel over a few miles of land . . ." Caolin shifted in his chair and it squeaked thinly, as if Brian were groaning in his grave.

"You would give us Santibar?" whispered Palomon.

"If my position here were strong enough, I could ensure that by the time you are ready for war again, the fortress would be easy prey," said Caolin carefully.

"What do you want?" Palomon leaned forward.

For a moment the question hung between them. A candle spluttered as the flame reached a flaw in the wick, then resumed its steady glow.

"I need the support of the people of Westria . . . For instance, I could become very popular by giving them the head of the man who had Lord Brian shot down . . ." Caolin took another swallow of wine. "But I have no wish to deal with your brother, who from all accounts is a belligerent fool."

A smile flickered on Palomon's full lips.

"If I should . . . marry the Queen . . . recognize me as Lord of Westria. But for now, give me symbols—" said Caolin, "reparations in gold and an apology for invading Westria. Insist that you will negotiate only with me."

"My own people would take my head if I did that!"

"What are words? Do your people need to know exactly what was said? If you hint to your councilors of secret concessions they will support your interpretation of what occurred. And a trade agreement will regain you the gold . . ." Caolin's wine glowed like the stone in his ring in the candlelight. Darkness surrounded them, separating them from the world.

The Prince of Elaya was still frowning into his goblet. "But a public apology!" His nostrils flared with distaste.

"Your Army destroyed the fortress called the Dragon's Claw . . . I could delay its refortification . . ." Caolin breathed carefully, as if any movement would break the delicate chain of persuasion he was forging between himself and the other man.

Palomon drew back suddenly and set down his goblet with a click. "You offer promises, but you ask *me* to pay . . . and then to wait for you to keep your word."

Anger flared in Caolin's belly. Palomon jerked away as if

he had been struck. The Seneschal's ring blazed as his hand clenched on the table's edge.

"I have promised you—and I always keep my promises *precisely*, Palomon!" Caolin hissed.

The Prince of Elaya tried to laugh, but his heavy lids did not quite hide the trouble in his eyes. "I believe you . . ." he said softly. He bent to pick up a chesspiece which Caolin's movement had knocked to the floor.

"And yet—" he added, a gleam of real humor suddenly relaxing his face, "I still would like to play at chess with you!"

Caolin smiled and forebore to tell him that he already had.

IX

The Morning Star

Early morning light slanting across the Lady Mountain left the intricate silhouette of the nearer ridge in shadow while the blue-hazed farther slope soared luminous against the sky. The Master of the Junipers felt his throat tighten and he wondered why he was so moved. It was only rocks and trees, though it might for a moment seem a veil drawn across the face of a world whose substance was living light. Once, he had been able to see that world.

He heard a ripple of laughter behind him. Most of the Queen's household had come with them to see the infant Prince receive his milk-name. The party had crossed the Bay yesterday and passed the night at the foot of the Mountain, for Faris had refused to sleep at Misthall.

The Master sighed. He had not been to the Lady Mountain since Faris was married to the King, and she . . . what place could either of them go that would not blur before their eyes with memories?

He looked back. Rosemary and Farin rode beside the litter which was bearing Eric up the Mountain. Farin had slipped his harp from its case and was improvising while he rode, guiding his horse with his knees. Behind them came Faris, and Branwen with the baby bound into a basketry cradleboard slung from the saddlebow.

The cradleboard was indeed a work of art, with its woven patterns brightened by red and blue feathers from woodpecker crests and jays, with a white deerskin to wrap around the child. A woman with a face like polished manzanita wood had left it at the Palace soon after the baby's birth with the message—
"Now that one of our blood will rule the Powers of Westria, let him be cradled as a child of the people . . ."

Then Berisa had told them of the Karok grandfather whom her younger brother and sister had never known. A descendent of the tribal People who were the original human inhabitants of Westria would rule . . . The Master realized suddenly that such a thing had not been since before the Cataclysm. His pulse quickened and his awareness reached out to the steady spark that was the child, perceiving for a moment the wonderful confusion of shape and color that swirled before the baby's eyes as he was borne up the path.

Quickly he withdrew again. The baby would have enough to assimilate today without the presence of an adult mind. But not for the first time he wondered at the ease with which that contact had been made. If he himself had ever begotten any children he was not aware of it. Would linking have been as easy if the baby had been his? Could any infant be reached so? Or was this relationship special—the one blessing of this dreadful time?

Rosemary's warm laugh distracted him.

"No, Eric, we are *not* going to join the dancing down at the Sacred Grove!"

"But the Lords of Seagate always go there to celebrate Beltane. I'm strong enough . . ." Eric protested.

"And will you still feel so strong after you have played your part in today's ceremony?" she asked tartly.

Farin interrupted her—"Don't be insulted, Eric. What Rosemary really fears is that one of the tree-maidens will carry you away!"

Eric laughed. "I *have* heard stories . . . Beltane is like the Feast of the First People in that way."

The Master smiled too, for he had served a year in the Sacred Grove and he had his own memories of the dancing at Beltane.

Sound shimmered from Farin's harp, silencing them. He began to sing:

"A King went out hunting, out hunting alone—
One day in the springtime, when the grass it was green—
And found there a maiden who sat on a stone
With the flowers all around her so fair to be seen.

'Ah maiden, no one could be fairer,' said he—
One day in the springtime, when the grass it was green—
'Come now to my castle and dwell there with me,
With the flowers all around you so fair to be seen.'

*'I am Princess of Flowers, and may be no man's bride—
One day in the springtime, when the grass it is green—
But I'll be your love if you'll stay by my side,
With the flowers all around us so fair to be seen.'*

*The Kingdom lamented and counted him slain—
One day in the springtime when the grass it was green—
But the lovers alive in the greenwood remain
With the flowers all around them so fair to be seen."*

"If Jehan had stayed with me in the north, he might be alive today!"

Startled, the Master saw that Faris had urged her horse forward to pace beside his own. "My dear . . ." he began.

"Can't I be allowed to forget?" she asked bitterly. Pitiless, the morning sunlight betrayed the false color on her lips, glistened on the dusting of powder with which she had tried to hide the shadows beneath her eyes.

"You cannot reject the past without rejecting yourself, but you can live each new day one hour at a time . . ." He offered her words worn smooth in the watches of his nights—the litany with which he tried to exorcise his own memories.

She shook her head. "Not today. Today I must put on the Jewels. How can I do it without him to share the burden?" her voice failed.

And how can I speak the words and conduct the ritual, when I feel nothing waiting to receive my prayer? The Master's fragile content shattered. He struggled to keep from voicing his despair.

"Stop it!" whispered Faris. "Must I bear your pain too?"

For a moment grief reverberated between them. Then the Queen spurred her horse viciously. The contact broke as a covey of quail exploded from the brush beside the path and the black mare leaped forward.

The Master's horse snorted and stumbled as Caolin's mount shouldered by, and the Master flinched, glimpsing contempt unshuttered in the Seneschal's eyes. For a moment the two faces flickered between him and the road—the Queen's brittle mask of beauty, Caolin's face, fuller than it had been, with all the betraying lines smoothed away.

The Master's unease focused to a sudden passionate resentment of the confidence with which the Seneschal had gone after the Queen. He clucked to his horse to catch up to them, then reined in. No—not now, when Caolin's amused smile could distort every word he said. No, he must try to find Faris alone.

"I will come in a moment—only leave me alone!"

Her words still trembling in the brittle air, Faris stumbled to the summit of the Lady Mountain, listening to Rosemary's footsteps fade. Numbly she set down the case in which the Jewels waited for her touch. She caught her breath on a sob, then stilled again as she heard only the wind, tuning itself to the contours of the Mountain with a thin high note that wavered on the edge of sound.

Far below the waters of the Bay glittered blindingly, a restless reflection of the light that had fired the bowl of the sky to a translucent sapphire glaze. Light glanced from the waters, from facets chipped in the rock of the mountainside, from the polished surfaces of madrone leaves.

The others were gathering in the meadow, waiting for Faris to put on the Jewels so that the ceremony could begin.

She stared helplessly around her, remembering how she had stood on top of the Father of Mountains and seen Westria laid like a golden promise at her feet. But this sunlight burned her eyes. Across the water the Red Mountain seemed about to shoulder free of its crumpled foothills. The slopes that lapped the Lady Mountain heaved like the waves of the sea.

For a moment the world whirled around her. Her balance was gone, and she fell, bruising her knees on the stone. *What is happening to me? What have I done?* She felt the easy tears sting her eyes, but there was no one to comfort her.

A vagrant scent of sun-warmed grass caught at her memory. She had done this before—wept into the bosom of the Mountain because she feared the ceremony that would unite her to the King. But now Jehan lay lost in the shadows of the Sacred Grove, and she had come here to give a name to his child.

And I am still afraid of the Jewels . . .

The wind song had deepened to a low hum that seemed to vibrate from the solid rock beneath her. She laid her palms against the weathered stone. There was a power here too, she thought, that supported her without judgement or demand.

"Lady of the Mountain," she whispered, "lend me your strength!"

Peace built around her, as fragile as a bubble of blown glass. Faris held her breath, motionless upon the still point of the turning world.

Why are you afraid?

Faris sought inward for an answer, and shuddered as she remembered the sweet sense of power that had stirred within her when she put on the Jewels before, and the triumphant smile on the face of that other Faris who had looked out from her mirror, mocking her. Somewhere within her, the Lady of Darkness was still there.

Then the trill of birdsong, the hum of the bee's flight, even the murmur of the wind, dulled and disappeared. Peace, palpable and enduring as the mountain itself, barriered her from the world.

For a moment Faris waited, poised on the edge of commitment, then she moved into that clarity where will and need are one. She opened the box that confined the Jewels.

Power throbbed around her, shaking the fragile boundaries of her control. But the stillness of the Mountain remained within. She imagined it rising around her, an inner barrier which would distance even the seductive power of the Jewels. She put them on, then got to her feet, carefully, as if she balanced the whole weight of Westria, and started down the hill.

Men and women turned as Faris came toward them. She assumed her place across the circle from the Master of the Junipers and held out her hands.

To her left, Lord Robert waited, and Eric to her right, responding to her offered hand with a swift movement that set the embroidered arms on their tabards glittering in the brilliant sun. Rosemary and Lady Alessia completed the circle as they took the Master's hands.

Those who had come to witness the ceremony gathered around them. Faris glimpsed the flare of Caolin's crimson robe, and saw, standing at attention near his mother, the amber-eyed boy who was Brian's heir. She felt their excitement as one feels the distant throb of the sea. But she was still barriered against its force.

The Master's invocation drew to a close. ". . . and therefore, Maker of All Things, make us open to Thy will. For Thou art the source of all strength and safety, and our promises are only manifestations of Thy power." His voice wavered on the words. "In the Names of the four elements and of the Covenant of Westria, let us begin."

Hands unlinked. Lady Jessica stepped into the circle past the little table by which the Master stood, followed by Farin with the baby clasped awkwardly in his arms. The child squirmed and looked around him with bright dark eyes.

"My Lords, my Ladies—" the Master bowed to each side of the circle. "You have come here, in the names of the Provinces of Westria, to stand sponsors to this child at his first naming, and to pledge to guard him until he is grown. Will you undertake this trust?"

Agreement echoed around the circle, but Faris held still, held to her circle of peace until her part should come.

"Will you promise to care for this child as if he were your own?"

"I will . . ."

"Will you see that he is taught the history of the Cataclysm and the meaning of the Covenant by which we live?"

Question and answers sectioned the brilliant stillness, the Master's voice fined to a cutting edge by strain, the replies of the sponsors falling one upon the other like notes in a trumpet call.

"And when he feels himself ready to bear the name of a man, will you bring him to be initiated and sworn to the Covenant of Westria?"

In the blaze of noontide they stood shadowless. Light shimmered on Rosemary's golden braids, flickered coppery on Alessia's leashed curls, picked glints of bronze and silver on Eric and Robert's bent heads.

The Master's voice deepened, falling through the sunlight.

"What shall the child be named?"

Faris felt her throat close. Light swallowed her words. What name—what name could transform him from 'the baby' to a person whom she could not ignore? She had thought to call him *Dolor*, for her sorrow . . .

"Who are you?"

The baby turned in Farin's arms, and Faris could not tell if she felt the clear flare of his spirit, or saw light kindle in his eyes.

"Star . . ." her reply sang to meet that brilliance. "He shall be called Star!"

The infant was still watching her, something achingly reminiscent of Jehan in the brilliance of his eyes. But his brows were too straight for that likeness. He was himself . . . Her vision blurred, extrapolating from the baby's rosy features the broad forehead and muscled jaw of a man.

"My star! My son!" her spirit called to him.

The Master of the Junipers turned to the baby and bowed.

"I salute you, Morning Star of Westria, for someday you shall bear the Jewels of Power. Therefore we must do more than name you—you must learn to know the Jewels."

The Master's gaze lifted to Faris. She felt his tension eroding the surface of her control and tried to smile, drawing the strength of the Mountain around her once more.

Farin laid the baby in Rosemary's competent embrace. The Master took an earthenware bowl of corn pollen and traced on Star's forehead the circled cross of Westria.

"In the name of Earth I bless you, son of this land. Grow strong as its bedrock, fertile as the soil, upright as the growing things that seek the sun!"

Faris felt the earth quiver. Through the soles of her feet she sensed the layered rock beneath her, the network of roots that latticed the earth, the life that sprang in every leaf and blade of grass. But her fingers were already unclasping the Earthstone from about her hips, and that awareness faded as she laid it for a moment on the belly of her child. Star's eyes turned to her, round and astonished, until she took it away.

The Master carried the Earthstone back to the table, and brought a silver chalice of rainwater as Jessica took the baby from Rosemary and carried him to Eric. Faris turned after her, feeling her stomach churn as the Sea Star, without the Earthstone to balance it, began to wake.

I am your Mistress—be still! she thought swiftly, willing her muscles to relax.

"In the name of Water I bless you, son of the sea. Grow mighty as the pounding waves, responsive as the tides, gentle as the falling rain!" The water on the Master's finger made a crescent on Star's brow, partially wiping the pollen away.

Faris' breasts throbbed with milk, her ears roared with the sound of the sea. She remembered how she had been the sea, bearing this child to birth. Tears filled her eyes. But already she was unbelting the Sea Star, and touching him.

Farin bore the baby across the circle to Robert, but Faris fought for breath while wind blew back her hair. Her ears opened to the whisper of wind around the Mountain, the cry of a hawk miles away, to the aromatic scent of the incense with which the Master was blessing the child.

She bit her lip, struggling with the power of the Jewel. Her barriers were thinning, and she sensed the force locked in the crystal at her breast, fought the temptation to let it break free.

"In the name of Air I bless you, son of the skies. Grow free as the wind, harmonious as music, wise enough to name all things—even yourself when the time shall come!"

The Wind Crystal lifted from Faris' breast as if borne by its own silver wings. As she laid it on Star's chest the crystal and the child's eyes blurred in a single point of light. Through the rustle of voices came his cry.

Faris felt his confusion, sensed a tumult of images for which Star had no words, and poured toward him love and reassurance until he stilled. Then Jessica carried him toward Alessia.

As Faris turned to follow, sunlight blazed across her sight, kindling the Jewel of Fire to life upon her brow. She walked toward Alessia through air like a sea of flame, battling the awe of those who watched and the power that pulsed through every nerve until it seemed that she too would burst into flames. Her body was a shell of blown glass, too fragile a vessel to contain such a fire.

"In the name of Fire I bless you, son of Light. Grow terrible as the lightning, companionable as a candle flame, brother to all who are warmed by the fire of life."

Faris' fingers closed on her coronet. She reached to touch it to Star's brow. But suddenly the air between them seemed filled with flames.

"His gown is burning, beat out the fire!" A woman's scream echoed from past to present in her memory. *I must not let him burn!* Again Faris twisted in agony as the fire retraced its pathway up her arm. But still she reached for Star, not knowing if he were hers, or the housekeeper's child she had saved long ago. Then her hand closed on his cool flesh and she let go the Jewel of Fire.

Darkness . . .

Faris' mind still resonated with images of pain and splendor—the Master's anguish, Star's delight, the terrible beauty of the Jewel of Fire. She knew her brother's arms were supporting her, but she could not see. As the pounding of her heart stilled she understood that there was no fire, and that it had been her own son whom she had touched with the Jewel.

My son . . . the ferocity of her passion to save him astonished her. *I love him*, she thought in wonder, *my own sweet Star!*

"Behold, ye people of Westria, the Master of the Jewels

who is to come!" The Master's voice was lost in the cheering that washed over Faris, piercing her naked soul.

The baby began to cry and she heard the Master trying to comfort him. "My son—let me go to him!" she whimpered, struggling in Farin's arms. But no one heard.

"What is wrong with her, what can I do?" Farin's panic lashed her and she screamed.

"I will take her."

Faris felt her brother's uneasy relief. Strong arms lifted her. The voices faded, and presently the torrent of emotions that had battered her began to weaken, as if some other will were blotting them away.

"Be still . . ." Faris realized that she had been hearing that dry voice for some time, with her ears alone. "There is a wall around you. You cannot hear or feel. You are safe with me . . . I will not let the Jewels hurt you again . . ."

Faris shuddered, knowing how nearly the Jewels had mastered her. She felt the earth solid beneath her, and she breathed to the rhythm with which cool impersonal fingers caressed her hair. Gratefully she sank into the silent dark.

After a long time, Faris opened her eyes. She was lying in the shade of a laurel tree. Beside her, Caolin sat with his back against its trunk, one arm resting easily across his bent knee as if he had been there for a long time. As the laurel leaves flickered, sunlight revealed the carven features she had come to know so well, shadow dissolved them into mystery. Which face was his? She sighed as awareness of her own body began to return.

"How do you feel?"

She struggled to sit up. "My head aches . . . but numbly." Just as, she thought, the salves had kept the agony of her burned arm at bay. But this time it was her mind whose protective covering had been stripped away. Dimly she sensed the life of the tree, but nothing from Caolin, beside her. Had he also kept those other minds from touching hers?

"Caolin . . . thank you for protecting me," she said softly. "And thank you for sparing me your emotions now. Your barriers must be better even than the Master's used to be . . ."

His eye-lids quivered as if that had touched him, but he continued to smile at her. "I did what I could to help you," he said neutrally. "Are you ready to go back?"

Faris looked down at the meadow, busy now with people

setting up the feast. A blue curl of smoke threaded the trees.

"So many minds . . ." she shook her head, but her breasts were taut with milk, and her arms hungered suddenly for the weight of her child. "Where is Star?"

"With the Master of the Junipers, I suppose," replied Caolin. "Don't worry, they have probably fed the child. I am surprised that the Master has not grown breasts to suckle him!"

He is my *son!* Faris felt resentment flare, not entirely because she knew the agony that waited for her if the baby had no appetite to relieve the pressure in her breasts. "I have to go. Will you stay with me and help me shield?"

"We will not be separated by any will of mine," he said, watching her, "but there are those who will resent it if we seem too close."

"No!" Faris gripped his sleeve, seeing her promised protection being torn from her. Caolin did not move, but the wind-tossed branches loosed a flood of sunlight that blinded her so that she could not see his face. Her need spoke. "No, I will not let you go!"

"Rosemary, let go of me!" Eric thrust her supporting arm aside. He took several careful steps toward the horselitter that had been braced up on logs to make a bed for him and sat down, and only the pallor around his mouth and a rapid pulse beating in his throat told Farin what it had cost him.

"You are tired—we're all tired. I only wanted to help you . . ." said Rosemary quietly, still standing where he had left her.

"By protecting me like a hen with one chick?" Eric snapped.

The image of Eric flapping downy wings set a bubble of laughter growing in Farin's throat and he turned away to stifle it. But Rosemary and Eric took no notice of him.

"Such help will make me an infant again! Go back to the baby, if that's what you want—I am not your child!"

"No, thank the Lady!" she retorted. "I wish your mother joy of you when you go from here to Bongarde! And I hope you go soon, before I regret that I gave you your life again!" Shaking, she whirled, stood a moment trying to control her features, then stalked away.

Farin took his hands from his ears, held there as if they could dull the impact of the shouted words. Eric was staring after Rosemary, his face almost as flushed as hers had been. Somewhere farther down the slope a flute twittered mockingly.

"Don't tell me I'm ungrateful—" said Eric, glaring at Farin as he had glared at the Elayans on the battlefield. "I'm going mad, always being cosseted and cared for."

"Did you have to be so harsh?" asked Farin peaceably, leaning against the madrone tree. "Rosemary was exhausted already and the ceremony was a strain for her. You may be getting well, but who will take care of her if she falls ill?"

Eric eased down on the bed, wincing just a little, and pulled a pillow beneath his arm. "Take care of Rosemary?" he repeated blankly.

Farin shook his head in disgust. *She loves you, and if your brains weren't made of granite you would have seen it long ago . . .*

A rabble of boys dashed past them, followed by an excited dog. "Badger, you come back here!" a woman called.

Farin, wondering if she was calling a boy or the dog, turned and saw it was Alessia of Las Costas.

"My lady!" he scrambled to his feet and bowed.

She stopped, recognized them, and after a moment's hesitation marched up to Eric.

"Sir Farin, my Lord Eric . . . do your wounds trouble you still?"

Eric grimaced. "I am only a little tired—"

"Don't try to get up, lad. You need not pretend with me—I nursed Brian often enough to tell when a man is in pain." She held herself upright as a maiden, but there was an etching of lines around her weary eyes, and bitterness had worn its grooves at the corners of her mouth. For a moment her glance held Eric's, then he sighed defeat and lay back again.

"They tell me you were wounded at my husband's side." Alessia said.

Eric's eyes did not falter now. "My lady, I brought two griefs from that field—that Lord Brian fell, and that we were friends for so short a time. I think . . . I fought him before because he was what I wanted to be . . ."

"I believe you." Alessia said softly. A muscle twitched in her cheek. "I am glad he had so good a companion." She looked around. "Badger, come here!"

One of the boys emerged from the tumult, and meeting his mother's glance, came slowly toward them. His steps hastened a little when he saw who waited there. He had his mother's auburn hair, but Brian's belligerent eye.

"My son—give Lord Eric your hand."

As Badger began to comply, Eric tugged free Brian's ring, put it into the boy's hand and closed his fingers around it. Badger looked at him in astonishment, but Alessia grew so white that Farin put out an arm to steady her.

"Badger, listen to me—" said Eric gravely. "When your grandmother died, your father went to King Jehan and swore to be loyal to him, and the King gave him this ring. Now the King is dead, like your father, but when that baby you saw named today is grown, he will be *your* King. Now your father knew it would be a long time before Star can give you a ring of your own. So Lord Brian told me to bring his ring to you. Will you swear to serve Star as your father did Jehan?"

"I swear it," said Badger clearly.

Eric swallowed and added, "Your father was a good lord to his people and the best fighter in Westria. Do not forget him. And when you are old enough to swing a sword, come to me if you wish, and I will show you how to use it . . . If your mother agrees," he added uncertainly. Badger was nodding with shining eyes.

"You do us honor—I know no one else so worthy to teach Brian's son!" Alessia's eyes were wet, but her voice was steady now.

"Mama, the ring is too big," said the boy. "You keep it—I shall lose it if I try to put it on."

Alessia bit her lip and held out her hand. "We will get a golden chain, darling, and hang it around your neck until you are grown."

A ball flew past them and Badger's eyes followed it, though he held himself still. "Go now and play—" Alessia told him. "I will stay and talk to Lord Eric for a while."

But for several minutes no one spoke at all. Farin's nostrils flared as the wind brought a scent of roasting meat their way and he wondered if he could leave to get something to eat.

"I hope you did not mind . . ." said Eric finally. "Lord Brian asked me to take the ring . . ."

"Mind?" Alessia's brows bent. "I wondered about it, but I supposed the ring had been on my lord's body when they burned—"she broke off and sat down on the edge of the bed as if her will were no longer quite sufficient to hold her upright. Wind rustled in the madrone leaves overhead, then passed on.

"They told me only that you found them, Sir Farin—" her

gaze returned to Eric. "But no one knew how it happened. Tell me how my lord died."

His eyes on the ground, his scarred hand clenching and unclenching in the blanket, Eric began to speak. Listening, Farin's mind peopled the barren battlefield with warriors. But they seemed distant now, their anguished faces ennobled by the sunset glow. Even the figure of Brian, scything his way through the ranks of his foes, was shadowed with tragic beauty by his approaching doom. *Not an epic but a lament . . .* thought Farin.

In the mists of the morning, Lord Brian stood proudly, but now in the darkness . . . He closed his eyes, searching for the line that teased him and the lift of the haunting melody.

"And then I saw him fall—" Eric finished, resting his forehead on his crossed arms. Mourning doves cooed in the madrone tree, lamenting the slow fall of the sun.

"Why cannot I believe it was only the chance of war?" said Alessia. "I know that even the greatest tree may be brought down. But the Seneschal sought my lord's death before . . ."

"What?" said Eric and Farin together. Eric sat up again.

For a moment Alessia frowned, then met their eyes. The westering sun kindled flames in her russet hair. "My lord swore silence to the King, but they are both dead now . . . I do not think that oath binds me. Last fall Caolin forged a letter to make King Jehan think Brian a traitor, then arrested and would have killed him but for the intervention of the King!"

The wind was blowing harder now, chilling the brightness of the afternoon. Farin ground the heels of his hands into his eyes to halt the tears and the rush of memories he thought he had locked away. *"That* was what he would not tell us! That was why he went out into the rain!"

"Farin, what is wrong?"

But now in the darkness . . . Farin's inner lament was halted by the spoken words. He looked up, saw through a haze of tears Jessica, and Robert looming behind her. Their eyes went anxiously from Farin to Eric and Alessia.

"Did you know that your brother took the fever that killed him going out to save my lord from Caolin's treachery?" asked Alessia in a tight voice.

"Lord Robert, did you ever learn who betrayed the plan that Caolin's Deputy persuaded you to follow? Did you know that Caolin had sworn Brian's death? Brian told me so," said Eric, croaking with the effort to keep his voice low.

Farin's heart began to pound, heavily, like a distant battledrum.

"Brian and the Seneschal were always quarreling," said Robert, the worry lines deepening around his eyes. "The Lord of All knows what I would give to know what went wrong, but what proof have you that Caolin . . . I cannot believe—"

"What can't you believe, Lord Robert?" asked Caolin.

The hand of a traitor has stricken him down . . . Farin's throat closed. After a moment Eric's dropped jaw snapped shut. Caolin surveyed them all with a sardonic smile on his lips, but there was no smile in his grey eyes. The wind whipped his robes around him like a flame in the sunset light.

For a moment there was no sound but the rustle of the wind in leaves, as if the trees themselves were whispering tales of treachery. All of them stared at Caolin. Farin wondered if he looked as guilty as Eric, as defiant as Lady Alessia, then thought, *but we are not the guilty ones!*

Lord Robert was the first of them to stir, assuming the dignity of the Ramparts as if he had drawn their protection over him from three hundred miles away. Lady Jessica clung to his arm.

"I will believe nothing until I have proof before me, my Lord Seneschal," he said mildly. "I suggest you do the same."

Some of the menace went out of the air and Farin dared to breathe. But he felt the tension in Alessia, as if sparks would spit from the waves of her hair.

"I am not so moderate," she hissed. "You may think yourself secure with Brian gone, but his spirit cries out against you."

Caolin shook his head gently. "I pity your grief, my lady, but Prince Palomon's crossbows killed your husband, not I . . ."

"But your servant told them—"

Farin clutched at Eric to silence him, stepped in front of the bed as if his slim body could hide that of his friend.

"Is this by any chance a conspiracy?" There was an edge to Caolin's soft laugh.

Staring resolutely past him, Farin saw his sister approaching with the baby in her arms, followed by the Master of the Junipers and Rosemary. The world seemed to slow. He had an eternity in which to watch Faris' expression change, to hear her ask the inevitable question, to recognize his own dread.

"I think they do not like Jehan's choice of a Seneschal . . ." replied Caolin.

Farin winced as the Queen's terror lashed him, sensed the

desperate appeal with which she turned to Caolin and saw the gleam of triumph in the Seneschal's pale eyes as he smiled at her.

"Yes, I want him gone, and more than that!" cried Alessia. "I want him to pay for my husband's death!"

Faris turned on her—"And who will pay for the death of mine? Brian forced his way into Jehan's sickroom and after their quarrel Jehan fell sick again—Lord Brian deserved to die!"

"Faris!" Farin's protest was echoed by the Master of the Junipers, but Faris did not seem to hear them. Everyone was talking at once.

"But Faris," Eric's exclamation rose above the rest, "did half the army deserve death too? Would Jehan—"

She glared at him. "Do you think your scars give you the right to change Jehan's will?" Star had begun to whimper but Faris only held him more tightly.

"You are all trying to confuse me!" the Queen's gaze moved from Eric to Alessia and the others while she fought for breath. "Are you trying again to seize independence for the Provinces now that Jehan is gone? May the Jewels destroy me if I alter the disposition Jehan made of this land! Caolin is Seneschal, and a united kingdom is my son's heritage. I will defend them both if I have to replace every Lord Commander in Westria!"

The baby had begun to shriek protest at the unleashed emotions crackling around him. The rush of wind through the trees echoed the voices of the crowd that had been attracted by the argument.

"Faris! Be still!" The voice of the Master of the Junipers rasped across the clamor. "Accusations should be aired in Council, not in a public brawl. You cannot attack the Lords of the Provinces this way!"

Faris stared at him, awkwardly patting the baby, whose face was purpling with rage.

"My Lady—consider Star—" the Master said more gently. "Your anger is upsetting him." He held out his arms to take the child.

"No!" Faris stepped backward until she bumped into Caolin, whose crimson robes flared around her in the wind like a nimbus of flame. "Perhaps I cannot deal with the Provinces now, old man, but I can deal with you! They only want my kingdom, but you would steal my son! Jehan's will made no provision for you, and I think you have stayed here too long!"

LADY OF DARKNESS

Farin tried to reconcile his knowledge of his sister with the madwoman he saw. The Master's face was bared like a skull in which only his eyes lived.

"Faris . . ." his whisper was lost in the wind.

"I am your Queen," she shouted, "and I tell you to go!"

The light went out of his eyes. "Very well. I cannot stop your self-destruction. Only remember your own words when you despair and call out for me, for I shall not be here!" He spoke as if the wind had shaped itself to words.

"I will make my own mistakes, then, for I swear I will deny my own name before I see your face again!"

The Master turned away.

"So . . . the great adept of Awahna, the pride of the College of the Wise, is humbled at last!" Triumph blazed through Caolin's control.

The older man paused a moment, looking up at the Seneschal. His shoulders twitched the words away. Farin strained to hear his reply.

"You are alone now, Caolin . . . for your own sake be careful, and remember that Jehan loved you."

Silenced, Caolin looked down and the Master continued to walk away. Rosemary ran after him as his grey-brown robe blurred into the shadows under the trees.

Caolin put his arm around the Queen, stroking her hair. After a few moments she stilled and let him lead her away.

Farin felt his own strength leaving him and he clutched at the madrone tree. The light was fading, but the sky was still scarred with bands of fire.

"Robert, that man is dangerous," said Jessica firmly. "I know that Jehan trusted him, but he is dangerous now."

Lord Robert sighed, looking after the receding figures of Caolin and the Queen. "Perhaps, but without evidence, what can I do?"

"And if you *had* evidence?" asked Alessia.

"What do you mean?" asked Robert. Jessica took his arm, and as Alessia began to talk the three moved away.

Eric's trembling shook the framework of the bed. "Has Faris gone mad? How could she do that? How could she be like that?"

Farin shook his head. "I don't know . . . I don't know her anymore . . ." He sat down on the edge of the bed. "But I'm glad you are going home. Jessica is right—I'm the Queen's brother, which should protect me . . ." he paused, wondering if the woman who had banished the Master of the Junipers was still his sister in any sense that had meaning now. How cold the wind had become.

"Well, you and Robert and Alessia should be safe in your own Provinces . . ." he went on, "but I'm glad that Caolin didn't see Rosemary with us today."

"Rosemary?" Eric's hand tightened on Farin's arm.

"Caolin knows now that *we* are his enemies—" said Farin patiently. "If he could bring Brian down in the midst of his Army, what could he do to Rosemary alone in Laurelynn? We'll keep looking for evidence for Robert, and send word to you in Bongarde if we have any success."

Eric's eyes glittered in the shadows. "I'm going back with you to Laurelynn," he said abruptly, looking across the field. Farin saw Rosemary coming slowly toward them and bit back his reply. Perhaps something good might come out of the disaster of this day.

As he stood up a last ray of sunset slanted beneath a cloud and flared on the Jewels of Westria, still lying on the altar where the ceremony had been.

Caolin looked down at the four Jewels of Westria spread out upon his table, glittering in the candlelight. He had not realized that they would be so beautiful. For two days they had lain hidden in his saddlebags while he fought the desire to go and look at them and the fear that the Queen would open the redwood casket she had brought home from the Lady Mountain and find the pieces of common stone he had put inside.

But now he stood on the Red Mountain, and the Jewels gathered and returned to him all the light in the room. The stillness seemed to increase the weight of the darkness outside.

"*I* have the Jewels . . ." the candle flames bent to his whisper. Light stirred in the depths of the Earthstone like new leaves in a forest stirring in the sun as Caolin turned it back and forth between his long fingers. Deliberately, he laid his palm across the surface of the stone.

He felt a strange heaviness, and a prickling whose source he sought vainly until he realized that it was not a physical sensation at all. Scarcely daring to breathe, he set the Earthstone down.

At the College of the Wise, the other students had set messages for each other in the rocks of the path and discerned strange tales from twisted bits of metal left from the ancient times; but to Caolin they had only been metal scraps and stones. In the ceremonies they had used him to handle objects too charged with power for any of them to touch, as a man without nerves to sense pain might be asked to take a hot kettle from the stove.

Quickly he reached for the Sea Star, and felt a tremor in his own belly. For the second time power tickled the surface of his soul. Carefully he put the Sea Star on the table again and stepped back a little, staring hungrily at the Jewels.

"I can *feel* them!" His voice cracked on the words as his mind leaped inevitably to the question of what would happen if he put them on. The hairs lifted on the back of his neck and his skin chilled. *No—you are not their Master* . . . He remembered the apprehension in Jehan's face whenever he put them on. *They are too dangerous . . . keep them safe . . . keep them here . . .*

Caolin pulled the curtain aside and looked out. But the wind had drawn a cloak of cloud across the stars. He could hear it sighing across the mountainside as a man sighs for some forgotten loss. Where was the Master of the Junipers now?

He had feared him for so long, and in the end how easily he was rid of him! Caolin let the curtain fall, his eyes drawn back to the Jewels.

"Well, old man, what did you expect me to do? You have left the Jewels, and the Queen, and the kingdom in my hands!" He laughed. "Well, I will guard the Jewels—and the Queen? I think she is ready to come to me . . ."

He remembered how Faris had clung to him and tried to imagine embracing her, but his mind conjured only memories of Jehan kissing her, image flowing into image until he saw only the slow turn of the King's head, and an echo of old passions darkened his eyes.

I wanted Jehan . . . he answered the question Palomon had set him at last, *but he is gone, and the world is an empty house which I must furnish somehow* . . . All that remained of Jehan were his kingdom, his Queen, his power. By taking them, could he touch Jehan somehow?

"But they will try to stop me—that bitch Alessia and Robert and the rest—I must marry Faris so that I cannot be dismissed . . ." *And the Jewels?*

Their beauty teased him, but he shook his head. Yet perhaps

there was a way he could draw on their power now . . . His gaze moved to the door to his temple, that he had not opened for almost six months now.

Dead air flowed from the open door. The stale scent of the incense Caolin had used in his ritual set nightmares stirring in his brain, his barriers powerless against visions that came from within. He waited, trying not to breathe, until the candle he held burned steadily once more.

Then he gathered the Jewels in a cloth and took them inside, setting each on the altar of its own element, not pausing until his foot struck against the boar's head that still leaned against the altar of the Lady of Fire.

No . . . he shook his head, denying his memories, and set down the Jewel of Fire. But the glass eyes of the boar took fire from the candle flame and followed him. *You killed Jehan . . .*

"No!" Caolin shouted then, grasped the dead thing and stumbled through the other room and flung open the door, his muscles straining painfully as he cast the boar's head wheeling into the darkness to disappear somewhere on the slopes below.

Shaking, he collapsed into a chair. The door slammed behind him; his mind reverberated with that accusation, in Brian's voice, and in his own.

After a time Caolin forced himself to get up. The wind of his passage had blown the candles in the temple out, but the scattered glitter of gold and bronze from the Jewels on the altars reflected light from the other room. Carefully he locked the temple door. The wind had increased, rattling the catches of his windows as if it sought a way inside. Shivering, Caolin drew his blankets around him and lay down.

Jehan . . . oh my dear lord . . . how simple things were when I only grieved because I could not find the road to Awahna, and you told me that you loved me . . . He comforted himself by recreating that first encounter, and in the midst of his memory, slid into sleep.

He was walking in the forest with Jehan, all the past gone like some evil dream in the sweet interplay of speech and silence . . . Their voices soloed to the orchestra of whispering trees and distant waterfalls. Grey cliffs rose above the pillared pines, converging toward a blaze of azure sky that marked some wonder that the trees still hid.

"Are we going to Awahna now, my Lord?" he asked.

Light dawned in the King's face. "Caolin—I have always known what you desired."

But Caolin saw his shadow, suddenly, stretch black upon the path as changing hues of light streamed from behind him. When he turned, there were four brilliant figures beckoning—tree-brown, sea-blue, wind-silver, red as fire—their eyes were gems, their fingers shone with power.

In his ears, a whisper from Jehan—"Awahna holds the Jewels' reality . . ."

But Caolin had no will to move until they faded like a rainbow in the sun. Then he turned.

But then, Jehan was gone.

Caolin woke in the dim emptiness between night and day, his body shuddering with soundless sobs, for Jehan's face was still vivid before him, and now he remembered how much he had lost.

The Master of the Junipers stirred painfully. The fresh damp smell of the air told him that dawn was coming even with his eyes closed, but his muscles were stiff with sleep and the strain of the two days' swift walking it had taken him to leave the lands of men behind.

For the price of a blessing, a trader from Seahold had sailed him all the way to Rivered with his cargo of salted fish. Since then he had been afoot, pushing himself onward. But now he was in the mountains, and though the Lord Commander of the Ramparts was called their guardian, men did not rule here.

A bird called, three notes rising in a question and breaking off, as if she were afraid to wake the sleeping world.

Be still! the Master told himself. *This is why you came away. Be still and forget everything that is not here and now . . .*

He opened his eyes. A pale golden light was diffusing across the grey sky, like hope in a weary heart. He made himself get to his feet, shivering, and turned slowly clockwise, saluting the guardians of the four directions and lifting his arms to the lifegiving light of the sun as he had done every morning since he entered the College of the Wise. Then he began the danced meditation that balanced the body with the forces of the universe.

The Master's foot slipped on a loose stone and he came to a halt, gazing unseeing at the trees. *Has even this failed me now?*

First it had been a shadow between him and the Mistress

of the College. Now he understood why her leadership had faltered. How could she counsel the priests and priestesses of the College to teach and correct the people when she herself saw only emptiness at the heart of things?

It was hard enough to get through life without carrying other people's burdens, and in a world that no longer held holiness or glory it hardly mattered what one did. How many others in the College had followed her through loss of faith or laziness? How many others throughout the land? Was he the only one who had been deluded?

The Master sank to his knees, his hands digging into the earth. After awhile his sight cleared and he saw that his fingers were clenched around something green—a withered acorn out of which a seedling grew. He sat back on his heels, staring at it. *That is no delusion. It cannot know the dangers, yet still it seeks the sun.*

I was seeking Awahna. Like the seedling, despite all evidence, there is something in me that longs for the Light. Carefully he patted dirt around the little tree and moistened it from his waterskin. Then he bent to drink at the little stream near the place where he had lain down. In his pouch were a knife and flint and steel. He knew where things grew in this land that would keep life in him. For a while . . .

The Master straightened, gazing at the misty silhouettes of the hills emerging into the brightening day. Somewhere among them the road to Awahna lay. Logic told him that he would never get there.

But as he gazed upward he smiled, for the mountains were filled with light.

X

Dream—and Nightmare

Faris slipped toward wakefulness as Star stirred in the cradle beside her bed, her emerging awareness replaying the events of her dreams. She watched herself move through a richly colored world of animate forms whose meaning hovered on the edge of understanding.

The baby squeaked, then gathered his strength for a wail. Faris stretched out her hand to the cradle, setting it rocking as she sat up.

"There, my love—be still—I'll feed you soon!"

Her dreams still glowed in her memory. *I ought to tell Farin,* she thought, but he was not speaking to her these days. *I should write them down . . .*

She reached for a fresh diaper and bent to change the baby. When she was finished she opened the window, breathing deeply of the cool dawn air. Already the weather was warming, though it was not yet June. Too soon, the morning freshness would disappear.

But the damp air set her coughing—she had been very ill for the week after Star's naming, but she had hoped to be over that by now.

The baby, realising that his hunger was still unsatisfied, began to cry again. Faris carried him to the rocking chair, pulling down the loose neck of her nightgown to bare her breast. Her nipple hardened in the cool air and she sighed with pleasure as the baby's lips closed on it and her milk began to flow.

She held him close, stroking with wondering fingers the dark silk of his hair. A thrust of her foot set the chair to rocking. Vaguely she remembered that there had been a time when she had not loved him, as she remembered the quarrel after his naming—like a bad dream . . .

Softly she began to sing.

> *"Oh why are you fretting, my darling, my child?*
> *Are you not yet to this world reconciled?*
> *Lie still now and listen, for music is near*
> *And the harping and piping will banish all fear . . ."*

She should send for Farin, she thought. Star burped and let go of her breast and she shifted him to the other side.

> *"And are you yet waking? Upon Mama's breast*
> *Lay your head, and her heartbeat will lull you to rest.*
> *Your father will bear you to sleep's shining hall,*
> *And there you may hear the best music of all."*

Her voice faltered on the last verses but she forced herself to finish.

"My little one, *you* will never feel your father's arms around you unless you meet him in your dreams . . ." she whispered, blinking away tears. But Star had fallen asleep, his pink mouth a little open, tiny fingers clutching a fold of her gown. Gently she detached his hand and laid him back in his cradle, suddenly desperate for something to distract her from her memories. The dream . . . she should record it.

She looked around her for paper, saw only Jehan's Journal, which she had not opened since Star was born. There had been blank pages at the end. Faris had meant to tear out the empty pages, but seeing Jehan's writing again her movements slowed, a sentence caught her eye and she began to read.

> *. . . a lord must have more than courage. He must govern*
> *with justice, judging himself no less rigorously than*
> *the least of those he rules . . .*

The words were written hesitantly, with much crossing out. But Faris recognized them, remembering how Jehan's voice had rung through the Hall when Eric was invested as Lord Commander.

He must act not from prejudice or even preference, but must give the accused the benefit of the doubt until he traps himself, and then pronounce what the wrongdoer himself has chosen for his doom . . .

The notes broke off, then, and after a little space she saw another line whose strokes were heavy and even as the calligraphy on a warrant of execution.

But who will judge me?

"Oh, my beloved," Faris said softly, "for what fancied sins did you blame yourself? And if you deserved censure, what of me? Our child will be my judge if I cannot preserve his heritage." She riffled back through the pages of the Journal as if seeking inspiration, but found only a carefully copied poem.

Fair as the lily flower, fairer than the dawn,
Thou, whose grace with beauty fills my days,
Fair as the springtide when winter's cold is gone,
Lady still grant me on thy sweet face to gaze . . .

Abruptly she closed the book, having no need to search her memory for the night when Jehan had sung her that song. After a few moments she turned to the mirror on her wall, examining her reflection. "Jehan is gone, but I am not. Am I still beautiful?"

The face that glimmered in the glass was no longer that of a girl, and yet it was not old despite the silver in her hair. Stripped of softness, the lines of her cheek and jaw seemed ageless. Faris thought—*I am a woman now*, and then, *will I live out my life alone? Do I want to?*

Jehan himself had told her not to mourn him too long, but where could she find a lover who would be worthy of his memory? Whom could she trust not to take advantage of her love?

Eric? No—she must not take him from Rosemary a second time.

Caolin? The thought teased her imagination. She could hardly imagine that cold man stirred by passion, and yet he had been kind to her. How astonished everyone would be . . .

No, she thought, some would be furious. Memories of the Naming Feast began to surface and she saw once more the anger in the eyes of Eric and Farin as they confronted the Seneschal. Why did they hate Caolin? Did they hate her too? Even the Master of the Junipers had deserted her. She had been ill and terrified that afternoon, surely he must have known that she had not meant him to go!

Star snorted softly and turned in his sleep. Faris sighed. "I can live without a lover, but not without love . . ." She touched the cradle gently, and as it began to rock the baby stilled. "My little Star—you are the only one whose love for me is sure!" She frowned. "Somehow Caolin and the others must learn to be friends again as we were when Jehan was alive."

Caolin's eyes moved quickly down the page.

. . . and so it would give me great pleasure to have you as guest for an evening of music on the last night of May . . .

The Queen's handwriting skimmed across the paper, the pen strokes light and apt to swirl unexpectedly.

Caolin folded the invitation carefully and set it on his desk, nodding to the messenger. "I will send her my answer."

"We were discussing the refortification of the Dragon's Claw . . ." Ercul Ashe reminded him. "You must authorize release of the supplies." Papers rustled in his thin hands as he began to list the resources that would be required.

Caolin thought of the elaborate language of the treaty Prince Palomon had signed, and the very simple promise on which he had given the Elayan lord his hand. A memory of candlelight warred with the sunshine spilling across his desk.

"I will authorize supplies, but not for the fortress—it is the road that must be repaired," he told his Deputy.

Ercul Ashe looked up. "So that they can attack us more easily next time?" Some emotion stirred beneath his still features like a hidden fish in a lake, but his voice was, as ever, neutral.

Caolin frowned. "Elaya will not attack. Both countries need the trade. Make up the list for me to sign." He listened absently as his Deputy's pen scratched across the paper, then opened the Queen's letter once more.

An evening of music in the warm night air . . . Would there be colored lanterns as there had been at the Feast of the First People almost a year ago? And would Faris lie down for him as she had for Jehan? He felt his flesh stir, remembering how the King's hands had moved upon her body. Faris was the Queen. Surely she would be something more than the other pieces of female flesh that had come from Jehan's bed to his own. He had touched no one for six months.

This woman had been Jehan's . . . Resolutely Caolin suppressed recollection of the dreams of the King that had haunted him since he had taken the Jewels. Surely they were no more than the results of his own self-doubt, now, when everything he had ever desired was coming to his hand like a hawk to her master's fist—the Jewels, the Queen, the land of Westria.

The door opened suddenly. Someone spoke from the shadows of the hall.

"How domestic! How refreshing to come in from the dusty streets and find you sitting cool and peaceful with your dog at your side!"

Caolin's hand moved automatically to cover the letter as he looked up. His eyes narrowed, but he relaxed as he recognized Ordrey, who booted the door shut and dropped into a chair. Ercul Ashe sniffed at the faintly alcoholic atmosphere that surrounded the other man, and continued to write.

"I did not expect you today," said the Seneschal. "Are you tired of your holiday?"

"No. But I would enjoy it more if people could forget the damned war . . ." Ordrey stepped over to the sideboard and poured wine into a goblet. He drained it in one swallow, filled it again and took it back to his chair.

"What happened?"

Ordrey shrugged, then glanced mockingly at Ercul Ashe. "I wouldn't visit the taverns for a while, dear colleague, if I were you . . . Do you know what stories they are telling about the battle of the Dragon Waste?" He sipped at his wine.

Ashe stopped writing and Caolin stilled, alerted by some tension in the way the Deputy gripped his pen. *Does he suspect how he was used?*

"You're not going to ask me how the gossip goes? You feel that the Lord Seneschal's chief Deputy has no need to fear the murmurings of lesser men?"

Ercul Ashe started to add a word to his list and his quill pen split, splattering ink across the page. He reached for another and began to trim it with precise, vicious strokes.

"Ordrey—" Caolin began a warning.

"People know who suggested that wonderful strategy to Lord Robert." Ordrey said kindly, avoiding Caolin's eyes. "I scarcely dare admit I'm acquainted with you, much less that I went with you on that ill-fated journey." The penknife jerked and half of the new quill drifted to the floor. Ercul Ashe sat, staring down at it. Ordrey began to laugh.

"Ordrey, be still!" Caolin's anger throbbed in the air. He held Ordrey's pale eyes until the flicker of amusement in their depths had died, waited until Ercul Ashe's dull gaze sought his as well. Ashe was a fool, but no one could learn anything from him. Ordrey, on the other hand, knew everything. Caolin wondered whether his loyalty would equal Ronald Sandreson's, if it came to questioning. Eric or Alessia would give much to learn what Ordrey knew.

"If you are frightened we must send you to safety . . ." said Caolin softly. "When Ercul manages to finish this list he is making, we will need a courier to take it to the border. You should be safe enough on the South Road!"

Ordrey began a theatrical grimace, then schooled his features, meeting Caolin's eyes. He set the goblet down.

"And what about me?" asked Ercul Ashe.

"You?" the Seneschal raised one pale eyebrow. "But you have nothing to conceal . . ."

"If Ordrey has nothing to conceal, why did Caolin send him away?" Eric pushed himself to his feet and took a step toward Farin and Rosemary. Concern flickered in the girl's eyes, but Eric had been out of bed for nearly three weeks now, since shortly after the Naming Ceremony.

"Perhaps they were both joking," she replied. "The man is Caolin's messenger—is it so strange that he should be sent off again? Surely Ordrey knows that nobody will harm him merely for serving as escort to Ercul Ashe!"

Eric crossed the room to Farin, who sat in his usual place on the window ledge. It was morning and sounds of carts and street merchants crying their wares drifted through the open window.

"No. Not for that—" said Farin slowly. "But there is *something* . . ." He closed his eyes, remembering the bewilderment in Ercul Ashe's face when the man had come to him that morning.

"For three days I have thought about it, Sir Farin, and I am convinced that Ordrey and my Lord Caolin were laughing at me. I lie awake and ask myself why?" Then the picture was replaced, as if he had turned a page in his memory. Farin

remembered Brian's camp, and a man laughing as Ashe struggled in his bonds.

"Ercul Ashe told no one but the Commanders what his idea was, before or after the Council of War," said Farin. "But I heard him say to Ordrey that Robert had accepted his plan. Dust can be sprinkled over a book . . . What if Caolin already knew about that strategy, and *Ordrey* betrayed it to Palomon?"

Farin looked up at his friends. Rosemary was frowning thoughtfully, but Eric's big hands closed and unclosed. *Caolin was wise to send Ordrey away* . . . thought Farin, watching him.

"Eric! You cannot go after him—not yet!" exclaimed Rosemary, who had been watching him too. She grasped his arm and abruptly let go again, coloring. "I'm sorry." She looked away. "I forget I'm not your nurse anymore."

Eric's hands stilled. A muscle twitched in his cheek as he looked down at her. "No. You are right. I cannot do anything until I am a man again . . ."

"Mousetraps and snares . . ." sang a hawker in the street below. "Live traps for every creature—mousetraps and snares . . ."

"*I* can go." Farin said into their silence. "We must find some real evidence, you know. Ercul Ashe will be watching his master now, but I doubt that Caolin will strew his floor with incriminating documents."

"But Ordrey knows you!" objected Rosemary.

"He knows the Queen's brother who plays the harp Swangold. But will he know a wandering bard who sings the common songs of the road? I'll darken my skin and pull a cap over my hair." Farin got down from the window ledge.

"I wanted to go in any case—I've another idea . . ." Two pairs of grey eyes turned to him expectantly. "With or without evidence it will be hard to move Lord Robert against the Seneschal while everyone is still praising him for winning that treaty from Elaya. We must turn the people against Caolin!"

"If you think you can do that, Farin, you grow as proud as he is!"

"What do you mean to do?" Eric sat down on his bed again.

"Well—" Farin flushed. "I have made a song. It's the song about Brian that you asked me for, Eric—" He took a deep breath and his light voice filled the room with a haunting melody.

*"The sun rose like flame through the mists of the morning,
Below, men awaited the doom of the day,
And saw, stretched before them their foe's camp
abandoned—
No life but the blackbirds and sparrows at play.*

*Oh where are the warriors, and where are the maidens,
And where is the hero who led them to war?
Their blood and their ashes now nourish the wasteland,
And the Lord of Las Costas will lead them no more."*

"The rest is about the battle, and there's a verse telling how a hooded man carried the word to Palomon, and asking who sent him there . . ."

Eric whistled. "Even the Queen's brother won't be safe once Caolin hears that!"

"Well, I wasn't going to sing it in Laurelynn . . ." Farin colored again. "But if an anonymous harper starts it in the south, and if people like it . . . the traders will carry it across Westria before two weeks are gone!"

"There's one problem," said Rosemary. "If you are tramping the South Road you'll miss the party Faris has planned for next week. What will you tell her?"

"Will she even notice I am gone?" Farin answered bitterly, remembering how his sister had struggled in his arms and how Caolin had borne her away.

"Farin! You know that's not true. Faris wants to say she is sorry."

Farin shook his head. "No. You read her invitation. She wants everything to be the way it was before. But the King is gone. Brian is gone, and she herself sent the Master of the Junipers away. Do you think I can sit beside her without her picking up everything I feel?" His pulse was racing.

"Don't you think *I* feel—" began Eric, but Rosemary interrupted him.

"He's right. He and Faris are twins. It will be hard enough for you and me to barrier our thoughts from her! But Farin, be careful," she added. "I've heard stories about Ordrey . . ."

Farin avoided her eyes, remembering the whispers he too had heard. His long musician's fingers curled defensively into his palms.

"Yes. Well—you two enjoy the party, but watch out for Caolin!"

LADY OF DARKNESS

* * *

Little lanterns shone among the green plums in the trees by the edge of the lake, sparkling on silver and crystal and glowing on the rich clothing of the Queen's guests. A glitter of light edged the wavelets pulsing outward from the barges moored just offshore as the musicians settled into place.

Faris glanced nervously around the semi-circle of chairs and cushions arranged to face the lake. Across from her Lord Robert and Lady Jessica were talking softly to Elinor of Fairhaven, while Master Ras of Santierra spoke to the concertmaster, who had not yet joined his consort of musicians on the barge.

Caolin had taken a chair to her right and a little behind her. He was dressed simply but richly tonight, in a new linen robe of dull rose worked with silver.

Rosemary and Eric had not yet arrived.

One of the servers knelt before her, offering a tray of goblets that held chilled wine. Faris took one, smiling her thanks, and drank quickly. Branwen had already told her that Farin had left Laurelynn. Closing her eyes, Faris could still see the resentment in the girl's face, as if the Queen had driven him away. Her throat ached—Farin had not even come to her to say good-bye.

Were Eric and Rosemary going to stay away too?

Then Faris heard Jessica call out a greeting and sighed in relief as she saw Rosemary coming through the lamplit trees. Her blue gown billowed as she hurried forward. For once Rosemary had left her hair unbraided and it cascaded down her back like a river of gold. Faris smiled. Surely tonight Eric would look at Rosemary and find her fair.

Eric was coming more slowly behind her, leaning on a staff. His eyes followed Rosemary and he joined her on the other side of the semi-circle from Caolin.

Well—at least everyone was here.

Faris gathered the folds of her sleeveless over-robe and moved to face the company, the corded silver silk dragging behind her. The interlace of peach and plum blossoms that bordered it gleamed in the lamplight, matching the peach-colored gauze of her undergown.

"My Lords and Ladies—" Faris waited as the conversations stilled, stifling a need to cough. "I thank you for your company. I hope that you will find the refreshments and the music we have prepared for you equally enjoyable." She gestured, and the concertmaster raised his wand. The first strains of music drifted across the water as she sat down.

Flutes and horns and viols sang out each in turn, then joined their voices in interlacing strands of melody. The white-robed servers moved gracefully among the guests, offering them patés and pastries, sliced fruit or cheese and a selection of wines. Faris' taut nerves began to ease.

Rosemary watched the musicians, but Eric was watching Rosemary. Yet he sat a little apart, as if he were afraid to touch her. Faris could feel his longing, as she could feel Rosemary's wall of unhappiness. Perhaps that was why the girl did not realize that what she most desired was within her grasp.

Faris smiled to herself, feeling like a village matchmaker. *And what match would I make for myself?* she wondered then. Without turning her head she could see Caolin's profile. His eyes were closed, his features modeled by his abstraction to an unaccustomed purity. *Is that the true Caolin? The soul hidden behind his perpetual mask?*

The music concluded and applause broke the stillness like the wingclaps of startled birds. Another composition followed, then an intermission when the servers offered new delicacies. The guests got up and stretched, and walked back and forth along the edge of the lake.

"Your musicians play well, my Lady—" Master Ras of Santierra bent before Faris, then straightened, his dark face shining. "But I had hoped to see your brother tonight—I have heard much praise of his skill."

"He had a sore throat and dared not come," said Rosemary, glancing sidelong at Caolin. Faris looked at her sharply—had Branwen been lying? But no—she could *feel* that Farin was far away. She turned to hide her hurt. Let them think she believed them.

"This evening is like something in a dream . . ." said Jessica, smiling kindly at Faris. "The air is so warm, and the lights on the water are so beautiful."

"I had an interesting dream a little while ago," said Faris brightly, seeking to fill the silence. The others turned to listen to her. Desperately she sought to recapture the vividness of the dreams she had recorded in the Journal.

"I was walking in a garden . . ." she began, "and with me went a horse, an eagle and a boar. Soon the horse galloped away, but the eagle rested on my shoulder and I fed it from my hand. Time passed, then the boar attacked the eagle and destroyed it. Then it and I were left alone together, and night fell . . ."

She looked at them helplessly. Perhaps Farin could have found words to recreate the fear and wonder of that dream, but she had not the power. There had been another dream that night, but what use would it be to try to recount it now?

"It has the ring of a prophecy—" said Lady Elinor. "Have you tried to interpret it?"

"Perhaps they could guess its meaning at the College of the Wise," said Lord Robert gravely.

"Perhaps," answered Faris. "I only dream . . . if any could tell me its meaning, I would reward him well." Suddenly embarrassed, she felt Caolin watching her and looked away.

Faris had feared that Caolin might quarrel with Eric or Rosemary, but everyone was keeping to generalities tonight, and if no one was swearing friendship, at least there was no hostility. Caolin had hardly spoken at all.

She fingered the milky opals in her silver necklace, her touch waking their rosy glow. *They are only gems . . .* she thought, *not the Jewel of Fire. Why does the air seem so warm?* She unclasped her over-robe and let it fall across the back of the chair. Her gown was cut low across her breasts, the full sleeves gathered at the wrists in the northern fashion instead of hanging free like those of the others. She envied the coolness of open sleeves—but if she had worn them they would have revealed her scar.

"Dreams can be strange indeed," said Master Ras. "Once I dreamed a mastersong, but when I woke I had no paper to record it, and after, I could never remember how it had gone. What about the rest of you?" He gestured around the circle. "What do you dream, my Lord Seneschal?"

Caolin lifted his head abruptly, something anguished momentarily revealed in his grey eyes. "I dream of the King . . ." he whispered before his gaze was shuttered once more.

Her heart wrenched, remembering her own dreams of Jehan, Faris signaled for the music to begin again. This time it was a group of singers from the Ramparts, miners who wove a close harmony around a melody as rhythmic as if it had been composed to hammer blows. Lord Robert put his arm around his wife and leaned back, smiling. Eric shifted uneasily on his cushions, as if pained by his wounds.

Branwen came through the trees with Star in her arms. Faris

felt her breasts throbbing in response to the sight of the baby and pulled down the neck of her gown to feed him. In a moment his fussing stilled.

"There, my son—" she whispered. "You will not starve. Mama will take care of you . . ." Her glance moved watchfully around the circle, where the music had stamped the faces of Caolin and the others alike with its own identity.

The singing ended. Jessica rose and came to Faris, bending to stroke Star's cheek. Then she smiled and folded her arms across her breasts.

"You remind me that it is time for me to feed my own little one. But I am glad we came. The evening provided a welcome interval of harmony."

"Thank you." Faris smiled back at her, once more astonished by Jessica's perception.

When they had gone the Queen called for the consort to play again. She finished feeding Star and gave him to Branwen to return to his bed. Then she whispered to the servers to leave the wine pitchers and go.

She refilled her goblet and drank again, her awareness expanding as the music went on. She could feel the pleasure of Lady Elinor and Master Ras, and Caolin seemed content. She glanced at the Seneschal's still features. *Do I really want him for a lover? Or do I only fear to remain alone?*

She bit her lip and focused on Rosemary, whose unhappiness was becoming steadily more apparent. The musicians were playing a popular song about unrequited love. When it was done, Faris signalled the musicians to be still.

"Rosemary—" she said swiftly, "we should let the players rest awhile. Do you remember how we used to sing together at the Hold?"

Her friend shook her head. *"You* have a lovely voice, but I have not sung for too long . . ."

"But I am afraid I will cough in the middle of the song," said Faris truthfully. "It must be a duet." She racked her memory for something suitable.

"Please, Rosemary, I would like to hear you sing," said Eric.

"You would?" Rosemary turned uncertainly to the Queen, her cheeks a little pinker than they had been. "What do you want to do?"

A fragment of melody surfaced. "The Parting Hymn that we learned at our Initiation and Nametaking," she said. Once more she saw the meadow at the foot of the Father of Mountains, and the ranks of young men and women flushed with pride in their newly chosen names. The hymn had seemed to express everything they had learned.

Rosemary nodded. "Very well. But your voice is higher, so you must begin."

Faris took a long swallow of wine, letting its sharpness quell her cough, and its warmth dissolve the last of her nervousness. Then she started, relaxing as Rosemary's warm contralto joined her in the second half of the line, then wove over and around her ascending melody.

> "Lest we forget, our voices join in harmony
> Once more before we part, before we part.
> What we have shared will never fade in memory,
> But live in the eternal present of the heart."

The tune shifted key in the middle so that the second verse started a note higher than the first.

> "May your path be fair, yet in the chain of living,
> Men are no more than links, no less may be—
> Blame not the world, for no way but by giving
> Yourself to her rhythms, may you be truly free.
> Our tangled lives are no haphazard blending;
> Strangers, we neither meet nor part by chance.
> Fortunes which seemed to whirl us towards an ending
> But add another figure to the dance."

Faris saw the others watching them and wondered, *In what pattern are our lives entwined now?* It seemed to her that Rosemary's voice faltered then, but she went on, soaring into the final verse of the song.

> "Singly we sway, unbalanced passions sundering
> Our hearts, and yet we hope, when all is done,
> To find ourselves, where is no need for wondering,
> Poised in that Love wherein all loves are one."

Rosemary stood up on the last line, fist to her mouth, staring at Faris. "How could you ask me to sing that—how could you, Faris, when you know . . ." she broke off on a sob, then gathered her skirts and ran off through the trees.

Eric struggled to his feet and stood staring after her, his face losing the little color it had held. Appalled, Faris went to him. "Eric!" she whispered urgently. "Do you love her?"

He looked down at her though nothing in his manner showed that he realized who was standing there. "Yes . . ." he said wonderingly. "Yes."

"Then in the Lady's name go after her!" Faris grasped his arm and pushed him in the direction Rosemary had gone. Faris sank into her chair, shaking her head, and reached for her wine. At least Rosemary would get her chance now. When she looked up again Lady Elinor and Ras of Santierra were standing before her, trying to hide their smiles.

"My Lady—now we must go as well. We thank you for your hospitality, and a most . . . entertaining . . . evening." Master Ras bent respectfully over her hand.

There was a silence when they had gone, broken only by a tentative croak from a frog in the reeds further down the shore, and the creaking of the barge.

"My Lady—" the concertmaster called across the water. "Will you be wanting us to play any more?"

"What?" Faris roused herself. "Oh—I am sorry. Of course you may go, and thank you. Your music was beautiful." She thanked them again when the rowboat had ferried singers, players and instruments to shore. Only a few of the little lamps remained alight now, like belated fireflies resting in the plum trees. The concertmaster bowed, then straightened, glancing uncertainly at Caolin, who was staring across the water.

"I would be happy to escort you back to the Palace, my Lady, if you will honor me . . ."

Faris smiled and shook her head. "There's no need. The Lord Seneschal will bear me company."

And then there were only herself and Caolin. The night was striking up its own music—the multi-voiced chorus of frogs, the tambourine of crickets in the grass, the humming of insects and the whirr of descending wings from those that hunted them.

The evening was over. Why then was she still sitting here with a sense of anti-climax souring her pleasure? She smoothed the silky gauze of her gown across her thighs, feeling the flesh beneath—the evening had been too warm for a petticoat. But had that been her only reason for choosing this gown?

She remembered what her mirror had shown her as she dressed for the evening—how the peach-colored gown had lent pink to her cheeks, how its soft folds had revealed the body beneath them . . . *I was going to be so fair he could not resist me,* she thought bitterly, *the one woman who would succeed where everyone else had failed.*

Caolin had not moved. His head was silhouetted against the starlit sky, his hands clenched in the folds of his robe. She considered the man—the pale silky hair cut short at the neck, his smooth skin and the lean height of him, like an image carved of marble and gold. Could these things attract her, who had known Jehan? Faris took a swift swallow of wine.

"I think that the evening went well . . ." she said aloud.

He turned to face her, the flickering shadows mocking her memory of his face. He spoke abruptly. "My Lady—did you know that I came here tonight intending to make love to you?"

For a moment she had no words. Her heart was thudding slowly, heavily. She pushed herself to her feet and took two steps toward him, standing where the remaining lamplight would reveal her body underneath the gown.

"Caolin . . ." she said softly. "My name is Faris."

His grey eyes focused on her, meeting her gaze fully for the first time. "Faris . . ." some of the tension seemed to go out of him with the breath. "Well, I will give you truth, Faris," he said as she tried to read his face. "I have loved no woman. I do not love you now."

Faris nodded. "I have loved only one man. But I think we need each other."

"I need you to maintain my position—" Caolin said bitterly, "to do the things Jehan left in my charge. I must be sure of you—do you understand?"

He was pleading with her. Faris shook her head in bewilderment. Did he want her to refuse him?

"I need your help to do as he bid *me,* and I do not want to be alone."

"But you were Jehan's!" he half turned away.

Faris sighed. "Do you think Jehan would disapprove?"

"No—I don't know!"

Must I do it all? The night had stilled around her, but suddenly Faris felt a surge of desire, and after a moment identified its source, as one might identify a fragment of melody, as Eric and Rosemary. She realized that she had dropped all her own barriers now. From Caolin she sensed faintly confusion and fear. Would he open himself if he made love to her?

"Caolin . . ." Faris reached out and took his hand.

He kissed her then, without gentleness. She had not expected his touch to bring her ecstacy, but she was grateful for his warmth and the security of strong arms around her at last.

After a little he released her. His face was intent, as if she were a problem he had to solve. He stroked her hair, then began to remove the pins, one by one, until the massed coils fell like shadow about her shoulders. Delicately, his finger traced the curve of her cheek, wandered over the smooth skin of her neck and across her breast, slipping beneath the edge of her gown and easing it over the curve of her shoulder.

Faris stilled, all her nerves flaring in response to a sequence which she had learned from Jehan. Abruptly she knew—*We have both loved only one man* . . . But she had no time to wonder, for Caolin was pulling her down on the carpets that had been laid over the grass, fumbling with his tunic and her gown. His body thrust against hers. Gasping, Faris lowered her hand to guide him and reached out with all the power of her mind for his, forcing her way through barriers weakened by his desire.

"Jehan!" She sensed his inner cry, and with the name something gave way in him like skin splitting along the line of an old scar. Caolin's body convulsed away from hers. Into her mind poured images—*a boar's head . . . the boar striking Jehan down . . . a woman who was and was not herself, whose flesh melted in a dark agony of fire* . . . Shrill laughter seared all the hidden places of her soul.

No—the laughter was Caolin's, crouched on his hands and knees above her while she whimpered and tried to curl away from him. His hand vised her shoulder. Faris shuddered with horror and pity, understanding now what he had done and how it had crippled him. The completeness of his former self-control was the measure of his violence now.

"You are the Dark Lady, come to torment me!" he cried. "I know you, Demoness—you were sent to destroy him, to destroy us both, but I know you now!"

Faris twisted and the thin stuff of her gown tore, freeing one arm. She struck out at him. "I am Faris—Faris the Queen."

He let go of her and sat back staring. His silence held her still.

"No—you cannot be the Queen," he said at last, "for you are flawed, and she was beautiful . . ." His voice had gone utterly without tone.

He has seen my scar! Her moment of comprehension was destroyed by her own hidden fears. Shivering, Faris tried to cover herself with the rags of her gown.

Caolin did not speak, and after a time she forced herself to look at him. He was still kneeling beside her, but the glow had gone from his eyes. Now, his gaze was that of a man who sees a serpent in his path.

"Caolin—" she whispered, but his voice absorbed hers as if he had not heard.

"You *must* serve me now." His calm was more terrible than his rage had been.

Faris sat up. "I am still Queen of Westria, however flawed," she said bitterly. "Have you gone mad, Caolin?" But of course he must be mad, after what he had done.

"Mad?" Caolin laughed gently. "You are the one who drove all your friends away—exiled the Master, earned your brother's hatred, drove Eric to another woman's arms. But it does not matter. I can compel you to do my will . . ."

He lifted his hand so that his ring of office caught the light of the last lamp. Faris stared at the ruby light. He moved it left and right, and her head turned. She understood what was happening now. He had done this to her before, and her will fluttered against his compulsion like a trapped butterfly. But his words resonated in her memory. She could not get free.

"You see?" Caolin laughed again. "Shall I make you walk naked through the streets of Laurelynn, displaying your scar? I have bent your will several times already, so that I could make peace with Palomon . . . you have no defense against me now."

His voice lowered, became more intimate. "Shall I order you to hold your son's arm in the fire? You *will* be mad, then . . ."

Faris stilled, her eyes fixed like a trapped rabbit's on Caolin's ring. In some untouched gulf of her mind her thoughts struggled desperately. *It is true . . . I must have consented or he could not hold me . . .*

She felt the invading pressure of Caolin's will forcing entry, as she had broken through his barriers moments before. She tried to scream as flames filled her inner vision, billowed around her. She heard a child shrieking in terror, saw fire lick at silken garments, fasten on the tender flesh beneath, as she had seen it when she was a child and again when Star was Named.

Lady of Fire, help me! She cast herself forward, beating the flames.

The last of the oil lamps went out.

The fire was gone, and the ruby spark that had held her eyes had disappeared. For a moment Faris blinked stupidly at the darkness. Then she scrambled to her feet and ran, blundering blindly among the trees.

Caolin's harsh laughter followed her. Without understanding she heard him say—"Are you afraid of me, Faris? You should be! I am the boar you saw in your dream! I destroyed Jehan!" He gasped for breath, then called again, "You will obey me, Faris, for the sake of your child!"

Sobbing soundlessly, clutching at the rags of her gown, Faris stumbled toward the Palace, pausing only to retch into the bushes beside the garden door. She pushed through it, then barred it behind her, shutting out the rasp of Caolin's laughter at last.

But she was already forcing herself up the stairs, though the breath seared her throat, not stopping until she reached Star's cradle. In the dim glow of the nightlight she could see the perfect curve of his cheek. His peaceful breathing was the only sound in the room.

Slowly the vision of his flesh blackening in the flames faded away. Faris' hands clenched as she fought the urge to clutch him to her breast. But if she touched him he would sense her agony and cry, and Branwen would come in and ask her what was wrong.

"No. No one must know . . ." Shuddering, she stripped the gems from her neck and ears, wrapped her chamberrobe around her, then locked the door to the adjoining room.

"I could accuse Caolin of rape—" The bruises where he had gripped her were beginning to throb. *If it only had been rape!* She had far rather have had him penetrate her body than this violation of her soul. Her stomach churned as she saw herself as he had pictured her—distorted and vile. *How could Jehan have loved me? How could he have made me Mistress of the Jewels?*

The Jewels!

Faris straightened, fire throbbing along her veins as she remembered their power. *Caolin called me the Dark Lady,* she thought, *now he shall see the Dark Lady indeed!* Unsteadily she went to her dressing room, and opened the redwood Jewel chest. She fumbled at the green silk covering of the Jewel of Fire.

There was only a chunk of serpentine.

Unbelieving, Faris snatched away the cloths that had wrapped the other Jewels, and found only stones. Had the Master of the Junipers taken them to be revenged on her? Or was it Caolin?

The room blurred. Her knees betrayed her, but Faris scarcely realized that she was falling. Her body grew rigid as her anguish exploded in a soundless scream.

In the Inn of the New Moon on the southern road, Farin woke suddenly, eyes straining to pierce the darkness, quivering with his sister's pain.

As the force of the call faded and the pounding of his heart eased, Farin thrust aside the cloak in which he had wrapped himself to sleep. He must return to Laurelynn.

Trying not to wake the other sleepers in the chamber, he picked up his pack and harpcase and started toward the door. He turned back to leave on his bed a few coins from the handful he had earned singing that evening, then opened the door carefully and went down the stairs.

Soon he was on the road to Laurelynn, shivering and searching the east for any sign of dawn.

The Master of the Junipers cried out in his sleep, then sat up, hands to his ears as if he could shut out the dreadful cry which his had echoed.

Faris! I must go to her!

Once more he seemed to see the tormented face with which she had sent him away, and he heard his own voice once more—*"Only remember your own words when you despair and call out for me, for I shall not be here . . ."*

He rested his face in his hands. He was days from Laurelynn. For good or ill, by the time he could reach Faris, whatever danger threatened her would be past. She needed help now. It had been a long time since he had asked anything from the Lord of Light. Did he dare pray for someone else? But he had abandoned care for his own life when he sought this wilderness. What happened to him did not matter now.

The Master composed his limbs for meditation, sent his spirit questing inward. He flinched at the drop into darkness, but he did not resist it now.

The abyss was measureless. After a time his own name was lost to him, and all memory of light as well, but still he held to the image of Faris. And then there came a moment when he was at rest. Warm darkness opened to receive him, and then at last he released consciousness of himself, and of her, and was free.

From the interaction of light and darkness the world is born . . .

The forest was beginning to emerge from shadow as light grew somewhere in the east of the world. The Master of the Junipers started, becoming aware of his own self-awareness, then he smiled.

Oh Mother of Darkness, help Faris now . . .

The darkness that had engulfed her lifted gradually. Faris forced herself to get up, shivering in her sweat-soaked robe. But her spirit hovered somewhere beyond the nausea and the cold and the fear, in a detached clarity in which mind and soul possessed an eternity in which to consider what she must do.

"I cannot let anyone know that the Jewels are gone—if the Master of the Junipers has them they will be safe, but Caolin would use my lack of care as more evidence of my madness . . ."

And he would be right, too, responded her inner commentator.

"And if Caolin has the Jewels . . ." For a moment she could not find words to express the consequences of that. In their brief traumatic touching of minds, she had seen enough to know that Caolin was now a sorcerer.

The Jewels tempted me to become the Lady of Darkness— to what would they tempt Caolin?

Faris shook her head. "I could take to my bed again, but how long could I refuse to see him? As soon as we met he would bind my will and I would be lost."

The Master of the Junipers warned you of this when he begged you to continue your training. You can barely barrier lesser minds, and Caolin may be even stronger than the Master!

"I wish I had died giving birth to Star—no one could have made use of me then!" The dark waters of the lake would give her rest.

And everyone would conclude you had gone mad from grief, and who would protect Star from Caolin?

No—whatever solution she found, it must protect Star and it must protect Westria. If her own survival were necessary to achieve these goals, then it would have to protect her as well.

Faris went back into her bedroom, needing to reassure herself that Star was still safe, then turned to the window. She shivered in the cool air, wondering how much time remained until dawn. She coughed and turned away.

"I have acted foolishly in the past, and who would believe my word against Caolin's? I must find a way to discredit him and prove my sanity!"

Suddenly Faris recalled Caolin's boast that he had destroyed the King. She forced her mind back to the events surrounding Jehan's death. She pushed damp strands of hair back from her face and reached for his Journal, seeking the final pages that she had never dared to read. The King had written a great deal after the boar had struck him down.

Oh my beloved! she thought, reading, *I saw you as a god—would you have been happier if you could have admitted to me that you were only a man?*

She went on, slowing as she reached Jehan's discovery of Caolin's treachery.

"Even then Caolin wanted power!" she exclaimed, her hands clenching on the book. "Sweet Lady! Why did Jehan leave me and the kingdom in that man's hands?"

She came to the last entry, whose writing wavered weakly, distorted by pain as if it had been written in the King's blood. *Because he loved him* . . . came the answer then. Faris reread the words aloud.

> My watchers sleep. How long have I been wandering? No—it is the fever, now . . . Where are you, Caolin? I touched your soul—But you are still there, and your soul burns like a coal in the ashes.
>
> Fire burns veils from my eyes. I did not mean to give you the leavings of my love. I loved you and Faris differently. What could we three have done together if I had only understood in time?
>
> I will give you my power and my Queen—even set my land in the balance to redeem the harm I have done. You and Faris must save each other, Caolin!

When she had finished, Faris closed the book, for Jehan had written no more. Then she cast herself on her bed and wept at last, for Jehan, for herself, and for Caolin.

"I tried—my dear, I tried! I would have loved him, Jehan . . ." she whispered brokenly. "And now your agony binds me. How can I save Star and the kingdom without destroying Caolin?"

Outside a bird twittered then fell silent again. Soon others would wake to herald the sun, and the moment when her decision must be made.

"If I learned to use the powers the Master always said I had, Caolin could harm neither me nor the child," she said at last. "But even at the College of the Wise we would be vulnerable to him or to others who might wish to use us in a struggle for control. There is only one place where I could study in safety. Awahna . . ." The lamp flared as if the name had given it new life.

"I will go to Awahna and leave Caolin with no competitor. For his own sake he will guard Westria. But he must not be too secure, so I will tell no one where I have gone!"

She choked down laughter, began to search hastily for the things she would need. Rummaging through chests, she thrust her silken gowns aside, for she was not going as a Queen. She took the plain tunic she had worn at the College of the Wise to serve as shirt and petticoat, and an old skirt and worn boots and a brown shawl of Branwen's.

What else? She scooped chains and bangles from the gem chest to trade for food upon the road. In a separate compartment she found the King's ring. Kissing it, she hung it around her neck on the chain with the golden cross that Jehan had given her.

Faint sucking noises came from the cradle, then ceased as Star found his thumb, but that would not satisfy him long. Quickly she folded a rough blanket lengthwise on the bed, began packing it with diapers and baby gowns.

Star whimpered. Faris stopped her work and forced herself to calm as she sat down to nurse him, rocking him gently as her mind cast back and forth over what she had done. Would it be enough to disappear? Should she leave some kind of clue for those with eyes to see?

When the baby was done, Faris changed and dressed him and laid him back in his cradle, where he followed her movements with bright dark eyes. Night was fading now. Birds sang cheerfully in the orchard. She picked up Jehan's Journal and tore free the pages on which she had recorded her dreams. To the last one she added a single line—

"Caolin has shown me the meaning of my dreams."

She placed the papers on the table. Then she tied the blanket roll and slung it behind her, drew the shawl over her head, and looked in her mirror a final time. With her greying hair braided down her back and the coarse shawl shading her face, she looked like a peasant woman old before her time. No one would connect her with the fair young Queen of Westria of whom bards sang.

Then she tucked Star in his blanket, and went out, leaving the door ajar. The eastern sky was brightening to gold. Faris felt her heart lift, fancying she saw the light of Awahna shining before her. Nothing could hinder her now, for at last she was going where she wanted to be. She smiled, remembering how she had dreamed that she set a laurel seedling in her garden, then carried it east to escape a storm and replanted it in the mountains where it grew strong and tall. Though he might never know it, Caolin had shown her the meaning of her second dream as well.

The sun lifted over the rim of the Ramparts a hundred miles away, and Faris and her child passed unnoticed through the gates of Laurelynn.

XI
The Trial

"My Lord I am sorry, but the Queen cannot be found." The Captain of the Guard of Laurelynn bowed and took a step backward.

"You are sorry!" Caolin turned on him, "She must be *somewhere!* Are your men blind? Surely in one day and a half a woman carrying a child could not get far. Send men to search all of the main roads within a day's ride of Laurelynn, and all the by-ways as well!"

"Yes, my Lord." The guardsman's brick-colored uniform jerkin was already darkening with perspiration. "But we have searched already . . ." he began, then faltered as the Seneschal rose from his chair. "Yes, my Lord Seneschal—we will look again!" Sweating, he backed out of the room.

I must find her before she tells anyone . . . Though the afternoon heat throbbed in the room Caolin shivered, remembering how his memories had been drawn from him when Faris touched his body, and his soul.

"My Lord Seneschal, I have couriers waiting if the messages are prepared." Another man stood in the doorway.

Caolin looked inquiringly at Ercul Ashe, whose pen completed a flourish as he nodded, folded the paper and added it to the pile on his desk.

"They are ready," said the Deputy. "One for each of the Free Cities." He stood, absently massaging his writing hand, while the man clattered down the stairs. The offices around them throbbed with orders and speculations, while the city buzzed like an overturned hive whose queen has been removed. A thousand voices repeated a thousand variations on the same refrain—

The Lady Faris is not in Laurelynn . . . The Queen and her child have disappeared . . .

"Should I begin to draft the formal proclamation now, my Lord?" The cool voice of Ercul Ashe breached Caolin's abstraction.

"What? Oh yes—I suppose we must tell them something." The Seneschal ran his fingers distractedly through his hair. Where would Faris seek help?

Caolin straightened. "Find someone who knows the cabin of the Master of the Junipers on the Lady Mountain and send him to look there!"

The Deputy nodded and called to one of the clerks who was waiting in the hall. Caolin felt the office spin around him and realized that he had not eaten since the day before. He poured wine and raised the goblet to his lips, but he could not drink.

If she had left a note accusing me I would be in chains by now . . . Caolin grimaced. *Why didn't Faris accuse me? Does she think that uncertainty will make me betray myself?*

He closed his eyes, but he could not forget Faris' pinched face or the disfiguration of her arm. She was flawed, he reminded himself. She should never have been made Queen.

Did I sense that Jehan had suffered some contamination? He wondered suddenly. *Was that why I destroyed him? It was her fault, then . . .*

"They found nothing when they dragged the lake . . . no trace of the Queen in the City at all . . ." said Ercul Ashe, the faintest question in his tone. Caolin rested his head in his hands, ignoring him. Where was Faris? What more could he do to locate her?

He had sent a message pigeon to one of his agents in the south the previous evening, when someone had at last told him that Faris was gone. He hoped that it would reach Ordrey. Gerol was with him—until they returned he could not even set the great wolf on the Queen's trail!

"It is strange that the Queen should have run off this way . . ." Ercul Ashe spoke again. "But illness can unhinge the mind. Did she seem well, that night?"

Caolin slowly lifted his head, staring at the other man as Gerol would have considered a trapped hare. "The Queen was quite unharmed when she left me. I do not know where she has gone. And I never lie . . ." he replied in a still voice. All the frustrations of the past two days focused on the Deputy's curious face.

"I spent half the morning repeating this to Lord Robert of the Ramparts while he wrung his hands because he did not know what to do." Caolin's voice gained in volume as he leaned across the desk. "And now, little man, will you make yourself my questioner?" he roared, easing around the desk toward Ercul Ashe, who scuttled for the door, his composure shattered at last.

The Seneschal stopped short as the door slammed, leaning on the desk with rigid arms. Pain throbbed at the base of his skull. He started to lick dry lips and discovered that his mouth had been contorted in a snarl. He shook his head, trying to evade the pain. All his energy had focused on finding Faris. But what would happen when she was found?

I destroyed Jehan . . . I swore to serve Faris and the child as I had served the King . . . I never lie . . .

Caolin's head drooped until his fair hair brushed the top of the desk and he groaned, knowing that once he had found them his own oath bound him to kill both Faris and her child. But no one must ever know—his own survival, Westria's security, depended on forever concealing what had become of the lost Queen.

Faris pushed her way through the willow branches to the edge of the road, coughing in the red dust that billowed around her, watching the diminishing figure of the horseman who had raised it.

"They are still looking for us—" she told Star, hitching him up against her shoulder. She shivered inwardly, wondering what instructions Caolin had given his messengers. She had to get off the road, to find someplace where she did not need to fear each passer-by.

"We should look for a place to spend the night . . ." she said stoutly. "I had hoped that we could stay with some farmer, but it is not safe yet, so soon, and so close to the road." She sighed, looking around her.

The haze of dust lent substance to the long rays of rosy light that slanted across the Valley from the western hills. There was a red-gold sparkle from among the reeds to her right where the Darkwater meandered in its shallow bed. If she followed it a little longer she would come to the fork where the Mercy rushed down from the mountains to join it, and the beginning of the Pilgrim's Road. Then she would be safe.

But she was not there yet, and though a ride from a farmer had shortened today's journey, she was still weak from a year's soft living. She had awakened aching in every muscle after a night on the damp ground, and her cough was back again. Tonight she could hope for no more than some thicket that might shelter herself and her child from the dew.

Faris climbed down from the raised roadbed, and began to make her way across the fields. Her skirts swished softly against the golden stalks of wild oats whose grainheads were already ripe enough to catch in the rough cloth as she went by. She breathed in the aromatic scent of sun-cured hay and was reminded of the fields around her home. Slowly, something in Faris' spirit began to ease. The drowsy silence of the land filled her until, like the world around her, she was ready for the evening's rest. She thought that though she had known both ecstacy and great grief within the past year, since she had met Jehan she had not known peace.

The golden land stretched before her, glowing as if it had absorbed the light along with the heat of the sun. It was as she had seen it from the peak of the Father of Mountains a year ago. But then she had been looking down on the earth. Now she was a part of it, and this small part which she could see yet encompassed the whole.

For a moment she forgot to move, suspended in the stillness, awareness turned inward as she sought a knowledge that barely eluded her grasp.

Awahna . . . Awahna was there—if only . . .

And then Star nuzzled against her neck and the moment was gone.

"Oh my baby . . . we shall have to take the long way after all!" she whispered, her eyes blurring with tears.

It was then that she noticed before her the overgrown wheelruts of a road. Curious, she followed its windings towards a clump of Valley Oaks. They framed a small building of whitewashed adobe, roofed with a motheaten thatching of reeds. But there were new patches of plaster on the walls. Someone still cared for the place, old though it was.

Cautiously, Faris opened the door. She blinked at darkness and a blaze of light which gradually resolved themselves into a shadowed entry and an alcove lit by a window that faced west. Her steps echoed on the worn tiles as she moved forward, trying to make out the hint of color on the farther wall.

Then the angle of the sun changed and the colors flared to life before her—a fresco showing a man, dressed simply in a robe of an adept, holding a staff as if he were a shepherd or a King. The artist had painted shadows behind him the better to display his aura of light. There were wounds in his hands and feet, and his eyes were like those of the Master of the Junipers. But his bearing was Jehan's.

Faris laid Star gently upon the low altar and bowed, for she recognized that she had come to a shrine of the Guardian of Men.

"Fair Lord, I thank you for this hospitality and ask your favor for my child . . ." she murmured, then stood silent until through closed eye-lids she felt the light fade with the setting of the sun and the Presence that had glowed within her awareness recede.

She straightened and carried Star to the other end of the little room, where she spread her blanket and left him while she gathered wood and cooked a simple meal of porridge and dried fruit. In the stillness of the night she dreamed that the Guardian had come down from the wall and was standing beside her, holding out his hand. He led her to an opening in the mountains where grey cliffs rose like pillars to an azure sky.

She had been there in her dreams, walking with Jehan.

But now the Master of the Junipers waited to welcome her. She ran toward him, laughing, *You see, I have found the way at last* . . . and opened her eyes to the golden light of dawn.

Sunlight filled Eric's chamber, but it was no brighter than the light in his eyes when he looked at Rosemary. Farin rested his forehead against the polished curve of his harp, repressing an urge to strike the happiness from those two glowing faces, as if they had no right to joy, with Faris gone.

"It's almost as if she knew something was going to happen to her—" said Rosemary softly, "and wanted to see us settled first . . ." Eric turned to her and lifted her hand to his lips.

"Faris is *not dead!*" said Farin. "Don't talk as if she were!"

Eric's face was troubled as he looked down at him. "Well, of course we all *want* to think she's alive—but the search has gone on for six fruitless days! How can you be so sure?"

Farin rested his chin on the harp and frowned. "There's something—a thread of awareness—between us. I felt her despair the night she disappeared. I would feel the pain of her death. Oh why did I go away?!" His fist struck the window sill beside him and he looked at it in surprise as the numbness gave way to pain.

Eric sighed. They had gone over all this too many times.

"She must have run away . . ." Farin continued after a little while. "She did that after our mother died." He sent a bitter glance at Branwen. "If you had given the alarm immediately—" he began.

"I didn't want to cause talk!" she exclaimed. "The Queen needed no more gossip about her odd ways . . . and when I found that Rosemary was not in *her* rooms I thought they had gone out together and forgotten to leave word!"

She looked reproachfully at Rosemary, who blushed and glanced self-consciously at Eric. Some detached part of Farin's awareness noted that he had been right to think love would make Rosemary beautiful. Even the flush of heat and the pearling of perspiration on her forehead did not diminish her new splendor.

He sighed, running his hand along the smooth curve of the harp. *But to me, Swangold is fairer still,* he thought. He had not believed that he could miss a mere instrument so much. Even if he had to paint over her gold to disguise her, when he took the road once more he would not leave her behind.

Farin stopped the thought, surprised to realize how naturally he assumed that he would be going away again. *Well, until I find Faris, there is no life for me in Laurelynn . . .*

He forced his attention back to the conversation.

"Caolin must know *something*—" exclaimed Branwen. "The concertmaster told me he left them alone together . . ."

"At Faris' request," answered Rosemary. "And the concertmaster would be quick to air any suspicions—he doesn't like the Seneschal."

They all jumped as a soft knocking rattled the door. Eric swung it wide, peering down the shadowed staircase. Farin stiffened as a shape materialized from the shadows—grey robe and greyer hair. He recognized Ercul Ashe.

The man eased into the room and looked behind him. "Is anybody there?" he asked anxiously. "I don't think I was seen."

"Why?" asked Farin, coming up to him and taking his arm. "Are you suspected?" His heart had begun to pound heavily in his breast. The Deputy had never been willing to come to him before.

"No . . . I am sure my lord is too distracted to think of me." Ashe sat down in the chair Eric offered him. "And yet—

I cannot tell *what* to be sure of anymore!"

"Is it the Queen?" asked Rosemary urgently, "Has Caolin—"

"What? No—I'd swear he is as desperate to find her as any of you. After all, his authority depends on his status as her minister."

Farin swallowed. "But you have learned something—" he asked softly, "something that we must know . . ."

"I think—" Ercul Ashe looked up at them with tormented eyes, and his voice became a thread of sound, "I think that my Lord Caolin has become a sorcerer!"

Farin repressed an urge to laugh. After all, *something* had frightened the little man.

"What has he done?" asked Eric, who did not seem to find it funny at all.

"Is it not sorcery to wear another shape than your own?" said Ercul Ashe.

Farin felt the hairs lift on his neck.

"He was angry with me for asking too many questions," the Deputy explained. "I thought he was going to strike me, and then it was not Caolin, but a wolf preparing to spring . . . I thought it was my imagination, then . . ."

"But not now?"

"No. Not since I remembered how people have mocked me, saying they saw me at times and in places I had no memory of. So I questioned them . . ." he forced out the words. "Now, I think that the Lord Caolin sometimes goes about in my shape instead of his own.

"He has *used* me! He has used my face and my reputation to serve his need without my knowledge or my will. I was only a convenience . . ." Lines etched in his face by years of dutiful service were dissolving under this strain.

Farin swallowed and looked away, not wanting to see the older man's shame. He wondered, *How would I feel if my lord had defiled my loyalty so?*

"But Master Ercul—why would he do that?" asked Eric at last.

The Deputy Seneschal sighed. "I can think of one reason. For a time I had meetings with an agent of Prince Palomon's— nothing treasonous—it was only to feed false information to Elaya!" he added, seeing the look on Eric's face.

"When war was declared my lord told me to stop going, and I was glad. But—" he looked around the circle of intent faces, "the keeper of the Inn of the Three Laurels tells me that I continued the meetings until after the peace talks, when Prince Palomon returned to Elaya!"

Eric was pacing back and forth like a caged mountain lion. "I always thought that Palomon's apology came too easily—" he observed harshly. "What do you suppose Caolin promised in return?"

"Unless we find written evidence we will never know," said Rosemary.

"And unless we can prove that Caolin is playing at sorcery, all the witnesses in Laurelynn can only swear that they have seen Ercul Ashe!" Farin objected.

Rosemary leaned against the window ledge, her bright hair backlit by the afternoon light. "I wish the Master of the Junipers were here. He would know what powers the Seneschal has . . ."

"What about the Mistress of the College?" offered Branwen. "When the Council meets in two weeks she will be here. Could she examine Caolin?"

"I hardly dare ask her—" said Rosemary, biting her lip, "and if Caolin has become so powerful, I wonder if she would succeed."

Farin moved away from them, feeling suddenly cold. Had Caolin used sorcery on Faris? He had imagined the Seneschal strangling her secretly and bundling her body into the lake . . . But what if mental violence had caused that anguished cry?

I would have protected her! he thought, and then, *But I was not here . . .*

"I must go—" said Ercul Ashe. "I am expected."

"You have done more than we could have hoped!" exclaimed Rosemary. "Be careful—you must not let Caolin suspect your change in loyalties."

The Deputy Seneschal got stiffly to his feet, drawing dignity around him. "My loyalties have not changed," he said simply. "I serve Westria."

Some impulse of responsibility drew Farin to accompany him down the stairs and watch him disappear into the crowd. As the young man turned to go in a man with the bearing of a soldier limped by, leaning on his companion's arm. They were singing—

> *"Alone with the ravens, a warrior lies wounded—*
> *He is shaking with fever, his blood stains the ground.*

> *He groans with the burden of farewells unspoken,*
> *Knowing not if by friend or by foe he'll be*
>   *found . . ."*

Farin's lament for Brian had come to Laurelynn.

Faris laid the back of her hand against her forehead, then readjusted her broadbrimmed hat against the sun. Did she have a fever? Her skin was hot and dry, but so was the air she breathed. Sun striking the rock cliffs to either side of the road made a furnace of the arroyo the Mercy had cut through the hills.

Her pony stumbled and Faris pulled him up with one hand, clutching automatically with the other at Star, who lay bound against her by her shawl. She had bought the beast, and her hat, at a holding near the town of Gateway with the last of her silver bangles, but though riding had eased her feet the animal walked no faster than she could, and its jolting gait made her ache in every bone.

But she had seen no searchers for several days. Had they forgotten her already? She coughed harshly and dug her heels into the pony's sides.

For four days she had followed the Pilgrim's Road through the billows of the foothills where the crimson of the earth overpowered the dull green of the occasional live-oaks or pines. But the mountains rose ahead of her now, ridge upon shadowed ridge of fir and spruce and pine.

Faris groped for the exaltation that had sustained her at the beginning of her journey, but it had been drained from her by the endless weary days. Now the road was climbing steadily while the gorge became deeper and the cliff fell away abruptly to where the Mercy frothed white over the rocks far below. The height brought a welcome breeze, but Faris' head still ached dully, and she blinked at the glare. She looked down, and dizzied, closed her eyes again.

If I were to fall no one would see. No one would ever know what had become of me . . . Faris shivered then and hoped it was from fear. Star squirmed and protested, and she forced herself to loosen her grip on him.

"I cannot be ill! I must not—not now! What would happen to you?" she cried. "I have been traveling too hard, that is all. I have been on the road for almost two weeks. I should find somewhere to rest. Awahna cannot be so very far away!"

But the thin air of the mountains seared her lungs, and the road wound onward to the end of the world.

"The Lord of All be thanked that the testimony is over—I thought they would be thinking up new excuses for not finding Faris till the end of the age!" Rosemary leaned back against the painted pillar that supported the porch of the Council Hall and sighed.

"I am thanking the Lord for you, Rosemary!" said Eric seriously. "If you had not asked your father to suggest a noon recess, Caolin might be Regent by now. Of course Lady Alessia and I would have voted against him, but I don't know about the others. He made it sound like such a *reasonable* suggestion . . ."

Rosemary laughed. Farin hoisted himself up on the railing and sat kicking his heels against the rungs. The rose-colored bricks of Laurelynn looked faded in the noon glare. It had been three weeks since Faris disappeared.

"This afternoon's debate will decide it for good," he said slowly. Too vividly, he remembered how the Seneschal had looked, with his fair hair cut precisely to skim the little upstanding collar of his loose linen robe. He had not seemed to notice the heat, thought Farin, feeling perspiration make a rivulet down his back.

"I think that Caolin has made a mistake," said Rosemary. "Given time to think about it, people who tolerated him as Seneschal may not want to see him on the Regent's throne."

"I hope so," answered Farin. Men and women were still coming out of the Council Hall, talking excitedly. Farin fanned himself with his loose sleeve, wishing the clouds banked in the west would cut off the sun, or build up to a storm—anything to break the tension that had been building all day.

"But can a Regent function without Caolin? *I* would not want the job!" exclaimed Eric, running his fingers through his tumbled hair.

"We expected Faris to do that job," Farin said bitterly, "and to bear her grief for Jehan as she bore his child." He felt suddenly chilled and alone. *Oh my sister . . . will you ever forgive me for deserting you?*

"There's always Robert . . ." muttered Eric. "He might do it if there were no other acceptable choice, and if someone testified against Caolin. Oh, I know I promised not to call on Ercul Ashe unless I could protect him from his master," he answered Rosemary's worried frown, "but if Caolin remains in power I cannot help his Deputy, and without the little man's evidence how can we break the Seneschal's power?"

"*We* may not have to . . . look!" Farin pointed to a slash of crimson that wove through the multi-colored tapestry of the crowd—Caolin and his staff crossing the courtyard to the Chancery. But people were edging away from them. Farin could feel their suspicion, their curiosity. Someone cried out, "Remember the Dragon Waste!" Then they heard a snatch of song that strengthened until the words of the chorus came clear.

> *"Oh where is our Lady, who once walked in beauty?*
> *And where is the Star who brought hope to our sky?*
> *Oh ask the red spider who spins in the City—*
> *With so many secrets, perhaps he knows why . . ."*

Farin saw Caolin stop and stare around him until he in turn recognized the group on the porch. Farin clutched at Eric's arm, shaken by the malice in the Seneschal's eyes.

"It's not fair—" he breathed between fear and laughter. "I didn't even write that verse to the song . . ."

The people fell silent, watching Caolin pass, remote and lordly, seeming equally oblivious of their praise or blame.

"What would they do if they thought he might become Regent over them?" asked Eric, frowning.

Farin bit his lip. His stomach was bitter with the knowledge that the journey which had cost him his chance to help Faris had not even bought anonymity. Not that it mattered anymore . . . The place in his soul that had been empty since the death of the King was filling now with hatred for Caolin.

Fragments of new verses began to surface in his mind and the world steadied around him. "I will tell them," he said, smiling thinly. "And I think that Caolin may soon be very sorry he asked for that job."

"No—you must not."

Farin looked around and realized that Branwen had joined them. He wondered how long she had been there.

Her tone sharpened. "You know that the Seneschal never forgets an injury. Let someone else bring him down!"

Farin swallowed. Branwen had grasped his arm and he was uncomfortably aware of her body. He could not help but remember the night before the boar hunt when he had lain with

LADY OF DARKNESS

her. But that did not explain the terror in her eyes.

"Somebody must try," he spoke as gently as he could. "Would you rather that Caolin's anger fell on *them?*" He gestured toward Eric and Rosemary.

"Yes!" hissed the girl. Her blush had paled and every blemish showed on her sallow skin.

Farin pulled his arm from her grip, understanding now why he had been avoiding her. Her desire stifled him, heavier than the humid air. She not only wanted his body, she wanted *him*.

"I will be safe enough. I am leaving Laurelynn to search for my sister as soon as this Council is done."

Spots of color flared on Branwen's cheeks. "I thought I had only your harp to compete with. I should have known that my real rival was the Queen."

"You had what you wanted—" Farin replied furiously. "And that was as much as any woman will get from me!"

His hatred for Caolin, his guilt for having failed Faris, his love for the golden harp, merged in a single moment of vision in which his future stretched before him like a fair white road. Thrusting Branwen away, Farin jumped down from the porch and began to push through the crowd.

The people of Westria moved to let him pass, whispering his name. Farin began to smile, memory of his quarrel already fading. For the crowds would still be waiting when he returned with his harp—waiting for him to move them to his will as he played for them.

Caolin considered the councilors of Westria enthroned on the eight sides of the Council floor, and the representatives of their Estates who sat on the rising benches behind them.

How shall I move them? he wondered. *How shall I shape them to my will?* He rose with the others as the great horn was blown and the Council declared to be in session once more.

Now . . . he thought, feeling his mouth dry and the blood tingle in his veins. Was this how Jehan or Brian had felt, facing their foes across a battlefield?

"This morning we discussed mounting a search for the Queen that would cover the entire kingdom," said Caolin. "Since this must affect all of your territories, I would like to request the Council's authorization." He looked at them inquiringly. *And when they find her?* He shied from memory of the orders he had given Ordrey.

"I thought that this morning we were discussing the Regency, my Lord Seneschal," Alessia observed tartly. Her basilisk eyes glittered beneath the dark fires of her hair. "There is still a motion to be voted on."

Caolin suppressed a sigh. He had hoped to distract them from that, since his move to gain power in name as well as in deed had failed. He shrugged deprecatingly. "It was proposed as a matter of convenience. But it was my understanding that the Council felt it too soon to consider such a move."

"Yes, surely it is too soon," said Lord Robert eagerly, looking up from his study of the polished slates on the floor. "It is barely three weeks since the Queen . . . went away."

Caolin sniffed. If Robert was his competitor for the Regency he was certainly not enjoying the prospect. In the silence Caolin caught the sound of singing from outside the Hall. His glance went to the bench behind the Queen's throne from which Sir Farin had glowered at him for the past three days. The young fool! He should have taken steps to silence him . . .

Now Lord Eric was on his feet, looking to Rosemary for reassurance as he cleared his throat. "My Lords and Ladies of Westria—at the final Council of our King, Jehan named the Lady Faris as Regent for their child. But he added that if anything should go amiss, we must decide for the future ourselves."

Jehan! Caolin's glance fled to the shaft of brilliance that fell from the skylight of the Council Hall to the empty hearth on the floor, but he saw only the light of midwinter illuminating the worn beauty of Jehan's face. *Oh my dear Lord . . . why did you leave me alone?*

"This kingdom must have a leader who is chosen by law, not by default. Let us decide now!" Eric cried.

Caolin began to frown, but Frederic Sachs was on his feet almost before Eric had sat down, and the Seneschal relaxed again. A judicious combination of flattery and fear had made the man his servant long ago.

"You were the Queen's champion, my young Lord—do you now fancy the mantle of the King?"

Eric reddened. There was a spurt of malicious laughter from some in the crowd as Sachs went on. "Surely our Lord Seneschal, who has borne the weight of the kingdom since the King died, is best fitted to wield this power. Let him be confirmed in it!"

Sachs looked to Caolin for approval and the Seneschal tried to smile. But he realized that there was no way to avoid debating the Regency now. He winced inwardly as Lady Alessia took the floor.

"My fellow Councillors, I have felt closer to the Queen than any of you can understand, now that I guard my own son's heritage. But for that reason I can afford no sentiment. You see the empty places here which last year held so many good men." She gestured around the Hall at the gaps on the benches.

"Do you of the cities wish to take their places, as you accuse Lord Eric of wanting another's power? I do not believe so—" said Alessia, "I believe we were all equally grieved by the battle in which my lord was slain. Now we are weakened and when Elaya attacks us again we will need a warrior at our head."

Eric stood again. "The Guardian of Men knows that I have no desire for *anything* that was the King's!" he stammered, his eyes on Rosemary. "I would not take the Regency if you offered it to me. But I agree with the Lady of Las Costas. I would willingly follow my Lord Theodor, who is senior among us, or Lord Robert, who was our Commander in the war."

"A Commander who let half his army be slain?" shouted someone.

"Through following a plan suggested by Caolin's Deputy!" snapped Alessia.

Caolin felt movement behind him, but knew he must not turn.

"I didn't know . . . I didn't know . . ."

The Seneschal stiffened, recognizing the voice of Ercul Ashe.

"Be still, man," whispered one of his companions. "No one has accused you."

"No. I am lost . . ."

Caolin's hands clenched. The hysterical fool! Swiftly he cast back, trying to remember whether Ashe knew anything that might be damaging. The Deputy had been a clerk in the Office of the Seneschal when he himself took service there. For years he had been Caolin's most trusted assistant. No one must question him!

"Nay, my Lady—I accepted the plan," said Robert heavily. "The responsibility is mine. Yet Lord Eric spoke well. I will give my allegiance to my Lord of the Corona, if he will take the job."

Forgetting Ercul Ashe, Caolin leaned forward. It was coming now, for surely no one would choose a man who needed a staff to rise from his chair!

Theodor straightened in his seat as if his dead youth were returning to him. After a moment he smiled.

"I am grateful for your confidence, but even if the Council should offer it, I must not take this role. Last year Brian spoke of the dangers of having a lord who knew only some of his lands. I opposed his solution to that problem, but his analysis does apply to me," he sighed. "The Corona is so far from the kingdom's center that I could not serve as Regent without neglecting it. And I have passed the best of my fighting days. You will need a younger man to lead you—a man who continues to struggle even in the face of defeat because that is where his duty lies."

Lord Theodor levered himself to his feet. His eyes lingered for a moment on the empty thrones of the King and Queen of Westria, then he turned. "I propose to you, therefore, that Lord Robert of the Ramparts be made Regent of this kingdom until such time as we find the Queen or her son."

There was a tense silence when he was done. Caolin stared at dust motes whirling in the sunlight, thinking furiously. Who would have believed the old man could refuse? Now Robert would be forced to agree—already he sat with his head bowed beneath the weight of his approaching responsibility.

Who could trust so unwilling a candidate? wondered Caolin. *Is it so wrong for me to want the power? I could use it so well for Westria!*

The other members of the Council and their followers were watching him, now, in a stillness that extended even to the crowd outside. Caolin nodded.

"I believe that it is now my duty to call for a vote." He was a little surprised that his voice should be so even. As he looked from face to face, he wished he could have just a few moments alone with each of them before their choice was made. With his knowledge, and perhaps the help of the dark fire in his ring, surely he could compel support from them! But numbers protected them now.

"Is it the will of this Council that a new Regent for Westria be chosen at this time? And if so, who shall this Regent be?" Caolin took a deep breath and turned to the Lady Alessia, on his left.

"I vote to make Lord Robert Regent now," she said flatly.

Well, the Seneschal had expected that. "Master Sachs?" he asked.

"The Free Cities choose the Lord Caolin."

"My Lord Eric?"

"Robert was my Commander—I'll serve him again," said Eric quickly.

Caolin's eyes slid past the King's empty chair directly across the Council floor from his own, and he bowed to Lord Theodor. "As you made this proposal I assume that you vote for Robert?" he asked ironically, and hated Theodor when the old man nodded and smiled.

"And the College?" Caolin's heart began to pound as he considered the dark, ambiguous face of its Mistress. She, alone of that company, might have been able to compel truth from him. She was looking at him now with a detachment that was almost sorrow.

"The College of the Wise chooses the Lord of the Ramparts."

Because you can rule him as you will never rule me? Caolin bit back the words, turned to Lord Robert last of all.

"And you, my Lord—will you vote for yourself?" he asked gently.

"How can I feel worthy of this task?" Robert exclaimed. "Let me abstain!"

"How embarrassing . . ." said Caolin, striving to hide the hope that struggled for birth. *Perhaps, even now . . .*

He went on, "I must agree with you. And I think that when the Queen is found she will not be happy to learn that her office was usurped so soon. I vote to delay this decision until another time."

"The tally is three 'ayes', two 'nays' and one abstention," said the clerk. Comment rustled through the Hall like wind in the trees.

"Not much of a majority," murmured Caolin.

"Robert, you must change your mind!" cried Eric. "Listen to the people!"

Subconsciously Caolin had been aware of a mutter like that of an approaching storm. But it was voices, not thunder, whose confusion was settling to a rhythm, a chant . . . Lord Robert's name. In a moment everyone in the Hall was echoing it.

After Caolin had made Palomon sign the peace treaty they

had cheered *him*. *Well,* he thought with a remnant of self-mockery, *Palomon's concessions were as hollow as Robert's victory.* He watched the play of expression on his rival's face—alarm giving way to the grim resignation of a man who turns at last to face his foe.

Robert would not refuse election now. Caolin had but a moment to salvage his plans . . .

"Very well," said the Lord of the Ramparts at last. "I will do it, and may the Guardians of Westria help us all."

"The vote is four 'ayes' to two 'nays,'" said the clerk. "Lord Robert is chosen Regent of Westria."

Before anyone else could move Caolin strode toward Lord Robert. He needed only to convince one person now.

"My Lord Regent! So that there may be no doubt of your election, I do now pledge you my loyalty before the Council and people of Westria!" He moved into the shaft of sunlight, willing them all to see his sincerity.

"For fifteen years I served the King, and I know the weariness of the man who sits *there* . . ." he pointed at the empty throne. "It will not be lighter for Lord Robert because he bears only the staff and not the crown. In all the world there is no land like Westria, where there is such good ground for all the arts of peace to grow!" Caolin turned, addressing each sector. He was a little surprised to realize that he was trembling, for what he was saying was true.

"Our neighbors envy our wealth and our golden fields. And yet there are things here that cannot be defended with the point of a sword . . ." He stared at Eric, wondering if he could understand. Carefully he began to delineate the delicate networks that interwove to form the fabric of Westria, and the precise management that was necessary to balance them.

"Some of this you know, my Lord, for you have ruled a portion of the land—" he turned to Robert again, "but you will have much to learn." He bowed his head. "I think that the decision of this Council is therefore a wise one, for it leaves two to bear the burden which might have borne one down. That is why I offer you my service, my Lord!" He met Lord Robert's tear-bright eyes and forebore to add, *as I gave it to the King.*

Then he waited, schooling his face to show no sign of triumph, while Robert rose and held out his hand. "Caolin . . ."

"No!" shrieked Alessia. "You cannot confirm him, Robert—he is Brian's murderer!"

"No!" came an echo, and Caolin saw Farin standing in the doorway with his harp glittering balefully in his arms. "Faris fled from him in fear!"

"No!" Eric found his voice. "He has betrayed us to Palomon!"

Truth! The accusations struck Caolin as Palomon's arrows had struck Brian. *But there was no proof for them!* Shaking with fear and fury, he looked at Robert in appeal.

The new Regent strode past him onto the polished floor, shouting for silence in a voice that would have carried across a battlefield. It shook the Council Hall, and stilled the ominous humming of the crowd that had followed Farin.

"Those are grave accusations! You have chosen me to lead you, and so I tell you—substantiate them now or be still!" Robert stared. "Well?"

"My Lord was proud and sometimes prejudiced," Alessia spoke in a low voice, "but he did not lie. He told me that Caolin had forged a letter to make the King think him a traitor, and when the Seneschal's men would have murdered him, to save him Jehan went out into the rain and so caught the fever of which he died. And later, before the battle, Caolin swore to Brian that he would contrive his death."

"My Lord Regent, will you believe the ravings of a woman mad with grief?" hissed Caolin. Farin stepped farther into the Hall, and Caolin realized who had been leading the mob outside. Robert turned his anxious gaze on him.

"My sister and I are linked in mind, and the night she disappeared her terror awakened me!" Farin said simply.

"Are you sure you were not awakened by jealousy?" Caolin began.

"But the Seneschal was the last one to see the Queen," interrupted Rosemary. "In the morning there was only the note that said, 'Caolin has shown me the meaning of my dreams . . .' Faris was gone!"

The light that shafted through the windows seemed to have turned to fire. Caolin turned to Rosemary. "And where were you when all this was going on?" he asked silkily. "Why don't you tell us what you and the noble Lord Eric were doing in the bushes while the Queen suffered whatever befell her, alone." He ignored Eric's protests.

"You tell a fine tale to excuse your negligence, but several days' of testimony have proven that it was the Queen's desire to stay with me. By the Lady of Fire, my Lords, why should

I harm her? If Faris were here now you would not dare to deal with me so!"

"Lady Rosemary is my promised wife!" Eric exploded. "Anyone who accuses her of . . . of anything, will answer to me!"

"First you must support your own accusation. I believe . . ." said Robert distastefully. "Can you prove what *you* say?"

Eric exchanged glances with Farin. "I have a witness," he replied, "but I will not ask him to speak unless his safety is guaranteed."

Caolin stiffened. A witness? Witness to what?

Lord Robert frowned. "Very well, he has my protection . . . if he is here . . ."

"I am here . . ." The reply was faint, but Caolin heard it. Others heard too. The Seneschal followed their stares to his own sector of the Hall and saw, white as cheese and shaking like an aspen leaf—Ercul Ashe.

"No! You are mine! Who brought you to this treachery!" Caolin dared not move, for how could he even trust the ground to bear him, now?

"You did, my Lord Seneschal," said the Deputy, steadying. It seemed to Caolin that he was seeing him for the first time, a fragile ugly man who stood as if his spine were steel.

There was no sound as Ercul Ashe came down from the Seneschals' benches to face the Regent of Westria.

"Lord Caolin is a sorcerer who binds men's wills and blinds their eyes," said the Deputy. "I know an innkeeper who will swear that on an evening when I was in my chamber, someone who wore my shape came to his tavern to meet with Palomon's spy!"

"You are so terrified of being charged with betrayal of the plan for the battle of the Dragon Waste that you turn on me!" Caolin fought to keep his voice low, though a roar of outrage was building that threatened to drown out anything he might say. "You would have done better to trust to my protection, Ercul Ashe. *You* suggested the meetings, *you* were the only one who visited Hakim MacMorann, and what proof can *you* offer regarding what you said to him?"

Caolin turned quickly to Lord Robert. "My Lord Regent—" he said wryly, the tone of one adult to another. "Is this all the proof that can be set against fifteen years of service to Westria?

It is insufficient even to bring a case in a court of law!" He stared at the other man, willing his belief, for the fire that had filled the air ran in his blood now, demanding release.

Robert looked at the tumult around them, biting his lip. His face seemed suddenly as grey as his hair.

"You are right . . . there is no proof that can bring you to trial, Caolin," Robert said painfully. "But with the welfare of the kingdom on my shoulders, how can I let you remain in the office you now hold?" He gestured toward the ranks of hostile faces. *"They* will never trust you now, and if I upheld you they would not trust me!"

"No." Caolin shook his head. "You need me too much . . ."

"Caolin, I *must* dismiss you now . . ." Robert was pleading.

The Seneschal stared around him. "And do *all* of you agree?" The air throbbed with dark fire. As the silence grew he looked at them, marking his enemies.

Ercul Ashe, who had betrayed him. Alessia . . . Eric and Rosemary and her old father . . . the Mistress of the College and Frederic Sachs and the rest. He was shaken for a moment by the hatred in Farin's face, the image merging sickeningly with his memory of Faris struggling in his arms. And then he saw the Dark Lady he had embraced on the Red Mountain, and he knew that he was free to use Her power now.

He pulled the chain of office from his neck and flung it to the floor in a clashing of soft gold. "I would have served you to my life's end, but you yourselves have written the fate that will come to you now." With an effort he fought the desire to tell them he held the Jewels of Westria. He had warned them—when they saw their destruction approaching they would know from whom it came.

"You will go then?" asked Robert wonderingly.

"I will go, with no recompense for my services but the holding the Queen promised to whoever interpreted her dream." Caolin felt his smile slipping, and turned hastily.

"But where—" began Robert. "Stop him!" shouted Eric and Farin as one.

"Oh no!" cried Caolin turning on them, "No one shall ever hold me again!" Somebody shrieked and people scuttled out of his path. Power was throbbing in his veins, flaming along every nerve.

As he emerged from the Council Hall he saw sunset on the

streets of Laurelynn, and knew that like himself, the city already burned.

"I am burning . . ." said Faris clearly. "I am burning like Jehan, and soon I shall be consumed and float away." The air glowed around her like fire but she felt no pain.

And then Star began to cry again.

Faris jerked as if waking from sleep, staring around her. It was sunset. Ruddy light glowed on the slabbed trunks of the pines, and laid a golden sheen across the forested slopes below. She was in the mountains. She was sitting on the ground with her back against a tree. She was thirsty.

The baby still whimpered fretfully, but Faris had heard something else and remembered why she had stopped here. Leaving Star nestled in her shawl she crawled toward the rush of the stream, collapsed beside it and put her face into the water, drinking as if she could never be filled. After a little she managed to sit up again, and though the world still held the afterglow of a summer's day, suddenly she was shaking with cold. She coughed, bracing herself against the pain in her chest.

Then she crawled back to Star, and still shivering, put him to her breast. He seized her nipple, sucking painfully, but after a few moments he let go and butted frantically against her chest. Sweat began to run down her face.

"My little love, what shall I do?" She moved him to the other side, feeling the easy tears start as the milk in this breast failed as well, and she could only rock him when he began to cry once more.

Even in her weakness she knew that he was lighter than he had been when their journey began. His face was pinched, and after a few moments he seemed to lose even the strength to wail. Once more the cough tore her chest. She held her arm across her mouth and when she took it away saw that her sleeve was stained with brown.

The road stretched mockingly onward, golden in the sunset light. *Fool's gold* . . . thought Faris bitterly. She recognized her symptoms now, for she had suffered through two bouts of pneumonia as a child.

"We must find people. This road is rutted—someone must live near. They will take care of you . . ." Faris closed her eyes for a moment, marshalling her strength.

When she opened them again the light had deepened. In the sunset hush of the mountains she heard the barking of a dog. Shivering, she began to bind Star clumsily against her breast.

Her horse had wandered off two nights ago, or perhaps it was more, for the days were confused in her memory. But she would not have had the strength to mount it now. She crouched, shaking, fighting the temptation to sink down into the dreamless dark. *Help me* . . . she prayed to that darkness, and then for a little while was still.

"Hullo—"

Painfully, Faris looked up and saw a tow-headed boy about ten years old, with scratched legs and a faded home-dyed tunic stained with berry juice.

"Are you coming to visit us? We don't get many strangers—just pilgrims sometimes, from the towns. I have never been to a town but my father has. He is Gilbert Stonebreaker, and this is Stanesvale." He picked up his basket.

Faris gripped his arm. "Can you help me up?" she croaked, "I am ill—" The boy twitched like a nervous horse but he did not pull away. Awkwardly he helped her to stand and let her lean on him as they made their way down the hill. Dimly she was aware of a log house, the smell of goats and a sudden flurry of dogs. She staggered as the boy broke away from her and stood swaying, clutching at Star and praying that she would not fall.

"Mother, mother—there's a sick old woman with a baby—come and see!"

Faris felt strong arms go around her and forced herself to look up into a woman's face, with weather-ripened cheeks and merry eyes.

"Milk . . ." she whispered. "I must have milk for the child." The effort to speak rasped her chest and she began to cough. She let them take the baby from her, feeling rather than understanding the kindness in the woman's stream of words.

Then she closed her eyes and let the darkness surge over her at last.

Shadows leaped like demons from Caolin's lamp to the room's dark corners as he pulled out another drawer of files and began to add its contents to the heap on the floor. Somewhere men were shouting. Caolin stiffened, but the sound faded. His muscles eased and he began his work again. They had hunted him through the streets of Laurelynn while he took shape after shape to confuse them, misdirecting them at last to the eastern road.

Soon he would take the opposite direction. They would not think to look for him on the Red Mountain. He had come here one last time for his books, and to destroy anything that might set them on his trail.

That had been his intention. But that was not what he had done.

Caolin looked at the sheaf of papers in his hand—his notes on the officers of Rivered. They were Lord Robert's men, but he doubted that the Lord of the Ramparts possessed such knowledge of their background and performance, their ambitions and their secret sins, as he had collected here.

"All this is my work!" He saw the shelves with their bound reports and stacks of files, the fruits of fifteen years of service to Westria, realizing for the first time what a priceless repository they were. "Do they expect to steal my labor once they have cast me aside?"

But they have done it already . . .

The papers slipped from his grasp and he stood staring down at them, shivering a little, and knew that he had returned to his office because even now, after all his words of defiance in the Council Hall, he could not believe that it was true. This place of all others was his refuge, his battlefield, his own— where in the turmoil of the day or the stillness of the night he had used all his powers as they were meant to be used.

And I will never come here again . . . He ran a finger along the polished wood of his desk; touched the box of quill pens, like arrows in a quiver. He sank into the great chair behind his desk, settling into the comfortable hollows his own body had worn there.

"They hailed me as Seneschal and now they curse me as sorcerer," he said softly at last. "I would have given them everything, but they want nothing from me, therefore they shall have nothing of what I have done for Westria. *They* have named me evil, and evil I shall be . . . I have no choice, now . . ."

He got to his feet, held the lamp high and began to tip out oil over the pile of papers on the floor. He heard a door click, the echo of a footstep in the hall—he must not be found here! He groped for a new shape, visualized the little clerk who kept the door.

"Durren! What are you doing here? I saw a light and wondered—" the papers stirred as the door to the office opened and shut again. Caolin recognized the voice, precise and a little disapproving, of Ercul Ashe. He fought to hold Durren's form as hatred strung his nerves.

"Master, forgive me for not getting consent—I thought there might be some evidence here . . ." Caolin ducked his head submissively and began to sidle toward the door, setting the lamp back on the desk so that the farther end of the room was in shadow.

He reached it, touched the key.

"Very well. Did you find anything? Do you know where he is?" Ercul Ashe's voice sharpened as he peered at the other man.

"Yes . . ."

Caolin turned the key in the lock and slipped it into his belt, then straightened, letting the form of Durren slip away. The Deputy staggered back, staring at the man who had been his master. His mouth formed the word 'traitor' silently.

Caolin shook his head. "You are the traitor, Ercul Ashe— to Westria and to me." Suddenly he was entirely calm. He had accepted his destiny and been rewarded with the life of his enemy.

"I didn't know that Ordrey already knew the plan!" Ashe found his voice. "I was only your puppet—I was innocent!"

Caolin shrugged disdainfully. "Are you still bewailing that battle? It let me make a lasting peace where a greater victory would only have brought more war! I cloaked my deeds to hide them from fools like you, who would not understand how they served Westria!" He began to laugh harshly and laughed again, seeing Ercul Ashe grow pale. Shadows groped from the corners of the room.

"You call me traitor, but your tender pride has deprived Westria of *me!* If it *was* pride—" he peered at the Deputy. "What did they promise you for this deed? Worm! Do you think to take my place?"

Ashe shook his head. Another step backward brought him to the wall, and he stood, twitching, while Caolin mastered himself again.

"Do you know . . ." he said softly, "that once I killed a man whose only crime was loyalty to his master? And you have betrayed *me* . . . You claimed protection, but where are your fine friends now? Fate has given you into my hand. Sooner or later it will give me the others too."

Ercul Ashe licked dry lips, tried to straighten and stop the tremors that shook his body against the wall. "Are you going to murder me? I *was* loyal to you . . ." his voice cracked. "But you were different when the King was alive."

Caolin stopped short, remembering how it had been when he could look on Jehan and see the Lord of Light—before he had embraced the Lady of Darkness and been lost. *Jehan!* Darkness swirled around him and for a moment he poised, reaching out to the emptiness where love had been.

Then Ercul Ashe snuffled convulsively and Caolin's vision focused again.

"But the King is not alive, and no one can save you, or me . . ." He lifted his ring so that the garnet glowed in the lamp's dim light, caught the Deputy's desperate gaze. "You are your own murderer, Ercul Ashe . . . and your heart will stop at the touch of your own hand . . ."

He stared at the other man, using him as a mirror to build this image one last time, and as in a mirror, Ercul Ashe saw himself approaching with death written in his eyes.

Ercul Ashe stretched out his hand and rested one cold finger above his heart.

Staring into the other man's eyes, Caolin saw awareness return an instant before his body registered its agony. He drew back his hand swiftly, fearing to share the other's pain. But there was nothing, only the waiting until the untidy twitchings of the body at his feet were still.

"My Lady of Darkness, accept this sacrifice," he said dully. "Ercul Ashe, farewell."

He bent then and dragged the body to the heaped papers, splashed more oil across them and touched the pile with flame. It seemed to him that it was a fitting pyre. Fire pulsed back at him; light and shadow leaped and merged around him as if the room and all its furnishings were no more substantial than his lost dreams.

He groped for his bag and fumbled for the key. The flames were licking at the base of the bookshelves now. Then he unlocked the door and slipped like a shadow along the passageway, through the twisting streets, away from Laurelynn. Behind him the night sky filled with angry flames, distracting those who had been seeking him.

When he reached the Red Mountain and the Jewels they would know where he had gone. But it would be too late, then.

XII

The Way to Awahna

Suddenly, the morning air was filled with butterflies.
The Master of the Junipers missed a step and grasped at a branch of manzanita. Golden wings brushed his cheek and for a moment his spirit fluttered joyfully. Then a little breeze stirred his hair and swirled the butterflies into the pure azure of the sky. Reluctantly the Master's tethered soul returned to him, but he was still smiling as he looked down and saw the tattered carcass the butterflies had been feeding on.

There is nothing to be afraid of here . . . His breathing steadied as he realized that the body had been that of a deer. *Surely there are worse fates than to nourish butterflies!* Today was Midsummer. In the coming months the butterflies would mate and lay their eggs and die, and in the spring the cycle would begin anew.

Did I really fear to find Faris' body? He wondered as he continued down the mountainside. And yet what made him think he would find the Pilgrim's Road, much less the Queen?

On the second night of his journey he had dreamed of meeting Faris at the gates of Awahna, and waking, had been certain that was where she would try to go. But what if he had been wrong? He stumbled onward until he rounded a shoulder of the mountain and saw below him the winding ribbon of the Pilgrim's Road gleaming in the morning sun.

He stopped short, his heart thudding heavily in his chest. "Now, let me find a holding, and let them give me word of the Queen. And then I will be done with doubting Your purpose, Lord!"

"Why?" Caolin brought his hand down upon the stone parapet that edged the platform at the top of the Red Mountain.

He felt the shock of the blow, but no pain. His pain was all internal, now.

"Why was I raised so high if I was not meant to reign?" He had evaded his pursuers, but he could not escape the questions that tormented him. He leaned out over the sheer cliff face. Wind plucked at his robe, rocking him. Just a little farther and he would not be able to balance again . . .

Why not let go and bring an end to pain?

Below him Laurelynn shimmered mockingly in the heat of noon. Caolin sobbed, unable to look at it, unable to look away. His vision darkened—he saw the rose-brick towers of the city melt and run like blood into the river; the ploughed fields sprouted bones like stalks of corn.

Caolin collapsed back onto the platform, his fingers digging into the cracks between the stones. *They will not let me serve Westria and I dare not die,* he told himself. *I must do something so terrible that the things other men care for can never tempt me again!*

His laughter was muffled by the stones. Some still voice within him whispered that this was madness. But that was just as well, he thought, for he would have to be mad to put on the Jewels and wield them to the destruction of Westria! After a time he managed to sit up, aching in every bone. He shut his eyes against the burning noonday glare. *The Light rejects me! I must find shelter from the sun!*

Crouching like some creature of darkness caught out by day, Caolin stumbled back to the beacon-keeper's lodge. Margit tried to help him, but he thrust her aside, made fast the door behind him and drew the curtains.

Then he threw himself onto his bed to wait until the terror of the light should pass away.

Faris turned her head to watch the play of light and shadow that formed and then erased Caolin's face. She was lying in the shade of the laurel tree on the Lady Mountain . . . no, she was in a house, and the dappled light was cast by the sun that moved slowly across the rustling leaves outside. But where was Caolin?

She drew breath to call him, winced and remembered where she was and why. It was quiet now, but there had been some sound to awaken her—the heavy front door opening and closing again. From beyond the curtain she heard a murmur of voices.

LADY OF DARKNESS

"The blessing of Midsummer be with you. I am Megan of Stanesvale, the holder here." There was a pause. Outside, the wind whispered to the pines.

"The child in your arms—was he brought here by a stranger, by his mother? Is she still here?"

Faris' breath caught painfully and she fought to suppress the spasm of coughing that would prevent her from hearing that voice again.

"His mother?" said Megan. "I thought she must be, for all her silver hair. She came here yesterday, fainting with fever. The baby was starving too, but goat's milk seems to agree with him."

"Yes . . ." the other voice trembled. "Thank you. I have been seeking them."

Rough as granite and sweet as honey—Faris would have known that voice at the thin edge of the world. She let out her breath and the coughing took her, so that she scarcely knew when the curtain was pulled aside and the Master of the Junipers came in.

For a moment the shock of his recognition breached her weakened barriers—she saw through his eyes her sweat-matted hair and haggard face on the pillow, the thin hands that clutched the sheet. *Like Jehan!* he was thinking. *No, it shall not happen again!* The Master reached to test her forehead, held the fragile bones of her wrist to find her pulse. He felt fever, and a flutter like the heart of a frightened bird.

Faris forced herself to open her eyes, unable to bear his pain. "You're real!" her voice strengthened. "I thought I had dreamed you again . . ."

The Master looked down at her, his face working as he tried to return her smile. How thin and brown he had become! She saw now that his robe was tattered and frayed, his face scratched above the ragged growth of beard.

"I was going to Awahna . . ."

"Yes. I know." His lips twitched. "So was I." He began to examine her more thoroughly, his gaze growing abstracted as the physician replaced the friend. Faris tried to speak, found her mouth too dry, and had to wait while the Master gave her water from the earthenware mug beside the bed, then held her until she had finished coughing again.

"I must tell you why . . ." she said at last. "I had to go where Caolin could never follow me!" Swiftly, she told him what had passed between her and the Seneschal, pointed to her bundle, where Jehan's Journal still lay.

"I had sent you away, and there was no one I could trust in Laurelynn. What else could I do? I must learn enough to protect my child and save Caolin too!"

"Save Caolin?" the Master exclaimed. "How can you think of it? I felt your agony a hundred miles away!"

"And the pain of what Jehan and I did to *him?*" breathed Faris.

He slowly shook his head. "No . . . I saw Caolin daily and never guessed at the canker that was eating his soul . . ."

Faris lay back, breathing carefully. The bed seemed to be tilting beneath her. She struggled against the dark tide of fear. The Master held her hands until she could feel strength flowing from him to her.

"Before you can save Caolin you must save yourself." His voice had deepened, steadied—it was the priest's voice now. "You are the perfect child of the Maker of all Things. Fill your mind with the pattern of what you were meant to be!"

The picture he held in his mind began to take shape in hers; she saw herself as she had been last summer in Laurelynn, though even then, she could not remember having been so beautiful.

"The body reflects the mind. You must rule your own mind, and you shall be free."

"To wield the Jewels of Westria, the wearer must first rule his own soul," read Caolin. "He must know the qualities in himself that correspond to the attributes of each element. The Jewels will link him to all that the elements rule, but he shall rule the elements by self-mastery . . ."

Caolin set the book down on the table. In his mind something settled almost audibly into place. He looked around him, for the first time since early that morning seeing and understanding what he saw. It was nearly sunset, and the light that filtered through the curtains was red as fire.

Sometime during that afternoon he had left his bed and begun to read, seeking in that mechanical activity a distraction from the chaotic thoughts that would have drawn him into a madness from which he could not have returned.

He caressed the worn leather cover of the book. There lay

his answer—the power of the mind! It was his fortune, his defense, the one thing that had always been his own.

If he had put on the Jewels the night before, they would only have amplified his own hatred and fear. But tonight surely his mind's cold passion could master them. Despite the folklore that told how the Jewels would overwhelm anyone who had not been initiated to their mastery, he had found no evidence that their use required anything more than training and confidence.

Caolin began to walk around the room, easing muscles tensed by the hours he had spent huddled in the chair. Now he was remembering the contents of the books at which he had stared.

"This world in which we live is neither as solid nor as immutable as it appears," the *Book of Julian* had said. "It is a patterning of powers, and the Mind is the greatest Power of all. The master of the Jewels does not *use* them, he *becomes* them, and they become him—healing or destroying according to the health or dis-ease of the one who wields them. Let the Jewel-lord therefore search his soul well before he wears them, as he would search for any flaw in a sword that he has taken into his hand, for if there is a weakness, it will surely betray him . . ."

Had Jehan ever read that? Was that why he had feared to use the Jewels? And Faris, so weak that Caolin could rule her with a glance—how could she hope to use their power? *But I am strong!* he thought. *I have no hidden flaws!*

He pulled back the curtains from the window and opened it, breathing deeply of the cooling air. His eyes moved to the closed door of his temple, where the Jewels waited for his touch to awaken them.

"But I must go carefully . . ." He had raised his hand as if he were taking oath. Now he lifted the other and looked at them, shuddering. They were grazed and bloody, their whiteness streaked with grime. His robe was torn, dust-smeared. Quickly he stripped and poured water to wash himself.

The cool droplets glittered like the red stone in his ring. In the west, the sun was sinking toward a sea that glowed like a lake of fire. Soon, pastures in holdings all over Westria would blossom with the bonfires of Midsummer Night. But the power of the sun was broken. Men's pitiful imitations would not save them now! When Faris emerged from whatever hole she had run to, there would be nothing for her to rule.

Caolin dipped his sponge into the basin and passed it over his body again and again, letting the water dissolve all the evil memories of the past twenty-four hours as it washed away their stains, until only his purpose remained.

Washed, shaved and at peace with the world, the Master of the Junipers finished his portion of the Midsummer feast. The western sky still glowed with the memory of a brilliant sunset, but upon the long table, candles burned cheerfully.

"Papa—can't we light the bonfire now?" asked the oldest boy. The other two chorused agreement, glancing hopefully from their mother, sitting at the end of the table nearest the hearth, to their father, who brooded opposite her. The candlelight glowed on the pewter goblets, the rich grain of wooden bowls.

"Not yet—it is not quite dark, and Mica has not finished his pie," answered Megan. She turned to the Master. "The lady looks much better now."

The Master nodded. "Yes. The dandelion root tea you made for her has helped, and if your sons can find me chapparal, tomorrow I will brew an infusion that may clear her lungs. I think the crisis of her illness will come soon."

Star stirred in his cradle and Megan went to him, lifting him expertly to her shoulder while she reached for a leather bottle of the sort they used to feed motherless lambs. She sat down again in her carved chair, humming softly, and held the bottle for him to suck.

The Master considered the baby nestled in the mountain woman's arms and thought how easily he had adapted to this substitute for his mother's care. With his dark head laid against Megan's breast, he might have been her own.

"Even after the crisis—" the Master said thoughtfully, "it may be long before the . . . lady . . . is well enough to go on."

"I'm sorry to hear it," said Gilbert, the gruffness of his tone making his words ambiguous.

"So am I!" retorted his wife. "It does me good to hold a babe in my arms once more." Some old pain showed for a moment in Megan's face, and Gilbert's grim look softened.

"They tell me that you were wounded at the battle of the Dragon Waste," the Master of the Junipers said quietly. The woman might be holder here, but if only for her sake, he must win over her husband as well. Gilbert grunted.

"If you like, I will examine you—that child's father was a notable warrior," he gestured toward Star, "and I often tended him." The Master realized suddenly that though he might always carry the pain of losing Jehan, what he had read in the King's Journal that afternoon had lifted some of the guilt he had been carrying as well.

For a long moment the other man's eyes held his, then Gilbert tried to smile. "I had accustomed myself to going halt-legged till I die . . . I can wait until the lady recovers," he said.

Megan's smile showed her relief. "Last night in her fever the lady spoke of an enemy," she said. "Was that delirium? She would not tell me her name. Who is she, and what does she fear?"

The Master shook his head. "It will be safer for her, for you all, if you do not know. The child's father is dead, and there are those who will destroy both him and his mother if they are found." Faris had forgiven Caolin, but she knew his secrets now. The Master could not believe that Caolin would forgive the Queen.

"Did he die in the battle with Elaya?" Gilbert's eyes glittered.

The Master considered him. "He died in the service of Westria."

"Mama, it *is* dark now, and I am done with my pie!" said the youngest boy. His brothers pushed back their benches as their father nodded, and clattered after him to the door.

Gilbert rose, reaching for the staff that leaned against his chair. Through the window one star glittered like a jewel in the pale evening sky.

"I will watch by the lady and the child." said Megan to the Master. "Go with them and bless the lighting of our Midsummer fire."

Caolin lifted the taper to light the candles on the Altar of Earth, then moved to the altars in the other three corners of the room until his temple was filled by a steady, shadowless glow. His gaze rested on the Jewels, in that moment drawn as much by their beauty as by their promised power.

He had bathed and dressed in a clean gown of undyed cotton and eaten the bread and fruit that Margit had set out for him. Now, standing in the midst of his temple, he willed himself to calm. His masters at the College of the Wise had taught him better than they knew, he thought, and he had not wasted the years since then. As his breathing deepened he let awareness of all outside this room slip away.

"Through the power of my Will, I encompass all things. There is nothing in the universe that does not exist within Me . . ."

Caolin stood upright and balanced, each muscle at ease as he began to map the domains of the Elements within his own soul.

Who am I? What am I? At the college such questioning had been part of the discipline of the students preparing to journey on the other planes. But such travelling had been forbidden him, until now, when he had the Jewels to dissolve the cataracts upon the vision of his soul.

He had no mirror here, but he pictured to himself what a glass would have shown—a tall man, smooth-limbed and cleanshaven, with pale fine hair and eyes like the winter sea. That was the body Jehan had loved . . . But he was not concerned with his body now.

He considered the four altars and the Jewels they bore, stopped, facing north and the first of the elements. *Now, I am concerned with the shape and coloration of my mind and soul.*

He took a deep breath and stepped forward.

"I claim the Power of Earth, immovable, unbending. Like the earth I have endured the assaults of my enemies. I stand like a mountain peak in a storm; I am as hard as stone, and their swords shall shatter against my unyielding will . . ."

He paused, remembering the gentler qualities ascribed to this element—nurturance, permeability—but those were for women. Nothing in him responded to them. He set his hands against the naked stone of the Red Mountain that formed the floor of his temple, as if he could absorb its strength through the skin of his palms.

After a few moments he moved to the Altar of Water where the crystal flagon and the Sea Star alike refracted the candlelight.

"I claim the Power of Water: the force of the flood; the inexorability of the tide; the patience of the falling rain, for like the rain, my will can wear rock away . . .

"I claim the Powers of Air!" Caolin bowed before the third altar now. "For the power of the wind is the power of the will, and air bears the words by which I shape reality."

He circled back to the altar on which the Jewel of Fire cast back the candles' flame. "I claim the Powers of Fire: fire to consume my enemies; fire falling from heaven like a striking sword!" He willed away the memory of times when he had invoked the Lady of Fire to bless his love, for he could only call on the Dark Lady now. For a moment Her face glimmered within the Jewel, mocking him with Faris' eyes.

He had invoked power—the active, masculine strength of each element that corresponded to his own identity. The Masters of the College had preached the need for a balancing of male and female to control such forces as these. But surely they were mistaken. Power could only be mastered by power . . .

Quickly, Caolin bowed to each of the Jewels in turn. *When I have put them on I will call the winds, and strike clouds together to spark the lightnings. They who have seared me with their hate and cast me into the dark shall have their fill of fire and darkness!*

Light blazed suddenly in the darkness in which Faris had been drifting. Cool hands lifted her, drawing the sweat-soaked sheet away and sliding a fresh one beneath her. She bit her lip as the movement restored awareness of which joints and muscles, which bared nerves, were most vulnerable to pain.

Then they replaced the coverlet and tucked it snugly around her. Faris lay very still, waiting for her blood to stop pounding, waiting for the world to go away.

The candle moved so that it no longer hurt her eyes. "Can you open your mouth, Mistress? I want you to drink this now." Faris felt the hard rim of the cup against her lip. The drink was tart, with an aftertaste of peppermint. She drank again and Megan smiled.

"Thank you," whispered Faris. "Is my child well?" Her breast ached for the warm weight of him though she knew that she had not even strength enough to hold him now.

"Yes, he does very well. Tomorrow I will bring him to you." Megan waited until Faris had emptied the cup. "I will be going now—it is nearly midnight—" she said to the Master, "but you must call me if there is need."

He nodded. "Come to relieve me when it is dawn."

Faris felt a breath of air caress her cheek as Megan pushed the curtain aside and passed through. "I have been such a trouble to her, and to you too, from the beginning," she sighed. "If I had let you teach me to control myself and the Jewels, I would have been able to deal with Caolin . . ." Some memory stirred in her mind as she spoke—something else the Master ought to know . . .

"No—" he was saying, "we laid too much upon you too soon. But no failure is forever. Now you have to repair your body so that we can begin again. I know that you want to sleep to evade the pain," he went on. "But right now you need to be *here*, in your body, using all your abilities to heal yourself!"

"*My* abilities?" she echoed mockingly.

"Yes—" the Master said gently. "You have great awareness—turn it inward to comprehend your own ills. You respond to beauty—hold to the image of your own. You have a gift for right action in a crisis that a warrior would envy—use it to marshal your own forces against your foe!"

"What do I look like, to you?" Faris asked, as if he were a mirror in which she might see her soul.

The Master closed his eyes, deliberately misunderstanding her. "I see your body patterned in light, but where the colors should be clear and glowing and the energies should flow smoothly I see them muddied, trickling sluggishly as a river flows when men forget the Covenant and choke it with debris."

She sighed as he focused on her again. "What must I do?"

"First, you must become aware of the earth supporting you. Feel the pulse of her energies as if you were lying directly on the soil. Then, visualize a shaft of golden light flooding down from that place where all is brightness, pouring through you, filling you with power . . ."

As she tried to comply, Faris perceived a tingling along her veins, a varying pressure as if a wind were blowing across her chest and outward along her limbs. She realized that the Master of the Junipers was passing his hands back and forth a few inches above her body with a stroking motion, as if he were brushing grains of sand away. Imperceptibly her pain began to ease.

Faris' eyes closed. Her awareness focused on the movement through her body of those currents of power. *There is a battle going on within you,* came the Master's thought. *You must visualize the forces that will come to your defense.*

"You are the center of the circled cross, in which the elements are joined!" he said aloud. "Use their power!"

Faris felt a throbbing in her chest and found it easy to imagine the struggle there. She breathed painfully, concentrating on drawing the golden light to help her, and awareness of the world around her passed away.

She knew that she had done this before—this grasping and focusing of power—she felt the Jewel of Fire burning her brow, felt the surge of balanced energies as she and Jehan strove to drive back the unlawful flames . . .

Once more she was standing in the Sacred Wood, on the Lady Mountain, in her chamber in Laurelynn, bearing the four Jewels. *The Jewels!* She struggled to tell the Master, but she could not break free.

Caolin has the Jewels!

Standing on the platform at the pinnacle of the Red Mountain, Caolin unwrapped the four Jewels of Westria, named them and put them on:

Earthstone . . .
Sea Star . . .
Wind Crystal . . .
Jewel of Fire . . .

His skin prickled as power began to swell through his nerves. He breathed deeply, deliberately, images flaring behind his closed eyes. Then he trembled, for he felt something beyond the reach of his senses, like a sound too high for a man to hear, an itch too deeply set to scratch, darkness in which one might strain forever to see. Was his isolation too great for even the Jewels to break through?

Be still, he told himself, *be open* . . . *wait* . . . He stood, yearning for the touch of power as once he had waited for Jehan's mind to touch his.

And like an answer it came.

Caolin's shout ripped the air, reverberated across the transient woods and fields and through the imperishable framework of which the land called Westria was only the appearance that mortal men could see.

I am Master of the Jewels! I, Caolin!

In the Sacred Wood, the Lord of the Trees was aware of him. From the depths of the western ocean Sea Mother flowed upward to float on the surface, waiting. Perched on an outcrop of the Ramparts, Windlord half-spread his great wings to catch the first stirrings of the storm. And in the forested slopes below him, the Great Bear stirred from the shadows in which he had lain, grunting a question that rumbled like thunder across the night.

On the many levels of the Place men called Awahna, the

Powers that ruled the elements focused suddenly upon the Red Mountain.

And Faris, wandering between the worlds, heard Caolin's words, and crying out, broke abruptly from her dreams . . .

Startled into wakefulness by the shout, the Master of the Junipers grasped Faris' shoulders, calling her name. Her pulse was bounding like a frightened doe. Was this only a nightmare or had the crisis of her fever come?

"Be still—it is over now . . ." He squeezed the extra water from a cloth, laid it across her brow.

"No . . ." she got out at last. "Caolin . . . took the Jewels, and he has put them on!"

The Master sat back, letting go of her. Caolin and the Jewels?

"They . . . were the only thing left to him . . . of Jehan's," said Faris. "I am afraid of what he may do."

The Master stared at her. Her harsh breathing was the only sound in the room. He wanted to tell her that there was no danger—Caolin, who had failed to reach Awahna, could never hold the Jewels. But what if it had not been lack of ability, but some other, deadlier flaw that had kept him from his goal? The Master shook his head, fighting a horror, trained into him at the College, of the idea that one who was unsworn and uninitiated should touch the Jewels.

"I thought . . . he would be satisfied to rule Westria," Faris said a little more easily. "It is my fault. He is on the Red Mountain now . . . I must try to reach him." She closed her eyes.

"No! Remember what I told you! Your body could not survive if you left it now!" He stared at her, shocked anew at her fragility as she lay swathed in the folds of Megan's gown. "No," he repeated. "I will go to him. Will you promise to stay and watch by me?"

Faris nodded. "Until you return."

The Master leaned back in his chair and shut his eyes, shuddering as his spirit struggled to leave a body that was unprepared to let it go. There was a moment of anguish, as if he were trying to squeeze through a closing door, and then he was free.

He oriented himself, found the line of light that led toward Laurelynn. But he scarcely needed a guide—the astral plane pulsed with currents of energy that flowed toward a single point where a glowing crimson figure gestured his commands. The Master neared him and sent out a mental call.

For a moment the rush of energy faltered. Caolin stared at the Master, and the older man shivered, sensing the mixed passions in Caolin's soul. Did he realize what the forces he played with could do?

"*Stop—you will destroy Laurelynn!*"

"*I know . . .*" Caolin laughed. "*Did your mistress at the College send you to plead with me? It will do no good! The Queen is gone and Robert has cast me aside! Go seek the lost Queen and tell her that no one will rule in Laurelynn now. Find Faris, and if she will listen to you tell her how she has betrayed Jehan!*"

The Master tried to approach him but the force of the Jewels blasted him away. He recoiled along the path by which he had come and jerked back to awareness of his own body, clutching at the arms of his chair.

And in that unguarded moment Faris touched his mind and read all that had passed between him and Caolin.

"He was right—it is my fault! Others cannot fight my battles anymore."

Still dizzy, the Master shook his head. "You will give up your life for nothing. You cannot stand against one who wields the Jewels!"

"And if he is allowed to go on?"

"I think that the forces he plays with will overpower him at last. He will be destroyed . . ."

"He, and what else? What will happen to Laurelynn and the heart of Westria?" she asked. The Master swallowed dumbly, visualizing a shattered city beneath a sundered sky.

"You see—" she said quietly. "I must go to him. What does my life matter if Caolin destroys all that I was trying to preserve? He holds the Jewels, but they are not his. I *feel* them, even now. Perhaps they will still respond to me."

Faris ignored the Master's protest as she continued, "Everything is quite clear now. I thought to learn the ways of Power, but I was not made to endure a lifetime of the subtle struggles that surround the Crown. Only when the great danger comes do I know what to do. But I will live if I can, I promise you, for Star's sake . . ."

The Master's awareness reached out to her and he knew that this was not delirium. She was arguing like a warrior volunteering to stand rearguard against an overwhelming foe.

"I am going—" Faris repeated, "but I will fare more swiftly if you guide me, and more easily return . . . Will you help me?"

With sick recognition the Master remembered how Jehan had asked his guidance on the final road. But he could not deny the Queen's reasoning. He reached out to take her hand.

"Yes . . ."

Yes—wind creature—come to me now . . . Caolin reached for the cloud, calling it like some shy bird he wished to coax to his hand. Already he had forgotten the Master of the Junipers, for the balancing of the elements required all his attention. Delicately he nudged the western winds behind the cloudbank and commanded them to push it toward Laurelynn.

Every sense was bombarding him with messages—the pressure of grains of soil against the probing rootlets of a tree; the slow heave and suck of waves on the shore; wind singing through an owl's wing-feathers as it stooped on some hapless scurrying thing; a young man's arousal as he drew his girl away from the light of the Midsummer fire and into the shadows where their bodies joined—as the Jewels linked him to the life of Westria.

But he refused to acknowledge these things. As the power of the Jewels increased, so did Caolin's concentration. He had nearly forgotten his physical body now, for he had shifted unawares from the material stones of the peak to the focus of power which represented the Red Mountain on the astral plane.

Faris hovered above the sprawling rooftops of Stanesvale, exulting in the freedom of her energy body and the blessed absence of pain. She perceived herself drawn upon the darkness in lines of light, and only the luminous silver cord that emerged from beneath her ribcage connected her to the wasted physical body below.

The Master of the Junipers waited for her nearby. She could feel the life-pulses of tree and beast in the mountains, the dreaming souls of the people in the house. Love for them all welled in her heart, poured out to them and to her child, asleep in his cradle below.

But the power of the Jewels was drawing her. *I am ready, my brother,* she told the Master. *Let us go.* She took his hand, and they passed along the lines of light, toward the storm that swirled between the Red Mountain and Laurelynn.

"*Caolin!*"

For a moment his attention faltered. The lightning bolt meant for the gates of Laurelynn hissed across the river's surface like a thwarted snake and ignited a dead tree at the water's edge. Warning blazes flickered in the fields already, circling the town. Faris felt the people's terror, their bewilderment as they gazed at this sudden storm.

"Caolin! Please stop—for the sake of Westria—for the love you bore Jehan!"

When Caolin perceived her Faris knew it, for as it had been by the Lake of Laurelynn, his mind was open to her and she recoiled from what she saw. Why had she ever thought that he would hear? What had made her think he might obey? She shivered, and he knew her fear, and laughed.

"There is no name that you can call upon to stop me now! Were you hidden with that snivelling priest? I wonder that you dare to seek me here, since you fled from me before. Indeed, I welcome you—now you will see what your own act has done . . ."

She knew that it was true, that she had failed—failed him, failed Jehan, failed Westria. She stood alone and wretched in the dark.

"Stop thinking of yourself—" the Master's thought pierced her despair—*"you do not matter now."*

For a moment Caolin seemed shaken. Then he turned away. *"It is too late—the choices are all made. You cannot tempt me to repentance anymore. I am damned, and you can neither save nor stop me, for I am the Jewel-Lord now!"*

His attention left her, but she felt him gather up the winds, and fling bright lightnings at the city's spires. She felt the varied forces of the Jewels pulse through her, the familiar pressure of their power, as she had felt them in the Grove, and on the Lady Mountain, not so long ago.

Caolin reached out to move a cloud, and Faris swept it back at him, instinctively, as she would have brushed a hornet from her child.

She jerked at the backlash of power. Looking down, she saw white radiance flare at her breast, and at her waist, her loins, a blue and amber glow. Something burned like flame above her brow. Wondering, Faris knew she bore the Jewels. Though Caolin might hold the stones themselves, *she* had been sealed to them, and on this plane, she, also, held their power.

"Caolin!" her call rang through all realities. *"I can command you now—I, Faris, am the Mistress of the Jewels!"* She

struck aside the stormclouds, sent them thundering like maddened horses off across the hills.

Caolin stilled, and turned, considered her. *"I would have spared you, Faris, even now. But now I see I must destroy you too . . . Did you think this power was all my own?"* His gaze went inward. He was trembling.

Behind him, something blotted out the stars.

Vision reversed, made darkness visible—a woman's face, a cloud of mantling hair, eyes like dead coals, and skin a dully radiant veil across dark fires within. The Master whimpered. Caolin bowed. But Faris knew the face once seen in Caolin's memory, seen in her mirror once, in Laurelynn, when in despair she had put on the Jewels.

"I am the Queen of Darkness, and My power that of Eternal Night. This is My hour. Your dream of light is ended—you denied Me when I lay within, but will no more, who know Me for your twin . . ."

The Lady's laughter broke across the night, sucked backward in a glistening slick tide till reason slid foundationless; identity drowned, mad and drunken, in that shoreless sea. And Faris, drifting in that dark embrace, knew how Caolin was tempted, and understood . . .

"Faris, come away! Your body is weakening . . ." Faris clung desperately to the Master's appeal, to the syllables of her own name.

"Faris! You must break free!" The Master's horror of the Lady's darkness reinforced her own, and a sudden clear anger flared in her.

"I must stop Her or She will destroy Westria—She is the dark face of my soul!"

"To do that you would have to absorb Her into yourself again, and you have not the strength or the time . . . Faris, come back while you still can!"

Lines of light shivered across the face of the land as Caolin shook the foundations of Laurelynn. The air quivered with the renewed tumult of the storm.

But the eyes of the Lady of Darkness swallowed light. *"Come to Me, and find oblivion far deeper than the lake of Laurelynn . . ."*

"Lady of Flowers! Lady of Fire! Lady of Light!"

Faris reached inward for their images, for the Names of all the goddesses who had possessed her when she was made Queen. Brilliance blinded her, rainbows flared behind her eyes, refracting myriad visions, scents, and songs . . .

"Sister, we are here, we are you, we are One . . . Light and Darkness are the two wings of the world . . ."

And Faris knew Herself, and knew the thing that in her had been missing, and embraced the Darkness, and was made whole and free.

She was darkness . . . She was starlight . . .

She was the storm's fury, and the stillness at its heart . . .

She spread her wings above the city then, and Caolin's fury, striking her in vain, was now deflected to its source again . . .

Now the storm boiled about the peak. Faris felt Caolin's anguish and rage. Her thought sought him—

"Calm the elements, Caolin!"

"I cannot . . ."

"Then call them in a gentler form."

"I do not know how . . ."

"Then strip off the Jewels!"

There was no response from Caolin. The Red Mountain erupted in fire. Its slopes shook. Their quivering transmitted tremors across the land. Escaping his will, the Jewels rioted. The forces that formed the frame of the world vibrated, faltered, rhythm gone.

"I . . . will . . . not."

Faris felt his answer, his anger, his anguish that she could not ease.

She rose like a bastion over Laurelynn. She spread her protection across the battered land. The essence of the Jewels, that was her own, she set against their lawless counterparts—absorbing, enduring, transmuting, extending power in a thin veil that, pricked by Caolin's pain, failed finally—the Jewels struck again.

Then, suddenly, there was an ease from strain. The load that she had carried now was shared. Light stood against her darkness like a counterweight, and darkness balanced the beauty of her light. Action and reaction, partnered now, reimposed a rhythm on the world. For she was not alone . . .

"Oh, my beloved . . ."

"Oh, my severed soul . . ."

She knew him then—the sum of all her shattered memories—eyes alight with laughter, a caress, the scent of roses, the sweet mingling of half-awakened bodies, tender, tempered strength, transmuted pain . . . *Jehan* . . .

Touching him, she knew all that his written words had tried

to say, and he knew what Caolin was, what he would be.

"Beloved, we must help him . . ."

"Yes, I know."

For a last time their joined thought sounded, *"Caolin—we forgive you, save yourself now!"*

"You cannot forgive me—I destroyed you both! How can I forgive you?" Caolin's answer was plucked on the highest note of pain.

"Take off the Jewels, and live, until one comes to give and take forgiveness in our names!"

They felt his struggle as they felt the forces that tore at him, searing his body as they seared his soul.

"Help me . . ." on the edge of perception came the plea.

Faris and Jehan moved toward Caolin. Force and fullness, strength and subtlety, mated with the Jewels' warring powers and for a moment stilled them. Jehan and Faris blessed him with their love.

And in that instant of freedom, Caolin took off the Jewels.

Freed from that faint restraint at last, the Jewels joined with the powers they ruled, were whirled away—wild, unwilled were outward borne; dispersed in a last pure pulse of power . . .

The Jewels were gone. The Master of the Junipers, unshielding his awareness, could sense nothing but the varied manifestations of the elements they had ruled. The reverberations of the battle were already fading, and around him peace was settling on both the physical and spiritual dimensions of the land.

Dimly he could sense Caolin, like the dull glow of a coal burned nearly to ash. He was alive, but the backlash of the powers that had escaped his mastery must surely have devastated the mind that had wielded them. It would be long, before Caolin could be a threat again.

Before him, shaped against a sky that flowered with stars, the Master saw the King and Queen. They were shining, and he thought that all the times that he had seen them paired—in the Beltane ritual, at their meeting in the Great Dance in the Sacred Wood, enthroned in the Council Hall of Westria or bearing the Jewels as they faced the forest fire—all had been only foreshadowings of this mated sovereignty.

Then they moved a little apart. *"My beloved, I must go back now."*

The Master's joy ebbed as he looked at her. *"You cannot*

come with me . . ." he told her. *"The silver cord is broken— you have been away too long."*

The night shivered with her bewildered pain as Faris looked about her and understood that at some time during the struggle with Caolin, the ribbon of light that had bound her spirit to her body had disappeared.

"There is nothing left within that world for me—" the Master faltered. *"My Lord, my Lady, let me come with you!"*

"My dearest friend!" Jehan looked at him, returning in that glance all the love the Master had ever given him. His features were still those of the man the Master had known, perhaps more so—closer to being a perfect expression of the spirit that the Master had glimpsed in his face as he lay dying six months before.

"You are the only one of us left to guard the child, the only one who can preserve the memory of what we have done . . ." came the thought of the King.

"My Star! My child! Who will hold him now? I bore him, but you lifted him into life—oh Master, you must love him for me now!" Tomorrow, some child would find the ground strewn with crystals and never know they were the tears of the Queen of Westria.

"Keep him hidden and safe until he has grown strong enough to claim his inheritance. Let him grow free from those who would seek to use him, or spoil him as I was spoiled with too much false affection," added Jehan. *"Keep him secret, lest knowledge of him tempt Caolin once again."*

The Master hesitated, wracked by his own agony.

A light was growing in the eastern sky. The Master turned, and saw it was not dawn—the hills themselves were luminous. He saw a shining road that led between two piers of stone, and recognized the Gateway to Awahna . . . But he saw that the trees and waterfalls of the Valley where once he had walked had been only a veil to shelter mortals from the bright substance of Reality.

"We will return for you when your task is done. It will not seem long."

"It will seem long to me . . ." the Master assented at last. *"I will guard the child. But when he has achieved his kingship, I will follow you."*

And there came a sound . . .

His spirit stilled to hear the harmonies, that chord by chord built, yet were not resolved, as if the Lord of Air harped on the wind. Moving to that music, Faris and Jehan were leaving him. Their figures lit the dark, and shadowed glory on the living light. Across the harping, one clear trumpet call rang like a summons.

Voices answered it, and then the singers came, dancing like sunsparks on a rippling stream. It seemed to him that some had faces that he once had known. The Master wept because he could not speak to them, because he could not sing their song.

"Glory to the Lord and Lady, to the children of the sun— Glory to all living souls that manifest the Holy One . . ."

The music deepened. Earth became a drum, cadencing a new processional, shaken by feet too great for mortal earth to bear. The Master saw, and hid his eyes, but in his heart the gods were recognized . . .

"Glory to the Powers of Heaven, who rule the spheres in majesty—Glory to the Lords of Life who sit in splendor on the Tree . . ."

And yet he did not know when they were gone, for the Light was every color . . . it was none . . . the music was all melodies . . . yet still . . . and, gods and souls forgotten, his own will was lost and found within a greater one.

"Glory, glory, gloria . . ."

One came.

One moment was Eternity.

Darkness and Light, and all that was were One.

Epilogue

"Praise be to the Guardian of Men—you are with us again!"

The Master of the Junipers opened his eyes on a strange room that was luminous with the soft light of an opalescent dawn. The air held a moist freshness as if it had recently rained.

There was a movement nearby and Megan bent over him. He closed his eyes again, reaching for the phrase of melody that had shaken his soul, his mind grasping vainly at the words of the song. The light of this world was so much less than the illumination from which he had come.

"Are you ill?" came the woman's voice. "I went in to see if the lady had been disturbed by the storm and found you both like ice. It took an hour's chafing to get warmth into your limbs, and as for the poor lady—"

The Master forced himself to focus on her, realizing that his cheeks were wet with tears. He must tell her that he knew that Faris had already completed her journey to Awahna . . .

"No—" Megan sounded alarmed. "Don't try to speak. You are still looking at me from a hundred miles away." She poured tea from a stoppered stone jug into a cup and held it to his lips. It was hot, and gradually he felt awareness of his body return.

"I am sorry . . ." he whispered, then stopped, for how could he make this woman understand what had happened here?

"You do not have to explain," Megan said calmly. "I have no training in these things, but I am a child of these mountains, and I have seen too many folk pass to and from Awahna not to recognize the marks of the other world . . ."

She looked down at her work-roughened hands. The Master watched her, recognizing now a strength in her that was one manifestation of that power which he had so recently experienced in its pure form.

"What will you do with the child?" Megan asked suddenly, still staring at her clasped fingers. "My womb will bear no more, and that little one is already dear to me. If you have no other place for him, will you let me raise him as my own?"

He stared at her. The King and Queen had left him to guard their heir, but would it be safe to take him back to Laurelynn? Caolin still lived, and though his strength was in ashes now, he might one day recover his powers and with them the ambition that had nearly destroyed him, and Westria. When he returned to Laurelynn he must go to the Red Mountain to look for Caolin. He would need care, and now, defeated and vulnerable, he might even be healed, and Faris' sacrifice would not be in vain.

Yes, Caolin could be dealt with, but there were others, with greater right in the world's eyes, or greater desire for power, who might prevent the Master from keeping the trust Faris and Jehan had laid upon him.

He reached out to Megan with all the strength left to him, reading in her a strength and steadiness that came from the hills in which she had been bred.

"I think I could find no better fosterage—" he said at last. "Take care of him, for the sake of—" he had almost said, *for the sake of Westria* . . .

"For the lady?" asked Megan. "I will take care of him for his own sake, Master!"

He lay back then, fighting his exhaustion, wondering if despite all their precautions, she had guessed Faris' identity.

After a little the woman spoke again. "We have prepared the lady for burial. We honored her as well as we knew how— in a while, when you are able to rise, perhaps you will come and look at her?" she asked diffidently.

But it was bright morning before the Master went into the room where the body of the Queen of Westria lay, though drawn curtains left it dim. They had set candles of scented beeswax around her, and the bed was covered with asters, late poppies and varicolored lilies so that it looked like a meadow filled with summer flowers.

The Master gazed down at the body, seeing all the marks of her suffering cleansed away. Megan had dressed her in the robe she had brought from the College of the Wise, and combed out her hair to cover the pillow in mingled waves of shadow and silver. And yet this was only an imperfect image of the completed beauty he had seen in Faris' face the night before.

So the *Death* he had read for her in the cards so long ago had meant the death of the body after all, but it had also been in truth a card of transfiguration. Now the promise he had seen then was fulfilled, and she was the *High Priestess*, the Bride of the Prince who is no longer of this world, initiate of all the mysteries.

Let the elements take this body I have loved . . . he thought as his hands moved in blessing and farewell, *as they have taken the Jewels of Power she bore, and as her spirit has passed to the keeping of the Maker of All* . . .

From the next room he heard Star's small contented cradle-song, and Megan's lullaby. A light wind passed through the opened window and parted the curtains, and the Master was for a moment blinded by a haze of light. When he turned, the wind was swirling loose petals from the scattered flowers to hide the body, like the wings of butterflies.

Index to Characters

Emir AKHBAR, an emissary of Elaya to Westria.

Lady ALESSIA of Moonbay, wife to Brian of Las Costas, and later provincial regent.

ALEXANDER, King of Westria, father of Jehan and Jessica.

Sir ALLEN of Badensbridge, knight and holder of the Corona.

Lady AMATA, wife to Theodor of the Corona, mother of Sandremun and Rosemary.

Sir ANDREAS BLACKBEARD, squire to Charles of Woodhall, later holder.

ERCUL ASHE, Deputy Seneschal of Westria.

Lady ASTRID of Seagate, sister of Eric.

AURIANE "the Golden Queen," a third century sovereign of Westria.

Sir AUSTIN of Seahold, knight and holder of Seagate.

Master ALESSANDRO COOPER, head of the barrelmakers' Guild, Laurelynn, member of Commission sent to Santibar.

BADGER, milk name of son of Brian and Alessia of Las Costas.

BARNI, a huntsman in the service of Lord Theodor.

Lady BERISA of Hawkrest Hold, wife to Sandremun of the Corona, sister to Faris.

BRIAN, Lord Commander of Las Costas.

BRANWEN, maid-companion to Faris, in love with Farin.

CAOLIN, Seneschal of Westria.

CARLOTA, housekeeper at Misthall.

Sir CHARLES of Woodhall, a holder of the Corona.

Lord DIEGUES DOS ALTOS, a holder of the Ramparts.

Sir DIETRICK of Wolfhill, a holder of the Ramparts.

DURREN, doorkeeper at the Chancery in Laurelynn.

Lady ELINOR of Fairhaven, cousin of Lord Theodor, member of the Commission to Santibar.

Mistress ELISA, priestess at the Hold in the Corona.

Lady ELNORA of Oakhill, a holder of the Ramparts, guide at Battle of Dragon Waste.

ERIC of the Horn, Lord Commander of Seagate.

Mistress ESTHER, chief priestess of Elder in the Ramparts.

Sir FARIN HARPER (of Hawkrest Hold), brother to Faris.

FARIS of Hawkrest Hold, Queen of Westria ("the Lily of the North")

FIONA FIREHAIR, a legendary beauty of Westria.

FREDERIC SACHS, Speaker of the Free Cities in the Council of Westria.

GERARD of Hawkrest Hold, father of Faris, Farin and Berisa.

GEROL, a wolf, the companion of Caolin.

GILBERT of Stanesvale, husband of Megan.

The Mistress of the GOLDEN LEAVES, an adept at the College of the Wise.

GORGO SNAGGLETOOTH, a trader between Westria and the Brown Lands.

Lady GWENNA, wife of the Lord Mayor of Laurelynn.

HAKIM MacMORANN, a trader and spy for Elaya.

HAKON, Lord Commander of Seagate, father of Eric.

HILARY GOLDENTHROAT, a legendary poet of Westria.

Lady HOLLY of Woodhall, daughter to Sir Charles, later wife of Andreas.

HUW, Rosemary's owl.

JEHAN Starbairn, King of Westria.

Lady JESSICA of Laurelynn, wife to Robert of the Ramparts.

JAIME of Palodoro, a holder of the Royal Domain, packmaster.

Master JOAQUIN, Lord Mayor of Laurelynn.

JONAS FERRERO, a smith in Tamiston, in the Ramparts.

JONAS WHITEBEARD, a trader and spy for Westria.

JULIAN Starbairn, "the Great," third century King of Westria, founder of royal line.

The Master of the JUNIPERS, chaplain to King Jehan, adept of the College.

Lady KIMI of Longbay, a holder of Seagate, member of the Commission to Santibar.

Sir LEWIS of Marsh Hold, Herald of Westria.

LINNET, milk name for the oldest daughter of Sandremun and Berisa of the Corona.

MADRONA, former name for the Mistress of the College of the Wise.

Sir MANUEL of Orvale, Controller of Highways.

MARA, Queen of Normontaine.

MARGIT, a deaf-mute, servant to Caolin.

Lady MARIANA of Claralac, a former mistress of King Jehan.

Mistress MARTINA, a holder in the Royal Domain.

Mistress MEGAN of Stanesvale, a holder of the Ramparts, Star's foster-mother.

MICA, milk name for the youngest son of Megan of Stanesvale.

Sir MIGUEL de Santera, Commander of the Fortress of Balleor near Santibar.

MIK WHITESTREAK, bodyservant to the King in Laurelynn.

ORDREY, confidential agent for Caolin.

PALOMON STRONGBOW, Lord of the Tambara and Prince of Elaya.

PATRICK, Steward of Misthall.

PHILIP of Rivered, oldest son of Robert of the Ramparts, briefly Jehan's squire.

RAFAEL, squire to Jehan, killed by raiders in the Corona.

Mistress RAMONA, a priestess in Elder.

Sir RANDAL of Registhorpe, a holder of Seagate.

Master RAS of Santierra, Master Bard, member of the Commission to Santibar.

ROBERT of Holyhill, Lord Commander of the Ramparts.

Lord RONALD SANDRESON of Greenfell, cousin to Lord Theodor of the Corona.

Lady ROSEMARY of Heldenhold, daughter of Lord Theodor.

Lord RODRIGO MACLAIN, an emissary from Elaya.

Sir RUDIARD of Applegard, Ambassador from Normontaine.

Lord SANDREMUN of Heldenhold, son of Lord Theodor.

Sir SERGE of Greenforest, a knight of Seagate.

STEFAN of the Long Ridge, son of a holder of the Corona.

SOMBRA, Faris' black mare.

STORMWING, Jehan's white stallion.

TANIA RAVENHAIR, daughter of the Miwok chieftain Longfoot, in the Ramparts.

THEODOR of Heldenhold, Lord Commander of the Corona.

THUNDERFOOT, Eric of Seagate's black stallion.

The Master of the TIDEPOOL, an adept at the College of the Wise.

WALDAN of Terra Linda ("Mole"), a former soldier of Westria.

Sir WALTER of Wilhamsted, a holder in the Royal Domain.

WAREN, a clerk in the Chancery in Laurelynn.

THE STAR TREK® PHENOMENON

The *complete* Star Trek collection

including original novels...

THE ENTROPY EFFECT 49300/$2.95
THE KLINGON GAMBIT 47720/$2.95
THE COVENANT OF THE CROWN 49297/$2.95
THE ABODE OF LIFE 47719/$2.95
THE PROMETHEUS DESIGN 49299/$2.95
BLACK FIRE 83632/$2.95
TRIANGLE 49298/$2.95
WEB OF THE ROMULANS 46479/$2.95
YESTERDAY'S SON 47315/$2.95

and movie tie-ins...

STAR TREK—THE MOTION PICTURE 83088/$2.50
CHEKOV'S ENTERPRISE 83286/$2.25
STAR TREK II—THE WRATH OF KHAN 45610/$2.50
STAR TREK II—THE WRATH OF KHAN PHOTOSTORY 45912/$2.95
THE MAKING OF STAR TREK II 46182/$7.95

All available now from POCKET BOOKS

TIMESCAPE

If your bookseller does not have the titles you want, you may order them by sending the retail price (plus 75¢ postage and handling—New York State and New York City residents please add appropriate sales tax) to: POCKET BOOKS, Dept. STP, 1230 Avenue of the Americas, New York, N.Y. 10020. Send check or money order—no cash or C.O.D.s and be sure to include your name and address. Allow six weeks for delivery. For purchases over $10.00, you may use VISA: card number, expiration date and customer signature must be included.

636

Rowena

ROWENA MORRILL
The World's Most Celebrated Fantasy Illustrator

Describes in step-by-step detail the secrets of her amazing painting technique in

THE FANTASTIC ART OF ROWENA
by Rowena Morrill • 47055/$8.95

Rowena Morrill, winner of numerous awards, has painted her beautiful, sensual works for museum exhibitions, private art collections, books, magazines, and the 1981 *Tolkien Calendar*.

Now, for the first time, she reveals how she paints, in a gorgeous volume containing 26 full-color reproductions suitable for framing.

POCKET BOOKS

TIMESCAPE

Her works include THE DARKOVER SERIES and THE MISTS OF AVALON.

She is

MARION ZIMMER BRADLEY

World Famous Fantasy Writer!

Timescape is proud to bring you the first volume in her haunting new series, The Atlantean Saga:
WEB OF LIGHT 44875/$2.95

Also by Marion Zimmer Bradley

THE RUINS OF ISIS 46843/$3.50
THE COLORS OF SPACE 44877/$2.95

Now available from **POCKET BOOKS**

If your bookseller does not have the titles you want, you may order them by sending the retail price (plus 75¢ postage and handling—New York State and New York City residents please add appropriate sales tax) to: POCKET BOOKS, Dept. MZB, 1230 Avenue of the Americas, New York, N.Y. 10020. Send check or money order—no cash or C.O.D.s and be sure to include your name and address. Allow six weeks for delivery. For purchases over $10.00, you may use VISA: card number, expiration date and customer signature must be included.

672